T

QUARRY

PETER

WEBB

Grosvenor House
Publishing Limited

This book is published by
Grosvenor House Publishing Ltd
28-30 High Street, Guildford, Surry, GU1 3HY
www.grosvenorhousepublishing.co.uk

A CIP record for this book
Is available from the British Library

ISBN 978-1-78148-590-3

www.peter-webb.com

Artwork – Ian Wasden

Cover Photograph – Yuriy Poznukhov

Cover Design & Art Layout – Ben Rowe –
www.benrowephotography.co.uk

Dedicated to *Les M, Derek M* and *David J*
Three of the golden threads in the tapestry of my life

Acknowledgements

Literary efforts would come to nought without help and support. My totally inadequate but nonetheless very grateful thanks go to *Marjorie Webb* for services above and beyond the call of duty – *Ben & Kate Rowe* for such commonsense advice in my more airy-fairy moments – *Mike & Rosemary Gaches* for their invaluable criticism (once again) – *Dawn Flynne* for her support and continual encouragement – *Ian & Eileen Wasden* for their comment, discussion and support throughout this endeavour – *Fennel* and *Tigger* for never losing patience with me – My Mum and Dad, *Dennis* and *Doris Webb* for everything else

For *Kate R, Kate R, Ben R, Jake W, Rob W.*
What a family

My thanks are also due, once again, to *Ruth, Tamsin* and *Corrina* at Grosvenor House Publications for their unstinting support and patience; thank you.

Marjie. *Love and life became one*: thank you. X!

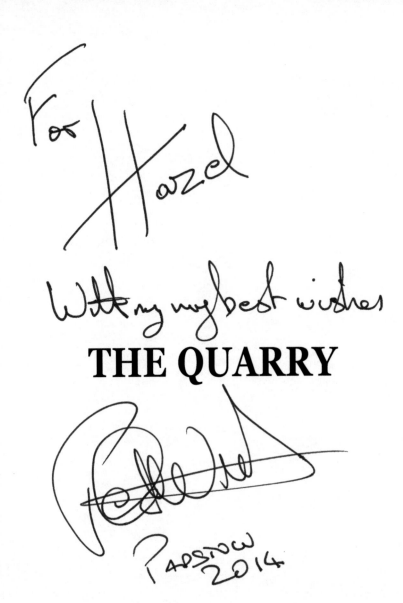

For Hazel

With my my best wishes

THE QUARRY

PADSTOW
2014

Chapter One
Month 12 – December 1984

The rain was falling such that it ricocheted a good foot off the pavement. Stephanie, shopping bag in each hand, was one in the shoal of people torpedoing for cover, all looking like a gang of freshly-surfaced otters.

"Here y'are, Alice." *Les, the café's middle-aged proprietor, looked round the crowded interior from behind the glass-and-Formica counter.* "There's not a lot of room."

"So I see; special offer on the tea?"

"No, it's the rain what's driven 'em in here."

Alice took the full mug. "Thanks, Les, an' I'm sure that aint the truth. Your tea's got a reputation as spreads from 'ere to Garston."

"So that'll be all of a mile an' half then, thanks for that."

"My pleasure. Much like me an' Christmas, I don't believe in buildin' up folks' hopes, saves a lot of disappointment in the long run."

She began to leave the counter as Les asked his question. "How's them youngsters of yours? Stratton family still scatter-gunned across the country and runnin' riot?"

She half turned. "Don't see much of either now..." *Alice's attention flicked to the café door as it careened open. A woman, masquerading as a shower-tester from coypu central and carrying two shopping bags leapt through its open maw, shoved it closed with the sole of her shoe and stood dripping on the threshold. After a brief glimpse and her muttered comment of, "That'll still be rainin' then," Alice turned back to Les. "Brian's still out in Ireland doin' what it is 'e does and Sydney's plannin' to take over the world from his bed."*

By the door, the woman waggled the shopping bags and the water flicked off them, liberally speckling the red-and-white linoleum floor.

Les shook his head. "Still no work then?"

"No, never likely to be neither; coal mines closin' all around. He's just one of thousands up north so no concern for him there, our good lady Thatcher's seein' to that."

The woman moved from door to café counter leaving behind a snail trail of moisture as she zigzagged her way around the crowded tables.

"Much longer an' he'll have to shift back down 'ere; though what he'll do then is anyone's guess."

"Move in and scrounge off you?"

"He'll get short shrift there, from my better half too; we aint got room for passengers." Alice glanced at the woman now standing alongside her. "You look soaked through, love, but it's only a passin' shower. We 'ave to worry when Les's cats start linin' up at the door in twos." Les laughed, the woman smiled and Alice pinned her folded newspaper under her arm and left the counter, moving to the café's only table with free chairs. "Thanks for the tea, Les."

"Y' welcome." Les turned his attention to the woman. "Yes love, what can I get you?"

"Coffee, please."

"Sugar?"

"No thank you; and no milk, please."

Les swivelled round to the coffee machine. "Unsweetened black comin' right up!"

While coffee was made Stephanie stood quietly dripping. She paid then looked around the crowded space for a seat. The only vacant one was opposite the lady who had just left the counter and she made her way across. "Would it be alright if I sit here?"

"'Course, love... you want to get that coat off, you'll catch y' death."

Dropping the bags, Stephanie shook the coat off her shoulders, doing a fair imitation of a soaked spaniel. She noticed Alice covering her tea with her hand.

"Oh, sorry, I didn't mean to drench you as well, sorry."

Alice smiled at her. "I thought I'd dodged the worst of it. Seems I were mistook!"

"Yes, sorry." Stephanie smiled back. "I can't believe how fast it came on. I know it's December and we should expect these things but, all the same... what happened to snow?"

"Ar'tic's got it all love." Alice closed her paper. "Pop y' coat down before you soak the rest of the folk in 'ere an' drink y' coffee... you'll feel a lot better for doin' both; so will we!"

Stephanie sat and cuddled the coffee mug between her palms. She looked up, smiled at her action and replied to Alice's amused expression. "Don't know why, tastes much better like this."

"Ar, all you need is a log fire an' footstool and you'll be set." Their gaze fell in unison on the shopping bags and Alice indicated with her head. "Been shoppin' at Garretts', I see."

"Yes, for cushion covers. Spoilt for choice there."

"Not bad for a small town shop is it? You'll be doin' some decoratin' then?"

"Well, one up from decorating really; furnishing. We moved here just over a year ago and I'm still trying to make a happy home... what was that poem? 'De-dah, de-dah... and I lack of household craft.'"

"Who said that then?"

"Don't know but it sums me up a treat."

"Can I have a look... at what you bought, I mean?"

Stephanie smiled, glad of the conversation. "Yes, 'course! They sort of reflect the one room I've got round to finishing; understated, you know?" She opened the bag and Alice saw the material.

"Oh, makin' your own then?"

"Yes, why, is that so surprising?"

"No, didn't mean to, you know, cast nasturtiums as they say, just, well you young folk usually buy them ready-made things these days, don't you? Unwrap 'em an' throw 'em at the settee."

"What, a young thing like me?"

"Well, not, you know, but, yes."

"Not often I get called young."

"Compared to me you're a slip-of-a-kid. It's just, you're modern."

"Young and modern in the same morning, goodness, I am having a good day." Stephanie looked at the brown cow-gown and fingerless mitts Alice was wearing. "You look as though you're working. Is this your lunch break?"

"I am, it is." Alice paused, smiled and nodded. "That it then?"

"Pardon?"

"My compliment from you. 'You look like you're workin.' You get, 'young and modern' from me, I get, 'you look like you're workin' from you..." Stephanie looked across the table for a few seconds unsure how to react then

4

saw the corners of Alice's mouth twitch. "Good job I've got a thick skin!"

"That came out all wrong." Stephanie laughed in relief too. "You look very smart... in your cow-gown and fingerless mitts. Paris fashion right there. A very good choice to go with the Fair Isle jumper under it."

"I think you'd best stop now, you'll have me blushin' at my good taste. What's your name?"

"Stephanie. Yours?"

"Alice."

"Very pleased to meet you, Alice."

"An' likewise, Stephanie. So, movin' on, you were sayin' about makin' your own cushion covers."

"Oh, yes... er... do you not have to be back... at work, I mean?"

"Gimme chance to finish me tea! You sound like Uncle Alan."

"Who?"

"My Uncle Alan, him as runs the stall." Alice smiled. "No, relax, Stephanie, the peasants aren't slackin'."

"Oh, no, sorry, I didn't mean..."

"I know, just raggin' you again. No, I've got another half hour before the whip falls."

"Oh, well, if..." Stephanie pulled the material clear of the bag. "It's just that no one sells exactly what I want in ready-made. Find that with all sorts of stuff and I just thought... you're sure this isn't me being boring?"

"No, not at all." Alice leaned forward to inspect the material.

Stephanie reached back into the bag and pulled out some edging strips. "And I got this to go with it. What do you think?"

"Lovely... good shade mix."

"Do you think?"

Both women looked up and smiled at each other as Alice nodded. "I do. That shade of cream sort of ages it nicely; goes really well with the tapestry pattern."

Day 12 – Monday 19th November 1985

"That bitch of yours up for matin' yet?"

Locked in silent struggle with a blackthorn spike embedded in his palm, Eric's question, out the blue like that, startled David and it took a few seconds to register.

"Erm... Oh, right; back on that are we? Still on about Jill?"

"'Course Jill, you daft sod! Who do y' think, Steph?"

"You have such a way of puttin' things, Eric."

"Well?"

"Well nothin'... How you even know when her season's due is beyond me... the terrier's, I mean. You want to get out and about more."

"A man on the 'unt for a replacement terrier has to keep one eye on the clock, one eye on the local availability and the other on the diary."

"That'll be three eyes then."

"Stop findin' fault, you know what I mean."

"Well, with all this eye movement you'll also know how much she looks forward to being lined; an' as for the terrier, well..."

Eric gave an audible smile. "I shan't tell Steph you said that but I'll make damn sure she gets to know." Both men now smiled as Eric continued, "Just that you ought to know, if you've been payin' attention to the odd comment, that I'm in need of a replacement for Patch. Arthritis has finished her for work now, poor mite."

"I do know. I seem to recall you startin' off in bloody October about it! For 'odd comment' read 'at every opportunity', an' I've told you at every opportunity that I don't know I'll use her again. It's gonna be such a bloody job to get that bitch mated after last time; not for the want of tryin' neither…"

They spoke together. "An' as for the bloody terrier…"

Then Eric pushed his point home. "Well, not wantin' to dredge up past events, but I'd think you'd want a replacement too, for Sack?"

"Ar." There was a pause as David collected his thoughts. "Got that bugger so bloody wrong, Eric. Never even saw her in all that chaff an' dust."

"That pump-action with the hair-trigger you insist on usin' didn't help neither."

"Just fits me so well."

"Maybe, but you should just try and crank it back a bit, y' know? You'll kill some bugger with it one day." David stared into the middle darkness and Eric softened his tone. "As things were, well, don't carry too much blame. Could've happened to any of us. Steph alright about it?"

"Thrilled."

"Like that were it?"

"Whole episode lacked a certain degree of merriment."

"She understood though, about how these things can sometime happen?"

"Did her best, ar, considering it was her baby."

There was another short silence. Eric lit up a cigarette and inhaled deeply. "Does 'er still just pee in the blue-brick yard when she's well in 'eat?"

"Are we still talking about the terrier?" Eric cough-laughed as David continued. "Ar. Yard's washed down every other day with Jeyes 'cos of the ferrets, so she reckons the stink from them an' the cleanin' hides her scent. Even then she keeps her tail tucked up for most of her heat."

"Well there you are then, all you've to do is watch her start all that silly stuff then you'll know she's ready!"

"No such luck! Fifteenth day is really all you get with that slippy little lass, and then only part of it. You tell me you know for a certainty the exact day an' time any of your bitches have started their season."

"Ar, there's a trick to that; not found it yet."

"Same with Jill." David took out a packet of sweets and he and Eric took one each and chewed methodically on them for a few seconds before David voiced his thoughts aloud. "All this started with Razor y' know."

"Ar, I know."

"Her first time. That's what buggered it all up. Someone should 'ave said about him 'cos I'd not know, only bein' on the estate five bloody minutes an' all."

"Ar."

"She's never liked members of the opposite sex much, but after Razor... Put her off it for good. I got Rascal over, Colin Spear's dog, when I thought she were right last time, just to see."

"Any good?"

"You seen any pups runnin' about of late? She turned on him with a move that'd startle a stoat; shook him 'til his teeth rattled, near killed the poor sod. Left him with a nasty gash on his throat."

"Bad?"

"Bad? Needed five stitches."

"Oh, that bad."

"Ar. And now word's got out about her. I talked to Guy Hurley, Lord Godson's head man, about usin' his Jack Russell, Barney."

"Nice dog, that."

"He is. Guy looked at me as though I were ninepence short of a shillin', said if he wanted his dog castrated he'd sooner go to the vet. He called her the prayin' mantis; some advert that is. Pups from Jill may be what's wanted but word's got round and she's fast run out of kamikaze studs. There's not one dog I've introduced her to that she hasn't lifted a lip at."

Eric thought for a moment then ran the options. "What about Percy Arlet's dog? Digger aint it?"

"Too big for Jill. They call him Digger 'cos he's the size of a JCB."

"The Spencer's terrier?"

"Small."

"Geoff Day's Border?"

"Scared."

"That Viper, Reg Patton's Border-Lakeland cross?"

David looked across at Eric. "Dead."

"Oh. Didn't know. When?"

"Last May."

"Oh, sorry to hear."

"As things stand, I'd 'ave dug him up."

Eric shifted his weight slightly, allowing the chill of the grass to attack his other buttock and pursued his objective. "Well, I think you're missin' the obvious."

"Meaning?"

"Meanin'... well, I thought, you know, I thought you might fancy puttin' her back to Razor again." There was a stunned silence from David. "Well, it were a success last time weren't it? The pups, you know?"

David finally laughed out loud. "Ha-ha! A success? I doubt she'll let that randy little sod get behind her again this side of Armageddon! She hates him with a vengeance; not surprisin' after the way he treated her."

"Ar, but she had pups!"

"Was how she got them was the problem, Eric! She went into shock after he nailed her! Her first time an' there's this... thing on top of her, all cock an' thrust, grabbin' her neck, growlin', slaverin'."

"Much like me with my Hattie."

David smiled. "I tell you, she hates him. They only get within a foot of each other now and she's bristlin', showin' her teeth."

"An' that's much like my Hattie with me." Eric shuddered. "Bugger but that wind's got up a bit chill, aint it? That'll snow tonight, mark me on that." Eric shuffled a little closer to the inadequate shelter of the autumn-trimmed hedge and peered through it. Perched on the bare branches of the hawthorn trees growing close to the roadway were several pheasants, their silhouettes plainly visible against a star-pricked, blackcloth sky. "Just look at them, stupid sods!"

David turned to look. "Ar. They've used them for the last couple of nights now."

Eric snorted in exasperation. "Stupid sods! There's a wood of firs behind 'em an' they're sat on them bare branches lookin' as big as bloody footballs. You wanna get them thorns down and on y' fire this next year, save a lot of bother... save us bein' out here for one."

"If not here then elsewhere. They make the most of them berries while they're about and they'll soon move into the firs when real winter comes. Anyway, they'll come to no harm tonight, bright as this. Only a raw recruit or nutter will be out poachin' tonight."

"Then why are we 'ere, eh?" Eric shook his head. "What you don't realise is they've got all day and night to get at these birds, poachers like Stratton and his ilk. The day's theirs to make of it what they will, an' that's mostly mischief. While you? You've got to sleep sometime. You should listen to some sense; talk to Liam and get 'em felled."

"A poacher of Alec Stratton's experience is the last bloke to be out on a night such as this."

Eric sat up a little. "Know that from chat then do we?"

David shook his head. "That chat never comes my way, Eric, you know that. Steph and Alice Stratton never discussed points of friction."

"Oh, yeah?"

"Yeah. I said, so did Steph... as things are it makes no odds now anyway."

"Why's that?"

"Steph's not been seein' much of her of late; Alice. I think the friendship's cooled a bit."

"Not before it's time neither; best off out of it."

"Maybe."

"What, you're not gonna tell me you liked your missus an' that Stratton woman bein' bosom buddies are you?"

"No. But... just seems Steph's lost some of her... I don't know, some of her... joy."

"What?"

"Nothin', forget it."

Eric stubbed his cigarette into the soil. "What d' you mean 'some of her joy'?"

"I said forget it... just leave it, eh?"

"Some of her joy?"

"Eric!"

"Yeah right." He paused. "So, you're not gonna cut them hawthorns down an' get us a few nights off then?"

"Oh, subtle."

"Well, are y'?"

"No! I'm not a one for cutting stuff down just 'cos it don't suit. Pheasants aside, there's thrushes... redwings, fieldfares; they rely on them berries to stock up fat for the winter."

"You're too soft by 'alf, you are. If they were mine, I'd be toastin' marshmallows over 'em come next December." There was a short silence as Eric resettled himself. "I should've bought one from that first lot."

"A marshmallow?"

"A pup y' soft bugger, a pup! I should've bought one from that first matin'. They were grand little 'uns, all of 'em."

David sighed. "You should've. I did offer."

"You did... an' wanted forty quid for the pleasure!"

"Bloody hell, Eric, you could easily afford it. You're the only man I know could commit suicide by jumpin' off his wallet!"

"When you get to pushin' sixty, youngster, you 'ave to watch the pennies, you'll learn that in time."

"What I have learned is that you're a tight-fisted sod." Eric grunted. "An' that litter were your chance, I did say to get in early."

"Ar, but, forty quid!"

"'Ark at you." David mimicked Eric but added a nasal whine. "'But, forty quid!'"

"Well, I'm backed in a corner now, Patch in retirement an' all, so I might just have to stump up the cost with the next lot."

"Have you not been here for the past conversation? I just said there'll be no next lot."

"But think of them grand pups... them grand pups of which you never kept a one of... nor Liam. Sold 'em all, an' at forty quid a bloody go, greedy bugger!"

"I'd been daft enough to promise too many folk. The four she had were three short of them as were wanted. Anyhow, we'd got three Labs an' two terriers; there's only so many dogs a body can afford to run."

"Only one terrier now though."

"Thanks for that gentle reminder."

"Right though, aint I?"

"An' you could see all this coming, could you?"

"Belt an' braces, youngster, belt an' braces."

"I'll bet you're a hundred per cent accurate in hindsight, aren't you?"

"I am, an' I'll tell you summat else that's a fact too. Fetchin' them two together - Razor, heart of a lion, Jill, killin' machine? Master stroke of breedin'; a master stroke!"

"Master stroke? What are you talking about? Master str... that's not flattery, Eric, that's bollocks."

"Grand pups though, weren't they? Got to be worth a second go."

David shrugged his shoulders. "Dunno..."

"And not wantin' to remind you..."

"Yes, yes, I'll be wantin' a replacement for Sack, yes, I heard you the last time, an' the time before that."

"Right though, aren't I? Both times."

"Maybe."

"An' it might even make the missus perk up a bit, eh? Get a bit of harmony back on the ranch; some 'joy'?" Eric took out another cigarette and lit it, the breeze forcing him to cup his hand round his lighter's reluctant flame.

David looked across at him. "You want to pack that silly lark in y' know. Everything in this county wearin' a nose will know where we are. You sound like a wind-broke horse when you're out beating as it is."

"That's it, take away all me pleasures. No terrier an' now no bloody fags neither!"

"I didn't say that... Christ, you don't leave off do y'? I'll have you burstin' into tears in a minute!" He paused, sighed. "Look... alright, all I will say is I'll have a talk to Liam. An' y' right, I will need another."

"You've finally seen sense!"

"Hold on, hold on! I only said I'd talk."

"Ar, I know, but it's the right thing, you mark me on that." Eric shuddered and repeated. "Bugger! It's cold, innit? What time did he say he'd be here?"

"Half eleven." David glanced at his watch. "Twenty past now... ayup, talk of the devil."

They got up stiffly, climbed the gate and moved to join Liam who had appeared through a gap in the tall hedge that bounded the road. Eric greeted him with a tugged forelock and a subdued whisper. "Evenin' Gaffer."

"You're being very servile. What d'you want?"

"Christ, can't an ordinary under-keeper be civil to his head keeper and not have an accusation of ulterior motives thrown in his face?"

"An ordinary under-keeper, yes. You? No. All quiet on the western front?"

David nodded. "Been so quiet you can hear the frost settle, or at least we would've heard the frost settle if Eric had stopped talkin'."

"Yeah, I've spent many a night out with him too."

"All quiet for you?"

"Without him, yeah. Nothin' doin'... night bright as this."

"Tell y' what," said Eric. "Let's all stand here, y' know, in the middle of the road and under this moon. Give everybody a real good look at our silhouettes, shall we?"

David looked at Liam. "That'll be a request to move then, will it?"

Disregarding this, Eric moved back along the road and climbed over the gate to settle once more behind the hedgerow. David threw a look at Liam as they heard Eric's continued conversation drift out from the dark. "Bloody damp's got back to this spot an' I'd just warmed it through."

They climbed over the gate to join Eric as David offered his opinion. "Such a pleasure, sharin' this night with you."

In the silence that followed they settled behind the hedge and locked into stakeout mode. It was Eric's voice that broke the lengthy silence.

"We was just talkin' Liam, weren't we, Dave, about that Jill and how best to get her an' Razor together again."

David sighed loudly and Liam's incredulity echoed it. "What?"

"You mean you were, Eric!" David turned to Liam. "I was just listenin' to him bleating on about it; I never got more than a word in."

"I can imagine."

"Ideal match them two though, weren't they? I've told 'im." Eric indicated David, still determined to get some sort of resolution to the discussion. "Ideal."

"Yes, alright, Eric, you've made your point. You want a pup," sighed David again.

"An' you do."

"So you say."

Liam joined in. "What, as a replacement for Sack y' mean?"

David looked from one to the other. "Jesus. It's a good job I'm not tryin' to forget about it. Yes, as a replacement for Sack, thanks for the reminder… again."

There was another lengthy pause as all three men looked out into the dark. Eventually, Liam spoke. "Well, not wishing to spoil this companionable moment but there's some rats to sort out tomorrow, in that cattle yard of Butler's, inside the lean-to, if you've both got nothing better to do, that is."

"I thought you'd dropped some poison down," said Eric.

"I did but then Butler wanted to use it for those store cattle he gets from that chap in Wales so I had to lift it before it really got goin'. Cattle are gone but poison will be no good now, not this close to shoot days. Give one of them guests' dogs a dose of the Warfarin an' we'll not be popular."

"Might make some of 'em work better, that or an eighth of an ounce of lead behind the left ear; either usually does the trick."

David shuffled a little in his seat. "When were you lookin' to do it?"

"After mornin' feed. Say… eleven?"

"Oh… erm…"

"There a problem, Dave; got summat on?"

"No, no, just, I was goin' shopping with Steph is all. No, I'll sort it out. She'll not mind."

"You sure?"

"Yeah, sure. We usually go… well, Steph usually goes of an evenin' but I thought I'd, y' know take a mornin' out an' go with her. Sort of get…" His voice tailed off.

"Some joy?" ventured Eric.

17

"Some what?"

"Nothin', Liam. Just Eric bein' his usual helpful self. Do you want me to bring all me buck ferrets along?"

"Just that big white 'un, Dave. He kills 'em well. I'll fetch along my couple of polecats; they've not had a day on rats for over three month now. We'll fetch our terriers along as well."

"What, Razor *and* Jill?"asked Eric.

"Yeah."

"Together?"

"Yeah, they'll be fine; we just need to keep on top of 'em."

"If you say so."

"Oh, now I get it; jealous 'cos you've not got one."

Eric snorted out loud. "Ha! Very funny that, you should be on the stage; there's one leavin' in ten minutes."

David got up "Right, if we're back on the subject of terriers, I'm off to check the far end of the Old Railway." He began to climb over the gate. "What time tomorrow, Liam?"

"Eleven."

"Right, see you both then."

Liam's closing remark drifted on the breeze to the departing David. "Yeah… an' don't forget that terrier of yours. With one short we'll need all the help we can get."

Eric's voice followed on. "You can't leave it be can y'?"

David called back. "Now you know what it were like bein' me this past hour."

Eric called out. "Oh, Dave…?"

After a brief pause, David arrived back at the gate. "Yes, Eric?"

"G'night." Eric smiled.

"It's just on five to twelve which means it's almost tomorrow, Eric. I've been up since five this mornin', this is no time for bloody jokes... if you're so bloody perky, Pinky, you walk the Railway an' I'll get off home to me bed."

Eric nodded in the direction of the gate-leaning David. "He's an idle sod he is."

"I'm an idle sod? This from a man still sat on his arse an' thinks he's had a hard day if he has to pick up the empty cartridges from round the pegs!"

Cutting the conversation short, Eric got up from the still cold, still damp grass. "I'm not listening to this rubbish. As instructed, I'm gonna walk the Railway, then I'll glance in at The Quarry. I've been up since half four this mornin', but I'll manage it." Eric climbed the gate and stood next to David. "An' you two wouldn't know a day's hard work if it jumped out of a hedge an' bit you in the ankle."

David shook his head. "Jesus, 'ark at you."

Eric disregarded him. "All the same the younger set. No stamina, no time to listen to the voice of experience."

"When the voice of experience talks, I'll listen," replied David. "Right, thanks for doin' the Railway, Eric. I'll do far side of The Clump an' the river. Oh, Eric, if you're at The Quarry watch out for them open tree roots on them tracks; in fact stay at the bottom of the drop. Man of your age, failin' eyesight an' all that, you could fall through one."

"Not with that paunch, he couldn't," said Liam as he rose from the grass, his joints silently shrieking in protest at having to move. "He'd get jammed in a hula-hoop. Right. I'll walk Cut-Throat Lane an' round Ling Mere then. That way we'll all be pullin' our weight."

The blackthorn barb in David's palm, forgotten during the past conversations, was now making its presence felt.

"I'll have to get this bugger out tonight, today... wherever we are; it's throbbin' like a Vincent Black Shadow."

"How'd you pick that one up?"

"Tryin' to get through the bottom end of Barton's Plantation. It's that thick I reckon there's an undiscovered tribe of pygmies in there."

"I'll bet they're the buggers who poached it last year, an' we didn't hear 'em 'cos they used blow pipes!"

"That weren't no bloody pygmies, Eric," added Liam seriously. "That was our friend Mister Alec-bloody-Stratton."

All three sighed inwardly and David shuffled his feet. "Ar, well..."

"Dave said Steph's not seein' Stratton's missus no more though, right Dave?"

"Ar."

Liam brightened a little. "Well, that's some good news then."

"Good-ish. I've just said to Eric, just made things not so hot on the home front of late, well, that an' this job... an' then Sack. Was just a bit... y' know? But getting better."

"The job?"

David shuffled his feet a little. "A bit, but more the Stratton thing, I think. The difficulties it were causin' for me, well all of us I guess, they've got to her finally."

"Steph reckons the pressure's come from us, does she?"

David looked across the fields and the chasm separating him from home and hearth. "Me, Liam, just me." He turned from the gate. "Hm... Right. See you both for rattin' tomorrow. An' we'll have some chat about gettin' this old codger a terrier, Liam."

Liam nodded. "Ar... an' you, if it'll help."

"Ar, maybe."

Eric moved past David. "Well done you two, sounds like you've heard the voice of experience!"

Chapter Two
Month 11 – January 1985

"Best Edwards on the market! Get 'em 'ere! Best Edwards! Ten pence a pound! Yes love?"

"Carrots please, three pound... oh, and a cabbage, Savoy, please."

"Yes, love."

The stallholder gathered the items and Stephanie fumbled in her purse, sorting out the coins. As she looked up she saw a face she recognized serving another customer further along the array of vegetables. The woman looked across at the same instant, smiled then turned back to her customer, flicking the brown paper bag of mushrooms over in her hands to seal it as she did so. Taking the money, she placed it in a leather satchel slung across her shoulder and called across.

"Know you, don't I? Stephanie aint it?"

The man tipped the vegetables into her hessian bag and Stephanie paid. "Thank you... Yes, in the café, that day when it was raining; you're Alice."

Alice moved closer. "Ar, Les' place, both got it right then! Did he give you discount?"

"Pardon? Er, who... no, I... er..."

"Thought not, that's our Alan." She looked across at the man who had served Stephanie and was now busy stacking parsnips on the display. "Y' tight-fisted sod! Give 'er ten percent, friend's discount, eh?"

A grunt and nod accompanied a coin passed to Stephanie.

"Oh, no really..."

"Go on, take it! Small change it may be but not to be sneezed at in these times. Way things're goin' it'll be all that bugger Thatcher'll leave us!" A gust of wind whipped a handful of sopping paper past their feet, flapping canopy and coat alike. Alice saw Stephanie shudder at its suddenness and temperature. "Cold enough for y'?"

Stephanie smiled. "Yes, plenty thanks."

"Thought so. Did you enjoy that last lot of snow then?"

"While it looked fairy tale, yes, but not with the slush it left behind. Bit of an Indian-giver is snow, I've always thought. You?"

"Indian-giver?"

"Yes, you know, promises one thing, gives another."

"Oh, yes. Can't say it's occurred to me before, but y' right." Alice smiled at her. "Ar, Indian-giver."

"See, Arctic's not got it all."

"True." Alice smiled at the reminder then indicated the hat Stephanie was wearing. "You knit that yourself?"

"Er, yes... why, does it show?" She touched the hat nervously.

"A less charitable person would say you were wearin' it for a bet; not me you understand, just someone less sensitive than me." Once more unsure, it took Alice's laugh to diffuse the situation. "Only jokin', Stephanie, just jokin' y'. Looks very nice, an' the stitchin', so neat. Can I see?"

Removing the hat, Stephanie passed it across. "Wasn't quite sure how to take that." She laughed a little. "Your sense of humour takes a bit of getting used to."

"You'll soon do that." Alice handled the hat. "That really is so neat. My handicrafts are on the scruffy side of rubbish

23

next to this. It's been a long time since I did any; one look at this an' I know why. Very smart." She handed it back.

A further blast of wind hit them and Stephanie shuddered once more. "I put on extra woollies but I think I should have brought a flask of soup as well."

"You should, then I could have scrounged some off y'. You said you were one up from decoratin' in the café. You all done yet?"

Stephanie was slightly flustered by the continued rapid changes in subject. "Sorry? One up from…?"

"Decoratin'."

"Oh, yes, I see. Yes I am, well, furnishing… cushion covers…"

"Ar, furnishin'. All done?"

"No. A little thing called Christmas got in the way… Well, Christmas and the estate shoot days."

"Best thing to do with Christmas, Stephanie, is smack its arse and send it on its way, I reckon!"

"I'm almost in agreement. Both of them made unfair demands on time and tide."

"Estate, you say? You work up there then; Barn Tor?"

"Yes. Well, not me, my husband, he's one of the keepers… you know; gamekeepers. I do bits in the big house, parties and such, when they need extra staff, but it's David who's employed there."

"David. That your husband…?"

"Alice, come on! There's custom waitin'!"

The shout cut Alice short in her enquiry. "Alright, alright, keep your 'air on!" She nodded in the man's direction. "My dad's younger brother, Alan. It's his stall."

"Yes, I remember you saying."

"He's too old for this really. My dad's way too old and he's had the sense to pack it in, but Uncle Alan, he insists on

keepin' on." Alice shook her head. "Soft bugger. I 'elp out on alternate days, more frequent when he's short staffed; no slackin' peasants here remember, an' the money's useful..."

"Al-iss!"

"Yes, I said alright! I said!" She turned to Stephanie. "See what I mean? Got to go, love, his whingin' lordship commands... probably just the same as yours, 'cept yours has got a better accent, eh? Maybe see you around here again? I'm on regular most weeks, an' there's always a bit of discount for preferential customers."

"Thank you, Alice. I'll repay the compliment one day." The wind gusted again as a hurry-up. "Bye."

"Bye, Stephanie." Alice waved tentatively and half smiled as Stephanie moved off towards the doorway of the indoor market.

Day 11 – Tuesday 20th November 1985

"Voice of experience! I don't think so," scoffed David as they split up to go their separate ways.

Within fifty paces the three keepers had put a hedgerow, the old orchard and a road between them, seemingly, hopefully, the only three people abroad at seven minutes past twelve.

After five minutes walking and part-way across the field, Eric glanced up. The sky was filling cloudy, gradually covering the glittering constellations that had jigsawed themselves together throughout the evening, and the temperature dropped as the breeze sharpened its blade on the woodland strop and rose in threat.

'That bugger's gonna snow,' he thought. 'I know it.'

The creatures living on the open fields, either by force or necessity, registered this threatened change in the weather too. Rabbits grazed a little quicker and moles, like hands in pockets, dug a little deeper.

Eric reached the edge of the Railway bank, his waterproof leggings making the stretch over the wire fence pull on his hip joints. But then he was quickly down the slope and the still comfort in the base of the railway cutting wrapped around him like a sleeping bag, relaxing his face and shoulder muscles.

Along this old trackway, now denuded of its iron rails and wooden sleepers but still covered by the weed-pocked, creosote-stained ballast that once supported them, were the skeletal remains of a dream ripped apart by Mister Beeching and his cohorts many years ago. Although they preserved the remote country stations, which gave an accurate map of the country homes of politicians, what they helped destroy was the Britannia Class landscape in the lives of suburban, short-trousered tykes with grey mothed pullovers, grubby knees and notebooks. These past runways of British Rail rolling stock were now just the winter roosting sites of wood pigeon, of fieldfare and redwing and here, on one of the estate's favoured drives, of pheasants; and tonight they were all in their allotted places.

Eric moved to the first of several straw covered feed rides dotted along this trackway, his line of vision out front, never upward for fear his white-orb face would alarm these dozing yet alert birds.

On the field at the top of the railway embankment, along the boundary hedge and in line with the keeper, a fox was also moving, as intent as Eric on not disturbing these hawthorn sentinels; not until he was ready. That moment would arrive at the spot where the railway track's shrinking embankment and the downward slope of the field became one. Here the hawthorns were lower and it would not be the first time an inexperienced pheasant had chosen this inadequate height to roost. A leap, a snap... it just might fill a corner of vulpine hunger.

Moving noiselessly along the straw ride, it was the moon's shadows that caused Eric's heart to slip out of gear. The shape of what seemed to be a crouching man shimmered to his right and, always one to get the priorities right, he gripped tighter onto his stick and stood rooted to the spot. His heart re-engaged immediately as hawthorn-bush-recognition shamed stalking-vandal-supposition but even so, suddenly, it felt quite warm. This split second halt, however, saved greater embarrassment for the hunting fox as, keeping to a steady measured pace, it emerged onto the rail track right in front of the immobile keeper. Indeed, had Eric's progress not been halted, these two night stalkers, both so quiet and intent on their own business, would have cannoned into each other; even so, the sudden, close appearance of man and beast caused some intestinal collisions. Their respective pulse rates bounced into turbo-mode as both moved out of their skin, stopped in their regard for each other, regained their composure then stood their ground, one in silent study, one in studied silence. The charm was broken by the wand of breeze; fox sniffed man and Eric was left with just pheasants for company.

After the briefest of pauses Eric moved on, glancing only to mark the track. A chat with David later in the morning would sign a death warrant and, four days later, this very fox would walk that very same track for the very last time, its progress through wood and life arrested by a carefully placed fox snare which would dress this complacent Reynard and take it out for one very last night of dancing.

Apart from this close encounter of the foxy kind, Eric's route along the straw covered spectre-track was uneventful and he finally melted into some thick hawthorn and bramble cover. Deliberately left to its own devices, this tangled growth obscured the Railway from any prying eyes using Raynes Lane. He pushed his way through these barbed hosts to finally reach the lane via a steep climb created by an in-filled bridge. A quick check told of no traffic on the move.

'Not likely, at,' watch-check, 'twelve forty in the morning,' he thought. 'Only fools and ne'er-do-wells abroad at this time, an' I know which I am. All clear!'

Eric was up and over the post-and-rail fence with an alacrity that belied his fifty plus years and he stood at the roadside for a lean-against-post cigarette, drawing a sound map of the locality as he did so.

He lit up.

'What was that? Owl kill? Fox pounce?'

Stiffened and alert, Eric's senses struggled to be the first to identify the sound. Time slipped into overtime but still nothing registered. The pregnant pause was on the verge of growing into an adult silence when he finally fixed the location after a further muffled sound.

'To the left... bottom of Stonepit Belt.' More noise. 'What the hell...?'

He moved toward the sound's epicentre as, crushed underfoot, the cigarette was left to become the target of interest for hunting song birds when dawn would break some six hours later.

Keeping the hedge as shadow-companion, he moved slowly, almost over cautiously for it seemed to him now that a violent struggle was taking place up ahead. On hands and knees like a hunting fox and near the bend in the lane that concealed the woodland's gateway, Eric drew ever closer to the aural drama.

The noise was clearly audible, a confusion of muffled grunts and yells. It was only as the cries of distress were rising to a crescendo that the rear end of the customised

Ford Zodiac parked in the gateway came into view. At the same time, the miasma of sounds became a recognisable, universal duologue:

"OhGod... Oh,yes!Yessss...!Yes!No!Ohno!OhGod!HM mmhmmhmm... Please? Yes, please... Oh! Oh! OOOO HHHH! AARRHH! Here. I. Cumm... Aa.a.a.aaaa... OO... OO... OO... HHH... UMPH...! H!H!Aaaa..."

The vehicle's wildly bucking rear end protested violently, its springs forced to undergo this unexpected human rally-cross and Eric's head dropped as the sounds stirred his groin, forcing him to concentrate fully on dismissing it; even a slight erection in waterproof leggings could prove terminal. Still on all fours, he crawled beyond the gateway, pausing only to carefully place his hand in an unseen dog turd left that very morning by a red setter blessed with an overachieving appetite and an underachieving bowel; this took care of any worries concerning an erection. Once past car and gateway he stood up, a handful of grass serving as makeshift towel.

Silence descended.

'Christ, I think he's killed 'er.'

The stillness spoke of exhaustion and loneliness both inside and out. Eric moved off to the right, along the belt of trees and its ditch towards the dark hulk that was Stonepit Wood, stopping only to swill his hands in the ditch-trapped water. As he reached the angled joint of Wood and Belt, he heard the car start and at the same instant felt, in silent blessing, the first snowflakes kiss his forehead.

He watched as the well-tested vehicle carried its scything headlights and exhausted partners back; back, possibly, to stammered excuses of punctures; of old friends met; back to excuses given to husbands, wives or partners who yearned, above all, to be told the truth.

—⚏—

"An' just what bloody time do you call this?"

David smiled as he entered the Home Farm yard carrying a leather-strapped ferret box over his one shoulder, a double-barrelled four-ten shotgun over his other, Jill tracking his pace, already aware of what was afoot. He looked at his watch. "Mornin', David, nice to see you! Not much in the way of snowfall earlier, were there? No, Eric, not much but you got the forecast right, well done. How are you...? No? That not the type of civilised conversation we're gonna have? Oh, right, we'll dispense with the usual pleasantries that we humans indulge in then shall we? Right. Well, it's eleven fifteen, Eric, why, what time do you call it?"

Eric turned to Liam. "Are you going to put up with him arrivin' late and talkin' to a senior and heroic member of the keeperin' staff like that?"

"If you'd bothered to ask you'd know the reason I'm late is twofold. First, I had to make peace with Steph about the shoppin', that were a feat in itself. I'm just glad she was reasonable about it, or as reasonable as a woman who's forgotten what her husband looks like can be."

Eric waited then asked. "An' the second?"

"You're looking at the keeper who's already picked up two foxes today. Yes, you heard right, two!"

"Died of old age then did they?"

"They were closer to old age than you'll ever be smokin' sixty fags a day as you do, but no. Both cubs of the year, an' it was clever fieldcraft what did it."

"Oh, right, cubs of the year... right. Inexperienced then, which explains it."

"Experienced or not that's two pelts that'll fetch sixty quid to the Christmas kitty, so just remember it when Santa comes callin'. Heroic?"

"Did you parcel 'em up as well then...?"

Eric interrupted Liam's question. "Never mind about him parcellin' up a couple of bloody fox pelts! I'll tell you both about the one he's missed in a bit. What about the real news of the day?"

"Which is?"

"You're lookin' at the keeper, the heroic keeper mind, who's just nabbed a couple of poachers, armed poachers mind, on Ling Mere, mornin' flightin' if you please!"

David looked from Eric to Liam. "What, you did... this mornin'; on your own? You're the one sayin' we should always be in twos or tell folk where you're goin'... I don't bloody believe it! Liam ?"

Liam nodded. "No, it's right. That young lad of Bradshaw's an' another from that travellers' caravan park out by Lord's Quarter."

Eric tagged on with the tale, eager to gain maximum praise for his efforts. "I just happened on 'em. I know Bradshaw's lad well an' I've seen the other about at odd times in the village, hangin' about with that lass... Erica whassername... Dyson, that's it! Richard Dyson's daughter; 'er as works in that butcher's... Taggart's, on the high street. Cheeky little sods."

"Oh, right. Lads. Inexperienced then; that explains it. What, were they throwing stones at 'em or summat?"

Eric scoffed at David. "You cheeky bugger! I'll have you know it were a risky old business; two of 'em an' firearms involved! I just went in instinctive like and faced 'em out, nary a thought for me own safety."

"What time were this then?"

"Just gone seven."

"Well I 'eard no shots an' I was feedin' The Railway then..."

"An' talkin' of The Railway, I saw charlie workin' the bank there after I left you pair, 'bout half twelve."

"What, on the track?"

"Just above. Were makin' for them low scrub thorns, where the field and bank meet. Lookin' for a cheap meal, I reckon."

"That'd explain the scent I got a couple of nights ago; thought then one was usin' the trackway. Right, thanks, Eric, that'll be three then."

"You've to catch it first, young 'un."

"I will. So, your poachers then... I said I 'eard no shots comin' from the lake this mornin'...?"

"No you wouldn't. They had a couple of air rifles, one-seven-sevens..."

David cut in, "Oh, bloody hell, air rifles! I thought they were usin' a punt-gun at the very least, the way you've built it up."

"A one-seven-seven can blind a body at close range, I'll have you know! Anyhow, I waded in, no thought for me own safety, disarmed 'em both then escorted 'em to the police house for Bob to sort; handy it bein' just down the lane from there."

"Christ, Eric, Bradshaw's lad's only fifteen an' I'll bet the other weren't much older! We're not talking Mick McManus 'ere."

"It's easy for them who weren't facin' the guns to scoff. The situation was riddled with danger, but I'd got it fully under control. I'm tellin' y' there were guns involved!"

David looked across at Liam, who just shrugged and smiled. "Some use you are." He turned back to Eric. "Did they not try and scarper?"

"For what? Young Bradshaw knows I know him, an' his dad as well, so it'd only get worse if he'd run... I'd got his rifle anyhow. He'd dropped it in some nettles the second he caught sight of me, but I clocked him."

"That's what's known as disarmin' people in the Cornby household is it?" asked David. "Pickin' up an air rifle from out the nettles?"

Eric ignored it. "I reckon it's his dad's. The coppers have got it now so he's in deep enough. The other stayed with him... I suppose it shows a level of support, a sort of honour among thieves, but my reckonin' is he couldn't give a toss anyway."

"Ar, the only whack he'll get is from his dad for gettin' caught," added Liam. "I tell y', the sooner them travellers move on the better."

"Gi' me a couple of nights an' half a dozen blokes an' I'll get 'em shifted."

"An' a stretch in prison to go with it."

"Gotta catch us first. Anyhow, once he'd been cautioned, I took Bradshaw back to his dad," continued Eric. "Pity the poor sod that. Then Bob marched the other back to the caravan site, an' you're right there, he'll get little change from them lot, but at least now they'll know this estate's on the case. An' not only them. Word'll get out and we'll see little trouble for a few days now, all thanks to my bravery, vigilance and direct action." He looked at them both. "Thank you, Eric, for doin' our job for us!"

David turned to Liam. "Not backward in comin' forward is he? Well, I suppose praise is in order. Well done, Eric."

"You're welcome, an' I guess it's a muted well done on the fox front. So, you're still late. Did you parcel 'em up?"

"It's important now is it, whether or not I parcelled 'em up? No, I left that to Steph."

Liam looked at him. "What, after tellin' 'er the shopping trip was off? You've got a bloody nerve."

"Well, as she was goin' into town, I thought she could post 'em." He looked at their expressions. "I was already runnin' late so I sort of asked her if she'd mind wrappin' them as well."

"Bloody hell! Half-a-job-Dave we should call you."

"Half-a-marriage more like!"

"No, she were OK about it... sort of... she could see I weren't strainin' at the leash to go when she mentioned it, shoppin' that is." David laid out the reasoning. "Sortin' the foxes out made me late as it were an' I rushed on, knowin' you'd be eager to see a decent terrier in action, you not havin' one an' all, Eric. I'd 'ave been able to wrap the pelts up if I'd not had your good self on my mind. Bloody hell, I even skipped a second cup of tea at breakfast to get along here as early as I could!" He looked across at Liam. "I'll not hold me breath waitin' for a thank you from misery-guts over there."

Eric grunted. "What's to thank you for? You just said Steph were alright about it, and there's no heroics in snarin' a couple of foxes... an' I've just said, you've missed one."

"An' none in catchin' a couple of kids with air rifles."

"Well, are we goin' shootin' rats or are we just to stand around 'ere an' chat?"

Liam picked up his ferret box. "Some would say that's all you were capable of doin', Eric, but I'd not be so unkind. And well done for this morning, both of you." He paused. "You don't think it might have been politic then, Dave? To go with Steph."

"No, it's alright."

"I don't want her gettin' further into a strop with you because of her lost friendship and then have you absent from the shoppin' trip on top of that. Don't want to have it spillin' over; have it makin' things difficult all round."

"Not all about you, y' know, Dave, see?" chimed in Eric.

"Never you mind that, Eric, it's for all of us. The last thing we want, the last thing either of you two want, is an unhappy missus. Not to put a too fine point on it, Dave, you've shot Steph's dog and lost her a friendship. Don't mean a thing to us, the friendship that is, the dog does but not the friendship, but to her? With that sort of stuff goin' on the last thing you want is to upset her further over summat we consider as trivial but she sees as the weekly shop."

Eric looked at David. "You know, for a bloke that's not married he talks a lot of sense." He stared at Liam. "Are you readin' the agony columns in Hattie's magazines when you pop in for coffee?"

Liam shook his head. "No wonder you're both makin' a hash of things."

"Don't lump me in with him! My Hattie and me are on the best of terms, it's this daft bugger that doesn't seem able to grasp the importance of keepin' the missus happy."

"Eric's right, Dave. Does you nor the job no favours."

"I'm sure it'll all come good." David hesitated a little. "Home landscape a bit mountainous at times but things are definitely better." His voice drifted off uncertainly as he finished, "An' I think she was fine about my missin' person act today..."

"Right, let's get on with it then lads; get an' kill some rats." Liam walked to his Land Rover. "You'll be havin' Jill up front, Dave?"

"Is Razor in the back?"

"Yes."

"Then yes."

"She's with Boss, Heinz and Kelly."

"Oh, the Barn Tor Sawmill in attendance, is it?" David looked across the yard. "That your Land Rover, Eric? You couldn't walk 'ere?"

Liam's look spoke volumes as he answered for Eric. "Eric's followin' on. 'Cos he's not got a terrier he's fetched along Simba."

"Oh, bloody hell, Eric!" David looked across at Eric's Land Rover almost as if he expected a dragon to leap out of it at any second.

"There'll be none of that sort of talk from you, my lad! If you'd priced that first litter of terriers at an acceptable figure none of this would be happenin'. Now you've to pay the bill for your greed."

"But bloody Simba! As if the chance of gettin' rat or ferret bit aint bad enough!" David sighed. "Bloody Simba? I should've insured me ferrets."

The Barn Tor Sawmill was Liam's pack; a kill-'em-all-collective consisting of Kelly, a Border-Lakeland crossed with a Pembroke corgi; Heinz, a black and white long-hair, whose coat looked like it was in mid-explosion and whose face looked like the result of a pug-bloodhound-poodle crash, and Boss, a fast and very willing to please out-cross, albeit one resembling the selective breeding attained by out-crossing a hare with a Rottweiler and adding a dash of Vietnamese potbellied pig.

All three dogs liked fuss and food in gargantuan amounts, loved the sofa when they could get it and killed vermin with an alacrity and pleasure that bordered on the decadent. None of them ever seemed to tire, would enter the thickest cover on the off-chance of finding sport and were a dab hand at thumping rats whilst simultaneously reading the last rites to rabbits. Kelly, Heinz and Boss were an invaluable aid on scratch days such as these; it was Simba's presence that rang alarm bells with David.

Simba was a yellow something or other of lax manners and morals who had gained a reputation as the dog to watch, but for all the wrong reasons. She was a fully trained manicurist, able, when snatching sandwich crusts from the unwary, to trim fingers and nails to such a degree that the next burglary would leave no recognisable prints. She had also graduated as guard dog first class, gaining her papers by going up and over the kitchen sink and on through the closed picture window above it in order to investigate the sudden noise in Eric's yard one winter. Outwardly friendly to other dogs and humans, nevertheless, inside, she saw them all in the light of fierce competition. Her only allegiances were to Eric and death, just not always in that order, for this was a dog that not only killed the rats but ate them too; David had every right to be wary.

"Well you just make sure you keep her on a lead and under some level of control, that's all," said David as he climbed into the front of Liam's Land Rover. "If I'd have known she were comin' I'd have worn me cricket pads and wicketkeeper's gloves... me box as well."

Eric moved off to his vehicle. "'Ark at 'im bleatin' on. You just need to look to your Jill, young 'un. There's a dog in the back there, one Razor by name, which bust her bubble last time they met; there's still scores to settle."

"For a bloke who wants a pup from 'em you're not doin' a good sales job," said David. "I just hope they get a rat or two before that bloody Simba eats them first then any stray cattle hangin' about!"

The three keepers drove off. Sport of one sort or another was in the offing.

—ᴍᴍ—

Given David's valid concerns about Simba, and Eric's reminder about Jill and Razor's uneasy alliance, the first session of ratting went well. Eric kept tight control of Simba and by the time they sat for a brief halt and a welcome drop of tea, ferrets, canine foragers and firearms had accounted for twenty six rats. In fact, to the delight of Eric and the annoyance of Liam and David, any flashpoints that did occur were, indeed, between Jill and Razor.

The sense of competition was always high between the two terriers, but past skirmishes of a sexual nature meant there really was no common ground between them now. Several times the two dogs had to be worked well apart as tempers frayed beyond healthy competition, even allowing a rat to escape in one instance when the two terriers squared up to each other. The day's results were still good however and, whilst tea was sipped in the lean-to, Liam indicated the remains of an old building, a one time livestock barn which sagged further along this main hedgerow. As with many such deserted sites nature had taken over the role of demolition contractor, and although slow to complete the contract she was absolutely thorough and never charged a penny for the work involved.

"You never know, the odd rat might've moved quarters. Close the day up nice if we can clear that too," said Liam as he finished a sandwich. The other two agreed and so, with flasks bagged and an assorted menagerie in tow, they made their way towards the old ruin.

After many years of neglect this once well-used construction had been reduced to nothing more than a backbone in the soil. In spots around this skeletal reminder of past dreams and struggles were piles of rubble and bricks too damaged even for the estate road menders to use; not all was flat however. Standing nine bricks high by eighteen bricks long, defiant to abuse and impervious to weather and subsidence, was the remains of a wall. Now wearing a jumper of ivy as intricate as any Fair-Isle sweater, it had played host to many creatures during its years of proud isolation.

Mice and insects had birthed, lived and died in both its shadow and security, the only earth they had ever known. Wrens and long-tailed tits had reared their offspring in its ivy seclusion. Owls had used it as a spotting post from which to launch low-level attacks and diurnal raptors had used it as a butcher's block.

On this day the wall was playing host to a very large, very brown, very 'buck' rat, as it had for the past two weeks. This mighty fellow had driven out the two long-tailed field mice lodged there just by his very presence. The tunnel he had usurped, widened and now called home was a shallow, short affair with an entrance-come-exit on either side of this wall; the one opening half-covered by a jumble of brick the other camouflaged by nettles as hot and as angry as the rat's uneven temper.

It was the perfect spot in which to create a den of domestic, macho, bachelor-rat bliss, and it was into this scene that Jill and Razor blundered.

The first the rat knew about the terrier's presence was a blast of hot breath threatening to ignite his rear end. It came from Razor's nose, only inches away from the heady scent of sport and eventual rodenticide. The buck rat shifted uncomfortably, weighing up the situation, deciding on what would be the best course to follow. Decisions were made for it when Razor eased back from the hole to allow in a little air.

As his eyes cleared the blindfold of deadnettle and grass, Razor caught sight of a determined Jill as she arrived at his side. As far as Razor was concerned their feud was only about sex but this was serious, she was after his rat. He rammed his nose back into the hole with a snarl, driving his snout home until the soil in the burrow cracked. Jill saw the rat's head appear through the broken ground and reached forward. Faced with Jill's purposeful stretch to administer oblivion, the rat was forced to adopt plan B which was to duck back into the hole and defaecate onto the tip of Razor's nose in panic. Not wishing to outstay his welcome, for the snip of the terrier's jaws was sufficiently close to give him a hurry-up as well as part his rump fur, the rat then squiggled through the tunnel toward the tradesman's entrance. Jill was the first to realise this escape attempt and, with catlike agility and a high-pitched yelp, she whipped round the wall determined to profit from Razor's blunder. Razor, tanked up on the heat of battle, heard her yelp, interpreted it correctly, pulled back from the hole and tore off round the other side of the wall. At this rate all three combatants would reach the other exit together... or as near together as makes no odds.

The rest of the lag-behind Barn Tor Sawmill were also alerted by Jill's yelp and, as one dog, Kelly, Heinz and Boss homed in on the epicentre of the action determined not to miss out on the sport. Simba, doing a fair impression of a kite, tried to lose the restraint of the lead and join them. The rat quickly made for his other exit hole where he knew a nearby patch of tall nettles waited to conceal him but, by putting on an amazing turn of speed, Razor arrived at this exit just as the fur-covered rat-missile rattled over the bolt-hole's threshold lickety-split. Razor was on the verge of snatching victory from the jaws of defeat, but the jaws of defeat had other ideas.

With the rat clear of the hole's entrance and skittling toward the nettles and freedom, a huge leap from Jill made up ground on both rat and Razor as she closed in for the kill. As Razor's head went down so the rats' went up, both combatants determined to get their fatal bite in first. Razor's teeth were right on target but so were Jill's and the rat, its mouth open to receive the approaching Razor's face, was taken slightly off target by Jill's initial hit. As her mouth closed round the rat's body, the rat's closing teeth were jarred away from Razor's lower jaw, but with hole-punch accuracy they closed on and neatly pierced the central rib of the terrier's approaching nostrils, grinding their way through cartilage and skin and meeting firmly in the middle.

Razor's teeth missed the rat altogether but the rest of him, as he braked and gambolled onward in forward momentum, did not miss the stand of nettles; his eyes and inner ears took the full brunt of the nettle's spiteful armoury. Throughout this confusion, Jill's grip remained tight. She braked right at the very edge of these nettles and began her first shake in accordance with page one of the working terrier's rat-killing instruction manual.

With a fixed point to aim at now, three of the four canine musketeers moved in to what they fully expected to be a kill. The fourth, a near levitating Simba, was making every effort to join in the sport and, with an almighty lunge forward, finally wrested the lead out of Eric's hand and sped off to what she fully expected to be lunch.

The pile-up, if it came, would be dogaclysmic.

All seven followers were stopped in their tracks by the almighty shriek Razor let out as the first twist of Jill's head rippled along the rat's body to reach its well clenched teeth. Even Simba, always one to dispute ownership of anything even vaguely edible, screeched to a halt and looked quizzically at her Master; Eric made the most of this hiatus and stamped on her lead. The second twist of Jill's head, which produced much the same sound from Razor, killed the rat outright, the force of the movement breaking its back, but its teeth held firm as it entered its death throes. After Razor's third shriek, the trio careered away from the nettles.

Razor was 'en pointe', trying to keep the body of the rat slack between him and Jill and wailing like a stuck pig, the blood spouting from his nose; Jill, her now wildly shaking head whipping the rat's body too and fro, was well into kill mode; the rat remained dead. This horror soundtrack and David's frantic shouts for Jill to "Leave it go!" were sufficient to keep the other dogs back and out of what now fast resembled a bad day at the abattoir. Shout as he would though, David's commands went unheeded.

—w—

Jill stood by her master, her bloodied face framed in a grin, her lolling tongue moving back and forth, her tail twitching from side to side, both appendages the metronome of her heartbeat as all three keepers surveyed the carnage.

"I'm really sorry, Liam," said David. "She's normally so, y'know, does as she's told... well, you know yourself. Can't understand her; sorry, Razor."

"The closest they've been for some months," observed Eric succinctly.

Parting the two from the remains of the one had been difficult. After a couple of tentative goes which drew further stentorian blasts from Razor, Liam removed his jacket and rolled the terrier up in it. Eric and David then prised the teeth of the rat apart with a couple of pen knives but, try as they did, they could not staunch the flow of blood issuing from the terrier's shattered nose.

"He'll have to go to the vets an' get stitched or summat, Liam," volunteered Eric. "He's in 'ell of a state. Looks like Brian London after the Porth Cawl brawl."

"My shout, Liam."

"No, Dave, good of you but no need. These things 'appen. I should've left him at home, should've known it'd end in tears."

"Then let me pay 'alf then?"

Liam thought for a second before answering. "Ar, alright. Thanks." He tucked the shivering Razor, still wrapped in the jacket, under his arm, gathered dogs and stick and moved off towards his Land Rover. "See you two later this evenin'."

They watched him go then Eric glanced at David and said quietly. "I think Jill won that round, don't you?"

David nodded. "I do."

"Evened up the score, wouldn't y' say?" added Eric sagely.

"Ar, I would."

"So, now they've settled up, nothin' to stop Razor 'avin' another go at givin' her some more pups then is there?"

Chapter Three
Month 10 – February 1985

"If y' goin' to the market can you get me another pair of them fingerless mittens, Steph? The others have got the palms out."

"What are you doing with them? That's two pair in as many months!"

"I'm wearin' 'em for work, that's what!"

Stephanie stepped out from the kitchen to the bottom of the stairs and called back in mock annoyance. "Well just stop it! Breakfast's ready." Returning, she busied herself with the final plating up of bacon and sausage frying on the Rayburn, and heard David coming down the stairs to join her. He sat, and she put the full plate onto the table. "Bread?"

"Yeah, ta." David picked up knife and fork.

"Tea will be brewed in a minute." She cut two slices of home-baked bread and put them on the tea plate next to David's breakfast. "Catch-up go well this morning?"

"Ar, fourteen hens, nine cock birds. Cold's brought 'em in. Let six of the cocks go, kept the one Chinese and the two melanistics back. Hens are all brailed and in the laying pen an' I've re-set 'n' fed for a second catch." He looked out of the large kitchen window. "I'll not hang about though. Looks like it could rain and I'll not want any birds getting damp and losin' too much in the way of feather."

"I heard you get up but the call of the pillow was too great, sorry."

"No blame there, love. Given the choice..." He placed one of the slices of bread onto the plate and began to dissect it amongst the contents. "I'll destroy this lot then get round again. So, you at market?"

"Yes, I've to get veg for the rabbit stew tomorrow."

"And dumplings?"

"'Course, don't want the worker walking out on me, do I?"

"No, you'll be courtin' disaster if the man of this house has to go without his dumplings."

"You have a way of making the most mundane sound saucy." Stephanie dodged David's attempted slap on her rump and placed a mug of tea on the table. "Enough of that, young man! I'll not be party to such frippery."

"And you have a way of making the most saucy sound mundane... You'll not forget me mitts, will you?"

"Not now you've reminded me again, no." Stephanie turned back to the Rayburn and a saucepan beginning to bubble. She pulled the pan back to simmer.

"What you got turnin' over there?"

"Eye of newt, toe of frog..."

"What?"

"Nothing, just some of that tomato cocktail... that recipe they used in Norfolk... for a flask."

"Flask? What, for goin' to market with?"

"Yes."

"Blimey, how long you gonna be?"

"I'm not. It's just... I met a lady who works there, couple of weeks back."

"You never said."

"I did." Stephanie looked at David and shook her head. "There's no point telling you anything, you don't remember

47

a thing I say." She sighed. "Pay attention, I'll try again. I told you I met a lady in that café off St. John's Road, the one that looks like it should be in a Hitchcock film; said that at the time."

"What, the one with the net curtains, looks like wassername was stabbed in 'em?"

"Janet Leigh. Anyway, she works on the market, not Janet Leigh, the lady, and I said then that it was cold enough for soup."

"I bet the owner of the café weren't pleased, you stealin' custom like that."

"You do this on purpose."

"What?"

"This! I said about the soup in the market."

"Oh. And that constitutes an invite does it?"

"Well, no, but… yes. She gave me discount for the veg I bought so I just thought I'd repay the compliment."

"With that recipe? Must've been some discount."

"Well, it's not just the discount and the cold. We seemed to get on right from the start."

"That café's some backstreet of a place. What made you go in there?"

"It was raining cats and dogs and I dodged in for coffee and shelter. Then I met her again on the market. That's when she gave me discount and, well, I've not exactly got much in the way of friendship out here, have I?" David stopped eating to concentrate on this. "Just nice to have someone to chat to, that's all."

"Ar, I know." He cut the sausage into portions and put the knife aside, picking up each segment with his fork and dipping it in the egg as he considered.

"Do you have to eat like that?"

"Like what?"

"*Like you're in some American film! It shows a lack of breeding.*"

"*Breedin'? I'm from the back of beyond, Steph, what your lot calls a guttersnipe! Only breedin' I've got comes from the mongrel backwash that make up my ancestors; thieves, vagabonds and footpads the lot of 'em.*"

"*Don't exaggerate, David. I don't know what your mother would say if she heard you talking like that.*"

"*We keep it from 'er...*"

"*David...*"

"*Her an' 'er dog fightin' friends.*"

"*That's not true and whatever your background it does no harm to aim higher.*"

He enclosed the egg-dipped sausage in a fold of bread and bit this mini sandwich in half, chewing as he spoke half to himself. "*Not difficult. My lot would need a ladder to climb up a snake's arse.*"

"*Must you, David?*"

"*Ar, I do. Look, you an' this... lack of friendship. Are you alright with it all? I mean, we've only been here a short while. There's Eric's wife. You get on with her don't you?*"

"*Hattie? Yes, I do, but she's on the other side of the park and when I get there the talk is all about the estate and the gossip. After a year, well, it just gets a bit... insular... no, not insular, sort of incestuous... no... oh, I know what I mean.*"

"*Glad you do, you lost me after you'd said 'on the other side of the park'. Sorry to hear you and Hattie don't get on.*"

"*I didn't say that! We do. I just... look, it's no big thing. I just met someone in a café then on the market who I get on with and who isn't connected to the estate, that's all.*"

"*An' I'm pleased you have, I wasn't getting at y'. I just didn't realize you was, y' know, sort of not enjoying it here.*"

"I am." She smiled at him. "How can I not? I'm with you."
David smiled back. "It's just that, moving from Norfolk to here just seemed a continuation of what we had... and before that, what we had in Kent."

"Yeah, well; Kent..."

"It was your first position and not easy, I know. But after that, I only made one friend during the five years we were in Norfolk."

"Ellie."

"Yes, Ellie, and she went with Roger when he moved up to Ayr."

"Well, he was after the grouse... an' she's his wife."

"Interesting way of putting it."

"Putting what?"

"It's not a solo thing, David. There's other's involved in these... strategies you keepers have. Like Roger... and you, about how you see your careers developing, how you want to better yourself."

"Better for us both."

"Yes, I suppose so."

"But it is, and we talked all our moves through didn't we?"

"Yes, but what I'm talking about now isn't about us, or you." She looked out the kitchen window. "It's about me... God, this sounds selfish. I don't explain things well."

"No, no, you do, it's just me an' my brain."

"You always create an escape route for me and my failings with that phrase."

He smiled. "We do our best."

She stopped for a moment or two to frame her thoughts. David continued to eat as he listened, using his knife now in deference to Stephanie's recent chiding. "Look, it's not about being here; it's about how I sometimes feel. As if I'm *just part of the household goods, chattels for want of a better word... and that what I want comes a poor second to what your job demands; and I know that's right. No, not right, just... just the way things work out, things like shopping, making friends. Things that may seem unimportant to most but which matter a lot to me... that I just get to sort out a routine, strike up a friendship wherever it is we are, get a bit of direction in my life and then it all gets lost. I just get a little lonely... no, not lonely, just a little distant from the... from outside contact."*

David had stopped eating again as Stephanie's explanation had unfolded and was now concentrating fully. "Crikey, Steph, you do come out with them! I'd no idea... you should've said." He held out his hand across the table and she took it. "Phoof... took me a bit by surprise that." He gently pulled her to the chair alongside him. "I get so, so sort of caught up in the job; I forget sometimes you spend most of that time on your own."

"There's no need to make a big thing of it, David, I haven't."

"After that little lot you've just come out with? I'd hate to see you really bothered then."

"I haven't mentioned it before, have I?"

"I wish you had! I don't cope with emotional avalanches like this."

Stephanie sighed, loosed his hand and shook her head. "That's what I mean; that's why I haven't mentioned it."

"What?"

"We start talking about me and end up talking about you."

It took seconds for this to register then David simply said. "Oh, yeah; sorry love."

"Then you apologise and I end up feeling guilty."

"Erm... what? Er...?"

She saw the bewildered gaze in his eyes and now she gave him an escape route. "No, no... look. Don't take all this the wrong way. It's not that I'm pining away or anything like that, it's just that I don't get the chance to make long-term friendships and that's because of your job. Not fault nor blame, just your job." She held up her hand to stop him interrupting. "Yes, I know, you've been working hard, working your way up and that's for us both. I know. But doing that means we have to always be looking for the next best thing for you; for you, David. And because of that you always put the job first."

"Not always."

"Yes you do. When was the last time you came shopping with me?"

"Well... that's just shopping."

"No it's not. It's more than that. It's time together."

"I..."

"And most of the friends we have are your friends."

"Well, yes, but, that's because they're connected to the job..." His speech tailed off in realisation.

"See? Listen, David Raymond..." He knew she was serious now because she hardly ever used his middle name. "I'm not complaining, that's the truth, but they are your friends."

"Yes, s'pose so."

"No suppose about it. They're you're friends who just talk estate talk. Well this friend from the café, this one's mine, and that's a good thing, I think. You?"

"Yes, I do. I know you're not much of a one for striking out on your own."

"No. Mother saw to that."

"Ar, I know. Look, I hope you know that what I do is for us both, but I'd not want you to be the one who pays the

price for that." He caught her look. "Oh, OK, continues to pay the price for that." She nodded in agreement as he stopped for a few seconds. Stephanie took the opportunity to get up from the table and return to the stove. "Do you like what we're doin', Steph?"

She removed the pan from the Rayburn and turned to the sink and the waiting flask. "I've already said. Who in their right mind would say no to all this? We've got the freedom to walk on an exclusive piece of ground, a beautiful country cottage in a beautiful part of the country... a life that's shared with the seasons; it's nothing short of idyllic, and I love it."

"Well I love it too."

"And me?"

"That goes without sayin'."

The words left her almost of their own accord. "No it doesn't."

This stopped him for a few seconds. "I know, sorry. Don't think anything on it; I just get wrapped up..."

"In the job. I know, I've seen you. I know what makes you happy... I just wish I did."

"Who said you didn't make me happy? I've never said!"

"No, I know but, as my mother keeps reminding me, I'm not as worthy a woman as a man deserves..."

"Steph, don't..."

"Just look at the time it's taken me to sort the house out."

"Oh, I thought you meant..."

"Well, yes, there's that too, but it's not always about that, apparently I've plenty of other inadequacies." David looked up surprised as she continued. "Look around, David. We've been here a year. Most other women would have been on their second set of matching curtains and cushions by now; my mother certainly would."

"What does she know. I have offered to help."

"Yes, I know, but if you started painting in the backroom I'd have to apologise to the neighbours for splashing paint on their kitchen window."

"I'm not that bad."

"Almost. You're always in a hurry to get out."

"Well if not me then maybe you could get your new friend in to help eh?"

"Bit early for that, we've only just met. But she has reminded me that, well, that there's a life outside of these park walls, you know?"

"I know."

"I sometimes wonder."

"I do know, honest."

"Hm. Well just remember, outside those walls the estate isn't the only topic of conversation and a friend who knows this would be nice; a friend of my own making."

"And you've found one?"

"I have no idea but she just seems to have a more balanced view of things that's all, more grounded."

David began to pull the second slice of bread apart and dip the pieces into the remains on the plate. "Well, would you feel easier if I told you I think I'd like to stay on here, for a good while?"

"You would?"

"Ar, think so. Liam's a good head keeper. Not a bully, not an arrogant liar like Crayford in Kent were. Remember him?"

"How could I forget? Don't know how you put up with it."

"No choice. Only doin' a year on your first shoot marks you out as less than useless for future work. As it was, three years was all I could do without committin' a crime on him." His face showed his disgust. "He was some kind of scummer. I'd see him hangin' round them guns, takin' the tips an' me knowin' I'd not see any of it, an' us strugglin' like we were. I thought, blimey, the things you see when you aint got a gun."

"You didn't really think that did you?"

"What, that I'd like to shoot him? I 'ad the odd flash, ar; when it involved you, saw how the lack of money hurt you. Ar, I did. Like when he used all the fox pelt money we'd built up over the previous year plus the turkey profit for buyin' himself that motor bike, so's he'd not have to walk his beat no more, lazy sod; remember?"

"I remember how it affected you. Not the details, but remember you were very bothered by it."

"Bothered? You could say that. Ar, I were bothered. Idle sod. Tried to tell me we'd made a loss on the turkeys we'd reared for Christmas so he'd used the pelt money to cover it, so I'd not have to pay anythin' meself. As if I didn't know where the money for that bike had come from. He thought I was stupid enough as to believe him; that we'd made a loss on the turkeys we'd sold? For Christmas? The only one who makes a loss on turkeys at Christmas is the bloody turkey!" Stephanie laughed in spite of the seriousness of David's face. "Not funny, Steph. Our Christmas box they were, them birds. Yours and mine."

"I know." She softened a little. "I seem to remember you having to ask your dad for money that year."

"Well there was no future askin' yours was there? It'd just confirm his suspicion that his one and only child, his lovely daughter, had married a waster."

"He doesn't think that!"

"Yes he does; y' mum more so. Go on, tell me it's not so." Stephanie stayed silent. "See? Like Master Crayford an' them fox pelts; they all think I don't know, but I bloody do."

"Good job we moved on then or I'd be a prison widow by now!"

David smiled. *"Not you. You'd've divorced me and become a gangster's moll after my first year behind bars!"*

"Stop teasing." They laughed easily together and it broke the tension. *"Norfolk seemed a good move though."*

"Was alright, but too one dimensional for me."

"'Terribly flat, Norfolk'?"

"That's a good description, well put."

"Not original, I'm afraid."

"Well its spot on. Partridge show well there, not pheasants. Like throwin' pancakes over the guns. No, here's different."

"How?"

"Just different. Like I say, Liam seems a good man. He's got a genuine love of things natural, an' it's a low-ground estate that's been a shooting hub for a hundred and fifty years; still shoot double guns. The lie of the land shows some of the finest birds in the country."

"Strange him not being married or anything."

"What, Liam? Hm... Seems at ease with it all though."

"Jealous?"

"Me? No way. He don't know what he's missin'."

Stephanie smiled at him. *"And Eric?"*

"Eric's alright too. Old hand, done his time, knows the job backwards. Easy to work with and he's not afeared to share the load. No, I think, I hope, I've landed on me feet here so if you've friendships on the make then I reckon they'll be good for a while; an' I'm happy you're happy with 'em 'cos you deserve good things."

As Stephanie smiled, gathered the flask and made to return to the stove, she stopped and placed her hand on his shoulder. "You're a good man too, remember that, and I'm glad you feel settled."

"Couldn't have done it without you, Steph. I'm what you allow me to be."

She lifted her hand abruptly from his shoulder. "That's a responsibility too big for me, David."

"You know what I mean."

"I do." Stephanie filled the flask and David finished his breakfast in silence.

Soup in flask, Stephanie closed the cap and placed it in a wicker shopping basket as David got up from the table and moved to the Rayburn. "Is there more tea in the pot?"

"Yes, like your mother's it's bottomless." David smiled at the family quote and poured a second mug.

Fetching her coat from the hallway and putting it on, Stephanie gathered her bags. "What time are you back for lunch?"

"Liam wants to repair the release pen in The Clump; that place the deer ran through last cock day, so I'd like to think about two. That OK?"

"Yes, fine. Something cold?"

"Hot soup for your friend, cold lunch for your husband? I'm worried."

"No need to be. Some more of that Cheddar you liked so much, from Gray's…" She lifted the lid on the bread bin to show him. "…And a fresh bloomer I made yesterday."

"That the cheese you got last week?"

"The very same."

"Then get a larger chunk, that was handsome that was."

"I noticed. A one pound block gone in three days."

"A square of that an' a sharp apple with a chunk of bread; meal fit for a king."

"See, not a cold lunch but a right royal banquet. Right, your highness, I'll pick up some Granny Smiths too then." She moved towards the back door. "See you at two."

She was out and gone.

—⁊⁊⁊—

The Market was crowded, as it always was on a Wednesday, and the green gabardine of roof canvas and side-sheeting drawn over to protect the produce from the worst of the weather only served to make the surroundings drabber. The rain shower had stopped by the time Stephanie arrived at the outskirts of the tented village but the wind had maintained its intensity and was busy flapping dry the stretches of rippling, damp market stall with the occasional more urgent gust.

She slipped the mittens into her bag as she left the relative warmth of the indoor market to brave the perils of the outdoor. Alice saw her approaching, waved and called out, "Couldn't keep away could you, eh?"

Stephanie smiled and waved back. "No, it's the lure of the veg that does it."

Laughing quietly, Alice brushed down her soiled cow-gown with fingerless gloves. "So, what can we get for you?"

"Er... OK. Carrots, please, couple of pounds... Er, a swede and a large parsnip. Four pounds of Edward's too, please... oh, and a stick of celery."

"Sounds like someone's makin' rabbit stew."

"Yes, how did you know that?"

"You're not the only one who cooks bun-stew round here, you know. Was the main meal most folk hereabouts were reared on. Only one they could afford, things bein' like they were back then for workin' folk. Poachers did a roarin' trade. An' this bloody Thatcher'll want it comin' back an' all, I know it. Parsnip and celery? Most would have a good guess at the meat what's goin' in with that lot. Dumplin's too?"

"Herb ones, yes."

"Herb dumplin's! You're spoilin' that man."

"I think I'd be party to a walkout if there weren't any."

"Same as mine. Easy to keep 'appy, men, aint they?" Alice winked and smiled. "They're like a carpet, y' know. Lay 'em right the first time an' you can walk over 'em for years." She winked again as Stephanie laughed. "I'll get your veg." As Alice returned with the potatoes so Stephanie removed the flask from her bag and showed it. "I see you brought some then."

"Said I would and it's cold enough to be good for a body. Can you risk a cup?"

Alice turned. "Oi, Crabby, I'm gonna 'ave a drop of soup with my friend 'ere. Do you think you can manage without me for ten minutes?"

Dressed in familiar brown cow-gown and flat cap, Alan turned to them. "What do you think I've been doin' for the past forty years?"

"Strugglin'?"

"Strugglin'! I'll have you know this stall's been a fixture in this market for the past twenty five years an' at Draymoor market for fifteen before that. Strugglin'... Just get on with y' chat, it's what you lasses are good at, save y' worries about me."

"Think I might've touched a nerve there," said Alice. "Let's get out the wind and sample a drop of your soup."

She led the way to the rear of the stall and, overturning two orange crates, beckoned Stephanie to sit. Shaking the *flask then unscrewing the top she tipped out its spare cup and poured two generous portions. Alice wrapped her hands around the steaming mug blew away the visible heat and took a tentative sip. "By all that's holy, that's some soup that is, an' spicy too!"*

"Too much?"

"No. just right. What's in it?"

"Glad you like it. Er, nothing much; four bottles of tomato juice, juice of a crushed garlic clove, squeeze of tomato puree, a teaspoon of homemade fish stock, five drops of Tabasco..."

"What's that?"

"It's a hot sauce kind of thing; you need to be careful how much you use... Er, a dollop of Worcestershire sauce, erm... salt, plenty of black pepper... a potato for the thickening, oh, and a good tumbler of best vodka."

"Bloody hell, that's some recipe!" Alice sipped more fully. "Where's that from?"

"Lord Orton's man, our last place in Norfolk, before we moved here. They served it between drives. Just the thing for a stiff pick-me-up in the winter."

"They know how to live them buggers, don't they?" Alice sipped deeply again. "Is there more then?"

Pleased her efforts had gained approval, Stephanie smiled. "Yes, here." She topped up Alice's mug. "Do you think we ought to save some, for your Uncle?"

Alice looked along the stall. "What, him? Far too rich, just bring his gout back on." She smiled at Stephanie and took a full swig.

"Be careful, there's a fair drop of alcohol in it."

"It'll take more than that to get me squiffy. This'll set me up for the rest of the day an' any alcoholic interference

will only help things go smoother." She wrapped her hands around the cup and looked at Stephanie. *"You're right."*

"What?"

Alice lifted her palm-cupped mug. "It does taste better like this. Thanks, Steph; you're a pal, a lifesaver."

Day 10 – Wednesday 21st November 1985

It was whilst early morning mooching, window-shopping almost, down by the Lodge Road Bridge that ran over the River Toyle, that Alec saw the several large parties of duck filing out of this natural supermarket.

The recent cold snap had obviously sealed up the local field flashes and small ponds, forcing these ever hungry birds to congregate on the only nearby open stretch of water in order to preen and bathe, pre and post their visits to the stubble fields in search of spilt grain or frosted potatoes. And now, after that recent light fall of snow the effect could only be heightened. Alec made a mental note. What was needed was a distraction.

As he sat in the snug of the Red Lion that lunch-time, eavesdropping on the tale told by Albert Crowe about the captured duck-poaching youths and of punishments meted out by irate fathers, Alec's mind pictured the duck he had so recently seen. He turned over the thought that estate vigilance would likely lapse after such a victory. To set the seal on matters he was aware, as he left the hostelry, of a cold breeze. This would add to the chill, keep the local ponds frozen and, more importantly, would make the ducks' direction of travel more predictable. All the elements and omens were pointing to Alec being able to pass go and collect two hundred duck, and he was ready to exploit the weakness.

―⚭―

The main thing to do now was remain still. He knew the site well for he had flighted duck here many a time before. Squatting on a small piece of protruding bank, just inside the cover of a long stand of Norfolk reed on this widened crook of the bend in the river, Alec's view was perfect.

With the wind at his back and well covered by these reeds, the large, thick thorn brake on the opposite bank gave good sighting cover. This evening the birds, forced to face the wind in order to parachute from sky to river, would have to approach the water blind, over the tops of these thorns. Using them as a measure he could accurately gauge just when the birds would be in the best position for a successful shot; in sport done under these clandestine conditions the bag must be easily gathered at close of play, and from terra firma, not have it float off downstream as aqua splasha.

Flighting duck had always been Alec's favourite pastime but it was also the most hazardous when you did it as he did – uninvited. Any unnecessary movement would alert the already hypersensitive wildfowl as they made their first circuit of the feeding spot, well out of gunshot to check out safety, so facing front and stillness were the order of the day. But this very need for immobility, coupled with a good breeze that twitched and rattled the reed cover, made pre-empting the arrival of keepers more tricky.

But for Alec, squatting silently in the lull – that deep outward sigh which accompanies the close of each day – in spite of the difficulties and risk factor, all was worth it just for the special pleasure of being a part of the cycle of the earth. It may only be something as everyday as the winter song of a robin or the less frequent scene of geese moving in formation across a blood orange sunset, but it was always enough to give this day, any day, an extra significance which sealed it in the memory; a personal note in nostalgia's diary.

Steeped in this particular evening's environmental symphony, as a season-ticket holder, Mister Alec Stratton had taken his place in the river's auditorium of reeds, soaking up nature's production and awaiting the first telltale sounds that would announce the wildfowl's arrival on stage; the whiffling of primary feathers as they played the air currents in the ducks' descent to the river.

Concentration fixed his stare.

Then he heard the first solitary mallard entering the scene.

Waiting his moment until the bird topped the thorns and was midway across the river he sent it crashing to earth behind him with a single shot. Pocketing the spent cartridge and reloading he smiled momentarily at his success then settled to await the next player's entrance.

The main thing to do now was to remain still but, involuntarily, Liam looked up from his straw hide on The Clump's feed ride as the sound of a single shot reached him. It seemed a long way off, yet nearby in its intrusion of the previous, prolonged silence.

'Could be anywhere,' he thought. 'Evenin' like this... stiff breeze...' He looked at the moving tree canopy above. '...Blowin' in that direction. Not shootin' on our ground though... Don't think so anyway...' He shifted himself on the straw-bale seat that had refused to warm up with the contact of his nether regions but had rather chilled him instead. Liam had now got to the stage where he was unsure where the bale ended and his backside began and the thought struck him, not for the first time; 'Do my piles the world of good will this.'

He knew the vixen's tracks, had even heard her calling for two previous nights, but she had failed to fall victim to the string of fox snares in the wood. Now Liam had made up enough time during the day to spend the approach to dusk ensconced in one of the bale stacks placed along the ride by David and Eric... waiting.

Evening was his favourite part of the day and this particular evening had not disappointed. For the forty minutes he had sat there, Liam had watched with pleasure as wrens, robins and dunnocks, oblivious to his presence, had worked over the damp straw of the ride in search of its myriad population of spiders and insects. Then, as dusk gathered and these tiny songbirds snuggled themselves into the pockets of pheasant-disturbed straw, ready to shelter from the promised harshness of the weather, he was reminded of the long winter of seventy three.

That year, on this very same ride, countless song birds and small mammals had responded to his pheasant-feeding whistle, so severe and prolonged were the snowy conditions. After the first ten days of this cold snap and with night temperatures regularly as low as minus fourteen, rabbits would hop out of the woodland cover at the edge of the feed ride each morning to take food directly from his open palm with velvet-gloved noses. A muntjac, too, had plucked up sufficient courage to enter the ride and feed, albeit from a distance. As the conditions switched from harsh to brutal and yet more snow fell, this deer and three companions were soon also feeding from the hand. Indeed, such was the glut of wildlife during feeding time that the whole scene took on a Disney-esque quality as the circus moved down the ride, trotting, pacing, jinking, flying and flowing around the moving feeder that was Liam Coyne.

But reasons and seasons change and the ride was now playing host to a different scene. Now the same keeper, absorbed in the memory of his life-saving visits of back then, was waiting to serve a death warrant of right now. Putting the sound of the recent shot to the back of his mind and facing front, Liam sat with alert concentration waiting for the signals that would announce the fox's arrival; the scolding of blackbird, robin or wren, the bark of muntjac, a scream of vulpine lust.

The sound had a distant familiarity. Like a high pitched whine it came on swiftly before he could fully place it. It was not until Alec saw their first investigative circuit that he made the connection.

'Teal! Not 'ere very often. Weather must be bitin' hard.'

Alec upped the gun as the gang of six birds bobbed and jinked their way to the river.

Bang! Bang!

The left and right barrels found their intended targets. As four remaining teal rocketed skywards so the chosen two folded up their canopy and plummeted earthwards, no longer able to resist gravity.

The double shot reached Liam and the permutations began to seep in. Mind maps were drawn as to the shots' position and the niggling possibility of threatened game on the estate began to twitch in the soles of his feet.

'Damndamn, fuck... Sounds like the river. Must be duck, this time of day... Lewis'? Could be... they normally let us know...'

Completely wrapped up in the essence of the sport, Alec eagerly awaited the arrival of his next target. It came on fast; a lone tufted duck yawing into the breeze as it approached the river.

Bang!

This evening flight was turning out to be as good as it gets.

The single shot decided things.

"Fuck it!"

The expletive was stated under his breath as Liam slipped cussedly out of the hide. Moving silently down the straw covered ride towards gateway and Land Rover, it was only by sheer chance he saw the vixen begin to glide, almost ghost-like, across the ride ahead of him.

The stock of the shotgun slipped into the caress of his shoulder as the fox began realisation's twist away, back into safety, back into the ditch from which she had so recently emerged; back into life. The first charge of shot hit her low, striking rear legs and feet and turning her sideways on, the next a split second later killed her outright, hitting her in the chest, the force of its impact pushing her into the ditch head first.

The double shot reached Alec as he waited his next opportunity.

He turned slightly, slowly to face its direction. 'Estate boundary somewhere... could be duckin' too, but a long ways off... Safe enough here for a while yet, I reckon.'

"You poor sod. See, if pheasants weren't your quarry then you'd not be mine."

Liam moved forward and drew the vixen's body up the bank and onto the ride, surveying her superb condition.

"Not your night is it? If I'd stayed in them bales…"

A single drake topped the thorn brake.

'Ayup, more mallard!'

Alec lifted the gun again.

Bang!

Liam gathered up the vixen and made his way swiftly toward the Land Rover. He needed to get on. It would be fully dark all too soon and the frequency of distant shots was a real bother now. Depositing his capture in the rear of the vehicle he started the engine and slipped away from The Clump and towards the river road.

He had originally thought to go to Barton's Plantation on the estate boundary and check the shots from there before committing fully but, still brooding on the plight of the vixen, it was only after the turning had slipped by at fifty miles an hour that he cursed and decided to go on to the bridge at Lodge Road instead. After a further few hundred yards, Liam dropped in behind another Land Rover, the number plate of which was very familiar. Flashing his lights he alerted the attention of Henry Saville and Malcolm Tolland and they both coasted into the verge. Liam stepped out onto the road and moved to the other vehicle as its window slid open. The yellow Labrador in the back barked a welcome and Henry's voice echoed from within.

"Shut up, Hoover, you noisy sod!"

Liam's face took up a wry grin. Henry and his dogs, particularly Hoover, were well known in the district. Only last shooting season, the happy-go-lucky Labrador had been mopping up praise from his master for bringing back several Barn Tor pheasants well after the drive had finished, seemingly wiping the eyes of the gang of professional pickers-up. It was only when he brought back a brace of birds tied together with baler twine did Henry realise the dog had been retrieving them from the rear of the game cart.

True to form on this particular evening, Hoover was showing his usual servility by barking, bouncing up and down on four pogo sticks, whipping the vehicle's rear door into submission with his tail and forcing his nose over Henry's shoulder towards the open window. Pushing his arm through, Liam acknowledged the greeting of the near-hysterical dog, his hand being liberally doused with spittle for his trouble.

"Evenin', Liam. You heard it too, then?"

Liam nodded. "Henry, Malcolm. Yeah. Wasn't quite sure where it come from at first..." Hoover lunged forward once more to get extra fuss. "Hello old fella. Is it on your ground, Henry?"

"Yes, I think so, not a hundred percent sure but... Get down Hoover!" Liam removed his sopping wet hand, flicking off the excess froth. "Sounds near Lodge Road Bridge. That's either us or the land on the other side, where the Sheffield syndicate shoot. Got that part-time keeper workin' it now. We've only just got back from hunting at Arleigh... Hoover, will you...! Stopped the lorry in the stable yard, stepped out, heard the shots, in the Land Rover and over here; left the girls to sort the horses."

"No peace, eh?"

"No, and no tea yet either."

"Decent day?"

"Aye. Not bad," replied Malcolm. "Killed two. One we had to dig for, the other we flushed from Captain Morris's coverts gave a good account of itself. The last of the day went to ground too, in that patch of gorse over by Shipley, on Rosie Ashton's place. Terrier boys were still at when we left."

"Light's closin'," observed Liam.

"Ar, they may have to leave it. Stanley will let us know later, I'm sure."

"Good day then."

"Yes, not bad but ground's heavy where it's thawed so, horses tired, hounds tired, us knackered and now this..."

A further shot snapped the links of their conversation.

"Like I said, no rest for the wicked. Right, we'll see if you've pitched the position right, Henry. I'll go back round to our boundary and walk along the river to the bridge from Barton's Plantation in case they try and leave that way. You gonna go straight to the bridge?"

"Yes. OK."

Liam turned on his heel. "Lights off."

"Yup." Henry closed the window, deadening slightly the noise of the once more hysterical dog that had sensed a move was imminent. A muffled shout of, "Shut up, Hoover!" made Liam smile again as he climbed back into his own vehicle and retraced his journey to the missed turning of earlier.

With five duck down, Alec was satisfied with his evening's work even though he had missed the last one. The breeze-twitched reed fronds had caused his eye to flick momentarily from the target and a miss was a sour note to leave the evening flight on, but the gathering gloom now told him he had better leave.

After twenty five minutes in one spot he was sure someone would soon arrive and spoil the evening's events. It was only the possibility of further teal in the bag that made him decide on just another five minutes…

Henry switched out the lights a full five hundred yards from the bridge, the engine ticking over as he coasted the final fifty yards to the gateway that led onto the bottom meadow.

He and Malcolm sat and peered through the failing light but a low river mist, well sheltered by the closeness of the thorn-brake, had wrapped its cotton-wool fingers across the field, obscuring any sight of river and reeds.

Liam arrived at the boundary of Barton's Plantation and jumped out. On his way down the bank that led to the river he disturbed four duck sheltering in the willows that dipped across the water like static swallows.

Up the birds went like rockets, then out and along the river towards the bridge. 'Blimey! Teal! Don't see them very often, weather must be bitin', thought Liam as he set out along the river bank towards the bridge.

Alec rose from his position, stiff but satisfied.

There had been no more birds for a while, the temperature was dropping rapidly and time really was up; overtime almost. He moved to the river's edge and the end of the curtain of reeds. The light and mist obscured his view so, after a short pause for listening, he emerged onto the field to collect his booty.

Liam moved along the river, scanning both opposite bank and the meadow ahead for signs of life.

Henry and Malcolm opened the Land Rover doors with exquisite quiet and stepped down onto the crispling grass.

Alec was collecting a second bird, another plump mallard, when he looked across the field and saw the teal lying only yards apart on the grass.

The sound of duck whisking across the sky made him drop his cargo, slip down onto his knees and tighten his grip on the gun as four teal swept out of the mist and across his line of vision. As he lifted the sixteen-bore shotgun for a final salute so he heard the unmistakable sound of a dog barking.

Rolling his eyes at the sound, Henry half turned and leant back into the Land Rover.

"Hoover! Quiet! You bloody hound!"

Frozen in mid-move, Alec slipped the safety-catch back on. 'Here comes trouble.'

Liam heard, located then named the faint barking. He smiled and shook his head in silent admonition. 'That bloody Hoover. He'll wake the dead. Scare off any poacher within hearin' distance... as far away as Derby.'

Henry's harsh whisper, coupled with a smack on the nose, stopped Hoover in mid bark, cowing him temporarily.

Pushing the vehicle's doors gently to, Henry and Malcolm left the vehicle containing the now silent and slightly chastened Labrador and climbed over the gate into the meadow.

Alerted to their position, Alec now caught sight of them, ghostly through the mist. They needed no labels, they were just the enemy, their intentions telegraphed by their slinking attitude as they landed on the field side of the gate and scampered to the river's edge.

He gathered up the dropped mallard and glanced again at the teal; his but someone else's already. A plan was formulating even as he trotted back to the reeds. 'What I need to do is keep the reed cover between me and the hunt; that means along the edge of the river, slip up the bank at Barton's Plantation, onto the road an' away home.'

Liam was now quite close to the bend in the river and by looking across at an angle, he could just make out the very faint beginnings of a belt of reeds.

Alec weaved along the river's edge, his movement disguised by the wind-snickering reeds. As he reached the upstream edge of them so he saw Liam. 'Shit an' derision; now we've got trouble.' He moved out and back, into the water, its biting grip making him draw in his breath as he moved away from the bank and deeper into reeds and river.

"Was that summat movin' just now? Up ahead… by the river?"

Henry whispered back as they moved in single file along the river bank towards the reeds. "Dunno, Malc; could've been Liam."

"Jesus, Henry, that bloody dog!"

Having seen Henry and Malcolm disappear towards the river and in such a secretive manner, Hoover reckoned it could only mean they were on the search for some sort of quarry and he was apoplectic with indignation at having been left behind.

In his tantrum, Hoover had now climbed into the front of the Land Rover where he leapt from one side of the windscreen to the other, barking and gazing after his mist-dissolved and much beloved master. As the dog's frenzy grew so the marks of saliva and the frequency of nose prints increased on the windscreen, further obscuring his view.

"You should've tied him up 'im at the stables."

Malcolm's unnecessary reminder nagged at Henry and he hissed back, "No time was there! My God, just 'ark to 'im!"

Liam reached the beginning of the bend in the river close to the reeds and slowed his pace; he figured this would be an obvious point of concealment for a poacher. He could clearly hear the cacophony being kicked up by Hoover and figured anyone else on site would be fully aware of their arrival so secrecy was of little use now. He called out, "You come to me Malcolm! Henry? Stay where you are so you can see the opposite bank!"

Moving up to then beyond the reed fringe, Liam rounded the bend and saw his two partners-in-scrum ahead. It was then his glance across the field was raked back as the unfamiliar met the familiar to stand out as if lit by a searchlight. "Hold on!" Liam stopped. "Keep lookin' Henry. You just move on a bit further Malcolm, so all the reeds are covered." Stepping out into the field, Liam picked up the two teal.

"What's that?" Henry had moved to Liam. "Couple o' duck is it?"

Malcolm joined them.

"Teal," replied Liam as the group gathered twenty yards from the river bank.

Having liberally plastered the majority of the windscreen with phlegm and spittle and sent his rear nails through the driver's seat in several places, Hoover was forced further over to the passenger side of the vehicle in order to see through an as yet unsullied portion of the window.

As he bounced off the edge of the seat and onto the door, his dinner-plate paws flicked the handle and, to his immense surprise and pleasure, the door shot open. Without waiting for an official invite the ecstatic dog leapt out of the vehicle and was swiftly up and over the field gate, intent on getting as much out of what was left of the day as possible.

"Don't see 'em round here very often, do y'?" asked Malcolm.

"No," replied Liam. "I put up some teal on my way down to the river; they headed this way. Can't be these though, they're cold. Shot a while ago..." Liam's voiced tailed off as he glanced across the field. "Ayup, 'ere comes trouble."

Henry followed his gaze. "Bugger!" He looked at Malcolm. "We didn't close the bloody doors properly!" He turned to Liam and offered a lame excuse. "Too much noise... Loves his shootin'. Come on y' daft sod, come 'ere!"

Pleased at having found his master and friends so quickly and at not getting an immediate good hiding, Hoover flung himself into a welcoming ceremony. Only after gaining fuss from all those present, twice, did he settle to some serious business. Although there had been no shots he was convinced there must be something to retrieve, and he moved closer to the river bank and reeds as conversation and concentration turned to consider where the shooting had come from.

"Could've been over the other side of the river..." Malcolm indicated. "Maybe been further down... who knows?"

"Close," said Liam firmly. "Those two teal lyin' near each other like that." He looked across the river. "They've flighted in this way, over them thorns, wind as it is. Maybe shot from in that thorn brake. If that bloody snow had held over a bit longer we'd have a map. No one came past me, I'm certain of that." He looked at the nosing Hoover. "An' I have to say, after all that noise, if they were over the other side when we arrived they're long gone by now; ayup..."

Hoover arrived at Henry's side, his face split by a grin as he proudly held the tufted duck. The dog circled head down. "Good lad, bring it on, good boy." Henry took the bird from Hoover's mouth at the fourth attempt and checked it over. "We've only just missed him; this one's still just warm."

Liam shook his head in frustration as he pointed to the thorn brake. "He, or they, must've been over yonder, on the syndicate's ground. Bird this warm? No way anyone scarpering off would've got past us if they'd been on this side, no way. Well, poachers they may be but, on that side of the river? Not a lot we can do. Part-time keepers are worse than useless at these times."

Amongst the reeds and cripplingly cold water, Alec shrank further back, out into the depths, feeling the water's sluggish, frosted tug welcome him in.

Dropping further back and kneeling on the gravel base, the water covered him to the bottom of his nose and now, as minutes and conversation ticked by, Alec waited for what he knew would come.

Having scoured the field and flushed with his success, the river was the next port of call for Hoover and he moved to the reeds. If nothing else there was bound to be a moorhen or coot skulking in there and it was such fun disturbing their peace.

Don't think it'll be worth hanging on any longer," said Henry. "Like you said, Liam, "whoever it was will be long gone by now."

"I'd reckon Hoover will have seen to that," added Malcolm. "Noise he's been making an' all."

Liam nodded in agreement and Henry needed no reminding of his dog's intrusion into the party. He was now also feeling the pangs of hunger, and to cap it all the cold was beginning to bite deeper as the warmth and excitement of earlier movement began to leave him. The feeling was mutual. Liam had not been home since lunch time and was eager to be off; there was a fox pelt to deal with before tea.

"I'll give you a lift if you like, Liam. Save you the walk back."

As one, the trio turned towards the gate. "Cheers, Henry." Liam was glad of the offer and it would also give him a chance to discuss the vixen of earlier. "I'll call over to yours tomorrow. We can let their keeper know and have a look in them thorns. Too late, I know, but we might find a cartridge case or two, if they've been sloppy. At least we'll have solved it."

Alec had been fully justified in his fears from the moment he was aware a dog had arrived on the scene.

Man only ever saw what he wanted to see or what circumstances and mood dictated... not a dog. Dogs inhabit a different world, a parallel universe almost; this was now a whole new game of catch.

Hoover mooched along the bank then stopped, catching wind of something... something...?

With his head rigid, his frozen death-grip on the necks of the two submerged mallard in his right hand, his ghost-numb grip on the shotgun in his left, Alec moved only his eyes. The first he saw of the dog was when it entered his line of sight and began to prowl the bank; then it stopped.

Lifting one front paw in parody of a point, Hoover slowly twisted his head towards the river and stood still. Their eyes met, locked onto one another's; dog sights man? Man sights dog.

In a move of delicate, gymnastic control which belied his nine years, Hoover leant backwards and took his full weight onto his hind legs to briefly describe the unicorn rampant as he slowly and oh, so, gently, swivelled his body towards the river. Lowering his front paws into the water, he sent a slight ripple, like the approach of a speeding torpedo, towards Alec's nose.

The dog was now rooted to the spot, tail ramrod stiff, rump raised up on the bank, front paws dipped frozen into the biting cold of the river. His senses were consumed by the half-vision reflected on the water's broken surface and lit by the dusky rising moon. Alec knew that to even blink now would be fatal; even such a slight movement at this distance would be sufficient to illicit a querulous bark.

The two protagonists looked deep into each other's eyes, into each other's very souls. The cold that had numbed Alec from chest to toes and was removing his lower jaw now began to gnaw its way into the front legs of Hoover.

Liam, Malcolm and Henry had travelled about twenty paces when lack of company was registered.

"Where's that damned dog?"

The question was heard by the quartet of humans with varying degrees of understanding, but the canine member that created a quintet had no sensory room left to register the query.

Liam looked around. "By the river... an' on bloody point by the look of it."

Henry's exasperated sigh escaped him as it had so often before where Hoover was concerned. "Oh, for God's sake... Leave the bloody moorhens alone! He's a bugger for 'em... Come on, Hoover! Leave it!"

Cast in bronze, Hoover stayed deaf, seemingly about to levitate with the tension.

Alec stared straight ahead at a fixed point beyond Hoover's head, his breath coming so slowly that he was on the verge of fainting. The water was raking at the very marrow of his bones and he knew with absolute certainty that the cold was going to ripsaw clean through them in a very short time. His lower jaw was set solid and the pain in his ears was so acute that it seemed to pierce his temples and eye sockets with laser sharpness.

"Come on...! Oi! Come 'ere and leave it when I call you!"

Hoover stood his ground. The water temperature was now making his front legs shake uncontrollably, the ripples lapping at Alec's nostrils like excited puppies.

Turning back towards the river, Henry's stride telegraphed his purpose and of punishments to come as he muttered to himself, "Bloody hell, dog. You deaf sod." Then his voice became laced with a volume brought about by the frustration at having to return at all. "I said come 'ere!"

Henry's shout turned the approaching mallard as they cleared the thorn brake, causing them to jink wildly to one side and climb skywards, quacking hysterically.

As Hoover flicked a look at the fast departing mallard, so Alec dipped his head under the water, his ripples blending in with those made by Hoover's shaking legs.

The dog looked back and if ever a member of the canine family frowned in puzzlement then this was he. With the space that had so recently held him spellbound now strangely empty, Hoover opened his ears to his master's fast approaching, fast rising voice. Pushing his front feet against the river's gravel bottom the dog heaved himself splashingly onto the bank and trotted somewhat stiffly towards Henry.

"Jesus Christ, you useless sod... come on! I'm bloody cold standing out here while you chase after moor'ens an' moonbeams!" Henry swung his boot at Hoover, who, slow to move, took the blow on his thick, padded rump. Giving a yelp he scuttled off towards Malcolm and Liam, seeking sanctuary. "Get off out of it, useless!"

Unable to stay submerged any longer, Alec chanced discovery. His head silently broke the surface and he took the measured, huge gulp of air his lungs had been screaming for.

Hoover turned at this ripple of sound.

"Hoovah! Don't you bloody dare...! Come here an' leave it!"

Henry's voice drowned any further desires the dog might have harboured about being tempted back to the river. With a sideways and slightly sheepish look at Henry, he continued to trot along with the departing trio, tail in the half-wag position.

Alec took his second gasp of air in time to hear Liam.

"No, no, you an' Mrs. Saville 'ave the teal, Henry. Malcolm will be happy with the tufty, livin' by himself, won't you Malcolm?" This was followed by Malcolm's unenthusiastic acceptance.

"How's that terrier of yours now?" asked Henry.

"Blimey, news travels round here don't it? How did you hear?"

"Saw Eric when we were loading hunters this mornin'; he was walkin' the boundary, checking traps I guess. He popped over to ask where we were drawin' today and mentioned about a disagreement over ownership of a rat. Razor alright?"

"As well as can be expected; looks more like Henry Cooper than Henry Fonda now..."

It was Henry's splutterings from the gateway that interrupted their conversation. "Oh, bloody 'ell! Look at the state of this motor! Where's that damn dog?"

Bracing his body for the first crippling move toward the bank, Alec heard a sharp yelp from the direction of the Land Rover which echoed his own yelp through clenched teeth as he forced his right leg to begin the journey.

He had only taken a couple of paces when he realised the two mallard were no longer in his grip. The cold had been so intense they had slipped away downstream without Alec knowing and he had to look to check that the shotgun was still there. It was, but only because his crooked finger was frozen solid round the trigger guard. Reaching the edge of the reeds, the mist and chilling night air on his soaked clothes caused him to inhale sharply.

The doors of the Land Rover closed and its engine revved to a high pitched whine as it turned out of the gateway, lights and heater on, and up the Lodge Road to homes and fires.

Alec began the three mile struggle back to home.

Chapter Four
Month 9 – March 1985

"Well, how about next Tuesday then? No market that day is there, and I've got nothing demanding on; Tuesday alright?"

"Only if you're certain." Alice lodged the last of the vegetables into Stephanie's bag. "Don't want to put no one out."

"You won't be. If we make it about eleven? I'll pick you up from your house."

"No! I mean, no thanks, there's no need. I can get a bus and walk from the village. Don't want to put no one out, like I said."

"And I said you'll not, Alice. Alright, I'll pick you up from the village bus stop then, how's that suit?"

"No, no… is there not a bus that goes nearer you?"

"Well, yes, there's the Green Line out to Denham. Goes right by the bottom of our lane, but they're so infrequent, only every hour I think. Village bus is every forty minutes. Just let me know what time and I'll meet you. Here's my number." Stephanie scribbled her telephone number onto a brown paper bag which she had separated from its stringed companions. "Just 'phone on Monday, I'll be in all day. Let me know the time." Stephanie gave one of her biggest smiles.

Pocketing the paper bag, Alice smiled by return. "Couple of extra parsnips in there…" She patted the shopping bag.

"...In case a rabbit stew beckons. I'll 'phone Monday and see you Tuesday then."

"Lovely. I'll provide coffee and cake, all you need bring is yourself."

Stephanie turned to go but Alice took hold of the shopping bag handle and prevented her. "You're sure about this, about me coming for coffee and stuff; you're sure?"

Stephanie smiled again but it was a little more quizzical than the last. "Yes, of course. You make it sound like coffee and cake was a clandestine operation, illegal almost."

"Close."

"What?"

Alice lightened the moment by laughing. "Ha! Nothing. We'll talk on Tuesday. I'll bring a home-made walnut loaf to add to the table. Is it strong?"

"What?"

"The table, is it strong?"

"Erm... yes, think so. Why?

"We're talkin' about my walnut loaf y'know."

"I can't imagine for one second that you'd bake anything that would be other than featherweight."

"Welterweight, y' mean! I'll bring some butter, help with the taste."

"Mine not good enough? I get it from Dobson's down the bottom there."

"Best there is. Right, see you Tuesday."

Stephanie turned to go again. "'Phone Monday, I'll have a chat with my table in preparation." She stepped out from under the tarpaulin into the light drizzle that had begun to fall and was immediately swept away by the press of market shoppers.

Alice looked at the empty space. "Steph, you have no idea..." A delivery man wearing a clear plastic rain hat over his already wet hair and carrying a large crate on his shoulder approached the stall. "Yes, love?"

"'Ere's cauliflowers."

Alice smiled at him and pointed behind her. "Crates, wooden."

"What?"

She shook her head. "Nothin' love, just my little joke. 'Ere, put 'em over 'ere, with these crates."

"Can you just shift them sacks of spuds then love?"

"What, with my bad back? You'll have me put it out again then you'll 'ave Mister Grumpy nineteen eighty five over there to answer to. Just pop 'em alongside the spuds, that'll do… an' that hat does nothin' for y', trust me on that."

The delivery man walked to where Alice was pointing, not even the ghost of a smile cracking his set face.

—⫘—

Eric bundled the last of the pine brash under his arm and walked towards the open rear door of the Land Rover, the back end of which was stuffed with more branches. He pressed them down, inserted the last armful on top and, on their release, the squashed branches sprang back up, filling the doorway completely. He looked at the jam-packed vehicle.

'Hardly room for the driver. Today's the day that Raquel Welch'll be thumbin' a lift dressed in her bear-fur thingy…"

He got into the driver's seat, turned the key and set off towards a distant gateway, the Land Rover scrabbling for grip on the wet slope of the wood's central ride.

As the bus moved off, Alice looked across at the sound of the horn.

Stephanie opened her door, calling as she leaned out to wave, "Do you know I can't remember when that bus was *last on time." She lowered her voice as Alice drew closer. "What did you do, threaten him with your walnut loaf?"*

"I would've done but I couldn't lift it up!"

They both laughed as Alice got in and they drove away.

—◊◊◊—

Even from that distance, Eric knew who it was. As he drew near to David's cottage he slowed slightly and slid the window back in readiness.

Two figures stepped out. One, Stephanie, he had recognized straight away; that hair and that figure, even under a fitted winter coat, was immediately recognizable. Of the other he was not so sure, but was immediately concerned at who he thought it might be. As he swept along the estate track that ran past the cottage so he leant on the horn and waved his arm aloft. Stephanie, on hearing this, turned and waved back; Alice on the other hand, after looking up briefly, turned quickly away... but it was enough; enough for Eric to have his suspicions confirmed.

His face set in a frown, he travelled along the road towards the laying pens and his pre-arranged meeting with David.

"Despite the sun, it's still a bit parky isn't it? Put your coat on any of those hooks and go into the warm. I'll just get the coffee off the stove and the sponge I made yesterday. Make yourself comfy in there."

Alice entered the sitting room as Stephanie disappeared along the corridor and into the kitchen. A coal and log fire was glowing beckoningly behind a tall fireguard in a spotless room, a room which lacked the scent of recent cleaning, of mad dashes with polish and rag before visitors arrived. This room was spotless because it was always thus; she knew it instinctively.

The cushions scattered on each of the chairs were dressed in familiar material. She smiled at the café memory then her eye was drawn to the mantle shelf and a string of photographs. Smiling people with dogs; smiling people with guns; smiling people. The photo of the man placed centrally, she thought, must be David, the husband.

The door opened and Stephanie entered carrying a laden tray and followed by a small, brown black and white mongrel suffering from tail frenzy. "I might have known you'd crab your way in here young lady."

Alice bent to stroke the dog which immediately threw herself onto her back to accept the fuss. "Who's this then?"

Putting the tray on a low table near the hearth, Stephanie scooped up the dog which immediately flicked over onto her back again to lay cradled in her arms, making Alice laugh. "This is my baby…" She nuzzled her head into the dog's neck. "My baby." Stephanie lifted her head and stood rocking gently from her hips. "Sack, meet Alice; Alice, meet Sack."

"Hello, Sack." Alice tickled the dog's tummy who in turn snuggled her head into the crook of Stephanie's arm with a couple of body twists and closed her eyes. Stephanie immediately lowered the dog to the floor.

"Oh, no you don't, little miss, you're not to stay in here." The terrier stood for a moment casting a wounded, wistful glance at hearth rug and fire then lifted her head to scent the covered cake. "Out. Go on. Into the kitchen. Go on… Sack, basket, now!" The dog took on a severely thrashed look and left the room. Stephanie shoved the door to with her foot. "Kids, eh?"

"Can tell who's in charge here." Alice looked at the tray and its glass coffee pot. "And real coffee too!" She rummaged in her bag and began to remove its contents. "Sack? Funny name for a dog."

"That's where David found her, at our last place."

"What, in a sack?"

"Yes, with two others. They'd been slung in the Ouse, the river that flowed through the estate. Both her litter mates were dead... well, it was so cold, but that one..." she gestured in the direction of the recently departed dog, "That one managed to survive. We took it in turns to feed her every hour or so over the following ten days and that's what we ended up with. David buried the other two under a hawthorn, middle of our old garden. Red one. Every year, when it blossomed we used to say, 'Sack, puppies are back....'" Her voice tailed off in reminiscence.

"This one's your dog then?"

"My baby. She goes out with David when he's dogging back and working hedgerows and she's a sharp one for furry stuff, foxes and such, but she spends most of her time here, getting under my feet." Alice smiled and after a few seconds, Stephanie voiced her thoughts aloud. "Funny how David deals in so much... well, death, I suppose, directly or indirectly, almost to the point where you think he's become inured to it all. But when he brought that pathetic little thing in and I took her on... well you would wouldn't you." She smiled wistfully. "Went to the local hospital, knew some of the staff there and they gave me one of those baby bottles... from the premature baby unit, fed her every two hours... she's been my baby ever since."

"How old is she?"

"Three now. She's such a sweet thing but has a yen for fire and cake. Well, who hasn't?"

Alice held up a cloth-wrapped something she had removed from her bag. "It may be you'll change your mind *after a taste of this 'ere loaf; have you got a butcher's cleaver handy?"*

Inside the laying-pen, David saw the Land Rover approaching from the yard end of the field and moved across to intercept it by the main gate.

Eric got out and untied the lashed rear door, calling as he went. "One more of these'll do it I reckon. You?"

"About." David indicated the expanse of pen. "I've got that last three loads well spread and the tin shelters are all up to scratch." He looked at the pile in the vehicle. "Ar, one more should do it. Do you want me to go fetch?"

"No, not unless you've got a real yearnin' t' be up there. I'm quite 'appy to be the errand boy."

"Suits me. I thought we'd do this then get coffee."

"That'll do." Eric looked across at David. "You gonna go home for it or did you bring a flask?"

"Flask," said David, pointing towards the centre of the laying pen. "You?"

"Home. Gotta split a handful of logs for Hattie so I'll get 'em done and stay on for lunch then get back over 'ere and start sortin' cock birds with you an' Liam."

"They need it. I told him yesterday there's a good twenty too many in here. Turf the buggers out to that holdin' pen early, they'll do as loss-makers."

"They will. Right, best get on." Eric moved off with an armful of brash and David followed suit.

After twenty minutes, he moved across to Eric. "You're quiet. If you weren't movin' I'd reckon you were dead."

"Nothin'..." He used his boot to seat a large branch alongside one of the low shelters that ran around the sides of the pen, then stopped. "Look... No way of lettin' this out gentle-like. I might be mistook, but I reckon your Steph

has got Alice Stratton as company up at your house. Got a good enough view to be almost sure."

David almost laughed. "Who... what, the Stratton?"

"Is there another?"

There was no laughter now. "She's never met her... not that I know."

"I'd ask again then 'cos I swear I've just seen 'er goin' into your place." Eric paused. "None of my business in the end who's friends with who, but... 'im of all folk."

"Steph did mention she'd made a friend, some woman who works on the market."

"Then that's definite. Stratton's missus works there odd days. Her uncle's got a greengrocery stall there."

"That fills in the gaps. Steph mentioned this new friend of hers had given her a few extra in the way of veg a couple of times... Bugger!"

"Nothin' much served by that. You'll just have to mention it and see how the land lies, won't y'?"

David nodded. "Yeah, I s'pose so." He sighed. "Didn't want this right now, not after our recent chat."

"What was that all about? Not that it's any of my..."

"No, that's alright. Was nothin' really, just Steph remindin' me about my priorities... you know, the job versus home? How she sometimes felt left out, lonely. How pleased she was to have found someone who she just... just got on with."

"There's my Hattie you know. She can always talk to her."

"Ar, I said as much."

"They saw a bit of each other when you first got here, not so much of late."

"No, I know." David glanced round the pen, giving himself time to pick his words. "Look... don't take this the *wrong way, Eric, it's just Steph said one of the reasons she liked this, this Alice woman, was that she was unconnected to the estate..."* He caught Eric's expression. *"Got that wrong then, but you know what I mean; that the talk wasn't all about estate gossip... I hope."* He stopped for a moment or two then carried on through a wry smile. *"That didn't come out at all well and you mustn't take any offence, nor Hattie, please. You've both been a real prop for us and I'm really grateful for that, we both are, can't thank you enough."*

"There's no need for thanks, David, we do it 'cos we want to."

"Yes, I know you do. I know. I'm making this worse by talkin'." He shook his head. *"Difficult balancin' act aint it, married life an' work life?"*

"Married life an' keeperin', y' mean, an' yes it bloody well is. Familiar territory for me; got a medal and a near divorce for it." He saw David's surprised reaction. *"Ar, I know, but it's not common knowledge and there's never been a reason to mention it. Take my advice; important thing is for you not to go in there like a bull in a china cabinet. That's the voice of experience talkin' there an' I only wish I'd been told the same. There's probably nothin' in it to warrant you givin' out anythin' other than a gentle reminder of just what's at stake 'ere, an' Steph probably has no idea who she is anyway... but I'll tell you this; I don't know much but one thing, Dave, the last thing this estate needs to do is give Alec Stratton an edge."*

He nodded at David who sighed. *"Pfhhh. Yeah, you're right. Don't suppose you'd like to do it for me would y'?"*

Eric laughed loud. *"Ha! I'd rather be fillin' me own teeth. No, this is one for you. Just go steady... oh, an' I'd tell Liam as soon as you see him; you know how small a world this game is. Someone from around will be sure to 'ave seen 'em, if not today then another time. Up front and head on David, only way to do it."*

David looked at Eric and smiled. "Thanks, Eric. Everybody else thinks you're a bastard but I think you're OK."

"You're wrong they're right. Let's get these branches spread then coffee and buns eh?"

They split up, both towing several branches behind them, cutting a swathe through the pheasants that had ventured out to feed from the hoppers during their chat.

"Do you have dogs?" Stephanie poured a second cup of coffee and handed it across to Alice.

"Ar, we've a couple of terriers. Not pedigree or nothin', just a couple of mutts, but they're lovely company now the kids are long gone."

"You say there's two boys."

"Ar. Brian. He's in the army doin' his second stint in Ireland."

"That must keep you nicely worried."

"It does. I mean, he's a big lad makin' his own choices but after that last mortar bomb in Newry... well, you never stop bein' a mum, do y'?"

"I suppose not..." Stephanie's voice tailed off.

"An' our Sydney's tryin' to find work after his mine were closed down a year ago."

"Oh, one of the many is he?"

"'Fraid so. Happenin' all over. Communities and lives destroyed... Strikes are all but over now; he never went back."

"Where was he?"

"Cortonwood. Was on strike almost a year to the day, held out to the last... fat lot of good it did him. Thatcher an' MacGregor, what a pairin'; butchers both. You can't tell me,

even if it does need doin', you can't tell me it was the right way to go about it. But then, never their lot as goes through it is it?" Alice added milk to her coffee. *"Always some bugger else's. You've no kids then?"* Stephanie's mouth tightened just a little and this time Alice registered it. She thought she had seen it before, something in Stephanie's eyes when she was talking about feeding Sack, but it was insufficiently clear; not now though. *"Sorry, Steph. Didn't want to open up anythin.'"*

"No. No, you haven't." She stopped for a moment, looking from fire to tea tray and back again then looked up. *"It's just... well, the thing is..."* They heard the back door open and the sound of a frantic terrier reached them. Stephanie stood up and opened the door into the hall. *"Is that you, love?"*

David's voice came back from the kitchen. *"Ar, it's me."*

"You're back early!"

"Got finished quicker than I thought... Sack, get down, good girl. Now, in y' basket. Go on! Good girl. Can I put the kettle on for us?"

"We've coffee in here, thanks. Bring a cup, come in and say hello to Alice." Stephanie tested the pot standing on the hearth with the back of her hand. It was still warm. *"I'm glad he's come back early for lunch, you'll get a chance to meet him."* She turned towards the door and called out. *"And bring a plate, we've walnut loaf here to spare."*

Alice smiled. *"If it aint the shock of seein' me then the walnut loaf'll do for him."*

A puzzled frown from Stephanie was broken as David walked into the room, mug and plate in hand. He paused at the open door then nodded in Alice's direction.

"'Ello, Mrs. Stratton."

Eric picked up the last of the split logs and dumped them into the wheelbarrow. Lifting the handles, he marched across the garden to an already well-filled log basket that stood by the cottage back door.

"These be enough, Hattie?"

A trim, late-middle-aged lady came to the back door and looked at the basket. "They'll see me through for a bit, but I'm bakin' Madeira cake an' a batch of madeleines after lunch so I'll soon be through them. Can you do me about the same this evenin'?"

"If I don't, who else?"

"Me fancy man."

"That'll be me again then."

"You think too much of y'self, Eric Cornby." She smiled. "Lunch is on the table. Wash up and come in." She turned from the door and went into the house.

Eric watched her go then called after her departing figure. "I 'ave to think too much of meself. No bugger else does!"

Hattie poured tea from a huge blue china teapot as Eric draped the towel over the back of the chair. "Not on there! The damp will mark the wood! Put it back where it should be." Eric grunted and put the towel over the Aga bar. "You've got the first of the bantams' eggs there, they started layin' today. Don't say I never give you anythin'."

"You never give me anythin'." He sat.

"We're not talkin' about eggs now, are we?"

"Might be."

She indicated the teapot. "An' this might be a diamond necklace."

They both laughed easily in their own company and Eric buttered the two slices of toast and removed the top from one of the boiled eggs. "Saw Stephanie earlier today."

"Oh yes? How is she?"

"Not to talk to. Just saw her as I passed by in the Land Rover with some fir brash for the layin' pens." He paused. *"She were with Alice Stratton."*

Hattie put the pot down. *"No! She weren't!"*

"Were. David said she'd mentioned as how she'd met a woman on the market…"

"Her uncle's got a veg stall there."

"That's what I said."

"What did he say?"

"Not a lot he could say. Said he'd bring it up when they met at lunch." He looked at his watch. *"Anytime now, I'd say."*

"What did you say?"

Eric looked at Hattie for a few seconds. *"I told him to go at it steady, like."*

Hattie put her hand on his. *"Voice of age and experience."*

"Age anyway."

"A good man. Now, eat them eggs before they spoil with the cold."

"David!"

"I only asked if she were any relation to our celebrated local poacher Mister Alec Stratton, Steph, that's all. Reasonable question, given the similarity of surnames."

"But she's a guest here, my guest!"

Alice held up her hand. *"Steph, Stephanie, David's right, it is a reasonable question."* She turned to David. *"Yes, I am related to 'our celebrated local poacher'; I'm Alec Stratton's wife."*

This revelation stopped all conversation. David stared straight at Alice, Alice looked at Stephanie and Stephanie *looked from one to the other. Eventually she spoke to Alice.* "You knew this might happen, didn't you? You knew you were Alec Stratton's wife, I thought you were just Alice."

"I am just Alice, but it seems I've a scar glows white whenever there's a gamekeeper in the room. I don't think I should have to apologise for who my husband is to everyone I meet, do you?"

"No, but I wish you'd said."

"Said what? You mean in the café? What, 'Hello, Stephanie, my name's Alice and my husband's a poacher, even done your place over in the past.' Would that've done the trick?"

"That's just plain silly, you know what I mean."

"No, Stephanie, I don't. I don't know what you mean. What my husband chooses to do aint under my control any more than what your husband does is under yours, an' before you say it, I'm neither makin' excuses nor pointin' the finger; I'm just tryin' to polish the glass so we can all see through it clearly."

There was a lengthy silence then Stephanie looked across at David. "So what does it matter?"

"Steph..."

"What does it matter if she is married to a poacher? She's not poaching here, is she?"

David tried again. "Steph, c'mon, you must see..."

"Is she?"

"You know as well as I do it's about more than that. Her husband is, has been, the bane of this estate for thirty years!" David looked across at Alice. "That's right, isn't it?"

"More like thirty two but let's not split hairs."

"See!" David sat back in the armchair and waved his hand dismissively. He studied Stephanie's face intently then sat back up. "*You must be able to see how difficult this is Steph. Mrs. Stratton, tell her.*"

"*I don't need anyone to tell me, David. I can see how difficult it is!*"

"*Look, can we just hold on here a minute?*" Both David and Stephanie looked at Alice. "*David... can I call you David?*"

He nodded. "*It's my name.*"

"*Thank you, David, and you can call me Mrs. Stratton.*" The silence that followed was finally broken by Alice. "*Joke,*" she smiled. "*Please call me Alice, an' believe me when I say that none of this is or has been a deliberate plan, not on anyone's behalf. We met in a café, Steph and I, in the rain. Steph shops in the market, I do occasional work there, we're having coffee together today; end of story. There's no inside knowledge being sought out, no plots being hatched... we're just two women having coffee and a chat. Now, if you want to read into that more than there is... far more believe me... then let me tell you, you are way wide of the mark.*" She looked at them both as she continued. "*If you're having trouble understanding this, eat a slice of my walnut loaf; it concentrates the mind wonderfully.*" They had been listening so intently to Alice that her last comment took time to register. Finally, Stephanie and then David began to smile. "*Look, I know this is very difficult. Can I just say I took to you, Steph, from the moment we met, before I had any idea who you was. I don't take to folk easy. Inclination to trust doesn't go hand in hand with bein' married to what everyone calls a rogue so, if you feel used in any way, feel I'm in any way to blame then I'm real sorry. Nothin' was meant by it but friendship.*" She turned to David. "*And if all this has made difficulties for you and Steph or anyone else, then I'm truly sorry for that too.*"

She got up from her chair. "Now, after all that and havin' to eat my own walnut loaf as well, I'm goin' to get off back to town, I've some shoppin' I need to do."

"No, Alice, you don't have to go!" Stephanie jumped up. "David really doesn't mind you being here, do you, David?"

Before David could reply, Alice drove home the point. "He's in a very difficult position, Steph, even you must see that. Best if I get the bus back. We'll see each other at the market... or the café."

"Hang on... just..." David stood up too. "Alice, look, if you want to stay, you stay. It's difficult all round, but you stay if you want, you're... welcome."

"Thank you that's very kind of you but, even so, I think it best if I went on back. Would you get my coat from the hall, David, please, the dark blue one with the hood?" After a look across at Stephanie, David went to the hall. "For the best, Steph, really. We're still friends. An' the master of the house has warmed a little to me. Let's just take it a little slower an' see 'ow things stand after a while, eh?"

As David helped Alice on with her coat, Stephanie went into the hall and came back carrying hers. "I'll run you into town." She held up her hand to stifle disagreement. "I'll have no one say differently; it's the very least I can do. I'll be back in time to cook tea, David."

"No, you take your time. I'm only checkin' traps and sortin' cock birds at the layin'-pen."

"I'll pick up some smoked haddock in town and do it with a couple of poached eggs apiece, and some fresh bread and butter. That alright?"

"'Course, if you can manage." As Alice and Stephanie left the room David called out. "Alice, you've left the remains of your walnut loaf here! Do you not want to take it with you?"

Alice looked back round the door. "You think, after luggin' it all the way up 'ere an' dumpin' it on you two that I'd be tempted to take it back, do y'?"

"No, guess not."

"No."

David smiled at her, picked up the loaf and went past Alice. "We'll gnaw our way through it then. Thanks."

He opened the kitchen door and the terrier rushed into the hall, all tail and tongue. Stephanie called after her. "Sack! Sack, get back in there...!"

"Leave her, Steph, I'll sort her out... Sack, here..." The terrier bounced like a circus dog around David's legs and he picked her up. She immediately flicked over onto her back. "You soppy bugger," he said, as the front door closed.

Day 9 – Thursday 22nd November 1985

The frost was becoming severe, the moon bathing the landscape in muslin light so clear the breath from the skirling vixen on Scholar's Hill, her whole body arched and hungry for sexual contact, could be clearly seen by Alec as he watched her from the cover of the broom thicket.

He had lodged himself deeply in this spark-sharp shroud forty minutes before sunset, content only with listening to the call of cock pheasant and partridge as they settled in their various roosting spots, his hunting desires tamed for the time being. The bitter wind of the previous night, conditions that had made duck flighting so secure and his poaching reputation so precarious, had dropped, but the memory of the thorough cold during his sopping wet journey home had left him stiff. What was scarier was that for the first time ever, especially after the close call with the dog, Alec had become aware of his age, of just what continuous nights out had done to his body. Yet, even though he was loath to add further to this legacy, here he was again.

He pushed the thoughts back. 'Bloody hell, old thinkin' Alec Stratton; old thinkin'! That'll finish you so it will. You'll get sloppy, then they'll 'ave y" The sound of partridges locking up as they jugged down for the night drifted across to him swiftly followed by the brag of a late rising cock pheasant. These night noises shook him from maudlin remembrance. 'You're late, you lot, near on full dark. An' a stupid over-announcement by quarry such as yourself as to your whereabouts. Everythin' with ears will pinpoint the places you've chosen; this vixen will for sure.'

To some the call of game birds going to roost just signalled the closure of the day's difficulties, the end of labours of love or hate. To others it was a fickle nature's gauntlet thrown down in challenge. Alec, along with the skirling vixen, was of the latter category but, with a night as bright as this and after his chill of last night, not even Elm Wood looked tempting. Indeed, it was only the unexpected arrival of the vixen that had kept him closeted in the furze break far longer than intended, and for no other reason than the sheer private pleasure of it all. No night work tonight. Tonight he was content just to sit back and watch the picture-book-silhouetted fox as she proclaimed her availability.

Having agreed with Eric and Liam the route he would take that night, the three keepers had parted and David had made his way towards Elm Wood. The hedgerow running to the wood's edge was reached without incident and now he moved along it, keeping as tight to it as he could, for the moon was so bright it was difficult to remain hidden unless he treated it as the sun and kept to the leeward side.

Crystal clear, the distant note of a skirling vixen penetrated his senses. 'At it early,' he thought. 'Not even December yet... Scholar's Hill by the sound of her. Cubs by middle-end of February if she gets lined this month... In that old sand hollow back of Symonds' place, I'll bet. Try an' beat the hunt to it.'

He stood for a moment and gazed across the valley. The view was ethereal. Hedges, trees, all the winter vegetation of dead grass and goldfinch-plundered thistles were visible in the light of the November moon. The frosting on the ground gave the scene a sculpted, Monet-like quality with giant cobwebs of mist stretched across the rumpled duvet of land that was the valley bottom, beyond which was Barn Tor's northern boundary.

Drinking the view in David walked the hedge, down the sloping ground towards the eastern boundary of Elm Wood and its nearby road, that night's first checkpoint. The wood's proximity to a ribbon of tarmac meant it was a prime target for grab-and-run poachers, even on a night like this.

The Scholar's Hill vixen called again as David, eighty yards short of the wood, dropped down into the three foot deep ditch running the length of the hedgerow. Flatworm and snail were dislodged to spin in the eddies created by his wellingtoned feet and the grass, steeped in the few inches of water in the ditch bottom, flattened as the near frozen sludge began its gnawing action even before he had settled. Instead of glazing over as they were wont to do during these lonely night vigils, David's eyes were able to rake over the valley below and to his left. He gazed across at the unaccustomed, stupefying beauty of the night panorama and tried to conjure up a description.

'Could see a moth fart at fifty paces in this,' he thought.

Alec began to move backwards, out through the arched gorse branches. After twenty minutes holding his position the cold had begun to tell, biting deep into feet and fingers.

He had thought to exit silently, making a slow semicircle away from the now silent vixen that was fully occupied in a session of post-skirling ablutions; but once clear of the shrubbery, Alec's stiff limbs reacted badly to the command of his brain. As his foot slithered along the flint-studded ground he lost all balance and fell crashing to the ground; the vixen catapulted forward mid-lick and whisked away over the hill towards Rickett's Farm.

He smiled and shook his head. 'Clumsy old sod.' Down onto the track that led to Raynes Lane, he step-stumbled, hips grinding their protest at cold and movement until the effort of his walking stirred his central heating switch and he began to grow warmer.

'That vixen'll whelp by mid February,' he thought. 'In that sand pit back of Symonds' old place. Bet them keepers will be enterin' terriers on 'em 'bout the first week in March, unless the hunt dig 'em out an' move 'em to safer lodgin's first.'

It was always his little finger that told David when it was time to move. A crushed nail in youth, a memento of sibling rivalry, meant that as the temperature dropped and the chill stabbed deeper so the colour bleached out of the finger and the digit lost feeling. That time was now and he would have stood up, but it was also now he sensed a change in his loneliness. Company announced itself, immediately discernible, moving from the wood and creeping along the opposite side of the hedgerow like the approaching ghost of marbling ice… but definitely here.

He dropped back into a squat as his hearing, now as sharp as a Siberian winter wind, finally gained confirmation. 'Yup. To the right an' comin' my way.' His mind began to race with possible permutations. 'Poachers come back to collect? No, would've noticed when I fed, was late on so I would've noticed. Not nettin' partridge nor coursin' deer, not in this moon. Snarin' rabbits? Noosed some pheasant maybe? Comin' away from the wood so whatever it was, the job's been done.' The steps were closer now. Careful, dainty almost. 'Two, possibly three. Bugger, no gun, no stick an' no bloody Eric. I'll stand and challenge when they get level... no, let 'em go by; follow to the pickup point, then... then what? Dunno. Hope summat occurs...'

David's breathing was controlled unlike his heartbeat as he stooped in the ditch unable to see, head facing front lest movement give the game away, waiting the moment. Then he breathed a silent prayer of thanks. 'That's no human or I'm no keeper. That's a fox... or a dog?'

Fox or dog halted exactly opposite him, now realising that it too was not alone. Not a-who, a-what or a-where, only that a-something was near. Now the competition was under way as both creatures strained to control muscles, lungs, heart rate and muscular tremble; to channel that negative power into positive recognition through eyes, ears and nose, each sense trying to outstrip not only each other but also those of the unseen enemy.

It could have been a drop of branch-mounted frost disturbed by David's body heat and plopping into the ditch. Whatever it was, he took the full force of the muntjac's first alarm bark and its accompanying spittle in his right ear. Cold had set his limbs but this in no way diminished the athleticism he showed as the sound gripped both heart and stomach and released a muscle spasm of Olympic proportions. On the opposite side of the hedge, the force the deer put into its first bark sent it backward and away in flight. It did the obverse for David, sending him vertically up from the ditch, his momentum depositing him on the grass at the field's edge yet still in the crouched position as a very breathy, "Jeeesussss!" escaped his freed lungs.

At the hedge's stile, Alec heard the muntjac's first bark and stopped.

'Someone on the move... Elm Wood way. Keepers most like.' The barking continued. 'They'll catch no one tonight, 'specially not me.'

He stood a few seconds more, listening to the muntjac's hysteria before shuddering once at the chill. He climbed the stile onto Raynes Lane that led to Milton and home.

The buck muntjac was massively surprised at the effect of his alarm call. So much so that it did not have the courage to continue barking until good space had been put between him and the strange, somersaulting-now-hunched creature on the other side of the hedge. Once sufficient distance was made the deer gave vent to its spleen by barking continuously at the distant form of David who was busy collecting both heart and dignity from the ditch. Gradually melding back into the wood's edge, the deer maintained its alarm call from the shadows. Now all other night creatures were certain just where it was – how it was – why it was – which it was, and they altered their timetable to suit.

David, still not quite knowing anything, squatted where he was. After a little time he began to unfold, quietly speaking as he did so.

"Oh fuck! Oh, me legs! Oh! Bloody 'ell!" The muntjac continued his barking. "Shut up you silly bugger, van-bloody-Goff could hear you!"

Rising to his feet, he made his way down to the edge of Elm Wood with all the grace of a clockwork toy. The muntjac, sensing things could possibly end badly, moved off deeper into the cover. As he did so his bark grew less and less bold, more and more questioning until, feeling safe once more, he fell quiet.

Turning away from Elm Wood and towards Raynes Lane, David threw a last glance in the direction of the now silent deer. 'That's it, nigh on give me a bowel movement then sod off. I'll return the compliment one day.'

After a stiff, six minute walk he topped the rise by Howard's Farm and David took in the ever changing panorama he knew so well. The whole of Raynes Lane could be seen under this moonlight, right up to the point where it disappeared through the gap in the row of trees that made up Stonepit Belt. To the left of the lane the fields sloped down to the Old Railway, to the right they ran slightly up hill to Rickett's Farm beyond which was Greys Copse and The Quarry. All was as it should be... except for that.

It may have been the light playing tricks on his eyes, but Alec reckoned there were at least a dozen partridge squatting on the newly rolled, winter sown barley field near the river.

'Hard to tell at this distance; maybe them ones I heard earlier. I'll come back another night, less moon, see if they're due for a little light cullin'...' He moved on, his joints almost complaining at that last thought, '...or maybe not. Two more miles and home to a mug of tea.'

The dark, unfamiliar shape took some minutes to register on David's pre-programmed brain. Looking but not seeing was a human trait that would guarantee a very short survival time to the majority of civilisation if cast into the wild environment to fend for itself. No mistake now though. Definitely a car, part hidden by the hedge, third of a mile distant; just off the lane in a gateway, a gateway whose track led directly to the Old Railway.

Even on as unfavourable a night as this every vehicle was suspect; parked here doubly so. The make and type could not be made out from this distance but gaining this information would not be difficult.

The route decided, David moved towards his target.

"So what did you reckon; locals or what?"

"Not sure." Liam shook his head. "Certainly weren't them lads you caught and who'd come back for a second go. Odd sound, sixteen bore or summat similar, no air-rifles involved."

"No way they'd have got past you?"

"No. None. I were there not five minutes after the last shot, Henry there maybe sooner... must've been in that thorn brake over the river."

"An' if they were in there then there's no hope of support from Timpson. He'll have been long gone home by that time of the day."

"Ar. I said as much to Henry an' Malcolm. Part-time keeper on there's about as much use as a racin' saddle on a donkey. I went over this mornin'. No one about so I slipped in and had a look without an invite."

"Anythin'?"

"No, not that I could see, not even a bald spot where someone had stood. I left a message with the farm manager over there, whatshisname, Anthony summat or other..."

Eric smiled. "Robert. Robert Davey."

"Ar, that's him. Told him to let Timpson know what'd happened and that I'd had a look. Said I'd pop round some other time... all a bit too late now though; horse's bolted."

"Stratton?"

"Dunno, could've been, he's been known to use a sixteen bore on occasions."

"What I thought."

"Well, if it were he'd have been long gone; Henry had Hoover with him."

"Ha! Right. Now I understand."

"Tore up the inside of their Land Rover 'cos he'd been left behind."

"Bet he were popular."

"Ar, he were." They looked at their respective watches together then smiled at the precision of their synchronised thought and deed. "How bad do you think things have got between them?"

"Who, Henry and Hoover?"

"No you daft sod. Between Dave and Steph."

"Some sort of warnin' about a change of subject would help, an' it sounds like you've written them into the divorce court already. What brought that up?"

"Just been thinkin' on it while we've been sat here that's all. The way David's been behavin' and talkin' of late, certainly up 'til a couple of days ago. On the verge of pear-shaped, don't you think?"

Eric gave the matter some thought. "Maybe. I know she's a bit... lonely like. David told me recent. Said she's been feelin' it for a while."

"Does she not see Hattie now?"

"No, not for a while; four... five months. Odd that. She complains about not seein' anyone yet doesn't want to see no one... if you get my drift. No one 'cept that bloody Stratton woman."

A silence followed before Liam spoke again. "Jesus but they're complex wildlife, women, aren't they?"

"And you'd know; a confirmed bachelor such as yourself. You'll be the font of all knowledge on things marriage-an'-feminine then, will y'?"

"One thing I do know for certain, Eric, is that, what, ten, fifteen years ago men were sure what women wanted; marriage, house, kids, steady husband. Now? Now we haven't got a bloody clue what they want... an' neither have they, but it sure as hell aint what they've got." Eric just stared, open mouthed. "No need to be surprised, just pay attention."

"Oh, right, an' that's it is it? You've worked it all out have y'?"

"As I'm not the one sufferin' at present, I'd say that I might have the answer, yes."

"What, not have a permanent woman at all? Good advice for me that is, an' about twenty six years too bloody late!"

"Well, I just hope all's well between 'em now. Last thing we need is big shoot days coming up an' a keeper with a rocky marriage."

"You're all heart, you are."

"What you mean?"

"Just listen to the way round you put those two facts."

"Oh, you know what I meant."

"Good job I knows you, Liam Coyne." They lapsed into silence once more, then Eric added, "Do you think one of 'em's had someone else?"

Liam thought for a while. "No, no... Steph's not that kind... an' not David. Apart from the fact he dotes on her, he never gets any spare time for dalliance, none of us do, the bloody job sees to that!"

"Not even with his missus by all accounts."

"Ar, so it would seem."

"But he was away in August, remember, on the grouse? Could he have bedded one of them housemaids?"

Liam spoke decisively. "No, not Dave, I've said; he's too much in thrall with Steph... no, definitely not Dave." Then added as an afterthought, "Anyway, we'd have heard from Mr. Macpherson, Lordy's man up there. He misses nothin'..." Eric yawned long and loud. "...Thanks. Always pleased when I see my conversation keeps the audience on the edge of its seat."

"Sorry, Liam... just knackered. Nothin's gonna happen tonight, I mean, look 'ow light it is! I'll bet that muntjac was barkin' at its own shadow; couldn't creep up behind a blind man in this lot. We've got the big days coming up an' were standin' 'ere like a couple of retired generals on a Bournemouth beach. I'm fucked, let's go 'ome."

Liam dropped his cigarette underfoot and crushed it out. "Ar, c'mon; up the wooden hill to Bedfordshire. I bet Dave's finished his round an' been abed for the past hour now. If I weren't so tired I'd drive round to his place and let a barrel off under 'is window, serve the bugger right. We'll look in at Barton's on the way round though."

"Why bother? With a good set of binoculars we could count the pheasant from 'ere!"

Both men laughed as they climbed inside the Land Rover. It was the cold of the vehicle gripping them that cut their laughter as Liam sucked in his breath. "Christ! It's warmer out than in!"

"Found the reverse on me 'oneymoon," replied Eric. "Mind you it was February an' in Scotland. I were fuckin'-freezin' while I were freezin'-fuckin'."

Liam smiled. "You'll never go to 'eaven." There was a short pause then he said, "I wonder how they got on walkin' them hedgerows over yonder today. I saw Malcolm over at Crowbury first thing; he'd got an invite. I think they was after a few partridge."

"An' as many of our pheasant as they could knock over." The engine fired first time and they drove away, minus lights, for the pillow run. Eric looked out over the moonscape. "Nothing stirrin' is there, not even a spoon in a mug o' tea."

The frost-scorched grass crunched like gravel under David's feet; silence and invisibility in conditions such as these were the prerogative of the owl. He knew the tale of his travels would be revealed in the morning by the burn marks, but not having learnt to levitate that was unavoidable. Even the fox with all his woodcraft hadn't learnt how to fool Jack Frost into telling a lie during these hoar nights.

The quarry loomed large now and the recently flailed hedge only gave David fractured inadequate cover, so much so that he was forced to drop ever lower to the ground.

Within twenty yards of its quarry, the Scholar's Hill vixen dropped ever lower on to the frosty carpet, pushing her belly hard onto the newly rolled, winter sown barley field.

The Perdix clan had been given much to consider after today's date with the Crowbury shooting party, but the safety offered by the failing light was only partial. Now all the covey could rely on for their protection during the dangerous hours of darkness was absolute stillness. To help with their disguise, the seemingly friendly moon shimmered through a high haze of mare's tail cloud, making the birds resemble a group of molehills. But it was with blatant disregard for their situation that events conspired against their camouflage of colour and immobility, showing the partridge for what they truly were. It was inevitable that the cloud's shroud would drift from the moon's face at some point in the night and allow its unfettered light to brag of the bird's vulnerability, and so it did. At this very instant, to add injustice to injury, the mischievous mist currents from the nearby river passed the bird's scent on like a baton and the vixen picked up the information it carried concerning the birds position, number, sex and, most importantly, their health.

David reached the edge of the gateway on hands and knees. Fifty yards of such movement across the frosty ground had made them wet and cold. Now he went down on his belly to crawl the last ten yards. After a swift glance, he shimmied across the vulnerable gateway under the floodlight moon and reached the front of the intruder's car. He lifted up slightly to peer through the gap in the gate's bars to check the number, but noises from within caused him to freeze his position.

'Don't know the car.' Movement from inside the customised Ford Zodiac made the springs to creak and twist, signalling '*ready*'.

He read the registration plate. 'Don't know it.' The puzzle was considered as David, fully preoccupied, searched his memory.

"Hang on; I'll 'ave to 'ave a piss." The man's voice was followed by a peal of female laughter, signalling '*steady*'

David sighed. 'It's a bloody courtin' couple. Might've known.'

The female of the party sniggered her reply. "Just piss-proud then are we?"

"I'll show you piss-proud when I get back, just get y'self ready."

"If y' can find it in this cold."

"Y' cheeky sod!"

The click of the rear door catch signalled '*go*'.

David snatched a look at the going-on-going-back choices. Neither was appealing but he chose onward, beginning to roll the rest of the distance to safety, but even his split second delay for assessment and decision made him late of leaving. The rear door opened fully to release the flatulence of foreplay as the occupant stepped out into the frost chilled air.

Caught in the open, halfway between car and hedge, David cut his losses. Ceasing movement, he curled into the kneeling foetal position, face hovering over the frosted grass, the top of his head barely a couple of inches away from the bottom bar of the gate. He could now only rely on absolute stillness and the camouflage of his black donkey- jacket. 'I'll be arrested for a peepin' Tom,' he thought. 'Bugger it, why me?'

"Bloody 'ell, that's cold!"

"Well, shut th' door!" The car door closed with a click as chilling as the weather.

With gloved hands over his head, David pressed his face into the frost and groaned inwardly, silently. The frost-peppered ground crunched underfoot as his nemesis moved closer.

The contest was on.

Slithing along by the gentle movement of just her hind legs, her underbelly only millimetres from the frost-thickened grass, the vixen kept her approach towards the covey of partridges constant both in speed and direction. Although her body undulated slightly with the exertion of movement her head was motionless, eyes unflickering as they assessed with acute precision the chances of a successful conclusion to the night's work. Then breeze blabbed again and the familiar and welcome smell of dried blood reached her nose causing her to stop and reassess.

The vixen slowly lowered her head and gently licked her nose, wiping clear the last message like chalk from a blackboard. A gentle lifting of the head allowed the message to be rewritten, reread and double checked. She drew in the molecules through her nose and each syllable of scent was now fine-tuned so the exact position and direction of the wounded bird, together with the extent of any injury, could be logged and allowed for, included in the equation of hunter-versus-hunted.

After careful consideration a slight adjustment of her position aimed her away at an angle, away from her first choice of dinner. With this minute alteration the vixen locked her senses and radar onto the reselected victim, a pricked bird from Crowbury's hedgerow walk of earlier. Like a flag of state the scent of dried blood coming from the bird's leg and right wing drifted along, a pennant in the brutal breeze. As the vixen moved on ever more carefully and in a straight line, for sideways movement was easier to detect by ever-wary prey, so both partridges sensed the subtle shift in emphasis.

The original quarry, a fully fit hen, relaxed slightly. The injured bird stiffened, sensing the full force of the vixen's decision and her own inability to deal with it.

Still clinging to the thin veil of hope that immobility spelt safety, the partridges lodged themselves tighter to the ground as the tester of their faith grew closer... closer.

The contest was on.

The wait was interminable. At first David was convinced the man had moved off to the left and the doubtful privacy of the hedgerow. The noise he heard convinced him otherwise.

Cranking his head slightly, he peered through the fingers of his gloved hands and looked into the brewer's waterfall streaming through the gate's bars and onto the frost laden grass just inches from his head, the spots of rebounding moisture causing his eyelids to flutter.

The distance was just right and, with rear legs folded tightly for the final spring, decision and action melted into one. The fox's first explosive movement carried her airborne and fully six yards towards the chosen target. The once stationary partridge-firework burst into a star shell pattern as each bird blazed into the thin, cold air. The vixen's rear paws hit ground after her initial leap and she combined this forward momentum with an upward thrust that carried her eight feet into the air. Slower to take off than her rocketing covey-mates, the injured bird rose laboriously, seeking pity from the stars; their pity was as cold as the night.

As the other birds ripped away across Rickett's Farm and towards the Old Railway, each one concerned only with its own safety, so the vixen's macabre pas de deux reached its climax as she joined the labouring bird in its farewell to the fast disappearing covey. The weight and momentum of the back end of the fox now overtook her head as she steadied her mouth in order to bring a swift conclusion to this particular ballet. Taking hold of dinner she performed a single twist, the force of her ascent carrying her and the now palpitating bird well beyond the point of capture as her jaws closed tightly, signifying the fall of partridge-curtain. Landing on her side, the fox showered the air with frost crystals of victory, her personal addition to the night's firework display.

The beer-shower showed no sign of abating. 'Christ, he must've drunk that bloody pub dry.' David held his position, amazed at his luck at not being seen. The noise came to him a split second after it reached the urinating form above. Although not able to see, David knew the sound of partridge wings a-whirring.

"Jeeeesusss... what th' bloody...!"

The man's exclamation was timed to perfection. His spin round to watch the covey of birds as they streaked over his head and down the slope towards the Old Railway, created a scything movement which sent the urine splishing-splashing across the bars of the gate until it finally cascaded through a gap and onto David's jacket, gloved hands and head.

"Christ! Did y' see that!"

A muffled voice from inside the car answered in the negative.

The end of the bladder salute to this fly past was at hand. The final spurts to closing drips plummeted earthwards.

"An 'ole load of fuckin' birds! Flew straight over me; I almost pissed on me leg!"

The zip was only half closed as there was still work to be done. Steam was now gently rising from the surfaces soaked by the recycled beer, adding flavour to the porous landscape. The voice above David tailed away as the man turned.

"Frit th' bloody life outta me, I tell y'!" The car door opened and the tone changed. "Move over, 'ere I come!"

"I bloody well 'ope not!"

Shrieks of laughter dulled as the door slammed.

After a brief pause, David crawled off to the sanctuary of the hedgerow. Reaching the cover he rolled onto his back and stared up into the star-riddled sky.

"What th' fuck?"

The vixen knew she had to get under cover now. All sorts of visitors, some unwelcome, would be aware of the recent disturbance. Carrying the prize of effort, she made her way to the nearby hedgerow café and, lying in its shelter, began to eat dinner.

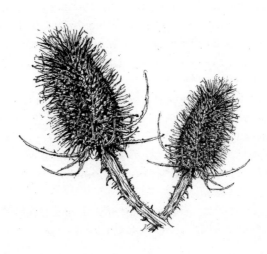

Chapter Five
Month 8 – April 1985

Out through the open back door, washing basket in hand, Stephanie sucked in the morning air. 'Perfect.' She turned back to the kitchen. "Sack! Out you come… butterflies!" Bounding out, Sack was glad of the early spring sunshine, glad of her mistress's permission to create havoc… just glad. The washing line was discharged of its overnight moisture by a deft hand flick and Stephanie began to hang out laundered clothes as the terrier penetrated the nearby shrubs in search of itinerant insects. "Not in there, that's where my hollyhocks are! Sack, out! Come on, out!"

"Don't want 'em damaged, do we?"

Stephanie looked up from the re-emerging dog and across the blue brick yard. "Eric! Hello! Is David…?" David appeared from behind the high section of wall. "David! You're back early, not coffee time yet, is it? Sack! Out of there!"

"Could be." Eric looked at his watch and smiled. "Lovely dress, Stephanie, you look real summery."

"Thank you, Eric."

David sighed. "Don't thank him Steph, he's just leerin' an' we'll never get away now, not now you've mentioned coffee."

"That'll suit me. Always glad of a bit of company."

"Me too," added Eric. "An' so pretty with it."

"Flattery will get you everywhere. Come in both, I'll hang these then put the perc on."

As Eric made a positive move towards the gate, Sack rushed over in preparation to do a formal inspection. David stayed resolutely on the trackside of the yard. *"Hang on, Eric! We were going to shift that fallen Scots pine..."* He turned to Stephanie in explanation. *"The big, one, y' know, with the double trunk? Fell across my release pen last week; Seer's Hill boundary."* Stephanie looked askance. *"I told you about it the other day."* He indicated Eric. *"Taken me twenty minutes to talk him into getting started; was gonna try and get it done before lunch. Now you've called coffee-time we'll be lucky to get it shifted by tomorrow week."*

"What's the rush? One thing I know about work, youngster, it'll always wait for y'." Eric entered the yard and took the full brunt of Sack's greeting as she leapt up at his legs then, as Eric bent to fuss her, flopped onto her back for a tummy tickle. *"Hello, lass."* Then he turned to Stephanie. *"You'll have to get him t' slow hisself down, Steph, or you'll be a widder be Christmas then I'll have to marry y'!"*

"I'd like to hear what Hattie has to say about that, Eric."

"She'll do as I tell her. I'll have you know, I wear the trousers in my house even if I do have to wash an' iron 'em."

With a second sigh of resignation David followed Eric through the gate. *"An' you want to give coffee to a bloke who's already forecast your husband's demise and is plannin' bigamy?"* He too came under inspection by Sack. *"Get down y' daft dog! All we need now is for Liam to turn up an' we'll have an estate full of pheasant with not a single keeper lookin' after 'em; perfect."*

"See what I mean? Get some coffee and cake down this young man's neck before he spirals into a depression and has us dressed in sackcloth an' ashes an' wringin' our 'ands

119

in supplication at the sufferin' of our poor lordship and master 'cos we abandoned our stewardship of his acreage an' its environs."

David looked across at him. "Do what?"

"Buggered up the estate."

David looked across at Stephanie and sighed. "See what I'm saddled with?"

Alec relaxed in the welcome midday sunshine feeling the warmth penetrate his clothing, soothing both muscles and mind. 'Perfect day for it.'

The winter had been prolonged, at times unkind, and spring had been reluctant to show its hand for fear of getting it chilled to the bone by a late frost. But now, at last, a definite decision had been made; the sun had grabbed its ball and come out to play and here, on the top of Seer's Hill, a spot Alec always thought was as near to the doorstep of Eden as makes no odds, it lit up the early greens with a vibrancy that was verging on the liquid.

Sat on the grass that reached right up to the bole of the oak tree against which he was leaning, Alec looked over the landscape of Barn Tor Estate and stretched luxuriously. Like the dog fox that moved over this hill under a different light, for this brief moment in time he was master of all he surveyed. This was his countryside; his countyside. Spread before him were the counterpane memories of his childhood, the scenes of his adolescent struggles, his adult triumphs and failures, and he felt as much a part of this blended landscape as the rooted oak.

The river below snaked its way along the valley floor like a discarded ribbon and he could see the faint scar of the release pen in the wood close below; insignificant in itself but to the observant it spelt out the very reason why this stretch of England was a shooting estate not a housing estate.

The spine of the landscape, of which the Tor was the highest part, ran across this corner of the county creating hills and valleys that were perfect for the showing of sporting game birds, particularly pheasant. Dressing the backbone of these slopes like the blankets of racing greyhounds, blocks of purpose-planted hardwood had been cosseted to maturity over the years and, throughout their growing time, any felling undertaken always had the sporting angle as a primary consideration. What shaped up from this attention to environmental detail were coverts of the greatest benefit to both game birds and general wildlife, and this dual role, safeguarded by generations of keepers, meant Barn Tor never had any need to fear the woodman's axe or the accountant's ready reckoner. Its value was in this natural ability to show superb sport, coupled with an opportunity for its owners and guests to 'Get on, Get honour, Get honest'. Through the munificence of Elizabethan aristocracy and God-given Edwardian finance, this oak tree's through line to the future had been assured and, by that same good fortune, Alec Stratton had been given larder, pleasure-park and spiritual confessor. As in life, however, nothing was certain and both onlookers had seen changes to set the heart racing.

Estate elms had disappeared, completely changing a landscape known to generations for generations, in a single year. On land abutting the very edges of the estate odd clumps of rough scrub had gone under the plough, odd clumps of plough under the builder, but not here, not on Barn Tor Estate. Alteration and abuse had been halted in the name of sport. This preserved firstly the surrounding landscape in general, secondly, this oak tree in particular, *and thirdly, Alec's single-most greatest pleasure in life; poaching.*

He stretched again. An afternoon of observation lay before him and there was plenty of time to enjoy it.

"I knew we'd not get away... you could talk for England, you could. Look at the bloody time, it's gone two!" The three keepers were making their way back to the laying pens and their vehicles, David remonstrating gently at the delay.

"Well, how was I to know there'd be walnut loaf an' butter as well as coffee, eh?" replied Eric. "I tell you what, my Hattie would like that recipe, or should I say I'd like 'er to 'ave it." Eric offered a cigarette to Liam and they both lit up. "Then this bugger turns up."

"You know this bugger. I can smell fresh coffee in the next county, an' with both your vehicles by the layin' pens it didn't take much to work out where you pair were."

"If I'd had my way we would've been long gone by now. We were only going to my place to collect tools. As things are, I doubt this old sod will be able to haul that paunch further than his Land Rover, not after four slices of that loaf an' three mugs of coffee."

"Good though weren't it?"

Liam nodded. "The loaf? It were that, 'specially with that bit of cheddar; no tea for me, that's for sure. You still goin' up to the pen Dave?"

"I thought I'd make a start at least. Try and salvage summat of the day. That tree's massive; it'll take some cuttin' up. Steph's gonna bring me tea up to the pen so I can crack on and get some of those top branches cut away... an' if I can keep this greedy sod away from my kitchen we'll try an' get it finished tomorrow."

"Can't do tomorrow, got those rearing pens to make. The jig's all set up an' if I don't break the back of 'em over the next few days you'll both be moanin' when first poults are ready for the rearin' field but the pens aint."

"Bloody hell, Eric." David looked at Liam. "See? I knew we should've got on today, an' I'll bet you want to slide off to do your traps now...?" Eric nodded, David sighed. "...Leavin' me to sort out the smashed pen as best I can and try to fit in a run round me own traps before dark."

"You youngsters! No idea, no stamina, that's your problem. In my day..."

"Here we go, 'in my day...'" retorted David. "...In my day what, Eric? Don't tell me, in my day we used to shovel twenty tons of coal with a bit of cardboard before breakfast, be smacked out shoeless to do a week's work in a day then get back to our gutter in time for a supper of a sound thrashin' an' sawdust before goin' to a bed of broken glass; is that it?"

"You've no idea how close to the truth you are. No stamina, like I said."

Liam smiled and shook his head. "Tell you what, do what you can today an' I'll start with the incubators a bit earlier tomorrow mornin' then come up to you; we'll christen it between us."

Eric was in fast again. "And who's left to help me finish them pens off then, if you two are off gambollin' in the woods for half the day tomorrow after he's spent this evenin' gambollin' in 'em with his missus?"

"Should've thought of that earlier, Eric," said Liam, winking at David. "How long will them branches take?"

"Well, if I can get the tops an' bigger side branches lopped today before I do my trap round then you and me should see it off in a couple of hours maybe. Can you fetch along your chainsaw as well?"

"Mine's in for repair. Can I fetch yours with me, Eric?"

"Well, I don't know. Mine's an expensive bit of kit y' know."

"I think it's the least you can do, havin' buggered up the boy's day for him like you have."

"Well, as long as you don't let 'the boy' use it. It's a man's piece of kit is mine; he'll only be sawin' his legs off at the knee if he gets hold of it."

"Eric, I tell you what; if I got to use your saw it'd be the hardest work it's had since you bought it. Thanks, Liam. I'll take you up on that. I'll do morning egg collection and wash 'em with bugger-lugs 'ere then meet you up at the pen at half nine."

"Bugger-lugs! He's no respect has this one. In my day..."

They had reached their respective vehicles now and they each mounted up like so many cowboys as Liam spoke over Eric. "Then we'll both get over and help you finish off those pens, Eric. That alright?"

"If I haven't done 'em all by then!"

"Ungrateful sod!" shouted David as he closed the door and drove off.

With a long slow sweep of the head, Alec traced the woodland edges from his elevated position and his thoughts ranged with his gaze.

He could see where the estate's woodland had been reshaped and nurtured, where whole cropping patterns had been altered in order to maximise the land's sporting harvest and knew it had been thus for the past one hundred and fifty years. On Barn Tor Estate it was as if time passing had been time slowed. Farming had been second-shelved in deference to game birds and this, in turn, had created a strand of the estate's DNA: the continuing dichotomy of keeper and poacher.

Keepers stocked the woods with game and sustained them up to the point where they reached the landowners' *game larder, via his gun, by age-old arts and woodcraft - trap, snare, gun and cunning. Poachers, too, used these age-old arts and woodcraft - trap, snare, gun and cunning, to intercept this straight line from keeper to owner and bend it their way... just a little.*

He gazed over the landscape and pondered the cropping patterns on display. A mixture of cereal, root crops and pasture smattered with livestock and shooting crops, the whole interspersed with blocks of deciduous woodland; the perfect example of agriculture working with nature, not against it. 'Farmers aint farmers no more,' he thought. 'All been lost in the chemistry set; taste of the year's first strawberry lost with it. Sellin' times and prices, big business that only cares 'ow much of the livin' countryside they own.'

Alec's thought process was interrupted by the insistent chatter of a chainsaw spluttering into life.

Standing astride the shattered release pen wire, David ripped through the first of the tree's side branches, the white wood-chips and scent of pine syrup filling the air.

After ninety minutes sawing, carting, sorting and stacking, he had removed and dissected a sufficient amount of the side brash to assess the damage. The tree was, indeed, massive and the crater left after the ignominious removal of the roots very deep. Two of the release pen's poles had been snapped like matchwood when the tree had fallen across the twelve foot high wire netting, crushing and folding it into an intricate if somewhat questionable piece of origami. The replacement of these poles was nothing to fret over; replacement of the flattened fence was. Its route through a large clump of snowberry would mean a full day of clearing in order to first release the old scrap wire then replace it with a new, full run of netting. Joining of wire was discouraged due to an inherent weakness and David sighed out loud at the prospect. "Bloody snowberry." Then, out of the corner of his eye, he caught a movement and looked up in surprise. "Oh, hi, Steph! Didn't hear you! You'd make a good poacher."

Stephanie smiled at him. "If you really didn't hear me then you'd make a poor keeper. Picnic here. Some of that beef from Sunday with mustard and a salad, plus Scotch coffee."

"Blimey, excellent, an' Scotch coffee. I'll be pissed!"

"Not you. Shall we eat now?"

"Yeah. Here, let me shift these tools an' the fuel can, we can use the brash as a cushion."

"Lovely scent of pine."

"Well, yeah. What did you expect, roses?"

"Cheeky." They sat and Stephanie unloaded the basket. "I thought we might take a walk up Seer's Hill after; when we've finished tea."

David looked up at the near summit then back at the pine tree. "Erm… yeah…"

"Oh, right." She sighed. "I'll rephrase that. I thought I might take a walk up Seer's Hill after."

"Sorry, Steph. I'd come with you, but…" He indicated the tree.

Stephanie shook her head. "Why should I be surprised at that?"

David looked sheepishly at her. "Need to get this sorted and the pen fixed. Time and charlie wait for no man."

"Alright for me though?"

"What?"

"Waiting."

"Oh, ar. Well, you know what the job is." Then he added as an afterthought. "You be alright, goin' up there by yourself?"

"I think I can find my way. Not as though I need a Sherpa or anything."

"Now who's being cheeky? I really would come with you but I need to get finished up here, or as near as dammit. After gettin' sidelined by Eric and his belly this mornin', I'm behind where I should be."

"Yes, I know. My fault. Shouldn't have kept plying him with cake and coffee."

"Not a fault, Steph. Eric's a bugger for coffee an' chat, Liam too. Don't matter who with."

"That does wonders for my ego."

"No, you know what I mean. Any excuse for gossip and he's there, especially if it's with you. And he were right, you look lovely in that dress.

"Better late than never."

"What, Eric?"

"The compliment... better late than never." David was about to speak but she talked on. "I'll be fine. I'll only be a short while. Just a look over the county."

"Ar, it's some view from up there."

"If you came with me you'd be able to share it."

David looked at the hill then back at the fir again. "Look, if you really want me to... but it's not as though I've not seen it before."

"Hm, there's a flattering reply."

"You're doin' it again, you know what I mean."

"Yes, I do."

He picked up her tone. "I didn't mean that, Steph, I meant..."

"I know, David." She sat on the brashing. "I know what you meant. Sorry, don't mean to be ratty." David joined her and they started their picnic in silence.

—◊—

David put his plate down and picked up his mug. "Well, that were some feast, our Steph. Don't know I'll be fit for work after that lot an' this coffee."

"Well, only do what you have to. I'll only be a short while, then we'll get back and have supper."

"Supper! I couldn't manage supper after that lot!"

"Fine. It'll just be me that has strawberry shortcake and Earl Grey tea then, will it?"

"Oh, bloody hell, Steph. I'll be dead of clotted cream arteries before I'm forty. Is that why you do it, to collect the insurance money?"

"Absolutely. You're worth more dead than alive and remember, nobody demands that you have two slices, you just do!"

"Your strawberry shortcake? How can I not? Anyway, the sponge is fatless, aint it?"

"That's some poor excuse, just have a little self-control my man."

"It's very difficult." He looked across at her, the late afternoon light dressing her hair and bare shoulders, the pinch of the dress at her waist emphasising her curves. "Not that you'd know anything about it. You turn out this stream of cakes and pastries and don't eat them. I don't think your figure's altered since we got together."

"I do eat. I'll be having strawberry shortcake with you later."

"Yeah one slice; one very thin slice. That's not what I'd call eating."

"What, like you, you mean? Seconds of everything and a pudding to follow. That sort of eating?"

"I'm a growin' boy."

"Outwards."

"There's no way I could do the workload I'm expected to get through and not stock up."

"I work too!"

"Yes, I know, and the reason you never put on weight is because you work as hard as you do but spend the day nibblin'. Nothin' even resemblin' a good square meal passes your lips in any given day. You force huge meals on everyone else..."

"I don't force you to do anything, you just do."

"...and you just nibble."

She stood. "Look, I'm away or it'll be dark and I'll miss the sunset. I'll leave the basket. Can you take it back to the Land Rover and I'll meet you there in an hour."

"Yeah, right. Take it steady." David watched her go then at the surroundings and spoke out loud again. "Bloody snowberry." Then his thoughts ran on. 'Get Eric down here to help trim this little lot, that'll slow the lecherous bugger down.'

Stephanie walked towards Seer's Hill to the sound of a restarted chainsaw aria as David moved along the fallen tree, revving the chainsaw in readiness.

Alec pinpointed the position of the noise and began to work out what was taking place down below. He knew the position of the release pen well and, from what he could decipher, it seemed as though work was taking place in or around that same pen.

'Probably damage to the wire; that or widenin' the feed ride... could be either.' What he was certain of was that the late afternoon's silence was being shattered by either inconsiderate keepers or foresters.

Stephanie walked along the riding. The wood anemone and celandine were decking the banks and open spaces and she smiled at the surroundings and her own luck at

being able to share in it. 'Nothing more I could want, really,'
she thought.

David finally freed the first top from the main bole which
lifted slightly at the release of the weight, the top falling
and rolling away to his left exactly as he had intended.
What he needed now was a second pair of hands to
complete the breaking down of the second large, very large,
pine trunk. That would be tomorrow, with Liam.

He looked out and across to Seer's Hill then at his watch.
'Might just have enough time to sort these other side
branches before Steph gets back, then drop her off; half
hour round me traps and home for a lid of tea and a slice of
strawberry shortcake... or two.'

The cessation of the sawing was welcomed by Alec.
'Barn Tor,' he thought. 'Last of the old school. No
Americans shootin' birds out of baskets here.'

Stephanie reached the footpath sign which pointed away to
the left, the hill's summit, and which also marked the estate's
boundary. She climbed the stile and set off up the slope.
Always a good spot for an impromptu summer picnic,
the hill was well used by locals as both lovers' retreat and
county spy-point. 'Be able to see most of the surrounding
countryside in this light, even the cathedral.'

David began to haul the large knot of brash aside in
preparation for an assault on more side boughs.

'Must have looked this way for a hundred year or more,'
thought Alec. 'As if the industrial revolution never 'appened.'
He coughed, breaking his thought train.

After a few seconds his gaze returned to the river line and he nodded in recognition of a thought now fully realised. As perverse as it might seem to others it was precisely because Barn Tor was old school that he came here, kept coming back. The shoot had a pedigree of class and style, and to be associated with that type of shoot, even as a poacher bestowed on one that very same pedigree. Anybody could rip off a sack full of pheasants from one of the commercial affairs where keepers were often of the five day week, eight hour day, feeding from the back of a Land Rover fraternity; there was no challenge in that. Barn Tor and the very few other estates like it, that was where the challenge lay.

Alec stared into this understanding for a while. It was the significant number of wood pigeons winging their way towards the bottom meadow on Carrick's ground that attracted his attention and broke his reverie. 'A sign of comin' bad weather? Not disturbance, not flyin' in that formation. Most birds are paired up by now. Old hands'll be on eggs, even the odd early chick. Could be just crop fillin' before roost; could be juveniles of last year without mates...' Whatever the reason the birds had alerted Alec's hunting instinct and he concentrated on deciphering the story they were writing in the sky. He was brought abruptly back to the moment by the sudden appearance of a woman in a summer dress stepping into the hill's arena.

The chainsaw fired into action again and David lopped off the side boughs in quick succession, flicking them clear with his foot as he worked his way further down the first trunk. He then shut down the saw and began piling the boughs on top of the stack of branches still bearing the bruises left by their recent picnic.

Time lingered mist-like along with their silence as they each looked across the twenty or so yards that separated them. At embarrassment level their silence was warily broken by Stephanie.

"Hello... erm, not disturbing you, am I?"

"'Ow do, Miss." Alec rose from his seat at the base of the oak tree in one easy movement. "No, nothin' to disturb 'cept idle time." He threw a glance in the direction of the recently silenced chainsaw. "Nice evenin' now."

Stephanie looked at him. 'Mid-fifties, full head of mid-length hair, classic good looks, kind eyes, held his figure well so must be fit,' she thought as she answered. "Yes. Look, erm... sorry, I can see you were enjoying the time alone."

"No Miss, really. Your company's welcome but, don't think me rude, nothin' to do with you, I was just leavin' anyway so you'll have the whole space to yourself." Alec continued to stare at her. This was some fine looking woman. That figure in that dress. Not someone he'd seen before; he would remember if he had.

"I don't mean to drive you away."

"You? Lookin' like that? Exact opposite." There was a short pause as the surprise of Alec's comment hit them both. "Sorry. Very forward of me. I'd best be off."

"I think that should be me."

"No, really, please don't be concerned, Miss. Was just a compliment, nothin' more."

Stephanie looked at him and felt no threat; the opposite in fact. "Accepted. I just wanted to look over the county really, using a bit of free time. Are you local?"

"Ar, born and bred. You?"

"No, I'm a relative newcomer."

"Anyone who wasn't born hereabouts will always be a relative newcomer, Miss, think nothing on it. No offence

meant but folk round here are slow to accept change. I've an aunt moved here over fifty year ago, still seen as a relative newcomer."

"Goodness, I've some way to go then."

"You'll fit right in, I'm sure." He smiled, Stephanie returned it. Alec held the contact then turned his gaze back to the surrounding countryside. "Can see the cathedral today."

Stephanie moved a little closer to the hill's edge and looked across to the distant city. "Yes, one of the reasons I came up here. The recent stone cleaning has worked wonders."

"Ar, glows beautiful in the sun it does. Right. These days need to be enjoyed; in company's nicer but alone will do. An' I reckon that's my slice of heaven for the day... An', as things are... you know, talkin' to strangers."

"Yes, very racy of me, and very chivalrous of you to recognise it."

"Well, Sunday papers are full of it..."

"Yes, of course."

"Ar. You could be a mad axe woman or summat." There was a short silence before Stephanie began to laugh quietly. Alec returned the smile again and they held each other's gaze before he broke the spell. "No, but serious now, you never can tell an' as charmin' as your company is, I'd best be off." He turned to go. "Oh, if it's alright, not too forward, what's your name?"

"Stephanie."

"Ah, right." He smiled and flicked another glance down into the wood. "Hello, Stephanie."

"Hello; what's yours?"

"Alec."

"Oh... Hello, Alec." Stephanie smiled slightly in realisation. "Right. Well, goodbye, Alec, nice to have met you."

"An' you, Stephanie, and if you're ever up here again... the cathedral?"

"Yes... 'Bye."

Alec turned and made his way back down the hill feeling the conversation had been short-changed.

Stephanie watched him disappear from sight as the afternoon sun hovered; like her it was seemingly reluctant to lose the moment. She stared back across the watercolour landscape to the far cathedral. 'Lovely.'

Minutes passed until she slowly turned in the direction of Alec's departure.

"Hmm..."

She walked to the base of the oak tree and sat on the grass that reached right up to the bole, leaning her back against its trunk. After twenty minutes she set off back down to the release pen, to Land Rover, to waiting husband, to home.

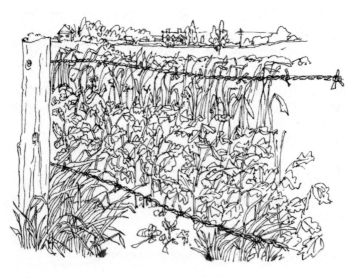

Day 8 – Friday 23rd November 1985

Parted kitchen curtains framed the panorama of a fast closing dusk and Alec's back garden.

'Can't believe this weather; one minute freeze an' breeze, then frozen an' still... now rain an' wind... and rainin' like stair rods right now. Them keepers can't know their arses from their elbows last few days. This weather keeps up, definitely worth a visit t' The Clump.'

The Clump was a difficult target for the poacher. Its closeness to the main coverts meant raised levels of vigilance which was aided and abetted by good transport access from both Privet and Raynes Lanes. Conversely, these factors increased its challenge to poachers of Alec's calibre. 'And with this lot,' thought Alec, 'The wind, the rain, the cloud cover? Too good to miss.' The collision of these natural events meant The Clump's playing field would be sloping just ever so slightly in his favour... just give it a little more time.

The Land Rover had been fired up and the wipers made to struggle manfully but futilely against the rainwater hem-lining down the windscreen. Falling steadily since late afternoon, by ten o'clock it was now cannoning off the tin cab and canvas back of the shoot vehicle, parked, complete with keeper posse, half way up

Privet Lane and just five hundred yards short of The Clump.

After a prolonged silence, David pulled a packet of sweets from his pocket and Eric eyed the bag.

"'Bout time too. Was wonderin' when you were gonna get them out. What are they?"

"You don't know what they are but your first consideration is how many of them you can get?"

"'Course. Never say no and you'll never starve so, what are they?"

"Blackcurrant and liquorice."

"Bloody hell, that's some combination is that. Will they help stave of this cold I've got coming on?"

"What cold?"

"This cold! Have you not noticed how peaky I've looked these past few days?"

David and Liam answered in unison, "No."

"No, you wouldn't. I've struggled on manfully though, no complaints, no moanin'..."

"'Til now."

"No moanin', just got on with the job, I 'ave."

David scoffed, "How your Hattie puts up with you, I'll never know."

"She knows a good bargain when she sees one."

"For bargain read cheap," said Liam.

"I suffer in silence me..."

"Then shurrup an' suffer."

"...In silence, and my condition isn't being helped by you denyin' me sweets." David offered the bag. "What are they like?"

David looked beyond the rummaging Eric to Liam huddled in the driver's seat. "Can you believe this? If you told him they was arsenic he'd ask how many he could eat before he dropped dead."

Liam shrugged. "Why not get him some then we'd find out."

David's grip closed round the top of the bag. "Steady on! They've to last all night these, an' I don't suppose you brought any, did y'?"

"Rely on you, Dave." Eric patted his coat pockets. "I've got a nub end you can 'ave... somewhere..."

"Eric, I don't smoke... Do you know, I do believe we have this conversation regular."

"Regularly."

"You sound like my Steph."

"Pity he don't look like her," said Liam.

Eric unwrapped the sweet. "An' I bet he takes about as much notice of 'er as he does of me."

"I take plenty of notice, you know nothing about it!"

"Oh, dear. Touched a nerve there, I think."

"No, just notin' the fact that you're talkin' about summat you know nothin' of."

"That right?"

"Yeah."

"Right. I'll remember that when it next comes to coffee time at your place. We'll see what Steph has to say about it."

"She'll say how it is."

"An' what's that?"

"That the only thing as buggers up our time together is the hours this bloody job demands, from all of us."

"That'll not be including Liam then?"

Liam stirred in his seat. "How come I'm being dragged into it?"

"Because you're the only one not carryin' the cross of a dissatisfied wife, that's why. Not my Hattie's favourite time of the season neither."

"All part of the bloody treatment. We all knew what we was takin' on when we signed up."

"Some of us."

"All of us."

David offered the bag across. "Liam?"

Liam shook his head. "No, thanks, you'll have enough bother feedin' the human piranha over there."

David took the wrapper off his sweet. "Can't even remember what she looks like some days, Steph."

"Woman like that... hard to forget, Davey-lad," said Eric as he screwed up his sweet wrapper ostentatiously. "Not my fault if your memory's failin' you, is it? Maybe the odd fag would improve it."

"If I was in need of the odd fag I'd not get it from you, that much I do know. You're the only man I know can peel an orange in his pocket." He watched Eric push the screwed up wrapper into the ashtray and offered him another. "An' if you sucked these sweets rather than crunched 'em up they'd last us a lot longer... 'Ere."

Eric rustled the bag again and smiled. "Ta, Dave."

Ahead of the vehicle an ash branch snapped and drooped across the lane causing Liam to exclaim, "Bloody hell! This is as wild a night as I've known for many a year. What the 'ell 'appened between last night's frost and teatime today, I'd like to know."

"A deep depression drifted in from the west..." began Eric.

"An' it's sittin' right next to me now," interrupted David.

"Yes, very funny, where'd you get that from, an early Christmas cracker? Sit still an' listen, y' might learn summat. As I was tryin' to say, a deep depression drifted in from the west; only 'ere for about twenty four hours then we're back to a bit of cold, might even snow."

"Christ," muttered Liam. "You can't keep up with it can y'? To be sittin' here in this we've got to be either mad or eccentric millionaires.

David and Eric both said, "Mad".

David slipped the bag of sweets back into his pocket. "Which is why we're all sitting here now, at twenty past ten, instead of bein' at home, relaxin'..."

"Shaggin'."

"Relaxin', Eric. Buildin' up our strength. Boys' Day then Lordy's big days to follow." Another blast of wind-chased rain smacked onto the windscreen. "I mean, come on, nobody in their right mind will be out in this lot."

"He's catchin' on fast, aint 'e?" Eric turned to David. "No one in their right mind is out in this lot!"

"Wouldn't hear 'em anyhow," Liam added. "Not if they were using a howitzer in the 'ome coverts we wouldn't."

"We'll never get back across the ford if we leave it much longer, y' know that don't y'?" Liam grunted in reply as Eric continued, "It'll be runnin' that full we'll 'ave to go up top of Privet Lane, round The Clump and back down Raynes Lane. That'll mean goin' through three sets of gates, an' I aint gettin' out an' openin' none of 'em, not with my cold."

The rain, lashed on by the wind, continued to hammer down forcing necks, like nose-tapped tortoises, ever deeper into winter woollies.

Plimsolls squeaked their displeasure at the treatment they were receiving. After twenty minutes in the unabating downpour, footwear and puddles were one and the same. Alec's clothes, once loose fitting and protective were now tailored to the point where the outline of his night time, smooth bore companion showed its voluptuous figure through the coat's folds and creases. Water trickled down the back of his neck.

There had been no need to dodge the unwelcome passing stranger for no one had been seen on his journey to The Clump which, as he plashed his way along the road's hedgerow, now loomed large.

To his right the wind was testing out the root system of the fir trees on the wood's perimeter, bending them severely one way then running round to the other side in an effort to surprise them, whipping their tops to and fro. Each drop of rain was stinging in its efforts to reach the ground before its companions, and Alec hunched himself even more as he topped the rise in the lane and the full force of the wind hit him sideways, trying to bend and snap him like the firs. Vision and hearing were limited. The lane's tall unkempt hedge could be made out for the first fifty yards or so, but then it faded into the weather's haze. Alec stepped smartly on, wanting to reach the shelter of the wood before his ears left his head in protest.

The keepers scanned their watches as one man and as one man realised that minutes passed belied seeming hours past.

"We'll give it 'til twelve then it's 'ome time," said Liam. He turned the key and the engine roared into life.

Alec stopped. The rain and wind made it difficult to locate and name the new sound, if such it was, from the continuing noise of branches clashing.

The need for silence and communion with his surroundings fell upon him and he squatted down in the hedgerow.

Liam switched on the wipers and the severely taxed blades sliced their way across the windscreen. "I'll turn it over again in a while, keep it warm an' dry."

"It's the only thing that will be," said Eric.

Liam switched the engine off and all fell silent.

Alec willed his senses to decipher the fragmented aural picture, all to no avail. He sat on. The town clock's chime of eleven fifteen was whipped by in the wind. Nothing. He blamed the weather which he considered wild enough to fool a hunting fox. He rose from the hedgerow and moved towards the gate that led into the centre of The Clump, draping his makeshift rope game-carrier round his neck as he did so. A long look down the ride was his salute to the wood as he made his entrance through the reluctantly closing gateway. Sidestep led to cover and first target as Alec removed the gun from its sodden shelter, accepting the quickening pulse rate as part of the job.

Watches were becoming self conscious after so much scrutiny. Was it home time yet? Must be, surely... Liam lifted his arm and jagged his sleeve back.

Alec lifted the shotgun at the lowest cock pheasant perched amongst others on the well stacked larch branches.

The rain drummed on the Land Rover roof, trying to find a way through.

"Twenty past," said Liam. "'Ome in a bit."

Eric took out his pack of cigarettes and David sighed. "Phhh... If you're gonna light up again then open a bloody window or we'll all choke to death, there's enough fug in here as it is."

Alec pulled the first of two triggers.

Sound and pheasant-fall became one, all nicely muffled by the weather. Now the next.

Eric's finger gripped the knob of the sliding window.

Alec's finger closed on the second trigger of the shortened .410.

As a curtain is drawn back to reveal a stage made ready for the play, so rain stopped, wind dropped and the sky splintered into a million fragments as the moonlight stabbed and seared through the colander cloud, illuminating the set below.

"Bloody hell, will you look at that! Gabriel's turned off the stop-cock."

The movement of Alec's trigger-finger was timed to perfection with Eric's opening of the vehicle window.

Unable to stop the gun's soliloquy, the first line was spoken.

Bang!

Alec winced and cowered at the shattering sound.

The shot echoed and reverberated through The Clump then, finding the tunnel formed by the Privet Lane hedges to its liking, it raced down the lane's throat entered through the vehicle's window and shook the three keepers by the shoulders.

Liam barked out, "The Clump... we'll leave the motor! Eric, you and David round the top side, Raynes Lane. I'll go into the flushing cover from this end and wait. Bring 'em on to me!"

They scrambled out of the vehicle.

"Pound to a pinch of pig shit its fuckin' Stratton! Take y' sticks," said Eric, always one to get priorities sorted.

Alec straightened up, the taught expression slipping from his face.

The speed with which the weather had changed left him bereft of belief and action. Like a cloud scudding across a sunny valley the storm had gone to be replaced by a still, bright, moonlit night.

Now decisions were necessary.

Past experience told him the Barn Tor keepers were more diligent than most, but the birds were here and so was he; easy pickings. And after that lot of weather he figured no one in their right mind would be out.

'Grab a few, then go'.

At The Clump's flushing point the fourth shot confirmed the position of the culprit to Liam. Now all he needed to do was sit and wait; Eric and David would do the rest.

"Oi! You there! Let's 'ave y'!"

Like the change in the weather, David's voice took Alec completely by surprise rendering him immobile for a split second. 'Alec Stratton,' he thought. 'You're gettin' sloppy.'

The seriousness of his predicament was then made all too clear when Eric's voice reached him from another angle. "Come on! We can see ya!"

'No you can't,' thought Alec. 'If y' could you'd have a torch on me! No dogs neither... Keep low, Stratton an' get out!'

He quickly closed the coat's zip to secure the pheasants; the gun was folded and shoved into his coat pocket in an instant. Keeping his head well down so as not to be recognised, Alec set off in the only direction left open to him, The Clump's flushing point. The chase was on and there was no mistaking who the quarry was.

David and Eric, hearing the movement and being fairly certain they would not be fired on, made no effort to conceal themselves; whoever it was had no idea of the welcome waiting.

Alec entered the thick cover fifty yards ahead of his pursuers. He crashed through it, briars and saplings begging him to stay and keep them company. David and Eric followed, thrashing the undergrowth with their thick ash sticks.

Victory was theirs.

After forty yards in the cover Alec dropped to his knees. With only a short distance to go before he reached the end of the cover and the valley below, where he knew a clear run could be made for home, something forced him to halt despite the activity of the two behind him.

Then it occurred. 'Two...! Bugger! You soft sod, Alec Stratton, there's only bloody two! Two... Number three's up front!'

He turned back the way he had come, moving on hands and knees towards the gap between the two fast approaching and wildly thrashing keepers.

Chapter Six
Month 7 – May 1985

"Sweet peas? Yes! Tent B! Far side, bay seven! It is marked, y' know! I put up the plan at the entrance if you'd bothered to read it... and park your van in its allocated spot; don't leave it there, they're all marked. Tinker! Tinker! Leave him alone!" The terrier studiously ignored the command, continuing to circle and jump at the man's legs.

Audrey Carlisle was the ideal person to run the Shardwell-by-Tor and District Annual Spring Horticultural and Produce Show; had been for the last nine years. She managed, organized, informed, arranged and ran the whole extravaganza supported, it had to be said, by an army of dedicated helpers, but no one was left in any doubt as to who was in charge. Only the foolhardy disobeyed her commands and they only ever did that once. Laws unto themselves, however, were her two Border-Lakeland cross terriers.

Tinker's attention was sufficient to make it increasingly uncomfortable for the man. But now, to make matters worse, he was joined by Belle, his litter brother. Both dogs circled and sniffed, inspecting the man balancing an armful of plants.

"Have you got cats? What!" The tone wasn't inquisitorial it was accusatory. "They can't stand cats, either of them."

"No, I don't have cats. Could you call...?"

"You've been near someone who does then! These two never make a mistake, much like me! They have an inbuilt dislike of cats, much like me; what! Can sense them, are you sure you haven't got cats?"

It would seem from their throaty growls that the two terriers were on the verge of starting a scrap over who owned this particular carcass. *"I am sure, yes and if these two will leave me be, I'll be very pleased to make my way..."*

The man's escalating canine predicament was of no further interest to Audrey however. Turning away she waved her stick.

"No...! No, no, not in there! You're in A! Tent A, what! That's tent F! Roses – shrub and hybrid T!" An elderly man with a stick in one hand and a box of magnificent rhubarb balanced precariously in his other looked across at her. Audrey's voice took on an exasperated tone. *"Look at the sign! You're in tent A! A! Oh, for goodness sake...! Tent Aaayyy! Produce! Tinker Belle! Come along boys!"* The two dogs were caught for a moment between their present point of worry and the tantalizing possibilities of something fresh. Audrey set off. *"Not in there, do you hear! Is he deaf or daft? What! Tent A!"*

A cursory snap at Belle by Tinker sealed the matter. They scampered off, overtaking Audrey in their eagerness to home in on their next victim.

David's voice reached Stephanie in the bedroom as she finished dressing.

"I'm away! Enjoy the flower show! It's supposed to be worth the visit, and you've got the weather for it."

"If it's so lovely then why aren't you coming with me?"

"'Cos these chicks have got to be de-beaked, Steph. They've already killed three and now they've got a taste... Oh, an' Steph?" She came to the head of the stairs. "Thanks for arranging to meet Alice at the show site an' not here."

"That's alright." Stephanie paused before answering further, but it was a pause filled with meaning. "I don't appreciate having to be so clandestine about my friendships, I really don't... but I understand how it could be misconstrued. For you, not me."

"Ar. Thanks. An' you do look lovely." David stared at her for a long moment then made a tentative start up the stairs. "She is welcome here Steph... Alice. I told her so."

"Yes, I know, I was there."

He stopped. "I know you were. So was I, it just... it does help if all your meetings don't take place in our front room... y' know, that they happen elsewhere too." His voice tailed off as he realized he was blathering.

"I've said I understand, David."

"Do you?"

"Yes..."

"Yeah, OK. Thanks."

He turned back down the stairs but her voice followed him. "Her husband may be your antithesis, but Alice isn't, remember that. She's just my friend and I value her company and conversation."

"Ar, I know, so you keep tellin' me an' I believe y'... honest."

"I sometimes wonder."

"I do." His avoidance technique was not lost on Stephanie as he broke the conversation's thread, taking the last couple of treads in one as he went into the hall. "I'll be off then."

"Yes, OK. Where will you be? The day looks set to be a hot one. I'll bring some tea along when I get back and we can have a picnic if you like."

He came back to the foot of the stairs and smiled up at her. "You understand me so much better than I understand you... why is that?"

"That's what we do well. Women. We understand people. We want to know all the little details given out... except I get lost when it comes to concentrated housewifery. Then I seem to run out of battery."

"Not true, Steph. This house is always spotless and the contents comin' from the kitchen are never anythin' less than superb." He patted his stomach. "There's proof if it were needed."

"Don't let what I do confuse you; that's a habit not a skill. I'm a creature of habit. Never step outside of the parameters... predictable as a clock."

"Do you want to?"

"What?"

"Step outside of them parameters... not be predictable?"

"No... don't think so, too... scary. Sometimes think it would be exciting, different, would make me feel... different. Maybe that's what I enjoy about being with Alice. Nothing predictable with her. On any given meeting anything could happen."

"Do you envy her that?"

"Yes. That... bravery, for want of a better word. Wish I had it or could recognise it in me, not that I'd want to use it but it would be... reassuring, to know it was there, within one's capability so to speak." David looked at her, the recognition of something newly discovered in her eyes. "I don't explain things well."

"No, no, you do, it's just me an' my brain."

She smiled at him for what seemed, to David, to be the first time that week. "We do have one thing in common though, Alice and I."

"What's that?"

"The details, people, like I just said. We both pay attention to the little details."

David smiled at her. "I'll try to pay attention to the detail too then."

"If you succeed you'll be the first man to achieve it."

"Ouch!"

"Picnic?"

"Erm... yes, that'd be great; thank you."

"Where will you be? Rearing field?"

"No, they're all done. I'm with Liam in the old pig sties at the back of the village for these. Should finish de-beaking by half two, three-ish..."

"Oh, well, if you're going to be that close to the show site do you want Alice and me to keep away?"

"Steph..."

"Well, I think it's a valid question considering our recent conversation."

"No I don't want you to keep away! It's hardly likely we'll see anything of each other anyhow; we'll be in sties and you'll be in tents."

"I know it's my first visit but I don't think I'll be all that excited; it is just a flower show after all." David looked at her bemused. "We'll be in tents? Intense? Oh, never mind."

"Oh, yes, I see. Oh, very good! Wasted now you've 'ad to explain it. Sorry, effort for nothing. Anyway, then I thought I'd take a walk over to the brook on Cut Throat Lane with some of that old planking from back of the sties there. I've *a tunnel trap to replace in that gateway. By the pole bridge over the ford."*

"Uh-huh."

"One of them bloody sheep put its foot through the old trap tryin' to squeeze through the gap between the hedge and the gate. Smashed the tunnel an' the tie-peg."

"How very inconsiderate of it."

"Weren't it. So, meet me there about five?"

"Does it have to be done today? If you left that you could come along to the show a little later."

"Ar, I know... but, well, it's best to keep on top of stuff, an' we are havin' a picnic, you know."

"Yes, I do. Thank you for sparing the time."

"Steph..."

"What about the lock-up on the rearing field?"

"I'll have to fit that in after our picnic. Liam won't mind if I'm a bit late."

"How kind of him. OK. Five it is. Do you want anything special?"

"Steph..."

"What?"

"Nothin'... You're just so..."

"Negative?"

"Well, yes. You know the pressure's on for me this season and..."

"And the least I can do is be supportive?" David looked at her but said nothing. *"Allow me my moments of negativity, David; they're all your job leaves me sometimes. Now, do you want anything special for tea?"*

After a short silence, David replied, *"Cheese, bread, an apple... that an' a flask of coffee will do nicely."*

"Forgot to get bread I'm afraid and not got round to making any either. See what I mean; concentrated housewifery? I've the remains of that last walnut loaf I made. Oh, I'll pick up something from the bakery tent at the show this afternoon, if there's anything left by the time I get there that is. Can you live on the promise of good things to come?"

"I can, but walnut loaf's fine, don't go to any special trouble."

She turned and made her way back to the bedroom. "It's no trouble. I'll bring along enough of whatever I can get for two. See you at the ford at five."

He stared at the empty space for a few moments. "Yeah, see you at five. Enjoy your show."

"I will. Enjoy your de-beaking!"

Opening up the metal cabinet bolted to the wall in the hallway, David removed a shotgun. He pocketed a few cartridges, re-locked the cabinet and left the house.

—⁓—

Alice waved from the far side of the home-made produce tent and Stephanie waved back. They met by the sponges. "I think they use a bicycle pump to get them as tall as this. Mine rise but not to 'alf this height. Potato flour, I'll bet that's what they use. Potato flour, mark me on that."

Stephanie frowned. "Isn't that cheating?"

"Only if someone else wins, apparently. You been 'ere long?"

"No, five minutes." She lifted her shopping bag into view. "I picked up a rye loaf and a couple of slices of fruit cake from the bakery tent then came straight on here." She lowered the bag. "Do you want to look around here or get over to the flowers?"

Alice closed in on Stephanie. "I think we'll leave, I'm feeling inadequate already. Let's do the flower displays then the craft section but by way of the bakery tent. I can get a French stick in there for tea. We'll get a cuppa later."

"Right, my treat, and a piece of cake too. There'll be some folk selling off samples of their wares in the café towards the close. We can find out if they taste as good as they look."

"If it is potato flour they've used we'd be as well havin' gravy than tea!" They linked arms and left the tent.

The afternoon was blistering its way slowly to what promised to be a postcard sunset and the three hours of de-beaking had taken its toll on both David and Liam.

Nipping off the end of the top beak and keeping the cannibalism of the crowded pheasant chicks to a minimum was a regular task. Today, however, with the gas heaters running inside the pens and the sun heater running outside, the job had become one of endurance and stamina. During their frantic efforts to carefully catch up the poults, a regular infusion of cider, chilled in the water barrels kept in the sties, helped with the endurance side of things. Any traces of alcoholic effect were immediately sweated out as both keepers juggled pheasant chicks and hot de-beaking pliers in the sawdust-laden air.

Job finished, pliers away, sawdust smoothed, David dangled his wrists in the barrel's razor-cold water to cool down and told Liam the tale of the broken tunnel trap. Liam said he would do the evening feed and lock-up on his own. David thanked him, dunked his head and shoulders into the barrel, flicked off the excess moisture and left the sties for Cut Throat Lane and the ford.

It was only as Liam had driven out of sight and David had collected planks for the repair job that his attention was drawn to the hedgerow that ran up to the show field.

He concentrated his gaze. That colour; could only be one thing.

Putting the wood aside, he picked up and loaded the shotgun and took another glance to confirm it. No mistake, that was definitely Marmalady.

"Do you want a scone or a slice of Victoria sponge?"

"How about both?"

Stephanie smiled at Alice. "Moment on the lips, lifetime on the hips."

"Clever girls who answer back only ever get a smack!"

"That an old country saying or one of your own?"

"One of my own that I'll carry out if you don't get a move on with that bloomin' tea!"

"Yes, right, can take a hint." Stephanie joined the short queue and Alice moved to find a seat for them both. Stephanie was soon back balancing a laden tray. "No scones left, lady in front got the last one so I got you a slice of sponge and a rock bun instead. That alright?"

"Fine." Alice eyed the tray. "I see you've not got one for yourself."

"No, well, allows me to feel superior about how much stodge you're putting away."

"Thank you for that." Alice pointed at the tray. "Will you be mum?"

"Yes, alright. Here, have a serviette."

"Anyway, girl with your sort of figure needs hardly worry about a couple of extra ounces, might make you look even better... if that were at all possible."

Stephanie put milk in Alice's cup. "What are you talking about?"

"You! Figure like that? You must have been well placed when they were handin' them out. Past the door marked sag-and-droop straight into the one marked pert-and-round."

"Alice!"

"You've the sort of looks an' figure most women would die for an' most men trip over for; their tongues in most cases."

She sugared Alice's cup. "What men?"

"Those hordes of chaps that pass us an' mentally undress you."

"What?"

"Well they're not looking at me!"

Stephanie poured tea. "And they're not looking at me either."

"Show's how much you know. That figure poured into that summer dress? All in all it's a problem."

Stephanie was uncomfortable with the conversation. "What's the problem with the dress?"

"There's no problem with the dress, the problem's with the men!"

"I think you're exaggerating."

Alice smiled and shook her head. "You really have no idea, do you?"

"About what?"

"Nothin', never mind. Let me try this 'ere rock cake an' find fault, eh?"

Rose Allen named the cat Marmalady. Found under an old shed, it grew from a brilliant orange tabby kitten into a very large, brilliant orange tabby she-cat.

The first time Eric saw her was as a kitten, playing happily with a dazed butterfly on the lawn of the Allen's small, neat front garden just two and a half years ago. Rose Allen had come to the door of their gatehouse cottage, possibly drawn by some sixth sense, and enquired ostensibly of Eric's health and temper. Eric made some remark about they were feeding the kitten too well, about how they needed to watch out for the road, it being so close, and they had parted; Rose onto the lawn to protectively gather up the kitten, Eric to a meeting with Liam where he would pass on the glad tidings.

Unfortunately, as with many felines before it, regular milk, meat and fuss did nothing to quell Marmalady's urge to hunt. The estate keepers soon became aware that, as the cat grew in size and stature so she was venturing further into the Barn Tor coverts, hunting quarry that ranged from mouse to pheasant. When David started on the estate, Eric had tipped him off as to the cat's depredations, but, either through good fortune or bad luck, Marmalady had yet to meet an armed keeper in a secluded spot. As the cat's hunting forays increased however, such a meeting could only be a matter of time.

That time seemed nigh today, for the cat had foolishly chosen ground close to the rearing sheds in order to try her paws at stalking a small party of bachelor cock pheasants quietly feeding along the hedgerow. Slotting into the shallow cart rut running parallel to the hedge, the cat had only just begun to creep along the channel, looking for all the world like a ginger slug, when David had spotted her and formed a plan.

Judging the distances, David figured he would not get within firing range before she was too close to the village showground, but all was not lost. Checking the gun's load, he gauged the degree of difficulty involved in circling the cat and approaching it from the show field end. If he got a wiggle on he could get the cat to run back towards the estate, thereby giving him a clear shot in a safe direction and allowing him to test the nine-life theory. He was just moving off, when over the hedge-stile, unannounced, unwelcome and definitely unforeseen, appeared Albert and Rose Allen.

"I'll have you know I am absolutely certain I left the hat there. I do not make mistakes, ever! It was placed on that chair and now you are using that chair so you must know where it's gone. What!"

Alice pointed out Audrey Carlisle to Stephanie in hushed tones "That's her there, shoutin', with those two terriers, stroppy one and stroppy two."

Stephanie looked across at Audrey then whispered to Alice. "Wouldn't want to cross her; that's a face carved from a solid block of confrontation."

The hat was produced by another stallholder who tried to explain he had removed it to allow the lady, who had complained of feeling faint, to sit down and recover. Without apology or explanation, Audrey snatched the hat back and began to revile the man for being so lax in coming forward.

"Weaned on a pickle, she were," said Alice. "Let's put some distance between us before we attract 'er anger."

"But we've done nothing."

"Exactly; ripe for attack we are. Come on! Jam and marmalade tent's through there, over the other side of the field." Alice pointed to the doorway and opened her shopping bag. "I've got a portion of that home-made French stick left in here."

Stephanie looked into the bag and at the ragged loaf. "I thought that was for your husband's supper?"

"It was." She smiled back and shrugged. "Could never resist the company of fresh bread. So, my diet's shot today. Let's try and do the free samples justice." They began to leave.

"Ah, Mrs Stratton, I see you've not entered any walnut loaf this year!"

Alice turned slowly on her heel. She smiled and nodded. "No, Mrs Carlisle, been too busy what with one thing an' another."

Audrey approached them and many relieved people made a pathway for her. "How very unproductive of you! I'd have thought you'd plenty of time on your hands, not working as you do. What!"

"I work on the market, Mrs Carlisle, you know I do."

"Part-time though, wouldn't you say?" Her voice took on an accusatory tone. "Your husband still... 'out-and-about' is he?" Alice was about to reply but Audrey was not interested. She had fixed Stephanie with a gimlet eye. "I don't think I know your companion."

Alice took Stephanie's arm and gave a saccharine smile. "No, you're right, you don't." With that she marched Stephanie out of the tent, leaving Audrey in her wake; but Audrey Carlisle was not to be outdone. She and her canine entourage followed swiftly after them.

David broke the gun's chamber waved cheerfully and walked across. At the same instant, heard but unseen, a group of cock birds splintered and cackled their way over the heads of the assembling trio. As a diversion to all this movement, David spoke to the arm-in-arm couple.

"Hello Mister Allen, Mrs. Allen! On our way back from the show are we?"

Rose watched the birds flick over their heads and glide effortlessly down a hedgerow and away. "Something's upset them... Yes, we are. Had a lovely afternoon." She looked at David's soaked hair and shoulders. "You look hot and bothered, covered in all that sweat."

"Been de-beaking in the sties all afternoon. Glad of a bit of air really."

Albert coughed. "Ah-ha! Not goin' to the show yourself then?"

"No, no time, things to get done. Steph's gone though. This'll be her first visit, you might've seen her."

Rose put her shopping bag of show-bought plants down. "No, we've not, but then, it's so crowded there, well, on a day like today, sunshine and all. You want to get over there, some lovely displays in the W.I. tent..." she indicated her shopping bag. "...And some good bargains on the plant stalls."

"Maybe the next one."

Albert spoke over them both. "Never mind flower displays and bargains, Rose, he wants to take a bit of time out for hisself and that lovely wife of his, flower show or not." He turned to David. "You think 'is Lordship will appreciate you more for workin' yourself to a standstill seven days a week on his behalf, eh?" David was about to reply but Albert continued on. "No, he'll not. You'll knock yourself out for 'im an' he'll only moan about you havin' time off for the sick."

Rose picked up her bag. "Enough of that, Albert Allen! Hope you get to the next." She stared at David and nodded so as to make her point. "And you have a nice afternoon..."

She indicated the buildings with another nod of her head. "...Somewhere else than here!" She tugged Albert's arm. "Come on, let's be off home."

David watched them disappear round the side of the building then scuttled back to look along the hedge. Marmalady was still there, checking the site of the recently departed pheasants. 'Cheeky little sod.' After a short pause the cat began moving slowly along the track and towards the far hedge and showground. There was little chance of getting beyond her for a safe ground shot now, but David reckoned he could still give the cat a big scare.

Up and along the opposite side of the hedge, he found a gap and pushed his way through. Sure enough, his calculations were right; Marmalady was just forty yards ahead. The cat took a look over her shoulder at the noise caused by David snagging his way through the hedge and, reasoning that a fireside chat and saucer of warm milk was the last thing on offer, began to run along the hedgerow towards the showground. David hoisted the gun to his shoulder and fired off two shots into the air in quick succession.

Stephanie looked at Alice. "One of the keepers letting fly by the sound of it."

Alice smiled at her. "I hope so. If it's mine we might have a bit of trouble on our hands!" They continued to move through the crowds and into the jam and marmalade tent.

The shots only served to add impetus to the rapidly retreating cat. Marmalady streaked away towards the first bit of visible cover, the rear flap of the jam and marmalade tent. She could hear the noise of chatter ahead as she wriggled under the tent's pegged skirt, but the recent explosions behind convinced her that chatter was better than dead.

Picking her way through the discarded delivery boxes and wrappings dumped under the trestle tables, the cat made her way as unobtrusively as possible towards the other side of the tent where an open flap promised escape. This direct march to freedom was halted by Alice and Stephanie who blocked the route, causing a quick cat-readjustment to be made. With a small leap beyond the barrier of legs and a jink right, Marmalady emerged from under the table and crossed the narrow aisle in front of Alice and Stephanie in search of another exit.

"Oh, look, that's the Allen's cat, Marmalady!" Stephanie said in cheerful surprise.

Making her appearance onto this same aisle and with perfect timing, Audrey entered with Tinker and Belle close by. The two terriers saw the flash of ginger, agreed with Stephanie's label and, emitting a duet-yelp set off to commit catricide. Their soprano yapping was echoed by Audrey's alto banshee wail for them to stop, and like a starting gun for a death race this signalled all hell to break loose.

Marmalady, deciding an aerial route might be the best means of escape, leapt onto a trestle table, bearing carefully stacked jars of local honey, in two balletic bounds. Belle scrambled his way under the drooping tablecloth, yapping in his exertions. Tinker obviously thought the cat had it right and, with a prodigious leap bounded onto the tabletop, just behind the cat. The cat had barely disturbed a jar, not so the terrier.

Landing heavily, Tinker could do little to halt his forward momentum. The tablecloth ruched and the terrier plus thirty four jars of two year old elderflower honey rapidly caught up the cat. Not wishing to crash over the precipice, Tinker back-pedalled and gradually slid to a halt; the table top contents, however, continued on over the edge. A split second later the tent was filled with the sound of crashing glass as the combined weight and speed of produce and puppy shoved cloth, jars, cat-and-all off the table and onto the floor.

Plummeting down amongst preserves and tablecloth, Marmalady landed not six inches from a very surprised Belle. To the cat's great good fortune the cloth draped over the terrier's face, blinding him momentarily. Like Supercat faced with a tall building, with a single bound she launched herself back and up, to the relative safety of the now denuded table top only to virtually collide with a seriously off-balance and equally surprised Tinker.

Audrey Carlisle yelled out in her most fearsome voice. "Catch the cat someone! Catch the bloody cat!"

Alice looked at Stephanie. "A bullet couldn't catch that cat!"

As the cat reappeared on the table top, Tinker felt his moment had come. Teetering on the table's edge, he made a brave fist of both snarl and lunge.

Handicapped though she was by her recent trampolining, Marmalady hardly altered stride in her tumbling flight. Fluffing out all her fur until she was as big as a battleship, she swerved at right-angles to dodge the terrier. As Tinker slalomed up, all teeth and panic but minus brakes, Marmalady kicked off from the table's edge, spat viciously, swiped out with her paw and performed a sideways roll of the utmost panache to complete her change of direction. The cat's well armed, well aimed blow tore open Tinker's forehead inflicting immediate searing pain and sending him back-pedalling *and yelping away from the cat's-paw-branding-iron. The now hopelessly out of control dog bridled back into thin air then down, amongst the debris, the tablecloth and his near hysterical brother; the loss of all semblance of sanity now followed.*

Setting off at high speed, the cat karoomed over the table tops as both terriers gathered their wits, dignity and vocal chords and set off in pursuit; any effort at care or considered direction of travel was cast to the winds by both dogs as they barged and charged their way under the tables, bishing and bashing the table legs in gay abandon. Ladies, customers and servers alike, vainly tried to catch, juggle and balance the tumbling displays caused by the immediate result of this cat-and-dog contretemps... alas, they were cruelly and very quickly outplayed. It was the toppling first table which caused a domino effect along the whole row of carefully arranged glassware and, once started, this tsunami of collapsing tables gathered pace, distributing contents every which-a-way as the cat surfed on. Jams, marmalades, beetroot, honey and bottled fruits of every description cascaded to the floor. Like an off-piste skier, Marmalady dodged just ahead of both domestic avalanche and pursuing terriers toward a partially open tent flap in a last ditch attempt for freedom.

Apoplectic with rage, Audrey took off after the rapidly departing trio as she registered the final table in the cat's path; the table holding the cups and vases for presentation. Scooping an unbroken two-pound jar of prize winning raspberry jam from off the floor, she launched it at the cat as it leapt the final gap to land on the cup-covered table. The jar missed cat... The jar overtook cat... Crashing into the silverware like a well shied mop-head the jar kindly cleared a path for the cat and removed the table's red cloth which fell to the floor, neatly netting both dogs.

With a massive leap along the now cleared route, the cat launched herself at the open flap just as the man carrying his prize winning box of rhubarb entered through it. He took the cat full in the chest, his reflexive action launching both walking stick and rhubarb high into the air as he dropped to the floor like a rapidly released anchor. It took only a couple of seconds for gravity to arrest their direction of travel; stick and rhubarb quickly fell earthwards crashing over and around him, box and all.

Using the man's head as a launch pad, Marmalady torpedoed out of the tent and melted into the safe haven of the boundary hedgerow that led to the church to the sound of the bemused coughing of the felled man, the muffled sound of yapping, cloth-wrapped terriers and the screams of their distraught mistress.

—⁂—

David saw Stephanie fifty yards distant and, patting down the last turf on the roof of the rebuilt tunnel trap with the shovel, walked across to meet her and took the basket.

"Good day at the show?"

"Before I reply to that, can you tell me, was it you who fired a gun near the showground this afternoon?"

"No. Heard nothin' neither. When were this then?"

"This afternoon... two shots. You heard nothing?"

David stood and scratched his chin, a look of deep thought on his face. He eventually shook his head. "Nope. Could it have been a car backfirin'?"

Stephanie looked at him for a long moment. "Doubt it. You heard nothing?"

"Nothin'"

"Hm. Right, well let me tell you about my day."

They turned back to the ford, David carrying the picnic basket and listening intently as Stephanie talked him through the events of Audrey Carlisle, Marmalady and the Shardwell-by-Tor and District Annual Spring Horticultural and Produce Show.

Day 7 – Saturday 24th November 1985

As Eric topped the Lodge Road bridge so his eyes fixed on a familiar figure sitting on the river bank and he slowed down. The spaniel curled up on the front seat rose in expectation, knocking the football rattle onto the floor.

"No, not doggin' back yet lass. A detour to make, a score to settle." The spaniel stared through the windscreen, her tail unconvinced that destination point had not been reached.

Last night's embarrassment of reaching the far end of the flushing cover with nothing to show for it but a dented stick fanned fresh flames in Eric's mind. Flooding back came the memory of the frantic rush they had made back into the wood as the realisation struck home that they had gone over the poacher... gone over him... and they each knew to man it was Stratton they had missed.

'An' here he is, twice as bold an' twice as ugly.'

That the poacher they had failed to catch and the fisherman now sat at the river's edge were one and the same, Eric had no doubt; none. He retrieved the football rattle and placed it onto the dashboard then got out of the Land Rover to open the field gate and exact payment.

Alec's concentration on the current-bobbing float was cut as he heard the click of the gate latch. He glanced over his shoulder and saw Eric swing the gate open. 'Ayup, here comes trouble. No bloody peace now.' He turned his head back to the float. After a few seconds, he heard the Land Rover rev into the field behind him and threw another quick glance away from his rod. Eric was now out of the vehicle again, closing the gate behind him. ''Ere we go. Looks like the end of my fishin' for the day.'

Eric kept his eyes on Alec as he nosed the vehicle across the field. 'I don't care if 'e 'as got a licence, I'll still kick 'im off.' The Land Rover swished its way through the blocks of scrub-rush that struggled to make a living against constant cutting, flooding and cattle damage, then Eric saw the bicycle, a new one laid on its side by a single tuft of hard rush not ten yards from Alec.

"Bought with the proceeds of his fuckin' night work no doubt, Spadger," said Eric out loud. The spaniel cocked his head to one side in recognition of the tone. "Well, 'e aint gonna keep this bloody profit."

Eric carefully steered the vehicle right over the bike, folding it neatly, creasing wheels, spokes and frame into a metal fan.

"Got a licence then?" Eric's words came from close behind.

Alec half turned to reply. "Yeah."

"Let's see."

"At 'ome."

"Then pack up and leave. Y' know you're supposed to carry it with you at all times." Alec rose in silence from his creel, pulling the line in at the same time. "Anythin' in the net?"

"No."

"Less time to waste then. Off y' go." Alec clipped the hook into the top eye then, fitting the rod in one hand, creel and keep net in the other, turned and was met by Eric's dazzling smile. "It aint much, but it's a start." Alec moved past Eric and on towards the bridge. His stride faltered as Eric's voice, the smile still audible in the diction, came from behind. "Don't forget y' bike." Alec turned back slowly as Eric expanded the point. "Y' bike. I don't want it clutterin' up the field so take it with y'."

Alec's eye caught the tangled mess of brakes, spokes and frame that had once been a bike but was now lying in the grass like a stricken wildebeest.

"I didn't come on a bike."

"What?"

"I said I didn't come on a bike..." Alec lifted one foot. "Shanks'..." He then pointed to another fisherman just two hundred yards further downstream, part hidden by a stunted willow just back from the water's edge. It looked as though he had a good size fish on, his rod bending as he stood to reel it in. "He did though." Alec turned away, waving a hand of royalty and dismissal. "See ya."

The elderly man was now happily netting the two pound barbel as Alec wandered past the Land Rover, saw the dog, stick and football rattle and smiled to himself.

'Doggin' back needed somewhere by the looks of it... that maize on Jackson's I'll bet, an' it'll take a fair posse of folk to do it, number of birds I saw on that road yesterday. Every chance that's where she'll be.'

"Come on, Jill! Out y' come, you idle sod!" The terrier scampered from under the hall stairs flicking her bed into an untidy heap such was the eagerness to answer her master's voice. "You ready, Steph? We need to get on y' know!"

Stephanie came into the hall from the kitchen wiping her hands on a cloth. "Just got to put my coat on."

"What took you so long?"

"You want tea when we get back?"

"Yeah, 'course."

"Then that's what took me so long."

"Point taken. Slip your coat on... get down Jill!"

"Is she coming?"

"Yup."

"I'm assuming we'll not be having the pleasure of Razor's company for dogging back then?"

David slipped his waterproof jacket on and pulled a stick from the collection in the tall basket by the door. "Your assumption is correct, oh all seeing one... which stick do you want? Y' usual?"

"The duck? Yes, please."

David removed a tall blackthorn stick topped by a carved mallard's head. "Not bad for a first attempt, was it?"

"No, not bad."

"Careful, you might actually give out some praise or encouragement."

"You know full well what I meant. It's a lovely stick, second anniversary present. Why do you think it's the one I always pick? Now stop fishing for compliments and tell me why no Razor?"

"He's still on sick leave." David leant the stick against the doorjamb. "It'll be another few days before he'll be able to sniff his own arse let alone summat else's."

"David, I don't wish to know the details, thank you! A simple, 'No, Razor's not well enough yet', would have been sufficient."

"That's what I said."

"No, it wasn't." She looked at Jill who was busy getting under David's feet in her excitement. "Sack would have loved this."

David smiled at her. "I know, Steph. An' I know it's no compensation, but you have no idea..."

"Yes I do, David. Shouldn't have brought it up, wrong of me. Been getting so much wrong these days, sorry."

"Not wrong, just still a bit raw for us both, you especially." He took her hand. "I'm the one who's sorry."

"And I am for you." Jill jumped up at them both, seemingly on cue. "Yes, and we've still got you, little miss; yes, I haven't forgotten." Jill wagged her stump of a tail seemingly fit to take off and grinned widely. "Yes, you're a sweetie, now get down."

"She better had be a sweetie 'cos you'll be workin' her today."

Stephanie looked at him in surprise. "Oh, me? But you usually do..."

"Ar... I know, but sort of compensation for no Sack... I'm takin' both Labs. That alright?"

"'Course." She looked at him. "That's very thoughtful of you. Thank you." She stooped to the frantic terrier and scrubbed her ears. "We make a good team, don't we, Jill?" The terrier barked and ran to the back door. "Hold on there, not quite yet. She's full of vim today. Will need a firm hand that's for sure."

"Down to you, I'd say, Steph."

"A remarkably unsubtle passing of the buck there. She just needs a kind word and a little T.L.C."

"Don't let her get away with anythin'. She's not made of candyfloss y' know. She's frisky 'cos she's not done much work this year that's all, 'cept that session of rattin'. Mass operations not needed 'til today. Eric says them Quarry birds are floodin' across the Bower Road for everyone to see, hence the three-line whip. Makin' a beeline for that maize on Jackson's place, he says; planted it there a purpose, I say."

"Jackson runs milkers doesn't he?" She started to pull her boots on.

"Yes."

"Friesians?"

"Ar, with a handful of Jersey's thrown in. Why?"

"So, he uses the maize for fodder, could that be the explanation?"

"Steph..."

"I don't think he put it in especially to spite Eric and attract his pheasants."

"So much you know. Listen. That farm's got near on seven hundred acres of pasture and arable, forty of which he always puts down to maize every year, for silage to feed his cattle on. OK?"

"Yes."

"So you tell me, Steph, why, with no increase in the herd and no intake of extra fattenin' stock, you tell me why would anyone put in an extra strip of maize a hundred and thirty yards long and thirty yards wide, but on our boundary so a good mile from the rest of their usual crop, eh?" Stephanie looked at him, nonplussed. "Funny that, aint it?"

"New feeding regime?"

"New feeding regime! You'd find an excuse for the devil, you would."

"Green manure?"

"Green...? I can't believe you! No one would know you're a keeper's wife. You need to toughen up, my girl."

"I am tough."

"No you're not, y' just smell strong. It's because Jackson's got wind of a way to gain extra sport for free, that's why he planted it there."

"Aren't we being a bit paranoid?"

"I'm not paranoid, just ask that bloke who keeps following me." She smiled. "Trust me, Steph; farmers are all the same."

"And stereotyping..."

"Are all the same. In the words of Blaster Bates, 'most of 'em would rip out twelve hundred yards of ancient hedgerow if they thought they could plant another ten row of spuds in its place; they think they're gonna live forever.'"

"Who said that?"

"Blaster Bates; comedian, an' he's spot-on. They're always on the lookout for a free ride."

"I think that's a bit of an exaggeration."

David pulled on his gloves. "Farmers and poachers, Steph, all the same."

"They're not all bad, David."

"Your time with that Alice Stratton turned you into the patron saint of poachers now, has it?"

This unexpected mention of the Stratton family stung Stephanie. "There's no need to drag that up again, David, and it's got nothing to do with my friendship with Alice..."

"Past friendship..."

"She was and is a friend, David. The fact I don't see much of her now doesn't alter the past. I'm not that shallow. I just don't see them in the monochrome texture you do."

"Mono what?"

"Monochrome... Black and white."

"Well why not say so?"

"I did. You just feign ignorance of these things to embarrass me."

"Not me. Wouldn't dare."

"Yes you would and I repeat all poachers, just as all farmers, are not all bad."

David wasn't listening now, he was muttering to himself inaudibly as he finished dressing. "Tarred with the same brush, always on the look out for summat for free and usually belongin' to someone else."

"This is not a good subject for you; poachers, farmers. You just get wound up. Never a good sign when you start to exaggerate." Stephanie bent low and talked to Jill who, apart from her tail, was stood patiently at their feet. "Let's get daddy in the fresh air and calm him down a little shall we?"

David smiled at her. "Yeah, right." He opened the door and Jill rushed out ahead of him.

"I'll slip my coat on and join you in the yard. And we still need to keep an eye on my dog!"

"Your dog?"

"You want me to work her today?"

"Yes."

"Then she's my dog 'til we finish dogging back and are home, I don't want her coming back here fit for nothing for two days because we've overworked her!"

David's disembodied voice floated back. "Yeah, yeah, stop fussin'."

—⁓—

The Land Rover bounced and splashed its way along the field track, shaking up its canine-human cargo with each dip and rise. At field's end, Liam got out and opened the gate as David pursued the recent conversation.

"What did he say then? I'll bet the sparks were flyin'."

Eric flopped the gearstick into neutral and pulled on the handbrake. "Well, not really. He weren't throwin' a party or nothin' but he was very understandin'. I just said I'd not seen it, below that line of rush as it were an' that I'd see it were replaced."

"Not rideable then?" said Stephanie from the rear of the vehicle.

"Not by one such as him, no. A circus clown maybe but definitely not a sixty-plus year old fisherman with a touch of the rheumatics."

Stephanie and Hattie laughed as David added, "The only saving grace was you bein' able to bugger off Stratton then?"

"Ar, sweet that were."

"Pity you didn't run him over too."

"David!" Stephanie's tone was sharp. Eric drove the vehicle through the gateway and stopped to pick up Liam. "There's no need for you to be so aggressive."

Eric threw a glance as David answered her. "It's alright everyone; Steph's linin' herself up to be the poachers defence council."

"And sarcasm is the lowest form of wit."

"Who's being sarky?" said Liam as he climbed back into the vehicle. "Shove up, Dave."

David moved across. "Me, apparently."

The atmosphere chilled a little and the remaining short distance along the road was completed in silence. It was only as the pheasant crossing-point came into view that Liam broke this lapse in conversation.

"Bloody hell Eric, you weren't kidding were y'?"

"No, I weren't, and they've been doin' that for the last two days, in spite of my efforts. Look at that lot, ladies!"

Hattie and Stephanie leaned forward through the curtain of dogs to peer through the windscreen. After a brief pause, Hattie asked the question. "Is he feeding in there?"

Eric answered for the three of them. "No, don't think so, Hat', but then, with that amount of maize, does he need to?"

She sat back. "Not a bit of it."

"You'll have to tap it back into The Quarry on shoot days as well, won't you?"

"We will that. Otherwise Lordy'll just be shootin' wood pigeon and crows on 'is main day."

"See, Steph?" David clicked open the passenger door. "Farmers, poachers; sniffin' out free stuff. We'll have to offer Jackson an extra invite to the cock day on the strength of this, which is exactly what he expects, canny sod."

Stephanie turned to Hattie. "Like a dog with a bone he is. That's been his sole topic of conversation since it came up this morning."

Hattie smiled. "Forty eight hours for me."

Stephanie turned to David. "Now who's tarred with the same brush?"

"Well, no use sittin' 'ere like a bunch of grapes is it?" Liam opened his door and all the pheasants on the road stood to attention. "Right. One of us can loop round the back and walk the maize through; that'll be you, Steph. OK?"

"Yes."

"The rest will join in as an' when. Once we're finished, I'll call round, let Jackson know what we've done and what we intend doin' come shoot days. I'll square it with his Lordship for an extra invite on cock day when I see him this evenin'."

"Told y'." David smiled at Stephanie.

"Been summoned have we, Liam?" asked Eric, his voice loaded with its usual derision. "Lordy speaks, 'e jumps."

Hattie chided him. "Eric Cornby, enough of that. You'd do no different, would you?"

"No."

"Well then."

"But I'd not jump quite as high!"

"Eric!"

"Never mind 'im, Hattie," said Liam. "What I was going on to say was I'm seein' him later today but he wants to see us all tomorrow. Eleven o' clock; talk through the Boys' Day."

"What, on a Sunday?"

"I'll take it from that comment that you'll not be goin' Eric?"

"What choice do I have? 'Course I'm goin, but... Sunday! I use Sundays to get fresh straw on the feed rides an' fill me feed bins."

Liam smiled at Hattie. "Now who's jumpin'? Has to be Sunday, Eric. The only day we'll get. He's away to London on Monday, not back 'til the day before the first shoot."

"What's he want?" asked Eric.

"Not sure..."

"Nothin' new there then. Same every year, but then, why break the 'abits of a lifetime?"

"Well, I sense a bit of a change this year."

"What makes you think that then?" asked David.

"Well, for one thing, Mister Stephen is out to impress. Wants to include a couple of girls in the line, so Lordy said. Lady Brenham's lass is one of 'em. That blonde one wore that light tan jacket last season. Turned all them left hand birds away before they reached the line."

"Oh, I remember her," scoffed Eric.

"An' that French girl, Baron Halle's lass." Liam got out of the vehicle, "Came 'ere last year as well. Had that mad, chocolate Lab... Benny or summat weren't it?"

David smiled as he followed Liam out onto the road. "Raisin."

"Ar, that's it, Raisin. Knew it were summat to do with fruit."

"Benny – Raisin. Yeah, names are almost exactly the same; easy mistake to make. We keep a bunch of Benny's in a bowl at Christmas, don't we Steph? Have 'em with the nuts." David looked across at Eric and rolled his eyes.

Eric closed the driver's door and went round to un-van ladies and dogs. "Wants to show off a bit, does he?" He unlocked the rear door and the canine flood swept out, ready to take on all-comers as the roadside birds began to make themselves scarce. Dog names were called on top of dog names as order was achieved, leads attached and conversation continued.

"Well, he'll have to learn to shoot first..." Eric's liver and white English springer spaniel made a beeline for the nearest hedgerow. "Spadger, come here!" The dog turned back reluctantly. "Good girl... although, if that French lass is anythin' to go by he'll have already learned to shoot summat!"

Hattie turned towards him. "Eric!"

"Well, it's right. All over him like fleas on a hedgepig last year." Eric took out a slip lead from his jacket pocket. "Pretty thing too... so Dave said."

David looked at Hattie and then at Stephanie, who was putting on a headscarf. "Wooden spoon time I think."

"All I can say is it's a good job Mister Stephen aint involved in the big drives... hold still dog!" Eric put the lead on Spadger and rambled on. "He makes a pig's ear out the simplest drive as it is."

Liam's face set a little. "This estate'll be his one day, Eric. He's the eldest boy and he's got to learn sometime..." It was as if more needed to be said, but time and place dictated otherwise.

"Maybe, but not on the best drives, not for a while yet, and only when he's learnt to shoot a bit better than his present standard."

"Which in your opinion, Eric, is?"

"Rubbish." Eric looked along the road. "An' if we don't get these birds shifted soon, there'll be nothin' for him to miss."

Its closeness to the boundary was the one overriding curse of The Quarry. Only three short fields separated the rear of this woodland from the road they were standing on and, as if in mimicry, the hedges that joined the wood and bounded these fields acted like pheasant motorways, the birds following them to congregate on the estate edge, ostensibly to peck up grit from the roadside but also for seeking out new feeding sites. It was this activity that attracted unwelcome attention... from all kinds of predators.

Along with the multitude of responsible citizens who used this particular road as a rat run to and from their places of work, people of a different persuasion and work ethic were also known to frequent the verge and hedgerows, so it was little wonder the keepers were keen to sort out this particular pheasant haemorrhage. The added incentive this year was that, aside from being run over by speeding cars or shot from the roadside by casual poachers, the birds could now be lost to their neighbour's new fodder crop.

The road was now clear of birds, the gathering threat being too much for them to countenance but, as the posse stopped, a bundle of thirty pheasants clattered out of the tall, recently cut hedge that ran away from the rear of the maize and headed off, over the road, back towards The Quarry.

"Bloody hell, that's all we need," said Eric. "A bloody fox or cat workin' its way into the maize an' not even a pea-shooter between us!"

"Weren't comin' to pick a fight, were we?" replied David.

"More's the pity. All comes down to one thing. Jackson were wrong planting this lot 'ere and well he knows it. Farmers! All the bloody same!" David looked across at Stephanie as Eric's tirade continued. "I don't know why you won't let us pour a load of diesel through it, Liam."

"Because Jackson will know who's done it; he's not that daft. The last thing we want to start on this boundary is a pheasant war."

"I'll give him war."

Liam interrupted him. "Let's just think peaceful and get these buggers on the right side." He stood for a moment or two and considered the problem. "Right, here's the drill. Hattie, we'll take the roadside hedges down to fifty yards short of the maize then stay on the road and tap us sticks on the fence. I want to keep them buggers runnin' back if we can, easier to control on the ground. Steph, over here and make your way right to the back of the maize. Wait for Dave's call then slip Jill an' follow her through, slow an' with plenty of noise; you got that rattle with you, Eric?"

"Ar."

"You 'ave it, Steph." Eric retrieved the rattle from the dashboard and handed it to Stephanie. "Eric, you an' Dave take the Land Rover to the other side. You go onto the field, Dave, about half way up the maize. When Steph's in line with y', move along level with 'er but stay out from the crop, you'll turn back any strays. You go on and dump the Rover in that old gateway of Jackson's, Eric. Drive the hedgerows back this way. Get Spadger to work the opposite hedge to you, that'll make up for the lack of beaters."

A second batch of birds flew up from in the maize. Most moved back across the road but a good few defied their lead and flew further onto Jackson's land, calling and chortling as they went.

"Let's sort this lot before we lose another load!" Liam's call stirred dogs and owners into action.

Aware that fun was afoot, Jill started pulling on the lead as soon as they had climbed the fence and were moving across the field. Stephanie flicked the lead.

"Heel-up, puppy!"

The terrier immediately moved back to Stephanie's side but her tongue was much less obedient and continued to dance and leap ahead of her mouth. They had only just reached mid point when a further half dozen pheasants rose from the maize and made an attempt at following the previous group. It was only the sight of Stephanie waving her headscarf that forced a change in the birds' direction.

David was almost in position when he heard these birds rise then saw them appear above the maize. They set their wings then jinked away from their original line of travel. 'That'll be Steph they've seen then. Good lass. Eric'll be pleased.' The Labradors watched the pheasants disappear below the maize horizon, tails wagging, tongues lolling.

Stephanie quickened her pace to the hedge in order to close off further escape attempts. Once there she picked Jill up, lifted her over the fence then swiftly followed. As she bent to unclip the terrier's lead, she heard movement in the maize; Alec Stratton stepped out not five feet from her.

David moved away from the crop and into the field, slapping his booted leg with his stick to announce that this way of pheasant-escape was closed too.

Both Liam and Hattie could see good numbers of birds running their respective hedgerows back towards the maize crop, and every now and then a bird would burst from one or other hedge, disturbed by the dogs.

"Bloody hell but there's some birds 'ere, Hattie."

"I don't think even Eric knew they were this thick on the ground. Let's just hope we can send them the right way... car coming!"

"Will you get back over there and seek-on, dog?"

Eric sent Spadger back across to the other hedge. They usually did hedgerows as a team and the spaniel couldn't understand why she was constantly being sent away.

He heard a car coming. "Sit up! Sit!" The spaniel dropped her back legs, tail still wagging, bottom hovering two inches above the ground.

The three looked at each other in their surprise; Alec smiling, Stephanie's mouth slightly open, Jill pulling to the extent of her lead before giving a single, surprised bark.

"That'll be Jill then."

"Alec! What the hell are you doing here?"

"Had to talk."

"Are you out of your mind? David's here... all of them! Oh, God, they'll see... you'll get caught... We'll get caught!"

"Steady on lass, only way anyone's gonna get caught is if you shout out I'm 'ere."

Stephanie hustled him back into the maize, dragging the perplexed Jill with her. "Don't be so stupid! One of them only has to alter their position and they'll see you... and me... God, this is madness!"

"Had to see you an' this seemed the best way."

"How did you know we'd be here?"

"Stands to reason. This many birds on the move from The Quarry, that rattle an' the dog in Eric's vehicle this mornin'; I saw him."

"I heard."

"Well, no prizes for fieldcraft there then."

"But... that's..." Stephanie faltered a little then eyed Alec. "Why?"

"Why what?"

"Why did you have to see me?"

"'Cos of something my Alice said, 'bout you, an' your... condition."

"Oh, damn! I told her not to mention it! Not to anyone!"

"She hasn't."

"She told you!"

"Yes, but as far as she's concerned I am no one, don't you see? Well, is it true? Are you pregnant?"

Stephanie paused for a moment. When she did reply her simple statement held a rainbow of conflicting emotions. "No."

"But, Alice said..."

"She was wrong! I... thought I was..." Alec began to speak again but she cut him off. "You haven't got me pregnant, Alec, OK? You haven't."

He stepped up close to her, placing a hand on her waist and pulling her towards him. "Steph..." There was little resistance from Stephanie. She dropped the rattle and they fell easily into a kiss, watched throughout by one very puzzled terrier. Stephanie felt Alec's body stir and she pulled back, gasping at the outcome of the meeting.

"Alec, please; what am I doing? This has to stop!" Tears began to form. "Please, it has to... I can't, won't..." He reached for her again but she stepped back further, pressing her palm against his chest as Jill bounced a little on her front paws, eager to be off hunting. "Alec, no! Please, we can't... you can't... this is killing me... It has to stop. Now!" Alec tried again but she cut him off once more. "Now, Alec!"

Liam slipped the lead onto his spaniel, checked that Hattie was in place and sent a call. "We all ready then?"

Eric waved from the opposite side of the maize.

David heard him and followed it on. "Steph! You there yet?"

Stephanie looked anxiously in David's direction and called back, "Yes...! Yes, just need to sort out Jill. Something in the maize... fox maybe... hold on!"

"Do you want me to come across?"

She bent quickly to pick up the rattle and flicked it over once. "No! No... Its fine, David. Thank you. Just keep an eye from where you are, let me know if anything runs out!" She looked pleadingly at Alec. "You have to go, Alec, and I can't see you again. Do you understand?"

"Steph..."

"Do you?"

Alec looked at the set of her expression then in the direction of David's last call. "Lucky sod."

"Not so lucky. I betrayed him."

"Ar, with me, and can I just say..."

"No, you can't!" She looked at him for a moment or two and Alec saw her look, something in her eyes. "Don't fret yourself. I'm to blame. It was me, and you have to go."

He took a couple of steps then turned back. "I hope it were worth it to you, Steph. It were to me."

"Taught me a lot, Alec." Alec opened his mouth to speak again but she flicked over the rattle again to cut him off. "Stop now. Just go!"

Alec shook his head then left the maize, ducked through the hedge and set off along it, deeper onto Jackson's land. Stephanie watched him go as David's insistent call penetrated her senses.

"Steph! Steph, come on! We need to start! Are you sorted?"

"Yes, ready!" She paused for a second to wipe her eyes before continuing. "Fox... just scampered back out of the maize. Ready now!"

"On you go then!"

Unclipping Jill's lead, a hand flick and call of "Get-on!" was sufficient to send the terrier scampering into the crop as Stephanie turned the rattle over again and moved through the maize, rattling the stalks with the duck's-head stick as she went.

Chapter Seven
Month 6 – June 1985

"So you're seein' her again then; today, I mean?"

"I am. We're to Leyton's Farm. They've an open day there."

"What, where them new-fangled alpacas are?"

"The same. A real rarity, only just started up."

Alec paused for a moment and looked at Alice. "To look at alpacas?"

"No, to look at Highland cattle... Of course to look at alpacas!"

"What for, you don't want one, do y'?"

"No. I'm going because Steph's asked me." Alice walked into the hallway to collect her shoes and stopped by the mirror talking almost to herself. "Though why a youngster with a face an' figure that'd stop traffic wants to be seen hangin' about with a dowdy old harridan like me, I'll never know..." She looked away and smiled. "But I'm glad of it."

"You're not a harridan."

She came back into the kitchen holding a shoe in each hand. "Thanks for that... one outta three aint bad. Steph wants to buy some wool, f' knittin'; says it very soft. She says they've brung some wool in from wherever it is they come from, 'til they get started with their own shearin'; spin it on the farm, an' she thought I might be interested."

"What's wrong wi' sheep?"

"There's nothing wrong with sheep!" She slipped her feet into the shoes. "Why the interest all of a sudden?"

There was a long silence as Alec gazed at the cleaned breakfast plate then sighed and pushed it away. Alice went back into the hall and came back with her jacket, checking the pockets before putting it on.

"This Stephanie, she my height, got really long hair?"

"Ah, now I see. So you have seen her then?"

"I reckon."

"And you're tryin' to tell me all you noticed was her hair?"

"Ar."

"Pull the other one."

"What do y' mean?"

"Because if it were true it'd be a first. Where did you meet her?"

"Bumped into her on Seer's Hill."

"So that's met then. When were this?"

"Couple o' month ago."

"And you chose to say nothing 'til now. What were you doin' up there?"

"Sear's Hill? I was up there just lookin' around. Up she comes, right to the top."

"You sure it was her?"

"No doubt. Same name, Stephanie. Hardly common round 'ere is it? Same... description."

"What do you mean same name? Did you talk?"

"Briefly, ar."

Alec closed up, aware which way the conversation was headed but Alice was not about to let it go at that. "Stop draggin' your tongue, Alec Stratton."

"Why's this so important all of a sudden then?"

"You're the one that opened it up, I'm just following through. You've always told me to guard me tongue.

Be careful who you talk to, you tell me, careful what you
say. Now here's you passin' the time of day with someone
you've just met."

"Bumped into..."

"Who happens to be the wife of a Barn Tor keeper!"

"So?"

"An' still you talked."

"No 'arm done; anyway, why's the difference?"

"No use tellin' you that if you don't know already. What
did you talk about?"

"Nothin' much. View from the hill... cathedral. I wanted
to bugger off quick."

"Not so quick as to stop you askin' her name. Did you tell
her yours?"

"Yeah, I think so... yes, I did."

Alice shook her head. "A pretty girl walks on the scene
and you start blabbin'." Alice put her things down and sat on
the arm of the chair, sighing. "Now she's got a line on you.
I was tryin' to keep all of this separate, as best as I could."

"All of what?"

"This! I told you, I wanted to keep all this other stuff,
her husband a gamekeeper mine a poacher, keep it all off
limits."

"How are we supposed to do that, reinvent?"

"No point now, not with you gettin' as careless as this."

"Careless? Careless how?"

Alice sighed deeply then spoke as if to a halfwit. "You
introduced yourself to the keeper's pretty wife, Alec.
The pretty wife of the keeper who looks out for the estate
you insist on poachin' over every winter." She sighed, in
exasperation this time. "What don't you understand in
all this?"

"She don't know me from Adam!"

"*I've just said she's a keeper's wife, Alec, 'course she knew who you were! You're up there on the edge of the estate, obviously 'country'...*"

"*What do you mean, obviously?*"

"*Take a look in the mirror sometime then report back.*"

Alec picked up his tea mug. "*Well, I'll tell you summat. This relationship of yours, it's leadin' us right into trouble.*" *He looked into the mug.* "*This is empty.*"

"*Then refill it.*" *Alice stared at him for a few seconds then got up and moved behind the armchair.* "*It'll only lead to where you're daft enough to follow, an' where you'll get caught.*"

"*Them keepers'll never catch me, that much I do know. I'm a mite too sharp for them.*"

"*Nowhere near as sharp as you're honed.*" *Alice picked up the breakfast plate and carried it to the sink.* "*She's my friend Alec, and if you do so much as muddy the water, I'll tell you now you'll be on your own. But then, according to you that's impossible, you'll never get caught, Super-Poacher, so no worries there then.*"

He chose to ignore it. "*Look, all I'm sayin' is you seem to be seein' a lot of this Stephanie... y' know?*"

"*I'm not seein' a lot of her, Alec! Maybe once or twice a month is all.*" *Alice stopped and looked at him for a second or two.* "*I'm not sure just what's goin' on 'ere, Alec Stratton. Is there another problem with this that hasn't surfaced yet?*" *Alec looked at her by return.* "*Well? Is there?*"

He picked up his mug again; it was still empty. "*No, not as such.*"

"*You must think I was delivered by the Easter bunny. What's the problem?*"

"*Well, I'd've thought it were obvious really.*"

"*Obviously not or this conversation wouldn't be takin' place, would it? Now, are you going to tell me what's goin' on in that pea-sized brain whizzin' round the vacuum that's the inside of your head or not? I've things to get on with.*"

"*You mean to say you can't see where the difficulties are?*"

"*Difficulties for who? For who? We're friends, Alec. Friends!*" Alec remained silent and they looked at each other. "*Right, well speakin' for myself there's no difficulty. I'm not the one who spends their nights out chancin' their arm over her husband's game, an' I'm not the one that risks gettin' caught…*"

"*I've told you, I've not been caught ever! Not never, nor will be… an' not by such as them!*"

"*First time for everything, they say.*"

"*You knew what I was about when we got married, an' before that, when we was at school, an' you're 'appy to eat the proceeds.*"

"*When we have them, yes! The fact most of the stuff you get is given away is neither 'ere nor there I suppose?*"

"*I've never done this for profit you know that, just for our pot and some of my friends.*"

"*So, we've established you don't do it for profit an' our pot's more often than not empty, so why do you do it?*"

"*What?*"

"*Well, seein' as how for the first time that I can remember you're willin' to talk about this, tell me.*" Pulling out a chair from the breakfast table, Alice sat opposite him.

"*Thought you needed to be off out.*"

"*I've time for this. Right, the bits of tree work an' log splittin' you do, the hedge layin' an' stone wall repairs, they hardly keep us in the lap of luxury, do they? An' it's not as if*" *you goin' out poachin' means we grow fat off the food or rich on the proceeds is it? So why do it... tell me?"*

There was a long silence then Alec replied simply. *"S'what keeps me 'eart beatin.'"*

There was another long silence then Alice said just as simply. *"It... what?"*

"Keeps me 'eart beatin.'"

"An' I thought that were me." Alice sighed and looked across at Alec for some time. *"So that's it, is it? That's supposed to make what you do alright for me, does it? Your beatin' heart."*

"Yes."

She got up. *"Well, I happen to really enjoy Stephanie's company. Terms not quite as strong as yours maybe, but that should make what I do alright for you too."*

"It's different."

"I'd like you to tell me where the difference is 'cos I can't see it. What you've just said is supposed to make it alright for you to continue on poachin', breakin' the law I'll remind you, but not alright for me to make a friend of a keeper's wife. Is that it?"

"Is it daft you are? He's a keeper, I'm a poacher!"

"We've done this, Alec! I'm friends with his wife. His wife!"

"Crikey... Can't you see she's taken you into her confidence? Tellin' you the tale of the old iron pot so's she can report back to the keepers about me so they can plan the next season? I'm the bloody quarry, Alice. Can't you see that?"

"Contrary to the opinion of your fan club, which consists of precisely one, the dissection of your every movement does not form the basis of my conversations with Stephanie! Never has, never will."

"Oh, yes?"

This hurt Alice and she leant forward, her fisted hands resting on the table. "Jesus, how did we get to this...? Yes! I'm your wife, Alec Stratton. Not perfect, not the drivin' force in your life, apparently, but I am your wife! An' if I thought you so much as suspected..." Alice tried to remain calm but her emotions were ruling her tongue now and it took several seconds for her to regain some composure; she needed to say this right. "I have never, would never, talk about what you do; not with anyone! Not with Stephanie, not with Alan on the stall, not even with your mother when she was alive, God help me... no one! But I'll tell you summat now. I've wanted to Alec. Many times I've wanted to and do you know why?" Alec stayed silent. "Because I hate every bloody second of it! There, I said it! Thank God! I've said it! I hate you doing it!"

A long silence followed this outburst. "You... hate me poachin'?"

"He heard me! Yes! Yes, Alec, I do!" She calmed a little. "I worry, don't you see? I imagine all sorts of things 'appenin.'"

"Such as?"

"To you! Not 'such as'! Happenin' to you, Alec Stratton!"

"But... I don't understand..." He stopped, staring into the middle distance.

After a short pause for breath, Alice tried to lay it out for him. "You're out late at night, breakin' the law, carryin' a shotgun an' bein' hunted by folk who could also be armed. Legally. So, you tell me, what do you think I worry about?"

"I can take care of meself."

Alice was stumped by this for a few seconds. "Do you really think this is what this conversation has been all about?"

"Well, hasn't it?"

"About you bein' a capable man who can take care of himself?" Alice sighed. "Just what we need to help the discussion along, male bravado."

She looked at her watch as Alec frowned in confusion. "Well for someone who's just told me they hate what I do it's an ideal opportunity to nip it off, isn't it?"

The second mention of this hurt just as much and Alice sat down again and spoke softly. "There's a lot been said this mornin' an' a lot of it'll need some thought from me; this one needs to be sorted right now. Do you really think I'd do that, Alec Stratton?" Alec was silent. "Well, do you?"

He looked at her for several seconds. "No."

"No. Right answer." She breathed in relief and moved to the door.

"How can you be so sure?"

Alice turned back and sighed. "Huh. About what?"

"That you're not being used."

"Because I'm a woman, Alec." He stared at her. "A man says, 'I wouldn't do it like that.' A woman says, 'Why are you doing it like that?'" There was a pause then she shook her head. "Do you even know the difference?" She went into the hall and came back holding her handbag then opened the kitchen door and allowed the summer air to rush in. "I'm away then. See you later."

"You still goin' to see them alpacas?"

"You still goin' poachin' this winter?" Alec looked at her but didn't reply. "Then yes, I am still going."

"You'll not be mentionin' our chat today though, will y'? To Stephanie?"

"Unlike you, I'm not as green as I am cabbage looking, so no, I'll not... but I 'ave to wish we'd never had it, this conversation."

"Because?"

"Because it puts a wedge between us, that's why. Summat we've never 'ad… an' I'm annoyed at you for doin' that to us."

"Then don't go."

"All that chat just to stop me goin' out for the day with a friend to buy some wool?"

"'Course not!"

"Good, then I'm off to spend the afternoon with 'my friend' Stephanie. They're the only folk as keep alpacas that I've heard of anywhere outside of zoos… There you are, you never know, I might even find summat to make for you with it, if the wool's good enough for a superhero that is."

With that she closed the door and walked down their front path.

Day 6 – Sunday 25th November 1985

The gunroom in the big house reeked of gundogs, gun-oil and governance. Liam reckoned it was the most central part of the house and so the most convenient for shoot meetings; Eric reckoned it was the place where the riff-raff could be secreted away from the delicate sensibilities of the ruling classes. Whatever the reason, the format was always the same. The keepers would arrive separately and on time; His Lordship would always be twenty minutes late; coffee was always served by Christopher, the butler, just two minutes before His Lordship turned up. This Sunday's meeting to discuss the drives for Boys' Day was just such a day.

"One of these times he'll surprise us all; 'ave the good manners to get 'ere on time," said Eric as he opened one of the gunroom drawers and took out a leather case.

Liam sat on one of the polished oak benches that lined each side of the room beneath pegs which held an assortment of cartridge bags, dog leads and wet-weather wear. "He's probably busy."

"What, busy every time we 'ave one of these sessions is he?" Eric released the buckled straps and opened the case. "Funny 'ow he's always 'ere in time for coffee though aint it." He was joined by David.

"Those the new pair of sixteen-bores of Miss Anne's?"

Releasing the fore-end from one of the sets of barrels, Eric removed a stock from its velvet grip and began to assemble the shotgun. "Ar. Got 'em last year."

"London auction, weren't it?"

"Ar." Eric re-clipped the fore-end into place and broke the gun as Liam looked across and gave the details.

"Lordy bid for 'em on the Friday, they delivered 'em on the Tuesday and she used 'em on them partridge at Lord Overton's on the followin' Thursday. Shot pretty well too, so Tom said, new guns considered an' all that."

"She's gonna 'ave 'em fitted though isn't she?"

Liam stood up and joined them now. "So she said, but you know what kids are like. Couldn't wait to use 'em, an' Lordy's not the man to stop 'er."

"Nor the kind of man to pay for the alterations neither," chimed in Eric.

David looked into the case at the other shotgun and ran his finger over the chasing on the action-plate. "She's alright is Lady Anne. A fair shot now..."

"For a woman."

David looked at Eric. "She's a fair shot now by anyone's standard. Might even make a good one, given encouragement. You loaded for 'er last year at Markfield's place didn't you? When Tom had that dose of flu."

"I did."

"I've only seen her from a distance and she looks like she's got most of it right. You must've got some idea as to what she were like, up close like that."

"She weren't bad. Needs to work on her balance a bit when the drive gets hot. Too small and light to cope with the recoil from the pair of cannons she had before; hasn't helped her footwork a bit."

Eric lifted the gun and looked down the opened barrels. "These are light, nicely balanced. All she needs is to get 'em altered proper and find a regular loader more fitted to her size, not Tom. He's suited to Lordy."

"Only just, I hear," said David.

"Ar." Liam nodded and looked at them both. "But Tom don't know anythin' about the partridge at present so, mum's the word, eh?" The two keepers nodded in agreement. "But y' right, Eric, she does want a regular, not me on a piecemeal arrangement. I missed the change a couple of times at Markfield's. She's that far below me, I passed it over her head!" They all laughed as Liam continued. "No, she were alright, and a nice sort too, very personable."

"Personable? Must 'ave come from the mother's side then." Liam took the gun and looked it over as Eric continued, "Nah, she's needed summat like these for a time now. That pair of twelves she had were made for the old Lord in the forties, an' that sums him up. He owns most of the county, has a daughter that maybe shows a bit of shootin' promise and what does he do? He gives a lass that weighs four stone soppin' wet a pair of twelve-bore shotguns that're almost as big an' as heavy as her; why? 'Cos they cost 'im nothin', that's why. He's as tight as two coats of paint."

Liam gave Eric the gun back. "I told Lordy that the first time I saw her out with 'em."

"What, that he was as tight as two coats of paint?"

"No, I wish. I said them twelves would put her off. He just laughed an' said she'd have to get used to 'em."

"Lordy bought these sixteens then did he? Saw the error of his ways?"

Eric laughed out loud. "Ha! You 'ave got t' be jokin' haven't y'? They came out of 'er money; Miss Anne's."

"Blimey." David took the gun from Eric and lifted it to his shoulder. "You forget just how petite she is, don't y'? Christopher told me the other day she were twenty three and I said, 'What, inches tall'?"

Liam laughed as Eric scoffed, "She's not petite she's a bloody pixie… Sounds to me like you fancy 'er."

"Not my type. Mister Gordon, Belfast's lad, him as shot 'ere last year, I'd think by the way they were behavin' he's her paramour."

"A what? What's a bloody paramour then?"

"Huh… Nothin', Eric; it's…" He shook his head. "A shag, Eric. She's got a shag."

"Well why didn't y' say so?"

"There's no hope for you is there?" David returned the gun to Eric. "Tom loaded for her last Thursday then did he, Liam?"

"Ar, Lordy's invite but he couldn't go at the last minute so he organised it and sent Miss Anne in his place." He looked at Eric. "On the ball, see."

"Ha!" snorted Eric. "A likely tale. He couldn't be on the ball if he were the maker's name."

"Well, he'll need to be sharp this next Boys' Day and that's a fact; we all will."

David and Eric picked something up in the tone and Eric voiced their thoughts. "An' why's that then? You make it sound like it's summat special this year."

"It is," replied Liam, and he went to look down the corridor before returning to them. "It'll do no harm to get it out the way before you hear it from the oracle. Save an embarrassin' explosion from you, Eric."

Eric eyed him suspiciously. "Bloody hell, you know how to set a story up, I'll give y' that." David returned the shotgun to Eric who broke it down and snugged the various components back into the case. "Let's be 'avin' it then."

Liam took a deep breath. "Y'know Lordy wants to string Boys' Day and his two-day session together this year, so we'll be shootin' Wednesday, Thursday and Friday?"

"Ar."

"An' that he wants to include part of your River Beat for Boys' Day?"

"Wednesday, Thursday, Friday an' part of the River Beat, ar, I know that," repeated Eric. "It'll be tight, close together like that but we've The Quarry to rely on as usual, for Lordy's main days..."

"Include part of your River Beat for Boys' Day," repeated Liam. "Do you not want to know which part?"

Glances were exchanged between David and Eric. They were not quite sure where this conversation was going but Eric in particular felt very uneasy. "I know which part. He does the duck. That's the part of the River Beat he does every year, then we move on to..." Liam stayed silent and Eric's eyes narrowed. "Wait on a minute... what? What does he want to do with it this year? Don't tell me, drive the duck backwards? Stand the guns on pontoons in the middle of the lake?"

"No. Nothin' so simple. He wants to include the first day through The Quarry as the boys' pre-lunch drive."

There was a stunned silence as David looked at Eric, Eric at David and then both at Liam.

Finally Eric spoke. "You are jokin' me, aren't y'?"

"Not the whole drive, I managed to talk him out of that. Just part of it. You know what he can be like, but we have reached an agreement."

"Agreement? What do you mean agreement? Which part of it?"

"He wanted to do the whole of The Quarry. I suggested just doin' a section of ground on the cliff-side. Y'know, cut into the wood about eighty yards short of the release pen; told him he needed to consider his main days. Lordy's colour drained at the thought of a lesser drive for him and his guests so he said right, just that end section."

"What... you've told him it's alright? Jesus, Liam!"

"I told him I thought Mister Stephen hadn't enough experience to be doin' a drive of that quality..."

"An' difficulty!"

"And difficulty. I told him to consider that it were first time through an' also consider the calibre of guests the lads usually invite, but he was adamant. 'River Beat, Coyne, including The Quarry', he said. So I made him compromise on the size of the drive. All you've to do is make sure you feed the birds late and close up the pop-holes, then he'll have a bit to show for sport but not the bulk of 'em. Right?"

There was a further silence and Eric, searching for the right words, looked away from the gun case, out of the gunroom window and toward the eighteen hundred acres of Barn Tor known collectively as The River Beat; his beat.

Made up by all the outlying woods and farmland, together with the river, three flight ponds and a small put-and-take trout pool, the beat also contained two of the estate's main coverts, one of which was a shooting prospect of legendary reputation; the notorious, exhilarating, treacherous, Quarry.

During its four hundred and eighty year life, this quarry had supplied the stone to build all of the oldest estate cottages and a greater part of the original manor house too. Quarrying had ceased on the site nearly two hundred years ago, the production of cheap and convenient bricks becoming a monetary saving too great to ignore. This abandonment sounded the fanfare of silence the local flora and fauna had been waiting to hear. In they marched, Dunsinane like, to reclaim what was considered their own.

Poppy, thistle and nettle set up home first, quickly followed by silver birch, elder and hawthorn. They held the fort until longer lasting species like sycamore and oak could stake a claim. In a relatively short space of time the soil covered areas were populated and this shrub-army was forced to explore every other surface in order to dominate the scene, including every crevice and fracture in the two hundred and fifty yard long cliff face. But, as with all takeover bids, this moving army of flora had stiff competition. The weather also put in an offer for the site and this battle for ownership had been raging since the quarry's closure.

Over the many following winters, driving rain lashed the cliff and rivulets of water rolled down the rocks until, gradually, the zigzag water trails it created flattened and widened to form rough tracks, one of them half way up and running right across the cliff face. Any boulders disengaged from under this track by this seeking water crashed to the floor many feet below, creating gaps and grinding out of fresh routes for the water to follow in its headlong dash back to the sea. To survive this disruption, any trees wishing to remain here were forced to send their roots deeper, widening once tiny fissures. Now the race for domination was really on, but for all the plants' efforts it was weather that triumphed most often in these silent battles.

Breaking away from under the larger trees that had managed to establish a home on the track and plummeting from brow to base, these falling rocks, some of them half a ton in weight, uncovered roots, laying them bare. Immediately, wind and rain, accompanied by their partner in crime, frost, moved in and picked at this fresh sore, probing at the rock, forcing more to break away and further reveal the bony tree roots to the open sky and air.

Often a tree would come crashing down, but sometimes the cliff-buried roots would be strong enough to support and feed the afflicted tree, long enough for yearly growth and strength to continue whilst leaving the exposed, now useless roots to paw over the drop like skeletal talons. Any infill left was teased out by rain and frost and the remaining filigree of gaping roots, projecting over the drop a full ten feet, gave the whole site a strange, malevolent quality in the crepuscular light of autumn. Many of the gaps in between the roots were plenty large enough for a man to fit through, however, if one needed to traverse the cliff face, for this was by far the quickest way to get from one side to the other without alarming carefully gathered or quietly roosting pheasants, then the crochet-work of slippery, algae-covered roots had to be crossed.

As far as pickers-up and beaters were concerned, The Quarry held the promise of a particularly hard, tricky day; to Liam and David it held the prospect of well-produced, high-flying pheasants; to Eric it was both these things and much more. Approached as a military campaign and treated with respect and discipline by beaters and guns alike, it could be coaxed to a climax of driven sport fit for fireside reminiscence. This was the nadir of Eric's beat, indeed of Barn Tor, and anything that threatened its success was anathema to him.

Eric looked away from the view, slipped the gun case back into the draw and closed it firmly.

"By bloody 'ell, Liam, this aint fair! With all due respect, Mister Stephen couldn't hit a barn even if I were to drag it behind me on a rope. Them Quarry birds are like starlings when they go over the guns!"

"That's a bit harsh, Eric."

"No it's not! And the way it's usually pegged an' now, with us cuttin' birds off from the pen like that, not to mention the noise of them guns gettin' in, not even twice the number of beaters will hold 'em back. They'll be in the next county before you can say, 'Whose fuckin' idea was it to drive it like this in the first place?'"

"Then we'll peg it different."

"How different?"

"Send the middle guns further back; open out the left and right ends. That way the birds will feel the pressure less, hang about long enough for us to drive 'em on."

"Bloody hell, he doesn't want much, does he?"

"That's only a suggestion, Eric. It's your drive and you know it best. I'll go along with whatever you think will work…"

"Cancellation."

"With whatever you think will work. It may even make us think a bit different too, about how we drive it in the future, eh?" Eric was silent. "Just might give us a new outlook on it. We've done it the same way for, what, ten years now?"

"'Cos that's the way it works best!"

"I know, but maybe we've got into a rut, you know, and now, 'cos of Lordy's insistence we've maybe a chance to see it from a different perspective." Eric was about to speak but Liam held up his hand to cut him off. "Just... just give it a bit of thought, Eric. We 'ave no choice in the end, it's his shoot and he's the boss."

"Thinks he is y' mean."

"Alright, thinks he's the boss, but let's use that to our advantage. Plant the seed an' make him think he thought of it. What do you say, Eric? I'd be grateful for your advice."

"Ar. Maybe." Eric paused and the other two keepers could almost see the cogs whirring. "Well, I hope you told him it's an untried drive. If we do it any way other than the usual, anythin' could happen."

Liam could see Eric had released his ire and was now thinking of the practicalities of a drive done differently and he smiled. "Thanks, Eric. An' Mister Stephen's not that bad a shot."

"He will be with that lass strung round his neck most of the day, I know it!"

"You may have a point there."

"I have..."

"But... look, Eric..." Liam walked to the far end of the gunroom and pushed the door to. "Before Lordy arrives let's understand this. It's what he wants. Let's not forget who pays for this lot. They're his birds and he wants Mister Stephen to do The Quarry on Boys' Day. When The Quarry comes up over coffee, an' it will, I'll see to it, we need to be positive and get him to play a full part. Don't let him get away with anythin'. He'll squirm when he sees the direction of the conversation but it's important that he takes on some of the responsibility of the decision hisself, almost as if he'd thought of it. That way he gets to share in the success..."

"Or failure."

"Ar, or the failure. And you never know, maybe it'll be a short sharp shock when he sees 'ow the kids 'andle the drive an' he'll drop it for next year."

"Too late by then. You know I've to get four drives off The Quarry this season don't you? And now there's this extra one."

"Part one."

"OK, part one, but you know he'll be the first to moan if the numbers are down late in December. The way them kids shoot, I'll 'ave more cripples than fit stock after they've finished. Has Lordy thought about that?"

"He didn't need to, I told him. That was when he put on his stern face. Said as how he'd told Mister Stephen he could do it this year, and that was what was gonna happen."

"I bet the miserable sod wouldn't do it for Miss Anne."

"Nope. Even as things are he wanted me to explain to the lads about how he'd made a concession 'to the keepers'; about cuttin' down the size of the drive like we are."

"And you told 'im what?"

"I told 'im it weren't my place an' that he needed to let the boys know sooner rather than later. Pulled a face like he'd swallowed too big a chip, but I was adamant about it, so he said he'd talk to 'em."

"What's the bettin' we get all the blame when he tells them? He's bound to phrase it so we look like the bastards in all this..." There was little point in pursuing the discussion but Eric made an attempt to rescue the situation even so. "Right, well, when Lordy brings it up can I shove in my quids-worth?"

Liam smiled at him. "You can. We're a team for the estate, but when it comes to your individual beats I expect you to take full responsibility, but remember, Lordy is Lordy...," Footsteps were heard. "Ayup, talk of the devil," said Liam as he moved to open the door. "'Ere comes coffee."

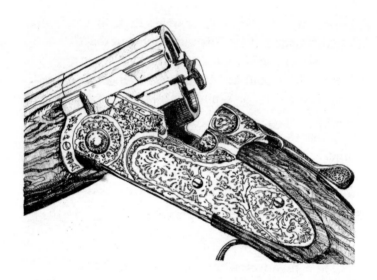

Chapter Eight
Month 5 – July 1985

"There she is!"

"Where?"

"There, just comin' through that hedgerow! Bugger if she aint got a partridge or summat in 'er mouth too, cheeky little sod!"

Crouched in the ditch alongside Eric and with the day just a half hour past dawn, David found it difficult to see the vixen and he rose up slightly to get a better view. "Oh, ar, I can see 'er now. Too far away for a shot though."

"Only just," replied Eric. "I knew there were one with cubs somewhere near 'ere! If we just sit a while longer she'll show us the direction. This much light she can't 'ave that far to travel."

"Quarter mile at most. She's makin' for that gateway by Lady's Copse. What do you think? In there?"

Eric scrubbed his chin. "I've combed it twice this year, found nothin', but there's old badger workin's in there; she could've moved in this week." The vixen flowed under the gateway and out of sight. "Give 'er a count of five then let's scarper t' the gate." Eric gathered up gun and feedbag and, as he stood, the bag slipped off his shoulder then down his body to the floor like a dropped lasso. "This bloody bag! Bust the buckle on the strap a week ago and keep forgettin' to buy another."

"Too tight-fisted to remember more like."

"I'm not made of money y' know, and I've a lot to think on, youngster. Lordy should buy these things for us; he's the tight-fisted one in this story."

"He does buy 'em, but only one a year. You insist on treatin' it like a polishin' rag an' that's what you get. The reason you won't buy one is 'cos the weight of your wallet's affectin' your brain."

"Never mind the smart talk, we've a vixen an' cubs t' sort out. C'mon!" Grabbing the bag in his hand, Eric clambered up the side of the ditch. David followed suit and like soldiers going over the top the two keepers left the ditch and legged it across the field quickly and quietly. They reached the gateway and peered round it just in time to see the vixen jink to her right and enter the copse.

"Got her!" whispered Eric triumphantly. "I'll call back later in the mornin', find the den then be back this evenin' an' bowl 'er over."

"Why not let me slip back home now? Get an' dig 'em out, pop the terriers in and get it done."

"'Cos she's at 'ome, that's why. No knowin' how many tunnels she'll have open; them old badger setts go on for miles. She backs up to protect them cubs there's no tellin' how long we'll be 'ere. I'll sort her out this evenin'. Once she's accounted for, cubs'll be no match for terriers on their own; they'll not know what a terrier is nor their way round that sett. Easy."

"Well 'Cymag' 'em then."

"That bloody stuff's too damn dangerous for me! Wrong breeze, puddle of ditch water and all of a sudden I'm layin' dead outside the den an' Charlie has to step over me corpse on 'er way to the next henhouse! Gun'll do a better job, an' I'll have her corpse to prove it. We'll bring terriers over *tomorrow and dig the cubs out, that way I know I've sorted the problem. Jill and Sack be up for it?"*

"When 'ave you known 'em not to be?"

"Never. For a sweet lookin' pair they don't take many prisoners when it comes to fox, do they?"

"Ar, killers come in all guises. Right. You want me here this evening as well, second string?"

"If you can manage."

"Yeah. Was supposed to be doin' the week's shop with Steph but she can probably leave it 'til tomorrow, or go on her own." They turned and began to retrace their steps to Eric's parked Land Rover. "I'll let Liam know the score so's he'll do the lock up in the rearin' field. What time?"

"Cubs might want to come out an' play, so she'll be with 'em. Half seven, eight?"

"OK. Do you want to meet up first or shall I go straight to the other side of the copse?"

"No need to meet. Get straight to that hedgerow that runs alongside Saunders' place, down in that ditch. That's as likely to be the route she'll follow if she does leave by the back door, but I reckon I've got the umpire's seat right 'ere."

"Right, half seven. If I hear a shot, I'll be over."

"Same 'ere. If all's still quiet by eleven-ish, I'll make me way over to where you are 'cos I know Liam wants to get out lampin' rabbits by half past."

David stopped walking. "Blimey, he never said! That'll be five nights on the trot."

"Mister Siddons has been on the 'phone. He reckons they're as thick as fleas on that pasture of 'is."

"That'll be all of six rabbits he's seen then."

"Ar, they see two rabbits an' multiply it by the leaves on a tree."

"Are we gonna get any sleep this summer?"

"Not if these furry little buggers keep breedin', no."

"I got into bed night before last, quarter to bloody four it were, an' Steph screamed."

Eric laughed. "Ar, an erection's a great alarm clock aint it?"

"No, I mean she shouted out 'cos she thought there were a strange man in the bed!'"

"There was, it were me a bit earlier!" Eric set off laughing again as they trudged down the hedge line towards the Land Rover.

—⁂—

"What, again? That's five nights in a row. Surely you've done enough for this week?"

"Not according to our Mister Siddons we've not." David watched Stephanie as she collected the last things from the washing line in their yard. "He reckons they're turnin' his pasture into a desert... or a dessert, not sure which."

"Why don't you get out with them?" She looked towards the corner of the yard where the ferrets were housed. A gang of kits were out, rolling and tumbling around the jill that was showing all the patience of a devoted mother. "They breed like rabbits and take enough feeding. Why not burn some fat off them and save these trips out every night?"

"It isn't every night, Steph."

"Good as." She nodded towards the ferrets. "Well?"

"We just don't get the time right now. Chicks an' poults all runnin' on at the same time, pens to get ready, still got barley and wheat to shoot foxes out of. The thing is we can roll over a good hundred buns in a night's lampin'. Couldn't even contemplate that with ferrets. Would need a whole day, and a whole day of ferretin' is a luxury we aint got."

"Then why do you let them breed... the ferrets? If you're not going to use them why let them have that last litter of kits?"

"'Cos I'll need some for the winter, you know that." David looked across at the hutch. "That jill's well past her best now and two out the three hobs have been run on rats so they'll be no use on rabbit."

"But that means you'll barely have time for a sit and supper tonight before you have to go out, not by the time we get back from shopping..." She picked up something from David's silence and raised an eyebrow. "What?" David stayed silent. "What?"

He cleared his throat. "Ahem... There's this vixen, on Eric's beat..."

"You're not coming shopping are you?"

David blinked a couple of times. "This vixen..."

"Never mind the vixen, David! I leave shopping until Thursdays because the supermarket stays open until eight. That means I don't have to take any time out of your normal day."

He swapped the mug of tea from left hand to right. "She's got these cubs..."

"Are you listening?" He had that look. "Oh... never mind, I'll go on my own, again."

"I'd come with you, Steph, but I promised Eric I'd give him a hand with..."

"Yes, I heard. You said you'd come with me last time."

"Well, I would've but those ridings had to be cut."

"And the last two times before that."

"I didn't! Did I?"

Stephanie sighed. "Yes, you did. This'll make it four times in a row."

"Will it? Four? Well, I'll definitely go with you next week. Promise."

"Only if you can keep it. I just hope Hattie understands too."

David grinned widely. "Thanks, Steph."

"Look at your face! It's like turning the children out for a little more play before bedtime." She smiled at him then a cloud passed over her face. "Not that we'll ever know it of course." She turned away from the yard and moved back into the kitchen holding up a hand in submission. "Sorry, sorry... came from nowhere, has done just recently, sorry."

David was at her side before she had reached the kitchen door. "Steph don't, eh? There's no need to keep remindin' yourself. It really is one of those things, not your fault nor mine. Nothin' you nor I can do about it."

"Me, David. Not you, it's me. You could sire a litter. It's me!" She left him and went into the kitchen.

David followed her. "OK, OK, so it's you, but it's not a thing you need to be wearin' a hair shirt for. It just happens you're not made in a way that allows you to have them... easily."

"Them?" She dropped the washing on a chair. "Children, David, they're called children, and I can't have them at all! And because of that neither can you." She stood at the sink, gripping its edge.

He could see her eyes were filling up. "Bloody hell, where did this lot come from? One minute we're smilin' about vixens an' shoppin' the next we're in the crèche from hell."

Stephanie pulled an envelope from under the clock on the window sill. "There'll be no crèche for me." She sat at the table. "I had the letter today... from the clinic. Written confirmation of the last tests."

David sat opposite her. "Oh, bloody hell, Steph. Why'd you not say so?"

"Don't know. Can't some days… can't."

He reached across the table. "Let's see."

Stephanie handed the envelope over and got up. "Do you want more tea?"

"Ar… please." He pulled the letter from the opened envelope and unfolded it. "You gonna 'ave another?"

"Yes. Tea… universal panacea, if you're English." She began to make the tea in the silence.

After a few moments of reading, David looked up. "See, they've given you a next appointment so all's not lost."

"Not going."

Stephanie's answer threw David and he looked at her for a long while before attempting an answer. All that came out was, "Look, Steph…"

She shook her head. "Not going. I'm not. Not any more."

"But… we've only been goin' to see them for a year."

"And the three before that, out east?"

"Well, yes, but these are new doctors."

"With all the old notes. Four years now they've pulled and prodded me about, and I hate that, David. I hate it… and I can't keep on… won't."

"Steph…"

"Won't."

David refolded the letter, put it into the envelope then back under the clock. He looked across at her. "Need a bit of air." With that he went back out into the yard and stood, arms folded, looking at the ferret kits as they played in the outer run of their cage. Stephanie finished making tea then carried out two mugs gave one to David then stood alongside him as they watched the gambolling ferrets in silence.

David eventually looked at her. "Well, OK, so you've had enough, I can understand that."

"Can you?"

He stopped for a moment to consider. "No... no, I can't. Silly thing to say but, look... you said it yourself, it's just written confirmation of the last tests they did and they said..."

"And the Norfolk and Norwich before that?"

"Yes, alright, and the Norfolk and Norwich lot before that. It's just... they all said more research is needed."

"You make me sound like a laboratory rat."

"Well you're not. It just means they're unsure of how to proceed."

"Ha! That's a good way of putting it."

"Unsure of how to proceed." Stephanie said nothing. "It's not your fault, Steph... the specialist said so, the consultant said so... they didn't say never, they said..."

"In so many words they did."

"No they didn't, they've said its 'unexplained infertility' and they were unsure how to proceed."

"I was there too, David, remember, and I heard what they said. They said 'the difficulty with unexplained infertility, Stephanie'... as if using my first name made some sort of bond between us... 'the difficulty with unexplained infertility is inherent in the name'. And they didn't say they were unsure how to proceed, David, they said although more research would be useful, given the combination of the present technology and knowledge and my particular symptoms, there was little they could offer by way of treatment or prognosis."

"Means the same thing."

"That could only be a man talking. When they say it's a case of unexplained infertility what they're actually saying is they haven't got a clue what's wrong with me, and

neither do they have a clue what to do about it. We'd be just as well going out and slaughtering a curlew on the first Sunday of the month as do any more visits to them!"

"Well, what makes you so sure your version's right an' not mine then?"

"Because the vast majority of men just pull out the bits that fit their beliefs. All they want is a solution and move on; I don't. I need to understand the problem even if I can't find a solution; which I have now."

"What, not tryin' anymore?"

"Yes!"

"Well, OK... OK, have it your way, maybe I heard it wrong..."

"You did."

"Maybe I heard it wrong but they did say new research was always findin' possible solutions, and when we've talked you said you had faith in the process, faith in them."

"I have... did..."

"That summat would turn up..."

"David..."

"Then there's always a chance, Steph."

"David..."

"There is! Summat could turn up. You could... I don't know, they could get a... I don't know, a new drug or a new treatment, it could even correct itself."

"That would be the second coming."

"But they said that it could!" He was desperate to be rescued; she could see it in his face, so she did her best to rescue him.

"David... My love, they told us that because they're out of reasons and explanations, don't you see? They feel they have to say something just to placate this hysterical woman who's been pouring scorn on their collective abilities and

technology for four years now because, in the end, I mean, you know, all she wants to do is what all mammals do with the minimum of fuss. Just. Get. Pregnant!"

"But they've given you another appointment."

She knew he was struggling with it all again but this time, instead of cushioning the blow, suddenly she was very angry with him. "You keep saying the same things, David, as if repeating them will make it all come true. It won't! They haven't got a clue! What is it with you? Have you not understood them... or me? Can't you see I'm sick of it?"

"I know, I... you've said as much before, I know."

"And every time you've jollied me along. 'It's alright, Steph; next time, Steph; chin up, Steph'. Well, no more!" She breathed deeply, trying to steady her anger. "When we first started out on this rail-line to hell it was alright, you probably got me through a lot of it because I wanted you to, but for the last eighteen months? Not then. It's dominated our conversation, our lives, for years, up to such a point that it now comes on from nowhere, like it did out in the yard, and I'm sick of it! I know, I know, I've said these things before, when I was really low, but now I mean it. It's not to be, I've come to realise it now. And all I really wanted to hear was the truth; not from them, from you! That you were sick of it all too, that you hated me being treated this way! But you haven't, and I know that's because you try to be positive all the time, for me; that you think you understand me, but you don't!" A silence followed. David stood, unable to contribute. Eventually, Stephanie carried on in a more measured tone. "Listen, let me... That was a bit unfair; I'm sorry... you deserve better, have been wonderful, but I can't do it any more." She felt her throat constrict and swallowed hard. "Can we change the subject please? Just for me, please, can we?"

"Ar, OK, we'll talk some more..."

"No. No more, just give me a bit of time; maybe then, but not now, please."

"Yeah... OK. I just thought..." He could see the bewilderment in her eyes, and the fear. *"OK, well, can we have another Labrador puppy then?"*

She smiled at him and shook her head. *"How can you stay so upbeat about it all?"*

"'Cos sometimes you can't."

This caught her unawares and she stepped back into the familiar to avoid yet more tears on this subject. *"Who's putting the poults away this evening?"*

David recognised the shut-down and went with it. *"Liam. He knows about the vixen. I'll be back about eleven. Any chance of a lid of tea an' a bun before I bugger off lamping?"*

"'Course. Hours you work, I need to keep you fed and contributing to your pension."

"Providin' I make it that far. Look, you sure you're alright about the shoppin'? If not I'll talk to Liam..."

"No, you go. I'm not good company at the moment anyway. Bit of an obvious statement that... You go, I'll be fine."

"Only if you're sure." She nodded. *"Right, well, I'm gonna check on the traps round the release pen an' trim back some of that hawthorn on the Railway, then I'll bugger off to meet Eric."*

"What about supper then?"

"When I get back." He put the mug down on the dustbin lid and took her hands. *"And above all of this, remember that I love you, Stephanie Clarke; eh?"*

"Yes, I know, David, I know."

"Do you?"

"Yes."

"Good." David collected his shotgun which was leaning against the wall. "See you later love."

Stephanie took its place, leaning against the yard wall to watch him go then looked at the still-frolicking ferret kits and spoke out loud. "How easy it is for you."

—⁓—

Moving through the car park, full shopping bags in hand, Stephanie was convinced more than ever that evening supermarket shopping was definitely a spectator sport. It seemed as though everyone left it until the last minute; there were never enough trolleys and the one she had placed at the end of the check-out had been quickly taken by a mum juggling with three small children. Now she regretted her Good Samaritan act as the handles of the loaded plastic bags cut and bit into her fingers. She still had a good fifty yards to go to reach her car when a man stepped alongside and slipped his hand into the bag handles.

"Here, I'll take that, you look fair tuckered."

Stephanie stopped abruptly and then her initial surprise gave way to realisation as she recognised the man from Seer's Hill. "Oh, hello!"

"Hello, Stephanie."

"I'm flattered you remember my name, Alec Stratton." They stood mid car park still sharing the weight of the bags. "No need to look so surprised. That is your name, isn't it?"

"Ar, it is. Alec Stratton at your service. Pheasants a speciality."

"Did you know? That I was a keeper's wife when we met on the hill? Did you?" He loosed the bag. "How did you know?"

"Bits I've heard about you, where we were... edge of the estate, the noise below in the wood. Not quite as quick as you knew who I were it seems. My missus been chattin' no doubt."

"She didn't need to. Your reputation precedes you... and my husband's a keeper so there's a strong possibility your name may have cropped up in past conversations, don't you think?"

"I'll bet." He gripped the bag again. "Look, let me at least take half an' help you to the car with this lot, I've seen pack mules carryin' less."

Stephanie smiled in spite of it all. "Yes, alright, thanks." She relinquished her hold on the two bags in her left hand and Alec split them, one into each of his. "Thank you."

They walked the rest of the distance to the car in silence, then Alec helped her load. "Your husband not about then? David, isn't it?"

"Yes, David. No he's work to do."

"A keeper's lot..."

"Is not a happy one? Not at all, just that he's got things he needs to get done. Why am I telling you this? You probably know more about his movements than I do."

"You make me sound like a peepin' tom."

"Well?"

Alec nodded. "Point taken." They stood for a few moments, both unsure how to proceed. "Well, it was nice seein' you again... my Alice were right."

"About what?"

"She said you had a face an' figure could stop traffic. Thought that the first time we met, you in that summer dress, think it more now." There was an awkward silence before Alec spoke again. "Sorry. Uncalled for that."

"No, no, I'm not so much a harridan as not to be flattered by the compliment. Thank you."

"That's the second time that's come up."

"What?"

"Harridan."

"What about it?"

"Nothin'." He leant against the car and folded his arms. "Do you know, in Latin American countries they applaud a well turned out woman. Applaud her when she walks into a restaurant or a hotel... front-thingy. None of 'em know 'er; they do it because they appreciate effort and beauty. You? You're worth a standing ovation."

"Now I think you have overstepped the mark. Not the comment but its content. I thank you again and will say goodnight."

Alec smiled at her. "Ar, goodnight."

He turned and began to walk away. He'd gone only a few yards when Stephanie's voice reached him. "How are you getting home?" Alec turned. "I mean, where's your car?"

"Not got one; can't drive."

"What, not at all?"

"No, never learnt. Never saw the point. Use a bike occasionally."

"Goodness." There was no thought given to what followed, she just heard herself say it. "Well can I at least offer you a lift... for carrying the bags."

Alec walked back to her. "You sure you want to be seen with the likes of me?"

"I'm my own woman, Mister Stratton. That much you will have heard from Alice. Now, do you want a lift?"

"Ar, I would."

"I'll take you as far as the Red Lion. That alright?"

"Fine. On the way you can tell me your life story."

"A life of missed opportunities and shopping trips? I think not. I believe yours would be far more interesting."

—⁓—

Something wasn't right. Nothing tangible, more ethereal... but certainly not right. Stepping over the last nipple-loosening cub, the vixen moved closer to the den entrance and inhaled deeply, her ears erect and radiating slowly through the four compass points of fox-safety; 'check; check once more; double-check the check; check again to make sure.'

There was nothing to be gained from her hyper-alert senses but she stepped back all the same, removing full teats from renewed attacks by the cubs. She turned and moved deeper into the den followed by the ever-hungry quartet of offspring; a deepening of shadows was required.

Eric looked at his watch. 'Ten past nine'.

He settled more firmly and lifted the shotgun onto his knees in order to cut any movement down to a minimum for when the vixen appeared, as she surely would.

Stephanie got up from the kitchen table, where she had been sitting for the past thirty minutes after putting the shopping away, running over the chance meeting with Alec in her head. He was not at all what she had expected; not at all. That he was older than her, a good dozen years older, only served to make him more colourful, made up of subtler shades than most men due to his history and background.

The drive to the Red Lion had been full of conversation and both of them had let their guard down a little, such was their enjoyment in each other's company. She had told him of her time at university; he had told her about how he and Alice had known each other since junior school. She told him of the best way to dissect mice; he had told her about his egg collecting days as a kid. She told him of how she once caught a grass snake near her home in Lincolnshire and kept it in an old washing tub but of how guilt had got the better of her and she had released it; he told her of the time he carried two kestrel eggs down from a nest in his mouth only to slip, clack his jaws on a bough and discover that both eggs were four days struck. She told him of how guilt had often been her downfall because she would have to tell people of things she had done when they did not need to know; he had told her of how his poaching had made him suspicious and untrusting of most folk. She told him how she had first danced with David at the university end of year ball.

"All flouncing frocks and semi-sophistication," she said. "Ignorant despite all that education." The memory made her smile and it lit up the inside of the car. He told her how he had first danced with Alice in the youth club.

"Not like they do now," he said. "Twenty yards apart an' tryin' to look like you don't care. Real dancin'. Rock 'n' roll. Hold a girl, let her know you know what you're doin'." His eyes sparkled in the reminiscence.

They were so involved in this swapping of detailed small talk it was a surprise when they reached the pub's car park, so short had seemed the travel time. As it was, he had sat alongside her in the car for a further fifteen minutes as they chatted on. Stephanie talked about how she should have stayed on at university and done a doctorate; Alec agreed, saying that then she could have had a look at his arthritic knee and making her laugh at the serious look he had on his face when he said it.

"Not that sort of a doctor," she had said.

"Too many nights out," he had said.

Then they parted. Her back to the cottage on the estate, him into the Red Lion.

'He really is a nice man. Open faced, great sense of humour... and lovely eyes...'

This was the thought that got her up from the table. She should not be thinking these things; should not have voiced the things she had to someone who was, ostensibly, the enemy. Not at all.

Stephanie put the kettle on the range and looked into the pantry. 'Bread,' she thought. 'Should make some bread...' She began to gather things together, placing them on the kitchen table in readiness. All was going to plan. She had measured, mixed and now the first proving was cloth-draped on the stand above the Rayburn. Next thing she was aware of she had drifted into the hallway, up the stairs and into the bedroom.

Almost automatically she pulled the dressing table drawer open, removed the top layer of nightclothes and stared at what was beneath. The christening dress and shawl looked as deep as a glacier, their reflected whiteness lifting the glow in her flushed cheeks. Stephanie pushed her hand into the material's folds and her eyes filled up.

"Oh my..."

The vixen settled in with her cubs for an enforced evening feeding session. She had plenty of milk; there was no need to fret on that point. Hunting had been good of late and the batch of young rabbits she had dug up on farmer Siddons' land last night, plus the inexperienced partridge poult she had managed to nab on her way home, had set her up for a while.

As soon as she had entered the den that morning the cubs had fallen on the bird, dragging it from her mouth and had set to with a squabble of adult proportions. Their needle-sharp teeth made short work of the bird. Any cubs that lost out in this hurried dismemberment quickly cut their losses and pushed tongues into the vixen's mouth whereupon she promptly vomited up the warm mix of young rabbit for them. As the last of this piping hot fast food had been scoffed so the cubs scrabbled for free space at the milk bar. The vixen had lain gently on her side to give each cub an equal opportunity, her metronomic licking of the feeding litter soothing them into a contented heap; her early morning routine, feeding the cubs in a tender nap... sleeping and waiting.

David reacted to the midges that were using his scalp as a supper bar and scrubbed at his hair. 'Bloody hell, that's warm tonight,' he thought.

The light was beginning to falter. Another half hour would render clear vision and shot almost impossible. He stretched his leg along the ditch and swapped the shotgun from left to right hand then resettled in a seemingly better position should the vixen choose this way of leaving her den.

Eric peered into the distant gloaming. In this light and against the thick hedgerow, even familiar objects elicited startled reactions. The Barn Owl, flicking its way along the base of the hedgerow caused him to sit upright and alert, then he relaxed a little and fingered the shotgun's safety catch back from foe to friend.

'If she don't get a move on it'll be a wasted night,' he thought.

The vixen twitched in her semi doze and the movement snapped the cubs from sleep to furious suckling in an instant. Their fast growing teeth completed the vixen's wake-up call and she rose to her feet.

Shaking the cubs off like so many burrs she flexed her legs, paws and tongue in displacement activity ease. Licking, appeasing and removing the cubs from her pathway she stepped gingerly towards the den's entrance, stopping on point just a few feet from its opening to rerun the check routine.

'I really should have given it to Oxfam years ago.' Stephanie patted the ruffled gown and shawl, wiping her dampened cheeks on the back of her hand at the same time. 'Or Save the Children... what children?'

Even given the outburst of earlier and for all her resolve, still it had a hold on her. It was not David's fault, she knew that. They both coped with it in their own fashion but she had often wished he would stop hiding all of the reality in a fog of optimism that was sometimes suffocating. It hadn't helped, when David was out of the consulting room collecting the car in readiness for home, that Stephanie had insisted she be told the worst-case scenario; that after four years of what she considered to be embarrassing hospital treatment, she deserved at least that. The specialist nodded and had said that privately, in both his professional and personal opinion, there was so little possibility of her having children she should just stop hoping for a miracle, accept it and move on. That what she was suffering by way of hope and constant disappointment was not a good thing for her. He should have been there, David, and she had neglected to tell him after. Not because she could not bear to see the look of defeat she knew he would feel, but because

225

she could not bear the thought of another round of jolly platitudes. Best say nothing and do as suggested; move on.

'Say nothing and move on? Well, you made a mess of that strategy, Stephanie Clarke. Your little scene of earlier put the tin lid on that one.' Her thoughts stirred at the reminder. 'Move on to what exactly? Well, there's David... and a life that many would envy...' Her thought train pulled into its usual siding, as it had done so many times over the past few months. 'Is that it? Is that what I 'move on' to?' Her hand instinctively exhumed the shawl and she stroked the material's folds once more. 'Well, that's one thing I can move on from.' She gently closed the crypt. 'No babies here.'

The vixen stood her ground not sure that all was well but not knowing why she felt that way.

Distracted momentarily by the bouncing cub at her front paws she dropped her head and licked the little one's face. This immediately brought on a deluge of siblings and she tried to distribute her attention over the whole gaggle of cubs; it was an unfair competition. She quickly closed the fuss-shop by turning abruptly back down the den's entrance tunnel, heading with some purpose towards a rear exit.

Eric was now having difficulty in making out shapes at ground level. The hedgerow base colour had been deepened further by the day's end, and it was almost impossible to see anything at all against its shadow.

David shifted once more and this gave him just a few extra minutes of vision over the brow of the field and against the rapidly fading skyline. Another five minutes or so and he would be unsighted.

The vixen reached a back door of the badger's den and stood at its threshold, nose, ears and eyes working overtime in order to confirm or deny safety.

A blackbird was sounding off near the opening, nothing new there. She listened longer and could hear the faint thumping of rabbits in a burrow further along the hedgerow.

The cubs had been shaken off a good few yards from where she now stood. They had returned to the central den where partridge wing-feathers and games of pounce were taking the place of their absent parent. All seemed quiet. Just a few more moments to confirm this suspicion and the vixen could get off and sort out breakfast.

Stephanie sat on the bed not sure what to do next, then the whistling of a crazed kettle penetrated. She looked at her watch. Twenty past ten. A look told her that the fast-fade of day had happened without her noticing. She stood up and went to draw the curtains, but stopped and gazed across the meadow to the distant village and at the house lights, street lights... and one particularly bright set of lights. 'Probably the car park of the Red Lion... Bread,' she thought. 'When all else fails make some bread.' She went downstairs to the kitchen and put her apron back on.

David lifted the gun to his shoulder but left the safety-catch on. The hair-trigger could catch a chap out and he really was not sure, in this light, just what he had seen.

Eric stood up and gathered his feed bag from the base of the ditch. 'Can't believe she's stayin' in tonight,' he thought. The feed bag slid off his shoulder and he cursed it under his breath. "Bloody thing! Don't even know why I brought it."

He climbed stiffly onto the field. Cradling the shotgun under his arm he switched the bag to his other shoulder. 'Meet Dave then 'ome an' a mug of tea.' Then realisation seeped back in. 'Oh, bugger, then bloody lampin'. Sod it!'

The vixen stopped in her progress along the hedgerow. Something was just not right here either. She lifted both paw and nose to rake the area for sign or scent.

The head movement confirmed it; charlie was on her way. She was just in range David figured, but he would like her to make half a dozen more steps in his direction just to make sure. He adjusted his hold on the shotgun and, with his finger well away from the trigger, gently slipped off the safety catch.

Stephanie moved to the back door and opened it to allow a little air into the stifling kitchen. She had stoked the range some fifteen minutes earlier and, what with its heat, the ambient temperature of the night and the effort she had put into the kneading, she was in something of a glow.

She knew what it was if not quite sure where it was, but that did not stop the vixen from whipping round and setting off back the way she had come in real and genuine haste.

David was certain the safety catch had made no noise but the fox had certainly heard something. As it was, and in his split second thinking time, he thought a shot was worth it. The feather-light trigger reacted to his slight caress and, cranking the pump action fore-end in a fluid move, two more shots followed one another in quick succession.

Eric was snapped to a standstill. Maybe David had been in the top spot after all.

Stephanie looked up from the butcher's block where she had been meting out further punishment to the dough as the distant sound of gunfire penetrated her senses. She moved back to the door and opened it wider, standing on its threshold, breathing in the night air and listening intently.

The vixen felt the BB pellets burn and twist their way into her rear legs as she scampered along and through the hedgerow in her efforts to avoid her nemesis. That her initial reaction had saved her from oblivion had not stopped some of the lead shot from finding their mark, and it would make lying on her left side uncomfortable for the rest of her days. Away and along the hedge she galloped, intent only on getting back to the den to protect her cubs within its relative safety.

Eric saw the vixen as she clipped the gateway in her haste to leave the site of danger. He lifted the shotgun.

David leapt from the ditch in his eagerness to pursue and discover the result of his shots.

The feed bag slipped off Eric's shoulder, jagged his arm and he fired the first barrel into the ground not three feet from him, supercharging the vixen's retreat.

David was halted by the closeness of the single shot. 'Maybe Eric's got her…'

Eric cursed aloud. "Fuck it! Fuckfuck!"

The vixen was deaf to Eric's protestations but David heard the muffled tones of rage even from this distance. '...Maybe not.'

Standing at the door for a few moments longer after hearing the fourth shot, Stephanie gently eased it to and returned to the dough.

—⦚⦚—

"She aint there, is she, nor them cubs?"

Kneeling at the den's entrance, David shook his head. "Nope. Jill and Sack don't miss a trick and if they've come away that quick then mum and babes have done a bunk. We should've sorted 'em out last night."

"No bloody terriers, were there?"

"Should've fetched 'em," said David. "I offered."

"Too bloody dark and too bloody late by then weren't it, an' we'd rabbits to lamp as well."

"Should've had a go yesterday mornin' then, when we first saw her; Jill! Sack! Come 'ere!"

"Too big a sett... Not gettin' her would be as bad as not tryin'. I did say."

"Bird in the 'and..." He slipped the leads over the soil-stained faces of the panting terriers, their look of disappointment palpable.

"That's it, go on, make me feel better about it why don't y'?"

David could see this was not helping and he tried a more conciliatory approach. "One of them things, Eric, not for the want of tryin'. You want me to slip 'em in again? Maybe they just passed her if she were backed up in a block-hole. Every square inch must stink of fox."

"No, no point. They were in long enough. If she'd been there those two would've connected. No, we'll bugger off."

"You'll catch up with her, I know."

"Ar, but not 'til after her next lot of damage, I'll be bound." Eric kicked his feed bag across the ground. "Fuck it... an' fuck them rabbits an' all!"

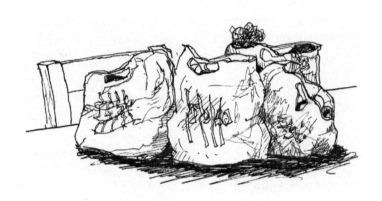

Day 5 – Monday 26th November 1985

"Ayup, that's a bloody big 'un! We should've brought the terriers in to sort this lot out!"

The wolf spider romped out of the disturbed pile of numbered, white-topped shooting pegs and made a dash for the whitewashed pigsty wall as Eric danced a jig in his efforts to avoid becoming its chosen retreat.

"Bugger me, I'd 'ave tied some string round me trouser bottoms if I'd known they were gonna be this big!"

David laughed at his antics. "An' this from a chap who drags fightin' ferrets apart with 'is bare hands."

"Ferrets is nothin'. All spit and stink they are, act decisive and you can easy wrestle them buggers to a standstill; but bloody spiders... They scuttle they do." He demonstrated with his hands. "An' that big an' all!"

"It weren't that big."

"I know it were!"

"You must tell a good fishin' story."

"No need to bring that up again." Eric eyed the slot now hiding the recently evicted arachnid. "That gap's an inch wide by three inch deep an' 'is legs are still stickin' out."

"It'll be a female then, that size."

"Sex don't come into it; y' could ride the Hindu Kush trail on that bugger!"

"You're off on the exaggeration trail." David jostled with an armful of the wooden stakes and moved to get past. "C'mon, shift!"

"I'll have you know I never exaggerate, I've told you that fifty billion times before. Jim-bloody-Corbett wouldn't have tackled a beast that big!"

"Jim Corbett! It was a spider, Eric, not a tiger."

"Paint stripes on that one and you'd be 'ard pressed to tell the difference." Eric began to turn over the remaining stake gingerly with his foot.

David went over to the Land Rover, parked with its back door open, calling over his shoulder as he went. "It was a bloody spider, Eric! How long you been afeared of them then?"

"I'm not frit of spiders, I just treat them ones as are the size of a Shetland Pony with a bit of respect is all, and you'd do well to do the same." He carefully checked then picked up the last stake and followed David outside.

"Can you manage that one on your own?"

Eric ignored him. "What I want to know is how come they get so big in such a short time? These shootin' pegs have only been 'ere since the close of last season, barely ten month, an' we're findin' wolf spiders the size of Scooby-bloody-Doo hidin' amongst 'em. What're they eatin', I'd like to know?"

"Any sheep gone missin' of late, M'Lord?" David bowed slightly and held the back door open for Eric to drop his single stake on top of those already gracing the rear of the vehicle.

"Now you are takin' the piss."

"I'm not; I'm merely continuing the flight of fancy you've begun with your tales of giant spiders."

"Never mind giant bloody spiders, we've to get a shoot day organised by Wednesday next."

"That were the most unsubtle change of subject I've ever heard." David tapped his head with his forefinger. "Seems to me we've got to the truth behind your arachnophobia."

"Arachno-buggery!" Eric left David holding the door and walked round to the driver's side of the vehicle. "Come on let's get these bloody pegs laid out an' ready for the slaughter of the innocents next Boys' Day."

"Yup, the real truth's comin' out." David closed the door and walked along the side of the vehicle. "That's what this is all about aint it?" He climbed in the passenger seat. "Nothin' to do with the size of spiders, is it? We're still smartin' about Lordy's decision to let the heir apparent shoot The Quarry first time through aren't we?"

"An' if it is?" Eric flicked the key and the vehicle roared into life. "Would I be wrong? No, I wouldn't. An' havin' to wrestle giant spiders in order to get ready for such a sportin' travesty doesn't help neither, alright?"

"Bloody hell, touched a nerve there I think."

"That'll be same raw nerve you've got about Steph then, will it?" Eric slotted the gearstick into first.

This mention of Stephanie, out of the blue, shook David and it was a couple of seconds before he answered Eric in a quieter tone. "Does it show that much?"

Returning the stick to neutral, Eric turned to David. "Sorry, David, there was no need for that."

"Does it?"

"Ar, it does a bit." Eric turned the ignition key to off.

"Good days, bad days."

"Like the curate's egg, is it?"

"What?"

"The curate's egg; some parts are excellent."

"Oh, I see. Ar, 'bout right that is. I try not to dwell on it, y' know. Get on with the job an' all that. Just, grabs me sometimes."

"Like Jaws."

David almost laughed. "Ar, like Jaws. Christ, this is maudlin chat."

"Maybe, but you need to get things right, Dave."

"No one knows that better than me… I'm workin' on it."

"Is she?" David looked quizzically at him. "Well, it's a legitimate question. If the solution comes from one side then it's no solution y' know."

"Ar, I do know, but, right now…" He shook his head as if to clear it of unpleasantness. "…Right now we've a drive to sort."

"That's all well an' good, but don't chuck y' future away on summat like this. This'll still be here when we've all long gone an' the graveyards are full of indispensible people."

"That's very profound, comin' from you."

"I have me moments. Few an' far between I know, but I still 'ave 'em. Think on it youngster. Look at what you have, what you want to keep and what you can and can't do without. Decide what you're prepared to settle for then make the decisions accordin'ly. There'll be compromises involved, always is, but at least it'll be you as made 'em."

There was a long silence. "Thanks, Eric." David smiled at him. "And by way of return, I reckon after Liam's chat with Lordy about Mister Stephen's ability to cope with The Quarry, not to mention his guests, I reckon Lordy will have passed these concerns on, that folk will concentrate all the harder, behave themselves like."

"Will they? Will they really?" Eric started the engine once more. "An' just when 'as Lordy ever listened to anybody before?" David drew breath to answer but Eric was not waiting. "Never, that's when. It'll be a right royal fuck up, David, an' you know it."

"That's the Eric I remember." They both smiled. "It's gotta start sometime for the lad."

"Maybe so."

"Well, look, let's stick to what we discussed with Liam and peg the drives accordingly. Quarry first?"

"Ar, I guess."

"Do it for the right reasons. Give 'em fair view and we can just hope folk are on their best behaviour, that they respect what's gone before 'em, eh?"

Eric slipped the gearstick back into first and snorted derisively as he drove away. "Pah! Respect? Word's not in their bloody dictionary!"

Stephanie spotted Alice by the far end of the stall, and after waiting for a few moments attracted her attention, motioning for Alice to join her, away from the gathered shoppers.

"Can I have a word, when it's convenient?"

Alice looked Stephanie hard in the eyes. "Do I know you?"

"Yes, I know, sorry. It's been a bit... difficult of late, one thing and another."

"One thing an' another, eh? That right?"

There was no shade of sympathy in Alice's voice and Stephanie squirmed a little. "I'm really sorry about that, Alice."

"So you said." There was an embarrassing silence then Alice added. "You're not lookin' for discount are y'?"

"Alice..."

"Yes?"

Stephanie sighed, paused. "What time are you off for lunch?"

Alice eyed her suspiciously. "Sounds serious does this; lunch. All this... this contact all of a sudden."

"Lunch?"

"Well, as y'know, I often grab a sandwich and work through, although you've probably forgot that. Can we not talk 'ere?"

Stephanie looked around at the gaggle of shoppers and shook her head. "Not really. Can I buy you a cup of coffee at the cafe, after your sandwich?"

Alice could see this was important but still she paused before answering. "Hm... Yeah... alright. I'll square it up with the boss and meet you in Les's, say half twelve?"

"Thanks, Alice."

"Only ten minutes though. As much as I can spare these days."

"Yes, ten minutes, thank you. I've some meat to collect and David's 'Shooting Times'. I'll get over there for half twelve. See you then... and thank you." Stephanie turned away and moved off along the serried ranks of stalls.

"What do you think? Will he see we've altered the position to make it easier... fairer, or what?"

"Fairer? We're talkin' Lordy 'ere, Dave." Eric looked along the graceful arc of shooting pegs fronting The Quarry. "An' yes, he will see... As for the rest of 'em, if they do it'll be the only thing they see right all day." He moved out a little from peg eight and eyed the treeline on the ridge up ahead. "Flanker will 'ave some sport 'ere, that much I do know. Comin' off the top like they do. There'll not be many but with this increased distance they'll be high an' knockin' on. Do you think we may even be too far out from the edge? Could make it a lean drive here."

David joined him and eyed the prospective flight line the pheasants would take. "Nah. Position's as good as any, plenty of clearance an' what comes will be committed by the time they see the gun."

"It's us as should be committed, lettin' kids such as these loose on a drive of this quality."

"They'll be fine, Eric, and you'll have Lordy to help keep 'em in check."

"Keep 'em in check? You and I both know he'll be as much use as a marshmallow tank."

"He's off again." David began to leave. "C'mon, let's get the next two drives pegged out before you get suicidal."

Eric glanced along the arc of pegs and called to David. "It's too late for worries such as that! It'll all end in tears! I know it an' so do you!"

"I've got you a tea."

Alice stood by the table in the far corner of Les's Cafe where Stephanie was already seated. "Crikey, all the way over here an' no cake. Looks like this is gonna be fun." Stephanie stirred her coffee and handed a paper napkin to Alice as she sat opposite. "Why is it folk that don't take sugar always stir their drink?"

"Mix in the milk?"

"You don't take milk."

"So I don't. That'll be a displacement activity then."

Alice sat. Placing her elbows on the table, she intertwined her fingers and rested her chin on her folded hands. "So, now, what's so important that I'm granted an audience after so long? Meetin' here like a pair of fifth columnists."

There was a lengthy pause from Stephanie before she finally spoke. "Alice, you know how much I value our friendship..."

"Christ, opening like that, got to be serious has this."

"Please... This is awkward enough without you breaking the chains of my courage."

Alice picked up her mug of tea. "Right. Carry on."

"I do really like you, we get on..."

"Got on. Haven't seen much of each other recently."

"No, I know, that's my fault."

"It is. Not mine. I 'phoned don't know how many times; tried to talk."

Stephanie bit her bottom lip at the reminder of excuses given, telephone calls ignored. "I know but we have the same interests..."

"Similar, not the same, let's not kid ourselves."

"Yes, alright, similar, but the same too." She paused again and sighed. "Bugger!"

"Not often you swear, Steph." Alice was now fully aware that she was being, if not unfair then unhelpful, and she softened her tone a little. "C'mon, out with it an' let's get this sorted. I've work to get back to. What's the problem?"

"It's Alec."

"Ah, all becoming clearer now. Wondered how long this would take to surface."

"I met up with him, Alice. Again, I mean."

Alice was puzzled at the unexpected turn of the conversation. "What? Sorry, not quite with you."

"Alec. Alec and I... we met up."

"I know..." There was a silence as Alice's jaw set. After a few moments she spoke. "Where?"

"Jackson's. Patch of maize, along the Bower Road."

Alice thought for a moment. "Jackson's, y' say?"

"Yes."

"Not Seer's Hill?"

"No… I mean yes, well not then, just… later than Seer's Hill… the back of the maize on Jackson's… the birds were all drifting across the road from The Quarry…"

But Alice wasn't interested. "Never mind the birds! What were you two doin' there?"

"I was there helping to…"

This was annoying. "No; you two. You've just said you met up with Alec at the back of the maize an' I already know you saw him on Sear's Hill! Now, do you calmly and quietly tell me why there's an increase of one hundred percent in your association with my husband, or do I cause a scene?"

"I met him at the maize…"

"Met up with him, Steph. To be a good liar you've got to 'ave a good memory. You said… told me you'd met up with him at the back of the maize, an' he told me he'd seen you on Sear's Hill…"

"I did too."

"Only after I dragged it out of you at the jumble sale. So, what happened in the gap between then and now that turned 'saw' into 'met up'?" There was no reply. "I want to know what's going on 'ere…" Her voice fast-faded in a well of possibilities. "Have you two been together in the gap between Seer's Hill an' the maize?"

Stephanie stared at her cup. "I was going to say, Alice, going to tell you, honestly. I just lost the courage. I…"

"I don't want to hear this… When, where?"

"I gave him a lift home."

"You what?"

"I gave him a lift home... well not home exactly. We bumped into each other in the supermarket car park. Alec..."

"My husband; call him my husband, you call him Alec too easy, an' it's scarin' me."

"Your husband. Yes, in the supermarket car park. He helped me carry my shopping to the car. It was heavy..."

"Never mind the weight! You bumped into my husband in a supermarket car park?"

"Yes. He was there, and I... I offered him a lift to the Red Lion."

"And he took it?"

"Well, yes... I offered..."

"In a supermarket car park. My husband."

"Yes."

"I'm amazed he knew where it was. So 'e gave you a hand with your shoppin'. An' then?"

"Just carried it for me and I just gave him a lift to the Red Lion. It seemed poor not to and..."

"That's not all, is it Steph?"

Stephanie went to pick up her cup, but faltered. "No, Alice, it's not all."

Alice had already worked it out but there was always the small chance she might be wrong. Not now though. She could read it and she was hit by the dread, the probability that her initial suspicion was right. "Don't you dare tell me that, don't you dare... an' don't you dare start cryin' on me! Oh, Jesus... not you..." For several seconds Alice looked down at the table top and wrestled with her breathing. "How could you? How?"

"It was all just a mistake, Alice."

Alice's voice rose. "A mistake!" Then she lowered the volume and leant across the table. "A mistake for what?"

"No, I mean, it was just, David was away..."

"I'll bet he was!"

"Yes he was. He was in Scotland and Alec came round to the house, to tell me you'd not be able to meet me."

"God, this gets worse! Why didn't he 'phone?"

"He said he couldn't remember the number and you were asleep, you know, with your back, and he didn't want to wake you."

"I bet he didn't!"

Stephanie wiped her eyes and face with her paper napkin. "I'm so sorry, Alice, I didn't mean anything by it."

"And that's supposed to make me feel alright is it?"

"No."

"Good, because it bloody doesn't, alright?" Alice got up to leave.

Stephanie put her hand onto Alice's to stop her. "No, no, I know that, and that's not what I meant. Alice... please. Sit down and listen to me. Please."

Their voices had grown louder again and Alice sat back down, stared out the window then turned to face Stephanie. Stephanie leant forward. "Alice, it wasn't anything to do with Alec. It was me."

Now Alice leant in too and hissed. "Fucked y'self then did y'? I really liked you Steph, you know, really; you were my friend."

"If I could change it, I would... turn the clock back... I can't. All I can do is own up, say I'm so, so sorry..." Tears began again.

"Took you a site long enough, didn't it? It isn't as though it happened yesterday, is it, an' I've had to all but wrestle it out of you, again."

"I was scared, Alice. Of what it might do..."

"To our friendship? Ha! Well you were right, weren't you?" Alice stared into her tea. "God… when you wouldn't answer my calls I knew summat were up. Not this."

"Whatever you feel is right, it's deserved."

"Apart from sick, what I feel is right is to slap you; right now an' real 'ard." Alice leant back in her chair again and looked around the part empty cafe. Les was fussing with mugs behind the counter and she paused to gather breath again and looked from cup to window to Stephanie. "You picked this place deliberate, didn't you; so as to avoid a slangin' match. Clever. I can't believe I joked about that with you barely a month ago. Takes two to tango, Steph, remember?" She stopped for a moment then spoke almost as an aside. "Our love life may not have been wonderful for a good while now but I've not forgot how it's done. Have you told David yet?"

"No."

"You goin' to?... Oh, my Christ!"

"What is it?"

"You... you're pregnant, with my…!"

"No, I'm not."

"Yes, you are! You told me, came to tell me… at the market. That was the last time I saw you…You said it wasn't David's!"

Stephanie's voice took on a commanding, demanding tone. "No Alice, I'm not! Listen! I'm not pregnant."

"You told me you couldn't 'ave kids…"

"I can't... thought I couldn't."

"But you thought you were?"

"Yes."

"With my Alec?"

"Yes. I told you the truth that day at the market. I've never missed my period, not ever."

243

"Jesus."

"I'm so, so sorry how it came about but not sorry for those three weeks... I'm not, and that's the truth. No matter now anyway; gone."

Alice looked into Stephanie's face which was red and blotched, her eyes swollen from her recent tearful exertions. "You think you're the only one? You're not. Millions of folk have had the same; me included." She saw Stephanie's look soften. "Don't! Don't even consider it makes us the same; it don't."

"I wasn't. I'm just... sorry."

"And I don't want your sympathy neither so don't you expect mine. I dealt with it, so should you."

Stephanie replied after a brief pause, speaking quickly, harshly, deliberately. "And you don't think I have? I have dealt with it, Alice... for years!" She clenched her fists and dug her nails into her palm to stop the tears; this was no time for tears. "I've wanted a child so badly, Alice! God, so badly. All I could think about some weeks. Kept me awake nights. It's been as much as I could do to be in the same town as a mother and baby never mind a shop. I've even thought of kidnapping, Alice. Kidnapping! Hated all my friends for having babies... still do; lost touch with them all. You all wonder at how I keep so slim? 'Cos some weeks I can't keep so much as a round of toast down because of feeling inadequate, of my failure, of guilt..."

"Guilt? Ha...!"

"Yes guilt, years of it! Years! Of false hopes... of letting people down. I've had pills, potions, injections, instruments shoved in every orifice, lying naked with just a sheet for cover... in front of all these people, these strangers, my husband while they mull me over, run their hands over me; discuss me like I'm a prospective

I don't know what. And every time, every single time, I've failed. I've failed me, I've failed David, the expectant grandparents-in-waiting; God, my parents... my mother... the damn doctors! Failed them all; for years, so don't you dare tell me I haven't dealt with it! I'd even managed to get to the stage of not caring... and then this...?" She slowed a little and her face softened in the memory but her voice still held its resolve. Even though it had been Stephanie talking they were both breathless. After a long pause, she spoke on, her voice softer but still simmering. "Do you remember, in the summer... you mentioned something about my figure, how lovely I looked?" Alice said nothing. "I said I didn't know what you were talking about; do you remember?" Alice stayed silent. "Well that was a lie too. I knew exactly what you meant." Alice raised an eyebrow. "I was the one patient all the student doctors wanted to look at, the one all the junior doctors wanted to 'examine'."

"Still lookin' for sympathy?"

"No, just..."

"Just nothin', what about me, hm? An' David? You thought you were pregnant; what about us?"

"For that short time when I believed I was? I'd have had it, Alice. I'd have had it. God help me, and damn you all."

Alice sat silently for a while chinking the side of her mug with a spoon. "So, you gonna tell David?"

"Don't know and that's the truth..." Then her eyes widened and she spoke in determined fashion. "Yes, I think I will. The guilt. Don't know when or how. What he'll do; he deserves better."

"So do I, Steph."

"I know, Alice, I know. You'll not say anything?"

"No. I've a right to, but no, I'll not."

"Thank you."

Alice almost laughed. "Don't thank me! It's not from a good 'eart, believe me!"

"No, I know. I'm so sorry. I still can't believe why... or remember what happened."

Alice sat up at this. "All sob stories aside an' talkin' plain, Stephanie, you fucked my husband, remember?" Stephanie began to fill up again. "I'm sure you should remember summat." Alice shoved across her paper napkin. "Any more of that an' Les'll be across. Dry up."

"Please, Alice, please forgive me. Can you? I didn't do it to hurt you."

"Well you failed. I trusted you. Who's the poacher now? Eh?" She turned in her chair and began to gather her coat and bag with finality this time. "Thanks for the tea; I've got to get back, things to consider." She busied herself then stopped and looked at Stephanie. "I suppose it says summat; that you had the courage to tell me. Can't have been easy, but don't expect thanks."

"Will you tell Alec? That you know?"

Alice thought for a while. "No, don't think so. I'd like to think he'll tell me." She smiled ruefully. "I defended you, you know? Defended you, to him." She turned to leave. "Should've listened a bit better. Seems he was the one needed defendin'."

"You make it sound like I hunted him down, Alice. I didn't."

"No? I'll tell you what it sounds like. We both know about my husband's chequered past but it's just pheasants are his quarry, whereas you...?" Alice turned and left. "Cheers, Les."

"Ar, see you, Alice" He looked across to Stephanie who sat back in her chair, pushed her coffee mug across the table and pressed the paper napkin back to her face.

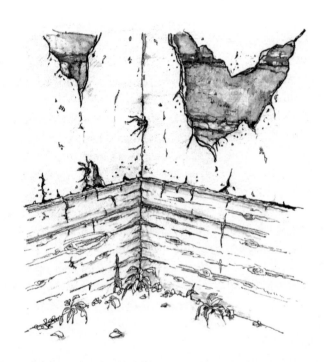

Chapter Nine
Month 4 – August 1985

"Will you go then?"

"I'd like to, if the offer's made official by Lordy. Never been on the grouse before, neither have the Labs so it'll all be a big adventure, for me and them."

Stephanie joined David at the breakfast table, tea mug in hand. "You mean, 'for both the dogs and me.'"

"Ar, for all three of us, an' I think it's very good of Liam, considering I've only been here a short time. By, but that's crackin' bacon our girl; from Taggarts'?"

"Yes, but from his own pigs this time. Still dry-cured but from his stock of Tamworths. First time he's bred them. Glad it's good, it cost enough." She sat opposite him. "Why doesn't Liam want to go then? He went last year. Head keeper and all that, they usually keep these junkets to themselves don't they?"

"Liam's cut from a different cloth; I found that out very quick."

"Quickly."

"Ar, real fast. He's alright about others goin'. Apparently two years of loadin' for Lordy on the grouse is enough for a body to bear."

"Doesn't Tom load for his Lordship on the grouse then? He does for the pheasants here."

"Ah, well, that's the thing see. That's why Liam's been doing it for the past couple of year. There's a feeling in the *camp that Tom's slowin' down a little, and nothin' affects Lordy's faith in his servants more than when they stop him gettin' what he considers to be his fair share of anythin' which, as far as shootin' goes, is most of it. An' all because his serf can't keep up no more."*

"Anymore."

"No, not no more he can't. Lordy had a quiet word with Liam about it just before I started 'ere, so Eric said. Said about Tom bein' alright for the pheasants and such but that he weren't quite nimble enough for the grouse 'don'tcha know.' Left it for Liam to tell Tom of course."

"Why am I not surprised at that?"

"Well, truth to tell he is gettin' on a bit, Tom. Lovely fella, knows the job backwards but... Anyway, like I said, Liam told him the score. But, what Tom don't know, an' this is not for gossip..."

"On this estate?"

"Ar, well, y' know what I mean. Anyhow, now Lordy's sayin' it'll not be long before he 'as to find someone else to load for the partridge too."

"Well why doesn't he find someone now, someone who can do the grouse this year as a lead-in to the partridge? Do you want more tea?"

"Just 'alf a mug, yeah. Ta."

Stephanie got up and moved to the stove, mug in hand. "So, why doesn't he?"

David tore fresh bread ready to mop the breakfast plate. "Because we're talkin' Lordy 'ere. This is a chap who makes his kids buy their own cartridges on shoot days, Steph. Eric said he's so tight-fisted he'd skin a turd for tenpence."

"David!"

"Eric's words not mine and it's for certain he's accurate. It'll take some jolt before Lordy'll even consider findin'

a partial replacement for Tom, let alone a permanent one. Cuts any possible cost down to a minimum."

Stephanie returned to the table, fresh-poured tea in hand. *"He'll pay you though won't he? On the grouse. You know, a 'thank you' at the end?"*

"Ah..."

"Can you tear me a corner and dip it in the tomato and mushroom juice, please?"

David looked at his plate still awash with the various breakfast juices. *"Have you not had breakfast?"*

"No, this is it."

"What, part of mine? This'll not be enough. You never finish any meal you start, you'll waste away."

"Well just be grateful that I'm tempted by the tomato and mushroom now."

"David tore and dipped the bread. "Not the way to go on, Steph, stealin' the food from a man's mouth."

"And a bit of the egg yolk."

"Jesus, I was looking forward to that!" He dipped it. "'Ere, don't say I never give you nothin'."

"Anything."

"Ar, nor that neither."

She took the bread. *"Thanks. So, you were saying, about his Lordship's attempts to save money. When I mentioned that he'll pay you, a tip, you went, 'Ah'. 'Ah' what?" She folded the bread and popped it in her mouth.*

"You're takin' a keen interest in the doin's of the estate all of a sudden. Why's that?"

"I'm not. I've always been interested."

"Not of late you haven't."

"You make me sound as though I've gone AWOL. I haven't. I am interested in what happens here, in you, and anyway you mentioned money."

"How come, of all the things we've discussed this morning you pick up on that?"

"Woman, remember? We're trained for it from birth. So, 'Lordy's attempts to save money' and 'Ah'; explanation please."

"I'm estate staff, just like Liam, Eric and Tom so we're already covered by the wages bill."

"Then where's the saving?"

"No tip to give."

Stephanie swallowed her bread. "What, he'll not tip you?"

"There's y' savin'."

"What? He gives his loaders nothing?" She looked at him in disbelief. "Will give you nothing for ten days loading?"

"Eleven if you count the walked-up day on the second Monday, an' no, he'll not."

"And you're driving up!"

"Yeah, but in his Range Rover."

"While he flies."

"Well, got to get guns, dogs an' kit up there somehow."

"Our dogs."

"Got to. That Ganymede of his is no use, not unless you want to find the rubbish bin."

"That's not the point, and I can't believe how blasé you are about it all! All that extra and nothing for it."

"No, well not in so many words, but it'll be a comfortable journey up and he'll reckon the tip is in the free board and lodgin', which I'm told is first rate."

Stephanie looked at him and shook her head. "Just make sure you get the money for the fuel before you set off or you'll end up paying for that as well."

"I will, an' now you know why he's so rich."

"And you still want to go?"

"Well, yeah. Just a new experience an' a chance to visit three different estates. An' the dogs'll be the better for it too; early season workout on a different scent... got to be good for 'em. Eric says it'll do me good as well. Freshen my outlook, he says."

"Why? What made him say that?"

"Don't know."

"Does he think you're not happy?"

"I am happy, who said I wasn't?"

"No one, I'm just puzzled as to why he said that. Must have come from somewhere; must have picked it up in conversation."

"Well, we chat, 'course, but it's just chatter, y' know? Nothin' dramatic."

"Hmm."

"It weren't!"

"So you say."

"Anyway, 'e said he'll maybe go next year if Liam's of the same mind; spread the load a little. I said I'd be glad to go this year... no, not glad, you know... 'appy to go... a bit 'appy, not massively, an' only 'appy if you felt OK about it... an' only then if..."

"Stop digging, David."

"Yeah. Right, yeah. I didn't want it to sound..."

"As though it was making you happy?"

"Erm..."

"The sort of happy that verges on the delirious?"

"Erm... yeah, sort of."

"And if I don't share your level of enthusiasm?"

He pushed the now clean, empty breakfast plate away from him. "There was a pattern on that plate when I started."

"Well?"

He picked up the mug. "I'll go anyway; there'll just not be many 'phone calls 'ome and definitely no stick of rock at the end of it." There was a short silence as David finished his tea then he pursued the matter. "Well, what do you think? Are you OK with it?"

"Yes-ish." Stephanie paused before continuing, "I'll miss you."

He brightened. "Will y'?"

"Well, your nuisance anyway."

"Oh, thanks." David stood up. "Anyway, look, time's gettin' on and we've birds to shift so, is it alright for me to sign up?"

"Yes. Yes it's fine, you go. At least you'll not be costing us anything to keep, and it'll mean I can get some household jobs done and not have to put up with you moaning about the mess."

"I don't moan about the mess. I just like things to be tidy, the way you keep 'em."

"It's a fetish with you."

"No it's not, you're my fetish. Always was, always will be."

"Flattery will get you everywhere."

"So it's alright, if I go then?"

"Yes, I said so didn't I? Just bring back a couple of brace for us."

"Right, but only if I get them as a gift. I'll not pay for 'em... so don't 'old your breath."

"And a bottle of decent scotch, single malt, if you please."

"That'll definitely be a buy-in! I'll get the keepers there to sort me summat out." He grabbed his waistcoat off the back of his chair. "Right, I'll get over and sort out the crates for the last batch of poults, though how I'm meant to throw myself around and catch 'em after that breakfast... What time for you at the rearing field?"

"About half nine. I'll hang this washing out first, put a second lot on then come right across. We'll be finished by the afternoon then?"

"Absolutely, don't want to be any later. The day's set to be warmer by midday and I'll want 'em in my pen long before that, otherwise they'll overheat. You can get off once they're crated up."

"That's good then."

"Something planned?"

"Yes, I was going to go to the jumble sale, at St. Mark's Community Centre."

"What, by yourself?"

"No, I was going to meet Alice there." David suddenly became very concerned with collecting his jacket and Stephanie spoke over his busyness. "Is that alright?"

"Yeah, yeah, fine. I just sometimes wish your mate was a couple of families removed from the cause of so many traumas on this estate, that's all."

"There's nothing sinister going on."

"I know that, there's no need to start in on it all again. I just merely noted that it's a very strange mix to be in, OK? Allow me my moments of insecurity." He paused, considered. "Really bugger it up wouldn't it, if I caught him; her husband."

"Truth to tell, I don't think it would."

"No?"

"No." She turned on the hot tap and opened the low cupboard door to get out the washing-up liquid. "I don't think Alice would choke on it. I mean, he's out at all hours, seemingly for pleasure, taking the risks he takes."

David put one foot up on the chair to fiddle with his laces and snorted. "Ha! For pleasure is it? Right... fine."

"Take your foot off there... and don't clam up on me."

"Well, what do you expect?" David dropped his foot to the floor. "This is the bloke whose 'pleasure' takes me away from you every night from the end of October until the end of February..."

"The rest of the year you do it voluntarily."

"Not voluntarily, it's the job, and it's him in the winter months."

"Not just him, David. Poachers in general do that."

"And that makes it alright does it?"

"No of course not, but he shouldn't be made to carry the blame for all poachers just because you know who he is."

"What? I don't understand any of that."

"Don't want to you mean. What I meant was that Alec Stratton only goes out for the odd bird or two. He's not one of these city slugs who come out mob-handed with the intent of clearing a wood of birds and slaying a keeper or two in the process."

"Succinctly put. Makes me feel a whole lot more cheerful about the comin' season does that."

"They're your words, David; I'm just repeating them back to you. And if I might say so, now you know what goes through my mind when you go out at night!"

"Point taken."

"But Alec Stratton's not like that."

"You seem to think you know an awful lot about this feller all of a sudden. I'll tell you what you don't know. You don't know that he's not like that."

"Yes I do."

"How? Because Alice said so? Now you're being naïve. None of us know how we'll react in any given circumstance." He stopped for a moment or two before continuing and Stephanie was aware this was new territory for him and so *for her.* "You think you know all about me, Steph, but I'll tell you summat you don't know; I threw Roy onto the livin' room fire once."

"What's a roy?"

"No, Roy. Our Roy."

Stephanie gasped then laughed in her reply, such was her surprise. "What, Roy?"

"Yup."

"Your younger brother Roy?"

"Yup. Onto our fire."

She stood for a moment or two, not quite sure how to react. "Was it alight?"

"Ar. A merry little blaze goin'!"

"You threw... you? But... why?"

"Because he wouldn't share his chewin' gum with me."

"Was it the last of the packet?"

"Not what was in a packet, what was in his mouth."

"What... you wanted some of the gum he was chewing?"

"Ar. Was all he'd got an' I'd got none."

Stephanie stood aghast for a few seconds. "You're pulling my leg, aren't you?"

"Nope; 'onest. Picked him up and chucked him."

She was near speechless now. "Well... what happened?"

"Dad came in when he heard the ruckus. Hauled him off, smacked me round the room... you know, the usual. Ruined our Roy's school jumper. Never did get me gum."

"I should think not!"

"No, he swallowed the bugger out of spite."

"I just..." *She considered the tale for a few moments.* "Well, it's not something I would ever have thought of you."

"An' that's just what I'm sayin'. He's never been caught, your friend's 'usband, Stratton, never been put in that *position, an' mild-mannered folk have been sentenced for some brutal crimes."*

"Alec Stratton wouldn't do that."

"I think you're in danger of romanticisin' this whole thing."

"How?"

"By classin' him alongside one of them nineteenth century, downtrodden, likeable country rogues. Them ones films and stories are so fond of. A sort of field sport Robin Hood who hunts for the pot to feed his starvin' family, who pits his wits against the cruel and brutal Lord of the Manor. He's not. He's just another thief who should find a better outlet for his talents... that bloody Roland Dowel's got a lot to answer for."

"Dahl. Roald Dahl."

"Ar, an' 'im." Stephanie shook her head and turned off the hot tap. "All of Stratton's skills, his fieldcraft, are all used to kill birds illegally."

"Which is what you do, the only difference is two letters."

"May be only a couple of letters to you, Steph, but it sets me an' 'im apart by a library." He thought for a few seconds. "Why doesn't she get him to stop?"

"Because he'd not listen; he's set in his way." She stopped abruptly. "He told her once; said poaching was what made his heart beat."

"He what?" Stephanie just looked at him. "Well, I've heard some bloody excuses for poachin' in my time but 'makes my heart beat' takes the biscuit."

"Well that's what Alice said and I believe her. Seemed tired, sort of resigned when she said it. Will that be us in another fifteen years time do you think?"

"What, me tellin' you I'm a keeper 'cos it makes me heart beat? I don't think so."

"But…"

David looked at his watch and cut the threads of the conversation. "Blimey, Steph, come on! Time's wastin with all this airy-fairy talk that's gettin' us nowhere. You're goin' out with Alice, I'll put up with it. I really do 'ave to get to them birds. Liam and Eric'll be wondering where I am. You'll be with us shortly, after the washin', right?"

"Yes, right… I will."

"Good, just be as quick as you can, eh? Them crated birds will suffer if the temperature gets up."

"Born with a death wish, pheasants."

"That's why I'm 'ere, to protect them from all the various predators…" He looked pointedly at Stephanie. "…Both animal and human that wants to see 'em dead before their time. I'm 'ere to prolong the inevitable but only long enough to get 'em dead on my say so."

"What a charming man I married."

David draped his jacket over his shoulder as he moved out through the back door. "Aye. You didn't know how lucky you were when you pulled me out the sherbet dip, did y'? See you later, twenty minutes tops!"

—⁂—

"Two weeks! Away for two weeks! There's lucky then. What I wouldn't give to be rid of mine for two days let alone two weeks!" Alice lifted the jumper from the pile and held it at arm's length. "What do you think? Might do for an indoor woolly when autumn comes."

After looking at it for a moment or two, Stephanie shook her head. "No. Someone of your high colour needs something brighter than grey. That will just accentuate your ruddy complexion; make you look like Mrs. Punch."

Alice put the cardigan down. "You really do know how to let folk down gently, don't you? You should stop sittin' on the fence and tell me what you really think!"

"My guilty conscience wouldn't allow it. At least I'd not tell you something looked good on you that didn't then watch you go out and look foolish."

Alice let out an exasperated sigh. "Huh…! I don't believe you!" She rummaged around some more. "I thought there'd be at least a couple of cardigans I could find here. I usually get summat to come 'ome with…" She looked at Stephanie. "…Up 'til now at least."

"Ah, but then I wasn't with you to act as guide and mentor, was I?"

"No, an' now you see my point."

"Do you want to go about looking foolish, 'cos if you do I'll just keep quiet?"

Alice stopped and considered. "Do I go about lookin' foolish?"

"No, but you'd be in danger of it if you didn't have your style-counsellor here with you."

"I know about style."

"If your recent choice of cardigan is anything to go by, I'd say what you know about style I could write on the back of a postage stamp with a six inch paint brush."

"That your guilty conscience breakin' perfectly good walls down again?"

"It is."

Hooking her arm through Stephanie's, Alice laughed. "Your guilty conscience will get you into real trouble one day, mark me on that. C'mon, let's get a cup of tea. Since you've been involved I've discovered a whole new look I didn't know I had, an' lost the desire to spend anythin' on it."

"So, style-counsellor and money-manager all in one."

"You will be if it's you as pays for the tea."

They made their way along the trestle tables piled high with clothes and bric-a-brac to where seemingly headless helpers served drinks through a partially roller-shuttered opening. Collecting two plastic cups of vaguely brown liquid, they sat alongside each other on the canvas chairs lining the side wall of the village community centre. Stephanie peered into her cup.

"This is definitely coffee is it?"

"What I asked for, black coffee."

"It's brown."

"It's the lights in 'ere, the fluorescents. Anyway you'll be able to tell when you get to the bottom."

"What, all the way to the bottom before I know what it is I'm drinking?"

"Ar."

"But, if I can't tell by the taste when I start how will I tell when I've finished?"

"Because they put more tea leaves in the tea than they do in the coffee. How you getting' on with knittin' that alpaca wool then? Finished the cardigan for David yet?"

"No, haven't even got a sleeve completed. The pattern's so complicated. There's so many strands of different shades of wool it looks like I'm juggling a spaghetti Bolognese. How about you?"

"Yes, well on the way."

"What, with that pattern you showed me a couple of weeks ago? Alice, I am impressed!"

"Don't be." Alice smiled. "I've 'ad two goes. Got as far as the top of the rib an' first cable before I realised I'd been usin' two different size needles. Been so long since I've done *any, see; rib looked like a field ploughed by a gang of piglets. Undid it, got the right needles, started again, got to the same place an' realised it was an unfair competition, the pattern were gonna win. I've undone it again and started to knit 'im a scarf."*

"Does he need one?"

"No, never worn one in his life, but he'll know better than to turn his nose up at summat I've slaved over for weeks." They both laughed. "No, he'll put up with the wearin', you know, when it's cold, when 'e goes out."

There was a silence after this as both women realised what Alice had just said. Stephanie eventually spoke. "Does he have to do it, Alice, go out at night?"

"Steph, we said, after Leyton's Farm..."

"I know, I know. It's just, Alec..."

"Oh, right. Alec. Of course, first-name terms. Seer's Hill, weren't it?" There was a long moment before Alice continued. "Why didn't you say you'd met him?"

"Because I didn't know it was him."

"Yes you did."

"Not straight away, I didn't."

"Find that hard to believe, but, let it pass. So why not say later, when you realised it was my Alec; my husband?"

"Well, there was no need... it was just a fleeting thing."

"Long enough for you to exchange names and chat about the cathedral."

"If you know so much why quiz me?"

"'Cos up to now you've been reluctant to talk about it, that's why!"

"Yes." Stephanie fiddled with her beaker. "Are you angry with me, Alice?"

"No. Disappointed, not angry. You should've said."

This was becoming difficult for Stephanie and she showed it by biting her bottom lip before answering. "Yes, you're right. I'm very sorry I didn't, very sorry if it seems I've held information from you. It really didn't register at the time and by the time it did it just seemed... unimportant, you know? I mean, it wasn't as though it's had any bearing on our friendship, has it? I realise I should have mentioned it, but it really didn't seem to be relevant and that's the truth."

Alice looked at her for some moments again before speaking. "I'll believe you, thousands wouldn't." Then she smiled. "So, what did you make of him?"

"Well, er... nothing really."

"Find that hard to believe."

"Why?"

"Stephanie."

"Well, yes, but I didn't, you know, didn't take a lot of notice."

"That'll be a female first."

"Alice, we spoke for all of ten seconds, not long enough to form an opinion about anyone." Alice held her gaze. "He seemed... nice, a nice sort, you know?"

"Summat else your ten seconds didn't tell you. Looks can be deceptive."

"Does he not see how his poaching makes it difficult, for everyone?"

"You really haven't been payin' attention, have you? I told you about it before, when we were at the alpaca farm, didn't I? About how there's nothin' he loves above poachin'. Not me, not the kids, the grandkids, nothin'. Remember? 'It makes my heart beat.'"

"Yes, of course I remember, and how upset you were about it."

"I was. Not a nice thing to be told. That what he has at 'ome is somehow lackin', unfulfillin.'"

"I'm sure that's not what he meant."

"You think what you like; I live with him an' speak from a position of privilege, an' that position has taught me summat else too. I've got no chance of makin' him stop so I'm not about to waste effort tryin.'"

"I just believe... I believe he and David would really get on if... They have so much in common."

"There's an arse-about-face statement if ever there were one."

"No it's not. It may seem like an oxymoron at first..."

"Like a what?"

"Oxymoron... arse-about-face statement."

"Why didn't y' say so."

"I just did. I said it may seem an oxymoron at first but I think they could both benefit from becoming friends." There was a silence as they both glanced around the hall at the woolly-rifling hordes. "Has Alec never thought of becoming a keeper?"

"Ha! There's an oil paintin' if ever there were one! We're dealin' with men 'ere, you know? Men. Cow-simple they are. Or as you like to call 'em, oxen-morons."

Stephanie laughed. "Ha! Yes. Agreed. But, why hasn't he? He has all the knowledge, all the skills; he just uses them in a different way from David."

"Illegally."

"Just a separation of two letters."

"What?"

"Nothing, something from earlier today. Surely it'd not be too big a step to make, even for a man."

"Giant. Well, you've met him, so..."

"Once and for ten seconds, Alice, and there's no need to keep underlining it."

"No, maybe not."

"Does it not bother you, all his...?"

"What do you think? What've I just been sayin'? 'Course it does, but I'm old enough to know better than try to change summat in Alec that'll leave me with a man I don't want." Alice stood up. "Enough! C'mon, let's see if we can find some silly hats to put on. C'mon."

Stephanie smiled and stood up too, glad of the excuse to leave the recent conversation. "Right, yes, of course." She laughed and showed her empty cup. "You were right, no tea leaves."

"Then it were coffee."

Stephanie peered into Alice's cup. "No tea leaves either, but you..."

"Yup. I ordered tea, got coffee but still believed I was drinkin' tea. Amazin' how they do it aint it? Off we go!" Alice crushed the plastic beaker, dropped it into a rubbish bin and dragged Stephanie by the arm, away in search of hats.

"Do you think Lordy'll say yes?"

"No reason to think otherwise."

David pulled the last empty crate off the back of the flatbed trailer, grabbing the second rope handle as it slid off, and followed Liam into the barn.

"Was just unsure whether he'd want the new boy on tour with him, you know. My guess is he'd prefer one of the older folk."

"Oi!" Eric looked up from the stack of crates out of which he was pulling the soiled straw from the recently moved poults. "Just you watch who you're callin' old folk! 'Ave you 'eard 'im, Liam?"

"I did, but I knew he wasn't talking about me." Liam looked across *"Were you, Dave?"*

"I wasn't talkin' about anyone in particular; it was just a general inquiry. Like it or not, I'm the youngest amongst us three." He looked across at Eric. *"In some cases by a long chalk."*

"There he goes again! I'll tell you summat youngster, growin' old is better than the alternative."

"There speaks the voice of Methusela."

"Mock on, children, mock on."

Liam dumped the crate onto the floor. *"Don't involve me in this battle of the aged."*

"I'm just tryin' to teach this babe in arms some valuable lessons on life."

"Oh, right. Such as?"

"Well for one, that at both ends of your life the success or failure of your day hinges on whether your bowels 'ave opened or not."

There was a pause then they all laughed. Eventually, David spoke. *"Thank you, Eric, for that gem. Quite how we got there, I'm not sure 'cos we were talkin' about Lordy and 'ow 'e may see me as not sufficiently interestin'."*

"Certain fact that, eh Liam? You're still wet behind the ears, young 'un."

David took off his jacket rolled up his sleeves and joined Eric in pulling out the soiled straw. Gradually the pile grew and the empty crates were ferried over to the waste-water runnel spanning the length of the barn, where Eric began flushing them out with a hosepipe. Liam collected the disinfectant for the final part of the cleaning.

"That'll do for you, Dave. Me an' Eric'll finish off, you get back to your release pen and check on them birds. Oh, an' thank Steph for 'er 'elp this mornin' too, won't y'?"

David needed no second offer. He quickly wiped his hands on a cloth, rolled down his shirtsleeves and grabbed his jacket. "Right. OK, Liam. I'll pass on your thanks when I grab a flask of tea from home afore I get over there."

Eric called across. "Ar, that's it, leave all the hard work with us."

David turned at the barn's opening. "Just followin' my dad's advice, he always told me to wear out the old 'uns first!"

"Any more of that an' I'll ask Liam to send me to the Cairngorms instead."

"Then you'd run the risk of incurring the wrath of Steph an' I'll tell y' now, she's not a pretty sight when she's riled."

Eric laughed. "Ha, I can't think of that woman bein' anythin' other than devastatin' David! You know it, I know it and so does everybody else round 'ere with 'alf an eye. Even today, covered in straw and pheasant shit she still looked great, didn't she Liam?"

Liam slipped the crate he was carrying up on top of the stack. "I have to say, he's right y'know." Liam looked across at David. "She's alright about it though, is she? The grouse... two weeks?"

"Yeah, she's... she's alright about it. Says she'll use the time to get curtains up an' such... decoratin'; spend a bit of time seein' folk. I think she's lookin' forward to it. It'll be the first time we've been apart since we were married. What's that... nine year, so it'll be a novelty for 'er."

"An' you."

"Ar, it will."

Stopping his work, Eric stood up. "I tell you what, knowin' the standard of folk round 'ere, I'd be loath leavin' a woman as well set up as that on her own for more than thirty seconds. What say you, Liam?"

Before he could answer, David interjected. "By the standard of folk round here, I'm assuming you're referrin' to yourself? You're the only one I know who has that glint in his eye every time he meets her."

"That's because you don't pay attention when folk come round. Liam dribbles into his coffee every time!"

"Only when Steph serves it though," *added Liam as he and Eric laughed together.*

"I can't believe you two! This is my lady-wife we're discussin'. If she knew, she'd have our testicles hangin' on a gibbet."

"Nice way to go though," *said Eric and laughed again.* "What you want is a couple of kids, calm you both down and give that lass of yours the matronly look; that'd slow down all the local lechers."

David smiled. "Ar, right, couple of kids... plenty of time for that."

"Not so much," *said Eric.* "What are you, pushin' thirty an' Steph about the same, even though she barely looks twenty? Take my word for it, you'll blink, do a couple of grouse sessions and all of a sudden you're near forty an' it's too late."

"Don't know that we want any... we'll see."

"All women want 'em, David."

Pulling on his jacket, David busied himself with waistcoat buttons. "Like I said, plenty of time yet..." *Eric was about to say something else but David cut across him.* "...An' in the meantime she's got curtains to hang, friends to see an', all things bein' equal," *he looked at Liam,* "I've got grouse to get shot."

Liam walked across. "You 'ave, an' I think Lordy will like a change of partner. Bit of fresh young blood."

He dropped his voice now and looked hard at David. "Your mention of Steph seein' friends while you're away. Does this still include a certain Alice Stratton?"

A second's pause then David nodded. "Yeah, so she says."

"Still on-goin' then?"

"Ar. She's seein' her today as well; at that jumble sale... St Mark's. They're just friends, Liam, and there's no need for anyone 'ere to fret about whether things are bein' said that shouldn't be." Eric had picked up on the conversation and moved over to them. "She'd never compromise us, not the estate nor me, never; I know it. She's told me they never discuss their 'usbands an' I believe her."

"It's been a subject we've talked about; me an' Liam. Aint it?"

"Ar, it is. We trust Steph, Dave, an' you, but we don't know this Alice and that's the scary bit. She could be as slithey a tove as her 'usband, leadin' your missus up the garden path."

"Steph's sharp enough. She's no one's mug and she'll let me know if she even so much as sniffs a set-up goin' on; her conscience wouldn't let her do anythin' else. Really. I absolutely trust her on this."

Liam smiled and nodded. "It don't feel right, I have to say. Havin' the wife of that... that, bugger on our land and friendly with the keeperin' staff to boot."

"She's not friendly with me, Liam, she's Steph's friend. Both of 'em knows exactly how I view it all but I owe Steph the right to choose her own friends."

Liam nodded again. "I've not mentioned it to Lordy. None of his business, not right now. But the minute I smell a rat or we get hit and the coincidences stack up it will become his business, Dave, make sure you understand that."

"I've told y', couple of kids is what she wants. She'll be too bloody busy to get involved in these daft friendships," added Eric helpfully.

"Thank you, Eric; we'll dodge the kids for now. I know I've only been 'ere two seasons but you know my stamp, Liam, you too Eric. I'd not be the one to let you down. Couldn't bear to do that; would kill me."

Liam and Eric were silent for a good few seconds then Liam smiled. "Funny old set-up. Let's just hope they never fall out."

"Thanks Liam. Eric." David left them standing in the barn's entrance as he walked to his Land Rover.

—‍∞‍—

"Goodness, now what!" Stephanie got up from the floor where she had been painting the skirting board, pulling the paint-stained shirt around her waist and tying the ends. Glancing in the hall mirror, she rubbed the paint spots from her cheek with the back of her hand as she went to answer the back door. "That's the second time this morning."

She opened the door to Alec who was standing back in the shadow of the wall. "Oh! Oh, er... Alec." Stephanie looked around quickly. "Is there something wrong?"

"Sorry 'bout this Stephanie, I just needed to get a message across from my Alice."

"You'd best come in before someone sees you." She opened the door wide and Alec moved quickly across. "What's so important?" She closed the door. "I was going to meet her in..." she looked at the kitchen clock, "...Three hours time."

"That's just it, you won't be. She's done 'er back in. Can't even get up off the bed."

"Oh, dear, poor Alice. But why are you…? I mean, she didn't think to 'phone?"

"I said I would, she'd mentioned about your man bein' away at the grouse, but I, er, I didn't know your number an' when I went in to ask her, Alice, she were fast asleep. An', er, an' I didn't think it was fair, you know, to wake her, her not havin' slept well last night like… so… so I come along, you know, to tell you meself."

Stephanie looked at Alec for a long moment. "You never had any intention of 'phoning did you, Alec?" He looked at her but said nothing. "Did you?"

After a lengthy pause. "No. No, I'd not."

"Why?"

"Don't know… just wanted to see you again, I s'pose; just thought…"

"What? What did you 'just think'?"

"I just thought, after you'd run me to the Lion that we'd… got on, sort of… Have I got this all wrong, Stephanie? I 'ave, 'aven't I?"

There was a long, long silence. Stephanie looked round the kitchen, into the hall then back at Alec. "No, not wrong. Look, this is really bad timing."

"I'd best be off. I can see it's awkward."

"No stay! Stay… for tea; just a cup." Alec hesitated, his hand on the door handle. "You can just stay for tea. You've come this far. I'll put the kettle on." Stephanie turned, filled the kettle and put it on the range. Alec released the handle but stayed where he was, just watching. "Grab a chair and I'll get the cake. Made a sponge yesterday."

"Are you sure 'bout this, Steph?"

"Yes, I distinctly remember breaking the eggs and sieving the flour."

Alec stood puzzled for a moment then laughed. "Ha! Got me there. All jokin' aside, you sure? About the tea and cake?"

"Yes, of course! You make it sound like a spy movie. It's just tea and cake. Sit down." She pulled out a chair and Alec sat. Cup-and-spoon-chinking-silence followed as Stephanie made tea.

He watched her move round the kitchen and eventually spoke. "Loose-leaf?"

"Yes, no teabags here, I'm afraid." She looked at the caddy. "What we had at home; I've never known any different."

"Makes a better cup, I'll be bound."

"I think so. Certainly better than putting a teabag into a cup and bypassing the pot altogether. That's why I always drink coffee when I'm out; can't bear the taste of what they serve up as tea these days. Should be strung up for mistreating a drink that's created a nation." She cut two slices of the sponge and put them on plates.

"You're looking at a guilty man then."

"You! I'd never have guessed. You seem too... too, traditional for that."

"Looks can be deceptive." Stephanie coloured a little and turned back to the teapot. "What you decoratin'?"

"Oh, er, the front room. It was a hideous orange and the wallpaper had the largest brown flowers on it that I've ever seen. A case of, 'either that wallpaper goes or I do.'"

"Ha ha! Very good."

"Not mine, Oscar Wilde." She poured the tea and held out a cup and saucer. "Bring it through, I'll show you if you like... if you're interested that is."

"'Course." Alec got up from the table. "I'll get the cake, shall I?"

"Oh, er, yes, please. Forgotten all about that." Alec moved up close to collect the cake, but took the cup and saucer from her instead. Their hands brushed in the exchange and suddenly Stephanie was aware it was very warm and her forehead was moist. "That Rayburn," she

271

said and Alec nodded. "Need it running all the time, cooking and such; but it's the wrong thing to have... at this time of year..." Her voice tailed off and she quickly picked up her cup and saucer and moved out of the kitchen, Alec following her along the hallway and into the front room.

The furniture was stacked at one end and, like the floor, covered with dust sheets. The windows were whitened over and a trestle table was placed in the middle of the room on which there were a couple of opened paint tins together with a brush and paint trays; all the walls were stripped bare and filler had been used in the cracks. Painting of the bright orange skirting board was partially completed.

'Probably what she was doin' when I knocked on the back door,' thought Alec as he placed his tea on the trestle table. "Blimey! Big job is this." He indicated the skirting board. "See what you mean, 'bout the colour."

"Yes, needs a volume control."

"Ar, bright aint the word. The new colour looks a lot calmer. What's it called?"

"Yellow."

"I know that, I mean... Right, got me again... you're good at this. I'll try again. Does the yellow have a name?"

"Primrose."

"Right. Nice name. You doin' it all yourself, no man to do the slog?"

"Not required... grouse has got him, as you already know. I've always done these jobs." She stopped and looked at Alec then changed tack. "Room's bigger than you think at first, from outside."

"Yes, they fool you, these old estate houses."

"They do; it did when I first saw it. There are four bedrooms upstairs and three of them would hold a double comfortably... Listen to me, I sound like an estate agent."

"Plenty of room for kids then."

"Yes… probably." She took a sip from her cup. "Is your tea alright?"

"Oh, forgot about that." He lifted it, took a sip then returned it to its saucer. "Ar, champion… that bit of cake we left behind would go well with it."

"Oh, cake, sorry, I'll just get it."

Stephanie put her tea down on the dust-sheet-covered mantelpiece and walked to the door. As she passed him, Alec took hold of her hand. "Steph…"

"Alec… this is…"

He pulled her to him and they kissed willingly then parted to stare at each other. Stephanie wiped the back of her hand across her mouth. "Goodness, Alec…"

He pulled her close again and as they kissed they sagged slowly to the dust-sheet-covered floor.

—⦿—

Stephanie sat up from the scuffed sheets and tried to pull on her underwear. "Oh, Lord! Lord… what have we done, Alec? Oh, no…!"

Alec sat up. "Got a bit away from us, I think."

"A bit away…? I have no idea what caused that! None!" Stephanie continued dressing in haphazard fashion.

"Good though, weren't it?" Alec's comment stopped Stephanie short for a moment, then she continued dressing. "Weren't it?"

"Alec… Alec this is no time to be discussing the merits of the… the, sex we've just had. I'm married… to a gamekeeper! I'm the best friend of your wife… oh, no, Alice! I'm so, so sorry, she mustn't know, oh, Lord…. Don't just lie there, get dressed!"

"Alright, keep your shirt on."

"That's just it, I didn't! Don't laugh, Alec, it's not funny!"

"There's some irony in this though, you must be able to see it."

"No, no I can't." She looked across at him. "Get dressed! There's no irony here just my own stupidity. Oh damn, damn! What was I thinking of? Oh, God, is that it? Am I a conquest...? Am I?"

"Steph, Stephanie! Calm down. That's not it at all, I was just commentin' on..."

"I know what you were commenting on! That you've... you've... you know?"

"What? I've what? Tell me."

"You've had sex with a gamekeeper's wife! Is that what I am? The ultimate quarry, ultimate conquest?"

"No! Don't you ever think such a thing! I didn't come 'ere to... you know..." He saw the look in Stephanie's eye. "Steph, I didn't, I swear."

"Then why did you? Tell me."

"Alice..."

"No, not Alice! Alice had nothing to do with it!"

"No, alright, it wasn't Alice. I just wanted to see you again and..."

"And have sex with me?"

"No! Nothin' was further from my mind... well not... Look..." Alec could see Stephanie was getting more upset and he began to dress with a little more certainty. "Look, Steph, it can't be helped, it just happened."

"Oh, that's original. 'It just happened!' Excellent defence at my divorce proceedings that'll be!"

"Who said anythin' about divorces? Crikey, Stephanie, slow you down! We slipped up, that's all!"

"I slipped, you grabbed."

"And you fought like a tiger to get loose, right? Look, calm down a bit. As far as I'm aware you've no intention of leavin' David."

"Absolutely! If he ever found out… God, I don't know what I'd do, what he'd do."

"No, and I've absolutely no intention of leavin' my Alice, so the only way they'll hear of this is if we tell 'em."

Now nearly fully dressed, Stephanie calmed a little, but was unable to stop her eyes from filling. "Oh, what have we done? It was all so, so lovely. Now I have to face Alice and be sunny… and David too." She looked around the room. "What a mess!" She lifted a corner of one of the dust sheets and wiped her eyes. "What a mess."

Alec put his hand on hers. "It'll be fine. Look, if anyone's to blame it's me. I shouldn't have come here."

"No, you damn well shouldn't!"

"No, I know, but I did. An' we chatted and ended up makin' love amongst…"

"Having sex!"

"You call it what you like."

"I will, and I say we had sex!"

"Fine, OK then, and we had sex amongst the paint pots."

"I'll have to change the colour. I'll never be able to look at that skirting board again."

"Does wonders for my self esteem does that. Never mind, I still enjoyed it. Didn't you?"

"Yes!" She had answered without thinking. "Yes. I did; it was… But that's not the point is it? Oh, can't you see?"

Her look of helplessness finally got through to Alec. "Yes, I can. Sorry, should've known better. But… I like you, Steph, and I mean a lot. I think you're smart, beautiful, clever, charming…"

She blew her nose on the sheet. "Not so smart, Alec, not so smart."

"No, it's me that's not smart, Steph, you're spot on. It was the right place, right time and wrong thing to do."

"Totally."

"Sorry."

She took a deep breath. "This can't happen again, it can't! Promise me you'll see it for the mental aberration it was and we can just... let it go. Promise me?"

"I'll try."

"Promise me!"

"Can't do that, you'll have to make do with me tryin'."

They completed their dressing in silence then left the room and walked along the hallway and into the kitchen. Stephanie looked out of the window, placing her hand against Alec's chest to hold him back. "How did you get here?"

He placed his hand on hers. "Shanks', how else?"

"Lord..." She removed her hand from under his. "Did anyone see you?"

"Steph... Steph... who is it you're talking to?"

"Yes, but..."

"No buts, Steph, nobody saw me, honest. The only thing that came anywhere near me was the Denham bus an' I reckon that were empty, never on time so no one ever uses it."

"I'll go out into the yard, look around just to make sure..."

"Oh, subtle, that. No offence, I'll stand my own dog, thanks." He took both her hands now. "And believe this of me, you really are some handsome woman Steph, and whatever the outcome, whether we run off together into the sunset or I never see you again, this afternoon were worth every second of anythin' that 'appens."

Stephanie coloured slightly again. "Oh, Alec, I can't, won't. We can't... Please, go."

Opening the door, he glanced around then slipped into the yard. "Take care of yourself, Steph. An' remember, it's our secret."

Stephanie watched as he disappeared round the yard wall and made for the fir copse that flanked the cottage.

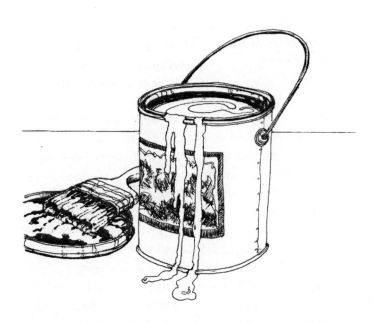

Days 4 & 3 – Tuesday 27th & Wednesday 28th November 1985

"It'll be a travesty, a bloody travesty, that's all I'm sayin'; an' what's my preparation for this travesty that takes place in..." Eric looked at his watch, "...ten or so hours time? Stuck in a pissin' Land Rover with you two."

"Really makes you feel welcome, don't he?" replied David. The night was dark, brooding cloudy with the residue of a storm just passed.

"Well you two are hardly a laugh a minute are y'?"

Liam looked across at him. "Tell you what; we'll both come dressed as clowns tomorrow night, how's that suit?"

Staring morosely out of the steam-sealed windscreen, Eric replied in a continuing monotone. "Oh, very funny that. Marvellous."

"Well it's better than listenin' to you bleating on about things you can't change," said David. "So the boys are gonna shoot part of The Quarry tomorrow. It's what's gonna happen, let's accept it, make the best of it an' move on."

"'Ark at him, will you? I'd like to see you take it as calm if it was your beat. You'd be round to Liam's sobbin' on his shoulder..."

"No he bloody wouldn't," interjected Liam.

"...Sobbin' on your shoulder and demandin' a recount. The trouble with you, Dave, is you don't seem to realise what's at stake."

"Chips? St Joan?"

"Oh, I see, all of a sudden it's you off with the funnies now is it?"

"What do you mean, all of a sudden?"

"Well, you've not been a bundle of laughs of late 'ave you? An' you choose now to brighten up, when the chat demands a serious tone. We're on the premier beat later today..."

David and Liam dived in, talking one on top the other. "The what?" "In whose opinion?" "Premier shite, more like."

Eric talked over them. "The premier beat on the estate if not the county, and what've we got? We got flyin' officer Fairfax in charge of it, that's what we got!" They all laughed a little as he continued, "Give us a fag, Liam." Taking one each, the two men lit up. David sighed and slid a window partially open then all three lulled into quiet introspection.

—⚥—

Fup!

The first suspected shot they heard was a two-fag break later from the direction of The Clump. Liam, David and Eric exchanged glances and slid the Land-Rover-sauna windows wide open to gain fresh-air confirmation of tobacco-air suggestion.

Like a squib in the next street the sound was heard again but clearer now.

Paff!

It almost denied its own existence, but the message was out and Liam was the first to reply to it.

"Fuck me, they're queuin' up this year. Come on!"

Paff!

As he moved along the bridle path toward the brook at Privet Lane, two brace of pheasant held tight by the loops in the rope hung about his neck and nestling inside his trench-coat, Alec heard it too... and the ones that followed.

Paff!

A second pheasant fell amongst the bramble scrub, was retrieved and sent sackwards by the poacher's helper.

Paff!

The fourth travelled the same way as the duo worked toward the top end of The Clump, sticking close to the ride. Their knowledge of the wood was not all it should be, but they were both wise enough in the night arts to know that to venture too deeply into the trees, then follow that with a couple of turns of the head in order to gain a better shot could make them a victim of disorientation, allow the branches to enter the mind, lose direction.

To that end these two had taken every precaution in these unfamiliar surroundings to stay alert and undiscovered. Keep near the riding; only take low birds; only take birds roosting above relatively clear ground; use a sawn-off .410 shotgun, modified with an old grease-gun cylinder taped to the end of the barrel to act as a makeshift silencer. All the preparation was good, the gun certainly quiet, but not quiet enough.

The keepers' Land Rover nosed its way through Privet Lane brook towards The Clump, lights off. The engine, set up for just such an event, was ticking over yet able to haul the vehicle along in a sleazy crawl without stalling and with the minimum of noise. No brakes were ever used on these outings; as on all such endeavours the vehicle was just taken out of gear and allowed to slide to a halt so that no lights showed. Using the grass kerb as a buffer it came to rest now with the front bumper overhanging the lane's ditch. Engine off, the two front doors opened like radar dishes and the whole human world breathed in... and listened.

To a fox even the background noise of the stuttering brook, its waters giggling across the stones strewn along the ford's base, would not have masked the two different sounds made by the vehicle's dripping moisture; but men are not foxes. Humans had gradually relinquished their critical aural abilities in favour of improved eyesight, fine-tuned from when they first began to stand upright to hunt the Neanderthal plains. Indeed, even the most modern of mammals, if cursed with the same level of present-day human hearing, would be classed as deaf. A fox may not be able to put a name to different sounds, but would recognise those made by water landing on soft surfaces, such as soggy leaves or grass, and water landing on hard surfaces, such as stone... or the stretched-taught material of a man's jacket.

Curled into a ball, folding air rifle tucked away, Alec lay motionless as the falling water droplets from the Land Rover's front bumper ricocheted off his shoulder.

Paff!

The effect was immediate.

Liam: "Topside of The Clump."

Paff!

David: "Too quiet for a twelve... that's a muffled .410 more like."

Paff!

Eric: "It is, an' workin' towards the topside; eastern end, above the valley."

A few more seconds.

Paff!

Then Liam spoke quickly, decisively. "Dave, you got change?"

"Yup."

"Right, back to the 'phone box by Baker's. Call Bob. Meet him at Raynes Lane end of The Clump, that's the way they seem to be goin'. You got your stick, Eric?"

"'Course he has," said David.

"The boy's right, I have."

"Right," said Liam. "You and me round to the end of the flushin' point, organise the welcome committee, eh? Let's go!"

Outing from the vehicle, Eric and Liam quickly disappeared around the bend in the lane. David started the engine. Doors still wide open, he backed away from the ditch. The billow of exhaust gases and steam from the well-soaked exhaust pipe caught in the backward air movement and were sucked under the vehicle, only to cloud down into the ditch and onto Alec. Unable to check the protest from his body, he coughed loudly.

The engine slackened off then collapsed into silence. David got out and bent low to check the underneath of the vehicle. 'Nothing'. Back in the vehicle, he turned the key the engine revved and he was away.

Alec curled tighter, closed his eyes and felt the ditch water seep gently into his trousers and plimsolls. 'No time for heroics now. Keepers will be up and down here like yo-yos with this gang of amateurs soundin' off... not to mention coppers. No. Best just suffer in silence and let things 'appen to other folk.'

Paff!

The fourteenth pheasant fell from a tree to the fourteenth shot.

In this last line of ash poles the gathering of birds was easier, the ground being clear of all but leaves. But this was a false prophesy. Had the poachers known the wood better they would also have known that, in their present direction of travel, the growth thickened gradually as it blended into The Clump's flushing cover.

Paff!

Consisting of serried ranks of snowberry, low cut laurel, self-set ash whips and bramble, it was from this very area that much choice Anglo-Saxon could be heard on main covert days. Beaters would jockey for positions on the outside of this homage to the Lost Kingdom, firstly to watch the superb sport and secondly to dodge the onerous task of moving birds from the thick cover that grew here in bearded profusion. Older members of the beating line pulled rank and the younger set were dispatched into this cover like so many terriers. Before long their youthful exuberance would be kept under tighter and tighter control. The vegetation gradually pressed them down, lower and lower, until they were forced to bow to the wood's superiority and move forward on hands and knees. Their compensation was in knowing that their strenuous efforts would be rewarded by gangs of well fed pheasants bursting into the air with all the majesty of a living firework display.

Many of these birds were just as short lived as a firework however for, down in the gully, some sixty feet below the flushing point, stood the line of guns... old hands and newcomers all a-tremble. To do as well as last time, to do better than last time, to impress, to re-impress, to show good form: and those guns on show for the first time trembled the most.

Depending on how they performed those assembled could either consolidate a tenuously held position or take their first step into a career in business, in the city, in politics, in power, and it had been thus for the past one hundred and fifty years. As the first flush of rockets with heartbeats left the Clump's flushing point and made for one's position no amount of prayer would turn them away, just as no amount of prayer would turn away the gaze of other guns. A rapid pulse steam-training through the ears was well known to many who had stood here before. Tomorrow your name could be on the lips of every serving diplomat in the western hemisphere... for one reason or another.

Brabham's Wood, The Quarry, The Clump; these Barn Tor pheasant drives were full of anecdote which had become as much a part of the national and local shooting fabric as the very trees and shrubs that grew on it. Each visitor was offered a rainbow of recollection and once the receptive were touched with it, it became part of their soul. It gave them comfort in old age, in sickness and in health and was their hearth companion; the one thing that could never be taken away, sold on the open market, taxed or defiled – their memories. These age-etched storytellers in turn gained a form of immortality by being able to say as they stood, backs to the fireplace, whisky in hand, remembrance in eyes that, yes, they were there.

In recognition of their service these people were remembered by the woodland's trees through having touched them and by the wood's trackways through having walked them; to have shared in its seasons, its moods and events to become part of a history that no petrified tree-ring could tell; the living landscape's story.

Paff!

As the poachers tied the string around the sack that held sixteen permanently roosting pheasants, so Liam and Eric arrived just outside the eastern flushing point of The Clump; a further anecdote was about to be imprinted on bark and soil.

Telephone call completed, David made his way to the Raynes Lane end of The Clump. Rabbits skittered off the tarmac surface as he drove at speed to where the lane met the main road. Lights off as he rounded the turn into Raynes Lane, David switched off the engine and coasted to the verge. A wait of four interminable minutes then followed until Police Dog Handler Bob Rice arrived; no siren, no fuss, just silent running. Plans were hastily made for this particular drive with the same precision as they would be on a shoot day; the quarry was different, the outcome no less important. It was as David finished quietly imparting his ideas that a further shot was heard.

Paff!

They were in no need of a reminder but Bob gave it all the same. "Still at it then." He rubbed his gloved hands together. "Goody!"

"With a bit of luck one of 'em will be that Alec-fuckin'-Stratton and we can nail 'im at last," David replied in like whisper.

The field vole which had suddenly become the all consuming interest of the tawny owl had been more than lucky of late. For starters, the wee creature had missed his lunch appointment with a weasel earlier in the week through the timely interruption of one of David's Fenn traps. Had the vole chosen a different route; had its weight been sufficient to spring the trap's plate; had the trap already been sprung by fallen soil or an intruding sheep's foot or been locked in a deadly embrace with an earlier lover... But the world is balanced on such coincidences. For the weasel, the dice were loaded differently. The trap was sprung as it crossed the plate and the vole had been able to go on its way, surviving and feeding, keeping itself in peak condition so as to become the prospective next meal of the hunting owl.

As in all games of chance the vole could only gain absolute safety at the expense of absolute secrecy. Moving swiftly along the verge and under cover of its drooping grass, the vole reached its diversion point scent line and, with blind faith that all would be as before, made the dash across the lane. It was not. The scurrying form was spotted by the gliding tawny owl; flight path and speed were rapidly adjusted and preparations for an emergency landing made.

The vole reached the verge on the opposite side of the lane and it careened through the first short strands of grass in its effort to reach the ditch and the beginnings of safety, unaware of the owl banking in anticipation, performing its overhead ballet to tumultuous silence.

Down the bank and into his face crashed the vole and Alec flicked out of the ditch like a released clay pigeon, one hand on his face.

The force of Alec's rapid rise from the foetal position caused the vole to be flipped up and away towards the brook. The fast descending, now very surprised tawny owl back-pedalled with a mighty downward push of its wings, his primary flight feathers brushing Alec's quiff into place and removing ditch water and leaf mould from his face with a stroke of the utmost delicacy. Alec gasped, sucked in air and owl-disturbed debris and dissolved into a fit of coughing.

It was at this moment the relief stockman, on his way back from Home Farm after helping to deliver a particularly difficult calf, turned the corner of the bridal path by the brook.

As Bob Rice tugged the hand brake to send the van jitter-bugging into the gateway of The Clump, headlights full on, Samson was left in no doubt of what was going down by Bob's command.

"Speak, Samson! Speak!"

For the first time since being unkennelled that night, Samson barked as Bob got out the van, moved to the gate and leant on it. He caught the sound of hurried silence and shouted into the wood something to the effect that they were known, located and would be wise to behave, otherwise the dog would be released.

Nothing.

David's lights blazed into the wood to Bob's left, and he too gave a warning shout. The answer came back in the form of rapid movement toward the eastern flushing point. Bob was round to the rear of the van and had the slightly confused dog on a leash in moments.

Samson was genuinely surprised. It was normal for him to eject himself like a bullet from a gun over the front passenger seat and out the van side door in hot pursuit. What he did not know was that out there were friends too. All fleeing humans looked the same in the dark and no one who had ever worked with Samson was allowed to forget that this was The Dog.

This was The Dog that had bitten the pretend criminal, one D.C. Charles, so hard during a village fete police demonstration that seven stitches had to be inserted into the gaping wound, but only after the nurse had dug around in it for fifteen minutes with multiple tweezers in order to remove the embedded material. This was The Dog that managed, by sheer speed and precision muzzle work, to catch and swallow a dropped, family size, lemon meringue pie, allowing only a two inch portion of pastry crust to hit the carpet. As P.C. Robert Rice once put it to the assembled keepers, "When I slip him, you best expect some serious shit."

The wood's gate catch was released as Bob and his mobile jaws entered The Clump. After sixty yards, Samson sounded a renewed variation of his pent up energies at David, who had tapped his way from the left corner of the wood with his stick, driving all before him.

David's greeting, delivered in hushed reverence, sounded more like a prayer than a request. "Jeeeesus, Bob! Keep a strong hold on that bloody dog!"

"You just worry 'bout them," replied Bob.

David's hand dropped instinctively to cover his groin. "I am," he said.

Setting off together, these three drove the quarry towards the flushing point, or at least as together as the now almost hysterical Samson would let them be.

The poachers, who had abandoned their booty and firearm in what they hoped was a secure hiding place – it wasn't; all was recovered by Eric the following day to become exhibit A – entered the flushing cover to find out why it was shunned by all who had previous knowledge of it. Briars and snowberry clumps grabbed at their legs and ankles, and the floundering pair flinched and winced as leaf-bare ash tops whipped back into their faces. No need for secrecy now, they knew the hunt was up.

In front of them, unbeknownst and in silence, Liam and Eric lay in wait. Behind them, well known and loud, was the sound of canine and human pursuers. A break to give heaving chests and straining ears an opportunity to regroup only served to make the sound of the dog's approach ever more clear to them, but now only twenty paces behind.

Alec had found the ten foot length of climbing rope in his father's workshop during the clear-out after the funeral. He had seen his father use it for lashing bean sticks to the cross-bar of his bike, and for several seconds he just stood and stared at it, the memory strong and the sense of his recent loss even stronger; this rope needed to be used. He stared at it for a good while, twisting it over in his hands, then, on the uppermost shelf, he spotted the jam jar with steel rings in it. By plaiting two rings, one at each end of the rope, it became a useful game carrier.

The rope was a little too long but he was loath to cut it. He measured both of the ends from his waist to the back of his neck, folded it at this point and pinched the rope together with some thin string. This would be the resting point on his neck, the rings, one on either side, reached his tummy and the excess would hang down his back in a larger loop. Now he could carry any birds and still have his hands free to continue to shoot; perfect. Tonight Alec was even gladder of the rope for though, as usual, it chaffed his neck with each movement, the birds lodged at either end of it made him look fatter, helping with the disguise.

To complete his subterfuge he began to act drunk... and slightly mad. He lurched to his feet, taking no notice of the staring farmhand who stood on the far side of the brook looking at this particular Kraken waking. Swearing and cursing as he rolled his way drunkenly towards the ford, Alec stared at the farm worker who had decided that discretion was indeed the better part of valour and had backed into the hedgerow. It was known that tramps used this bridle path as a short cut from village to village and, although pretty unkempt, they were a harmless lot. This one, however, seemed to be in dire straits. At midpoint in the brook the dishevelled creature hovered off balance, shouted something about having lost control of his bowel again, missed his footing and stumbled headlong into the water. Any impulse by the farmhand to rescue this poor unfortunate was quickly quashed as the drunkard rose immediately from the brook. The swaying movement caused water to slop out of the filled hood on the coat as the now sopping excuse for humanity, clutching his backside, shaking his fist at an unjust and unmerciful heaven and cursing the trees around him, staggered on past the hedge-hugging farmhand.

—ᴧᴧᴧ—

"My God, look at the state of you! What on earth happened?"

"If I told you, you'd not believe me."

"Look at the time!" Slipping out of bed and putting on slippers and dressing gown, Alice squeezed the hooded coat Alec had dropped over the armchair by the window. "It's soaked you are. Is the rest of you like this?"

"Pretty much, ar."

"Then you need to get into the bath or you'll catch your death." She began to help him off with shirt and shoes. "How the hell did you get into this state again?" She saw his look. "You think you were tidy when you got home last Friday? If you knew how to work the washer you might've got away with it; just dumpin' your soppin' wet clothes in the laundry box meant you didn't."

Alec sighed and sat on the edge of the bed. "Picked the wrong night to go poachin'."

"The way you've been goin' on of late every night's the wrong night."

Alec ignored it. "Amateur night. Place crawlin' with keepers and coppers; I 'eard a dog havin' a go. Come close to nabbin' me."

"What, the dog...?"

This was a first for them both. She never asked, he never told. She knew immediately the status quo had altered; he was slower to recognise it.

"Nah, the dog was after the other bloke. Keepers were close by though; near on run me over if they did but know..." He shut down now. "Nothin'. Nothin' to tell. Just got a bit wet is all."

Stopping in her efforts to remove the second shoe, Alice looked up at him. "Just a bit wet? Then it'll match the damp behind your ears. You think this can go on forever do you?"

"What?"

"You! Runnin' around the county thinkin' you're a ghost?"

"I don't know what you mean."

"Yes you do!" She sat alongside him. "I hate to state the obvious, Alec Stratton, but you're not half the man you reckon you are."

"Well thank you for that."

"You will thank me, one day. If you pack it in before they catch you, y' will."

"I've said before, they're not sharp enough to catch me!"

"They don't have to be sharp, you just get blunt."

Alec stared into the reflection of her words, willing a reply.

Nothing came.

—◦∭◦—

Day 3 – Wednesday 28th November 1985

Coming down the stairs, Stephanie called softly, sleepily into the kitchen. "Is that you? Are you alright?"

"Yeah, fine." David stood by the Rayburn, hands resting on its warm surface looking anything but alright.

"Look at the time..." She entered the kitchen. "It's gone half three. Boys' Day."

"Ar, I know. Don't need remindin'."

"You should have got back a little earlier then, tried to get a little more sleep. Where have you been?"

"Cop shop. Bit of success tonight. Got Bob and that bloody Samson on the job. He soon sorted 'em out."

The catch in Stephanie's voice was audible. "Oh, no! Alec? Alec Stratton?"

"Nah, worse luck. I wish. Coventry boys, both of 'em." He looked at her before continuing flatly. "You obviously don't wish."

Stephanie's expression was of a rabbit caught between fox and buzzard as she sank slowly into the armchair by the stove. "I don't know what I wish." She stopped for a moment then breathed deeply. "I can't do this... When you told me just, told me you'd caught a poacher, the feeling I had was wrong... The wrong way round. This isn't right, it's not right." She looked up. "Help me, David, please."

"With what, Steph? Tell me with what an' I'll do my best." She sat looking at him as he paused and released a shaky sigh. "What's got into you, Steph? Eh? How bad would it have been if I'd said yes? Yes, we nabbed the bastard, caught him red-handed and he's goin' down for it." He took her hand gently in his. "How bad, Steph?" She said nothing. David sat on the arm next to her, unsure of how to react but working on it. She gazed into the middle distance and gently shook her head. David loosed her hand and stood up, his back to the hot stove. "I'm out of things to say. I'm just... I just... I'm gonna make some tea, do you want one?"

"No." Stephanie looked at him for a few seconds. "Thank you."

He picked up and emptied the teapot of old leaves into the compost bucket under the sink. "Can't hang about, I've got outside coverts to feed before light, bloody Boys' Day to cope with an' all on that fifty minute nap I 'ad yesterday afternoon... Christ was it that long ago? An' I hate to state the obvious but its fuckin' poachers like Stratton have kept me awake all night Steph."

"But not him; and there's no need to swear."

He stopped in his tea-making and turned on her. "What's in a name? Eh! Jesus, what is it with him, Steph? With that family? Eh? What is it?" She didn't reply. "That's it, is it? Nothin'. Well I'll tell y' then. Samson don't care who they are an' neither do I, an' there's

293

every need to fuckin' swear 'cos I'm sick of it all! Sick of havin' to justify my job to Liam, Eric, fuckin' Lordy... an' you! All because you 'appen to be friends with a bloody poacher's wife!"

"Not any more, I'm not. Estate priorities have seen to that!"

"No they bloody haven't! That's just it! They haven't! You may not 'ave seen her for a bit but it's like walkin' on eggshells every time his or her name comes up. Jesus, Steph, he's even been round 'ere! Like they're a third person in this relationship! If I didn't know you better I'd say you'd had an affair with him!"

Stephanie snatched in her breath and the blood drained from David's face as he registered her involuntary reaction.

There was a mixture of silent collisions and cataclysmic internal realisation before David spoke.

"Oh, Jesus... Say it's not so, Steph. Say it."

"David..."

"Say it, Steph! Please... just, say it!"

"I can't. It would be a lie."

The crashing teapot shattered the frozen silence which followed.

—⚉—

The first splits in the material of night appeared, showing what colour petticoat the day would be wearing. David moved from sink to rubbish bin, the remains of the blasted teapot resting on the dustpan in one hand, the brush in his other. His face was pale and drawn; Stephanie's was too, but water marked. He dropped the broken china into the bin, replaced the dustpan and brush, picked up the kettle and began to fill it.

Stephanie watched him, the air still full of the explosions, explanations and discussions of earlier. She finally took her courage and spoke, "What are you going to do, David?"

He breathed in deeply. "Now? I'm makin' tea."

"That's not what…"

"Then I'm goin' to give the pen a light feed…" He looked at the clock. "All I'll have time for. Outside feed rides will 'ave to do without now. Then I'll come back 'ere, grab a bacon sandwich then away to Boys' Day."

"That's not what I meant and you know it."

"Well that's the present answer, alright?"

"No, it's not, David."

His eyes were wide, wild, full. "No more, Steph! OK? No more! Let's just stop for the moment, eh? I can't… Please."

"If you won't say what you're going to do then what do you want me to do?"

"I've just said what I'm doin'. I'm makin' tea."

"No teapot."

"I'll use bags…" He looked pointedly at her. "…From that box I bought that's been standin' in the pantry for ages. Make it in a mug. After that, I'm gonna need all my concentration to put up with Eric who'll have a face like he was weaned on a lime 'cos he thinks the boys are gonna fuck up his day. Bugger, swore again. Now, do you want tea?"

"No. Thank you."

"Thought not."

She could see the set look on his face. "David…"

With finality. "You don't want tea? OK. Get y'self back to bed. If you can see your way clear to fryin' the bacon for me at eight, I'd be most appreciative. If not then I'll get it meself an' see you this evenin'. We've decisions to make."

"Yes."

Then it came, simply, lonely, abandoned almost. "I'll sleep in the spare room."

Without waiting for a reply David returned to the stove, placed the kettle on it and pulled a single mug from the line-up in the wall cupboard.

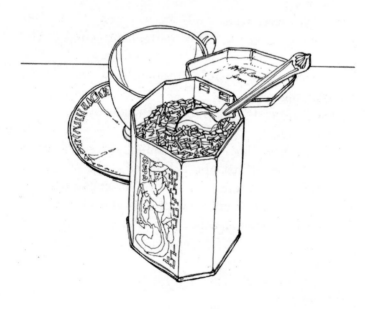

Chapter Ten
Month 3 – September 1985

"What you doin' in there, makin' your will?"

Stephanie turned swiftly toward the bathroom door, gripping the handle as David's knock and call penetrated her fully occupied senses. "No, no, I'm just on my way out... is it desperate?"

"No, I was just a bit worried; you've been in there twenty minutes now. You OK?"

"Yes, 'course... just a bit of tummy upset. Out in a moment." She heard him go down the stairs then concentrated back on her pocket diary and recounted the weeks then the days, just to make sure. No doubt about it, she was definitely, most definitely late. She rechecked the dates. The memory then the horror began to bite; of her fearing David's return, of excuses, borne out of guilt, that she had a urinary infection; of no sex between them since he had got home.

'Oh, Jesus!' She looked up and into the mirror and a bloodless face stared back as she spoke out loud this time. "Oh, God..." She slumped onto the closed toilet seat. "I can't be." Dread and exhilaration in equal measure swam inside her. She looked back at the diary, the sink, the mirror, the diary, the sink... finally at her stomach. Her hand went instinctively to it, cupping its imaginary future shape and then she pressed her palm flat onto it. 'Oh, no... stop it, you stupid... This can't be!' "I can't be...!"

"Steph? I'm gonna have to go!"

She stood up and became aware that her legs were shaking. 'But what if I am? A baby... a real baby...' She let out a long, almost tortured sigh. "Ohhh no, not like this..."

Climbing up a couple of steps, David called again. "Steph! I'm away love, are you really OK?"

"Yes!"

"You don't sound it. I'll stop on if you like?"

David's offer snapped her back. "No, you get off! I'm fine, I think it's just that blasted urinary thingy flared up again."

"I said you should go to the doc's last month, get summat for it."

"I know, I know. I thought the lemon barley would sort it. I'll maybe go if it keeps on. You get off or you'll be late. Will it be alright to skip lunch today?"

"'Course. I'll grab a couple of apples an' some bread on me way out."

"Oh, what about a drink?"

"Eric'll have enough coffee to float a dinghy, I'll be fine."

"You sure?"

"Yeah, 'course!"

"Home when?"

"It'll take the best part of the day to combine that field; five-ish?"

"Right."

She pressed her ear against the bathroom door.

She heard the call for Sack and the back door close.

She breathed a sigh of relief.

She slumped again onto the toilet seat.

—⁂—

Dust from the combine's rear chute billowed up and David moved slightly to his right to avoid the cloud of chaff.

His attention was focused onto a waving Eric some sixty yards away on the other side of the crop; David waved back and Eric pointed. Moving out from the line of the disappearing combine, he alerted Liam with a piercing whistle. Liam picked up the signal. David part opened the gun's chamber rechecked the load and snapped it to.

The combine was chomping away twenty yards ahead when it suddenly stopped and Mark Chayter, the driver, left the cab and began to whistle, wave his arms and shout. "Dave! Dave, your way!" The fox cub broke cover behind the combine and skittled across the fresh stubble toward the nearby hedgerow and safety.

David lifted the pump-action shotgun to his shoulder flicked the safety catch and his finger barely caressed the trigger. The cub made a forward roll to stretch out to the sound of his first and only shot. He held his thumb up to Mark and Eric then walked quickly over to retrieve the body. Back in the combine's cab, Mark set the massive machine into motion once more as further areas of fox-safety were chewed up and spat out.

The cub was a decent size, probably February born. At eight months old it was already capable of massive damage to the game on the estate, if the opportunity had presented itself. David turned it over with his foot. A dog, good coat, brush, well fed, so its mother had obviously been hunting well. He picked it up and held it aloft for Liam to see, then, with an eye on the combine's progress, he walked a few yards away from the edge of the standing wheat.

He dropped the corpse near his coat and alongside the feverishly active but securely pegged Sack, who pounced onto it with throaty growls. David quickly pulled another couple of cartridges from his jacket, slipped one into his waistcoat pocket the other into the gun's chamber, and moved back to the freshly cut crop line.

'Was that Alec? No, not possible, you're seeing things my girl.'

Stephanie stared down the length of the market stalls. The press of people made it difficult to focus on individuals but she was sure she had seen him. She turned to look down the opposite line of stalls. Alice was serving customers but looked up just at that instant. Stephanie pulled back quickly behind the canvas, her mind racing.

'What the hell are you doing here?' she thought. 'Why did you come at all? Guilt? Damn guilt! This is stupid and you need to go home, you know nothing for sure.' She turned and slipped back through the gap in the stalls. Coming out onto the next concourse she bumped into Alice.

"I thought it were you! Were you not coming to see me?"

"Alice! Yes! Yes, 'course. Just looked as though you were very busy. I was... was going to come back when things had quietened down."

"No you weren't, you've got no bag an' were creepin' off like a cat with a stolen fish! You ought to know it never gets quiet 'ere. I've a coffee break in five minutes, what say we grab a quickie at the van?" Alice smiled. "Come on; get yourself down to the stall before then, eh? We got some lovely early russets on offer, fresh in. They smell like Christmas. Come on!" Stephanie hesitated and Alice felt the resistance. "You alright, Steph?"

"Yes, no... I mean, I just don't want to seem like I'm... like I'm using you or anything like that."

"Usin' me! What you talking about? You'd never be accused of doin' that, your conscience would get the better of you. Now, stop this foolishness and come on!" She hauled on Stephanie's arm and trooped her down to the stall.

The combine was vomiting its load into the waiting trailer by the gateway, leaving the final, seventy two foot wide strip of wheat and its suspected vulpine inhabitants to the kind ministrations of the three keepers.

"Eric! To you... Eric!"

David ran the line of wheat straw, lifting the shotgun to his shoulder a couple of times as the half-glimpsed red quarry bristled its way along the shrinking strip of uncut wheat. Liam stood his ground some hundred yards distant, legs spread slightly for balance, shotgun at shoulder. Eric moved slightly back so as to give himself a clearer shot should the fox emerge on his side. David came to a halt and lifted his shotgun again. All three now looked cast in stone as they waited on the fox's next move.

Time flicked to overtime. Gradually the effort of holding guns at the ready told on arm muscles and all three began to relax their position. Eventually Eric called across to David.

"It's laid up! If there's more than one an' they spilt up we'll lose one of 'em if we aint careful. Drop back and let Sack in, Dave, this end, while the combine's away. She'll flush at least one bugger out."

Sack was at the extent of her lead, up on rear legs, tail and tongue wagging and ready for action when David got back to her. "Sack, get down, good girl, get down." He slipped the lead free of the screw-peg. "Come on lass; let's sort this ginger sod out, eh?" The terrier hauled David to the wheat.

As he moved back to the opposite end of the strip, Eric called across. "Liam! Dave's gonna turn Sack in!"

The call was acknowledged and Eric stopped thirty yards short of the wheat ready to move once Sack was slipped. David unclipped the lead on the near levitating terrier. "Get on, Sack!"

The terrier catapulted into the wheat, her bow-wave of movement as she snaked her way left and right in search of the elusive vulpine hoard made her progress easy to follow. Suddenly she stopped and David called out. "She's onto summat, Eric!" David's call coincided with the appearance of a second fox cub. Eric lifted his gun. "Watch the dog!" David's second call greeted the arrival of Sack in hot pursuit. "Sack! Sack! Leave it! Leave!" The terrier slowed to the command.

Looking along the barrels, Eric saw Sack in line with the shot and paused at David's repeated call. This hiatus gave the cub cause to believe in divine intervention; it was a cruel lie. The time gap was only introduced by Eric to allow a safer shot: to increase the angle between pursued and pursuer. The young fox came on sideways and he timed the single shot to perfection. The cub collapsed in an instant, only to have Sack fall on it before it had completed its second death roll. Eric held his thumb up.

"Sack, leave it!" David's call as he ran round to leash up the dog fell on deaf ears as Sack pounced and ragged the corpse. "Shot, Eric. Sack, leave!" He slipped her back onto the lead. "Christ, will you do as told!" The dog continued to growl at the lifeless cub.

"Ayup, Dave! Liam wants her back in, looks like it is a trio then; try an' beat the combine to it."

Moving rapidly round the wheat to his previous position, David indicated to the combine driver then slipped the lead again. "On y' go lass, find him!" Sack sprinted off. "Watch out for the dog!"

"Wet and warm it may be, tea it certainly aint."

Alice and Stephanie were leaning against the rear of the tea-and-fry-van parked at the far end of the market, plastic mugs in one hand, Alice with the remains of a bacon sandwich in her other. "You sure you don't want one of these? Tea's rubbish but the bacon's lovely, oak-smoked." Stephanie shook her head and remained staring along the aisles, unable to meet Alice's gaze. "What's up? You've not seen me for three weeks an' hardly say a couple of words when you do. You acted like you'd seen a ghost when we met up. What's wrong?"

Stephanie's eyes filled. "Alice... Alice, I've been such a f..." She was unable to complete her sentence and her shoulders shook in silent sobs.

Placing her tea and sandwich to one side, Alice took out a handkerchief from her apron pocket. "Steph? What is it? Tell me."

Wiping her eyes determinedly, Stephanie shook her head. After a few seconds she drew in a huge breath. "Alice, I've been really, really stupid. I think... I think I might be pregnant."

"Oh, that's... oh my God; but... you said a while back, about how you and David couldn't have kids."

"David's not the father."

Alice's jaw dropped and then she slowly closed it. "Bloody hell! That's it, drip feed the information out why don't you? You think... blimey, are you? I mean are you sure?"

"About what, that I'm pregnant or that David's not the father?"

"Both."

"On the first count I'm reasonably certain, on the second I'm absolutely certain."

"Jesus, Steph. Well, what happens now?"

"You haven't asked who the father is."

"Would you tell me?"

"No, not until it became absolutely necessary."

"Then no point in askin' is there, and it's none of my business anyway. So, I repeat, what happens now?"

"I leave it until I'm absolutely certain then face the music... with all concerned."

"Oh, bloody hell. He's married, aint he?"

Stephanie nodded and began to fill up again but forced herself through it. "My fault, no one else to blame."

"Oh, so the chap you did it with, where does he figure in this? No blame there, no, 'course not. Or maybe there was no one and it was an immaculate conception." Stephanie smiled briefly in spite of it all. "Well then, no need to be so 'ard on yourself. There's two folk involved in this an' he's got summat to answer for as well." She thought on for a moment. "Is there a future in it? For either of you?"

Stephanie gulped back her coffee. "Sorry, Alice."

"For what?"

"For dumping this lot on you. Not fair, needed to talk, just feel so guilty..."

"Of what? I've told you before about this. Us girls need to stick together." Stephanie began to cry again. "If we can't do that then we're in big trouble."

Stephanie was now crying silently but uncontrollably. All she could do was nod at Alice as she turned and made her way back towards the car park as Alice called after her.

"Steph! Stephanie...!"

Sack scampered and twisted her way through the crop whose stalks parted like a rush-hour crowd as she searched for the rapidly-running-out-of-space fox; she even caught a glimpse of its ruddy tail. It was only the approach of the combine harvester that caused the terrier to alter course in order to dodge the flashing cutter-blades and rolling spikes that were gathering the crop into its ever open maw.

Eric held his hand aloft and called out, "Hold up, Mark!"

Mark lifted the cutter and the combine bounced to a halt as he let it idle and left the cab, stepping out onto the side plate. He stood for a few seconds then traced a line in the crop with his finger.

"Dave! Making its way back to you… your side! Dog's up front, she'll miss it! Liam! Up here! On 'er way!"

David moved swiftly round towards the chaff chute as Liam stepped smartly along the crop line towards the front of the combine. At that same instant, with the cutter head lifted, Sack could see through to other end of the machine. Registering a flash of vixen, she cannoned under the machine's belly, cutting across the vixen's escape route. Launching out from the dust and falling straw, the vixen saw David lift the gun and flick off the safety catch and she did an about turn, back towards the wheat as a snarling Sack exploded from the crop alongside her.

—⁂—

Stephanie looked into the bathroom mirror and spoke out loud.

"You look like the wreck of the Hesperus. He sees you like this and he'll chunter it out of you in no time." She tied her hair back. "Wash and brush up, come on!"

After several moments spent with her face in the bowl of cold water followed by a liberal application of elderflower eye gel, she brushed her hair and began to put on a little make-up. The opening of the yard gate stopped her from completing her work. Leaning out of the bathroom window, she saw David enter the yard, a wrapped cloth in his arms.

"Hello, love, you're soon back. Not even half four. Where's Sack? Oh, no… where's my baby, David? What have you got there?"

David stopped and looked up at her.

"Sheet full of bad news, Steph."

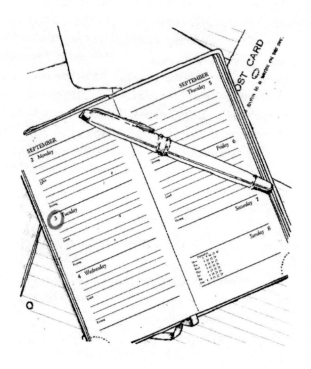

"'Ere 'e goes look. Goin' to get 'is marked deck."

Eric voiced the opinion of all three keepers. They were gathered a good distance from the main duck lake in readiness for the first drive of the day. His Lordship walked to his Range Rover to initiate the ceremonial peg allocation to the guns. This first serious morning of Barn Tor's shooting season may have been called Boys' Day, but it was anything but child's play.

The form, the show, it all had to fit an unwritten set of rules and symbolisms. These were the legacy of the Edwardian double-gun shooting party, and its inheritors, His Lordship's two boys Stephen and Edgar, were today's centrepieces.

For these young pretenders and their friends, freshly back from universities and boarding schools, bursting with enthusiasm and accompanied by giggling sophisticates, it was an opportunity to unload their social hamper stuffed full with the desire to impress. A chance to captivate the bevy of beauties who accompanied them; to cement future liaisons between the country's ruling elite; to keep the conveyor-belt of great English families moving. Or, as Eric once put it, "to fuck their way t' the top at the post-shoot party."

Tom, His Lordship's loader-chauffeur, left the others assembled by the game cart and moved over to join the three keepers. He was greeted by a communal, "Mornin' Tom".

"Mornin' all." He tipped his cap and gave them a knowing smile. "Ready for the surprise draw then, are we? I can't believe they'd fall for it each time, and they still use his deck every year. What a shower!"

"Kids, Tom," whispered Liam. "They're just kids, remember. Think they can rule the country an' not dry behind the ears yet."

Eric looked at the cartridge bag Tom had over his shoulder and gave a low whistle. "Bloody-hell, am I seeing right? Is that a new bag, Tom? Has he finally forked out for a new one then?" He squeezed the top flap of the bag. "Nice bit o' leather that."

Tom rolled his eyes. "Aye, 'tis that." Then he added in an over-loud voice. "An' no bloody good neither!"

Eric smiled. "That right? Looks alright to me. How come?"

Tom took on the voice of the expert, glad of an audience ready to appreciate the finer points of cartridge bags. "Well... look at it! Front lip comes over too far an' it's got a steel rim, so the front's that bloody stiff." He demonstrated. "See? I 'ave the devil of a job gettin' more than one cartridge out at a time. Like the monkey an' the sweet jar. You could turn it upside down and they'd stay put..." It was during Tom's continuing diatribe that, one by one, the keepers gradually became aware of His Lordship's frantic scrabbling in the glovebox of his Range Rover. "I've told him to chuck it an' let me get a new one, I have. But he won't, 'cos some daft bugger's give it him see. So it's a free one, see... tight fisted sod. I'll sort the bugger out one of these days though, so I will, then he'll 'ave to get a new one. Canvas, I'll be bloody bound-sure; like the last one we 'ad."

The scrabbling continued and Eric whispered eagerly. "Ayup. He can't find it; he can't find his rigged pins! That means he won't be able to draw peg number one for the duck, an' if..."

The group shushed Eric and listened further to the hysterical scratching as His Lordship tried to locate his peg holder. Gradually the collective smile spread.

"Now we'll see some bloody fireworks," continued Eric. "An' you'll be for the high jump, Tom."

"No, I'll not! He won't let me touch that little gizmo of 'is; always insists Christopher packs it for 'im. Well, he's not by the sound of things." Tom looked across to the other loaders whose conversation had also ceased. "Have the flankers been sent out?" Liam nodded. "Then serve the old bugger right. We're too far from the 'ouse for 'im to send back. Much longer and them wild duck'll be gone. He'll have to ask if anyone's got a set. Poor old Chris. He's never forgot to pack 'em yet... an' today of all days. First time through an' all!"

"It's about bloody time," said Eric. "He'd've been shot in the Wild West for the fiddle he's done with them pins over the years. An' all the guns who come here regular know just what he's like an' still they say nothin', creepin' sods. Almost makes doin' the part-drive in The Quarry worth it just to see his face, eh Dave?" The noise from the Range Rover grew until it resembled the desperate attempts of a terrier trying to get at a well-lodged rat. "You alright, Dave? You've not said two words since we met up."

"He's right for a change, you've been uncommon quiet this mornin'. Are you alright?"

"Yes, I'm fine, Liam. Just a bit of a headache."

"Booze."

"Lack of sleep, Eric. Just lack of sleep."

The continuing noise was just on the point of becoming embarrassing when His Lordship stepped from the vehicle. "Awfully sorry. Can't seem to find the peg pins. Has anyone else got a set?"

These last words were uttered as a throwaway line but his stunned audience was now fully aware of the significance of this invitation, the two sons in particular. They all reacted to the request with undisguised alacrity.

The team of guns and even one or two of the loaders moved as one to their respective vehicles, determined to cash in on this piece of good fortune. Eric indicated a three hundred year old oak in the park close by. "If they can't find any, what's the bettin' they fall on that oak with their collective pen knives and whittle a set?"

All were united in their search. They did not care who drew peg number one for the first drive – which meant getting the best peg at The Quarry, the day's third drive – as long as it was not Lordy. His Lordship's phrasing of "Oh, good," to the announcement that a set had been located certainly lacked conviction. His second "Oh... good," when he drew peg number four almost dripped contempt.

"Duck first drive," said Eric with badly hidden glee "They all get plenty there. That means he'll be peg number..."

Eric's celebrations were cut short by the arrival of His Lordship. "We'll move off now then, Coyne! I'll bring them in from the bottom corner of the lake, in silence as usual."

"Right M'Lord. Will you 'ave your dog with you?" asked Liam, knowing full well what the answer would be but feigning innocence.

"No. Not for this first one. I'm round the corner in the willow scrub. Peg four."

They were as happy as sand boys at the prospect, and Liam emphasised the number and looked at the gathered keepers. "Peg four! On that narrow bank. Right, Sir. You'll be wantin' a picker-up sent round after the drive then?"

"Yes, I will," replied His Lordship tersely. "I'll collect Ganymede after the duck drive."

"OK, Sir. Leave it to us." Liam cut short any further conversation. "Right beaters, load up! Stops with David! Cyril? Drop us at Hickman's farm then take the beaters' trailer round to the far side of the Ling. Holm Wood next drive so you'll be on the right side to go on stop by the laurel break. OK?" Cyril nodded and the whole scene swung into action. Guns, loaders and pickers-up went to their respective vehicles as the beaters filed onto the trailer and the day, for better or for worse, got under way.

The duck drive off Ling Mere went well considering it was first time through. The ducks' habit of circling before moving off to other open water meant everyone in the line got plenty of shooting. This year a larger than usual number of wild duck were mixed in with the reared birds and this made for testing shooting. Centre pegs here were of no advantage but, even as the first group of mallard rose up and came over the line of guns, so His Lordship declared his dissatisfaction with the day's proceedings. Guns often moved a step or two from their pegs in order to gain the best position for the next shot so, for the first few changes, Tom kept alongside. It was when the distance between them and their official peg grew, and they appeared round the corner that hid their peg from the rest of the shooting line, that Tom's anxiety increased. He touched his cap and murmured "Sir", at the young gentleman and his loader at peg five, as he and His Lordship moved along behind them, swapping guns as they went. This gesture was also repeated as they passed peg six.

With the drive's starting point being so far back, it was only when the beating line reached half way that word was passed along the line as to His Lordship's behaviour. Eric, on the right hand side of the beating line, moved out to the flank to take a look. Sure enough, there was His Lordship moving moth-like between pegs seven and five, banging away with the best of them and ruining everyone's concentration. No one was quite sure who was going to shoot which bird, and the confused outcome was leading to the same bird regularly being shot twice; the second time often when it was already dead. Meanwhile, the guns at pegs three and five were stretched to cover the gap left by an empty peg four. Flying true to form, the duck had spotted this weakness and were streaming through the gap.

Eric's voice rang out. "Stay by your peg, M' Lord, please!"

"Lordy won't like that."

Liam's comment reached David just as he thought it.

He didn't. Even knowing it would have been bad form to dissent in public when one was so clearly in the wrong didn't stop His Lordship from throwing a haughty look towards the disembodied voice. He moved petulantly back, shooting continually as he went and the final bag of duck spoke volumes about his behaviour.

Lordship and loader reached peg four just at the close of the drive and, as the keepers moved towards the line of guns for the pick-up, His Lordship scampered off to his Range Rover on the pretext that the ground around his peg had been very wet and he needed a change of footwear.

"What's he bloody doin', Tom?"

"Don't ask me." Tom was slipping the guns into their sleeves. "We was Flanagan an' bloody Allen goin' along that line! I didn't think he was serious at first, but it got bloody embarrassin' when it turned out he was. I'll try an' stop him, Liam, but you know what he's like. Makes me look a right idiot, don't he?"

Liam looked in the direction of the Range Rover. "Well, let's hope it was just a sulkin' fit after drawin' the wrong peg. Eric gave him a shout."

"Ar, we heard. He weren't keen, but knew he were in the wrong."

"Well, maybe he's got it out his system and he'll stop behaving like a baby that's lost its tit. Let's just hope." They parted company, neither of them at all convinced they had solved the problem.

"How's it gone then?" asked Eric, almost before Liam was within earshot.

"Well, you can imagine how Tom's feeling."

"Never mind bloody Tom!" replied Eric. "What about that daft sod with him?"

"Steady, Eric," said Liam, calmingly. "I expect it were just a sulkin' fit. Tom's gonna have a word. We'll just 'ave to 'ope he don't do it on the next drive. It's Tom I feel sorry for, tryin' to keep Lordy under control."

"He wants to stand his ground. Make Lordy come back to him."

"He can't do that, Eric; you know damn well he can't. Let's just see how the next one goes. Alright?"

"But, Liam..." Eric's voice was almost pleading. "It's Holm Wood next an' then The Quarry! What if he goes walkabout there? Then what do we do?"

"We'll adopt Plan B," said Liam as he moved away to the assembled beaters.

"Oh ar? And what's Plan B then?"

"Fucked if I know, I'm makin' this up as I go along. Geoff, Mark, Richard! Get round the far side of The Quarry, you're on early stop." He half turned and smiled at Eric. "Alright?"

Eric nodded in Liam's direction. "Thanks, Liam."

"Just tryin' to do what we can, eh? Cyril, take Dave plus another five to the other side of Holm Wood." He looked around. "Where's Dave? Anyone seen 'im?" The beaters around him shook their heads. "What's got into him today? He's not said two words, an' now..." David came over the gate that led away from the flight ponds, half a dozen mallard in his hand, wet, panting Labradors at his heel. "Oh, there you are. Where you been?"

"Collected a couple of runners and took these off the pickers up. Two are gonna stay on an' clear the other runners an' divers... that alright? Were you waitin'?"

Eric looked at him. "Not so you'd notice. How's that head?"

"Still on me shoulders. Just. It'll clear as the day goes on, but thanks for your concern."

"Mine?" Eric smiled at him. "No concern of mine. I couldn't give a fuck; it's Liam that's concerned."

"Enough chaps. Come on, we've got a big day 'ere, let's waste our concern on that! Right, Eric, you get off an' feed The Quarry. Join us in the line as soon as you can."

"I'm away."

"Cyril. Drop Dave and the rest off on them hedgerows leadin' to Holm Wood then take the trailer to The Quarry. Leave it by the big gate on Jackson's side, with the motor runnin', that'll make any birds think twice about buggerin' off; then make your way back to the

314

point of the wood and stand on stop. Come on! Let's get on with it!"

With The Quarry stopped off much earlier and fed much later than usual, the reduced number of beaters tapped the outlying hedgerows back into Holm Wood and then began to line out. Just as they set off Eric joined them and took his correct place in the beating line. His Lordship, officially at number six in the shooting line, should have done the same – he did not; should have felt satisfied with the amount of shooting coming his way – he was not. The drive was barely half way through when a message came back that he was once more taking a stroll. Eric turned to Keith Edwards, the beater to his left.

"I might've bloody knowed it! He wants them high birds he usually gets, them ones that turn back!" His voice rang out loud and clear once more. "Stay by your peg M' Lord. Please!" Eric turned back to Keith. "What the 'ell's 'e doin'?"

What His Lordship was doing was abandoning peg six and moving between four and five, giving a fair impression of Newton's Cradle, accompanied by a very confused and embarrassed Tom.

"He's not stretchin' his legs again, is he? Hold the drive!" Liam continued to mutter to himself. "All them bloody birds going out on the flank and no one there to salute them. This is gettin' bloody silly." Gradually the flood of birds dwindled to nothing as the line of beaters came to a standstill but continued to gently tap their sticks. Liam added his plea to Eric's, "Please, M' Lord! Stay by your peg!"

Liam's rank gave him much more authority and must have registered; it certainly did with Tom. His Lordship knew he was skating on thin ice now and his only possible choice was to return to his official peg. Followed by a very sheepish Tom, he moved back and the drive continued. The victory was a hollow one though, for, at the close of the drive, His Lordship was nowhere near his peg. Once again he had moved a distance of twenty yards towards the next peg down, which happened to be Mister Stephen's.

Liam heaved a sigh as he and David came together. "This is turnin' into a farce. If he fucks about at The Quarry we'll be facin' a disaster... ayup, here comes trouble."

"What the bleeding hell is he playin' at?" Eric joined them. "I can't believe he'd be so bloody spoilt! I want eight hundred today, I'll be lucky to get four the way he's poncin' about! Can't we nail his feet to the spot or summat?"

Liam nodded in sympathy. "Or drive a wooden stake through his heart. They're back at the vehicles havin' drinks so I'll have another word with Tom and one with him. Not that it'll do any good. Get the beaters on the trailer an' off to The Quarry. I'll see what I can do..." His voice tailed off as he left them.

Tom was alone again, where His Lordship had abandoned him after the drive. The guns were away in their sleeves and he was struggling with the new cartridge bag, complaining in mumbled tones.

"Like trying to pull cartridges out of a duck's arse..." He looked up. "Sorry Liam. I know, I know. I tried stayin' by the peg. I even moved back after each change; we ended up six yards apart after the fourth swap. If he keeps on like this I'll get through three pairs of boots, an' by the end of the day I'll be loading at Barn Tor while he's shootin' in

Lincolnshire! He just says, "Cam along Tom, nevah mind the keepahs, they won't shout at you old chap!", an' he's off! All 'cos he didn't get the right number at the start of the day. I 'eard him mumble summat about them bein' his birds anyway. You can't credit it can y'? It's his children that's out shootin' today... his kids; it's supposed to be their day!" Tom paused in his tirade then redirected his aggression onto the only available article. "An' this soddin' bag!"

Liam didn't push it. He knew the unenviable position Tom was in; Lordy on one side, the keepers on the other.

"OK, Tom. It aint gonna help you but I'll 'ave to go an' 'ave a word. Eric's fit to be tied. He can see disaster gallopin' over the horizon... so can I. Just do your best to keep him by that bloody peg. We've got The Quarry next, new peggin' an' all; he's got to stay put there. Any gap an' he'll wreck the whole thing an' I'll not be answerable for Eric then." They parted, Liam to face Lordy, Tom to face having to use 'that soddin' cartridge bag' for the next drive too.

On his way to the face-off, Liam mulled over the possible approaches he could make. Contrary to popular belief the days of serfdom were still very much alive and kicking in the Shires. The last thing needed in this situation was to go into it like a fox in a full henhouse and show His Lordship up in front of his family and guests, but the situation could not be allowed to continue. Liam knew it, the other guns, keepers, loaders, beaters and dogs all knew it; it just needed His Lordship to agree and the vote would be unanimous.

Liam moved towards the group of guns and loaders gathered by the vehicles. Most of them were having drinks, pastries and hot beverages and, as Liam strode over, everyone knew why he was there and who he wanted to see.

"Ah, Coyne!" His Lordship had obviously decided to meet the problem head on. "Very good day, what?"

Liam stopped several feet short. "Could be better, M' Lord. Could we just 'ave a word about the next drive? Slight change in the method, as you know, and I'd just like to make it all clear with you, Sir." Liam stayed where he was and it was obvious Muhammad would have to go to the mountain.

His Lordship left the group. "Yes, Coyne?" he said, loudly and with exaggerated bonhomie. "What's the problem?"

"As you know, Sir, after our talk in the gun room, we're to cut into The Quarry between the cliff and the release pen."

"Yes, and most grateful I am for you all agreeing to include it today, Liam..."

The use of his first name by His Lordship was an interesting gambit, but Liam was not going to be chummed into anything and ploughed on in the same serious tone.

"We'll be drivin' it a little left handed to allow for the new peggin' an' today's breeze. I just want to make sure..." Liam dropped the level of his voice "...Absolutely sure, that the guns stay in their position. Right through the drive. You know, by their pegs. From start whistle to stop. Otherwise we'll be pushin' the birds into empty spaces. The keepers have spent a lot of time organisin' this for today, Sir, for Mister Stephen an' his guests... All very new."

"Yes, and very grateful..."

"If you'll just 'ave a word with the guns, especially the newcomers, the younger ones. Make sure they all understand how important it is for them to stay with their pegs. Sorry to put the burden on you, Sir, but I know you'll lead by example and I'd much appreciate it." Liam paused for a fraction longer than necessary, then added, "So would Eric."

"Certainly will, Coyne. Leave it to me." With a beaming smile, His Lordship turned away and moved back to the guns. "Certainly will."

Liam was not quite sure he had been understood and he reran in his mind the process involved in setting up and completing the altered Quarry drive, but the more he thought, the more damage he could see His Lordship doing if he persisted with his present attitude. Eric was going to take some convincing too.

Eric was grateful that Liam had seen fit to make an early placement of stops at The Quarry, but even so, the recent difficulties with His Lordship were uppermost in his mind. "Did you have a word?" he asked as soon as Liam got close.

"Did the beaters bring back that maize on Jackson's?"

"Yeah."

"Many in there?"

"Enough for this drive on their own."

"Like that were it."

"It were. The stops are on the hedges that run away from the Quarry valley bottom, pen them buggers in. Did you have a word?"

"I did. But I don't know we were listenin' to the same programme. He seemed to take it all in 'is stride. My opinion? He thinks it's someone else's fault. No moanin', no shoutin', I've still got a job."

"Jesus, Liam, does he know it's the bloody Quarry we're doin' next?" Liam could almost see the anxiety in Eric's voice. "If this goes arse over tit we're in deep shit for the day, you know that don't y'?"

"What's this 'we' bit, Eric? From here on you're on your own!" His effort at lightening the situation was in vain. "We're doin' the best we can. I can't be in the shootin' line an' 'ere at the same time, neither can you. All we can do is hope he stands his ground. Dave will see the most 'cos he'll be Lordy's side; he'll keep us posted."

"If he's payin' attention, ar, but the way he's been actin' today?"

"I know, I know. If I get a chance I'll 'ave a chat. Bloody hell, it's like runnin' a crèche... present company... Right, let's get on with it." This last was said like the final words to the condemned man. Eric grunted and moved off toward the centre of the line of beaters. "Tell Dave we need to know as soon as anything's amiss. Impress it on him," added Liam to the slowly retreating, hunched back of Eric. "OK, beaters! Let's blank it through. And take it bloody steady!"

The line moved off, sticks tapping gently through the cover and over the ride where the guns would soon be standing, sixty yards from the quarry face. At the base of the steep bank a hushed comment came from Liam to the beaters. "Watch your step, don't do nothin' clever... an' if you have to use the cross paths on the cliff go real steady, watch out for them tree roots... an' no dogs that way! Up you go!"

With dogs kept close to heel the climb began; the noise from gasping smokers accompanied the team of canine and human exertion to the summit. Once on the top the beating team filtered off left to the drive's new starting point.

The blanking-in had gone without a hitch, and judging by the numbers of birds moving ahead, even in its reduced form, the drive promised to be memorable. By now, guns and loaders were moving into position and the doors to pheasant-escape were being sealed.

The sewelling – strips of brightly coloured plastic attached to a length of rope that stretched right along the edge of the quarry precipice – was put into place on its supporting sticks. When faced with this new addition to their once familiar landscape, plus the noise of the approaching team of beaters behind them, the pheasants would decide to sit tight. This meant the birds could be teased out gently, thereby prolonging the shooting, rather than have them leave in one big flush.

"I'll detail the sewelling-twitchers, Eric," said Liam. "Let Dave know we're ready. Take the centre; I'll go on the right flank."

Eric mumbled his way after the fast disappearing beaters. "Don't know why we're botherin'. He'll only fuck it up. I know he will."

"No you don't," said Liam, totally unconvinced. "Everything forward and trust in the Lord, eh?" Liam turned to the beaters nearby as Eric moved off. "OK. Geoff, Will, Adam, Derek; twitchin' duty. Keep the sewellin' on the move. Derek? You'll be nearest. Check regular on Lordy."

"I thought Dave was?"

"He is, but an extra pair of eyes won't go amiss. If Lordy starts a-waltzin' give us a shout, but make it discreet. You know discreet?"

"Ar, I do," he nodded in Eric's direction. "He doesn't."

"Cheeky bugger..."

"Discreet, Eric."

"Ar, righto, Liam," replied Eric without turning round or altering stride.

Liam blew his whistle to start the drive and Eric's voice sounded along the line. "Move on then flankers! The rest of y', keep the bend in the line as steady as possible. Watch the flanks! Let 'em keep ahead, an' keep them sticks tappin'. Short drive so keep your bloody dogs up! Let's go!"

This first section of the drive was over fairly open ground kept clear to avoid unwanted predators creeping up on the birds around the release pen. Progress was rapid, but as the flankers reached the start of the hawthorn and bramble fortress near the cliff's edge, so they stood still, tapping their sticks gently. The arrival of the rest of the beating team straightened out the arc in the line and the pressure on the gathered birds relaxed as dogs and beaters drew breath for the final act.

"About right, Eric?" shouted Liam along the line. "Can you see Dave?"

"Yeah, he's there! Do you want the far left an' right to go ahead for the first fifty yards, or what?"

Liam spoke to the beaters next to him. "Hang on tight here a minute." He moved along the line to Eric. "Keep the far side runnin' a bit ahead, that way we'll force more birds Lordy's way and he just might be satisfied."

"I've just seen a squadron of bacon sandwiches go across the field... obviously doin' some low level manoeuvres."

"Good to hear you've regained your sense of humour... and don't be such a bloody pessimist." Liam turned and made his way back. "It might work out alright."

Eric gave the beaters their final briefing. "OK. We'll move on then. Keep the right hand on a bit and when they start to rise, just stand still, keep tappin'. Get this wrong an' there'll be a surfeit of eunuchs in the county. OK? On y' go!"

The first beaters and dogs entered the hawthorns followed shortly by the rest of the team. Now larger numbers of birds left the cover and the sound of gunfire grew in intensity as the drive progressed. It was halfway through that Eric heard the first comment that guns five and six seemed to be graced with damn good loaders, such was the rapidity of gunshots. A few seconds later fuller information came back to him that His Lordship was on the move again.

Eric's face was as red as a rosehip with rage and frustration as he moved across towards Liam. "He's what! I don't fuckin' believe it! I don't fuckin'... I'll sort the sod out. Hold th' bloody drive! Stand still! All of y'! Just keep them sticks tappin'! Liam! I'm up front!"

They were on Eric's beat and Liam recognised the tone; Lordy was obviously spoiling for a fight and Eric was up for it; the shooting line was not the only place where form and standards held sway.

"Take it steady, Eric, you know?"

"Yeah, I aint daft, but this can't go on, both he and we knows it!"

"We do. Just go steady at it; right?"

The shooting had all but died away now as Eric moved to the cliff edge, nodding to David as he passed. "Thanks for the call, Dave."

Eric reached the sewelling line and called out, "Hold your fire, guns!" A few more steps and he looked over The Quarry bank to where guns five and six were standing in their correct places. Behind them were His Lordship and Tom, both looking up at the crest of the ridge, Tom blinking owlishly at Eric's sudden appearance.

The silence continued for several seconds, and then Eric ruptured its comfort.

"STAND. BY. YOUR. PEG. M' LORD! ... PLEASE!"

Eric faced the line for a full five seconds in order to drive the point home then turned on his heel to begin making his way back to the line of beaters with as much authority as he could muster. His step was frozen mid stride as His Lordship's dulcet tones came floating up to him.

"I am standing by my peg, keepah!"

Eric turned back, his head slowly leading the rest of his reluctant body. There, dead ahead of him was His Lordship's beaming face, his right hand holding one of his pair of Holland and Holland twelve bore shotguns, the left holding his number eight peg aloft like the battle standard of the Confederate Army.

"I carry it with me and push it back in the ground whenever we stop!"

Two more pheasants rose and fled backwards, over the beaters' heads. Eric stood; stared; returned to the beating line. As he passed David he snarled. "He's got a fuckin' nerve!" David just shook his head. Eric reached Liam in the line. "Did you hear that? Did you fuckin' hear that? The cheeky sod!"

"You've got to 'and it to him, Eric, that's some style out there. The drive's lost now anyway, that soft bugger's seen to that. Let 'im sort it out with the boys hisself. Shan't tell 'em the causes but we can make bloody sure they get to know, as if they don't already. Let's save a few for the next time through, shall we, Eric? Let's finish the drive?"

Eric caught the intonation in Liam's voice. He smiled. "Yeah. Let's finish the drive." Eric whispered to those who had a dog. "On the call, let 'em run in; remember the cliff. Count five then follow 'em on... at speed. Keep the left hand well forward." He waited a few seconds then gave the very audible and seemingly cheerful order. "Sewellin' line hold still! OK! On we go then!"

The drive may have been very short, but it was very spectacular.

With the dogs now allowed to run on and no movement from the sewelling line, the birds raced forward unhindered, lifting off from the cliff face to either storm over the waiting guns or flick over the beaters' heads on their way back to the release pen. Out front, as the first flock of birds burst forth, the extended left hand of the beating line forced them off and right, straight over the empty peg at number eight. On seeing this, His Lordship made a determined move, calling out, "Cam along Tom! Quickly!" His panic was further increased by the call of "Tally-Ho forward!" coming from the beating line, followed by a flurry of shooting around peg eight.

Some said it was the uneven ground that caused Tom to tumble, others that it was the shooting peg His Lordship had been carrying but had now abandoned. Whatever it was, both Tom and the entire contents of the new cartridge bag were sent sprawling and bouncing onto the ground. Attempting to rise from this semi-recumbent position, his foot caught in the strap of the cartridge bag and the upward pull, as he tried to stand, wrenched the strap clean away from the bag's side. In common with many of the old school, Tom never wore wellingtons when loading, preferring studded, well dubbined boots with spats. "Better grip," he was fond of saying. As he tried to disentangle himself and stay upright, his boot studs ground into the cartridge bag. The jig Tom danced whilst juggling with the second gun, scuffed the leather, tore the stitching and crushed the cartridges before he lost his balance completely and fell to the ground again. By the time he had sorted out the remains of the bag, the safety of the second gun, the usability of any remaining cartridges and stood upright, His Lordship was fully twenty yards ahead and holding an empty gun, having used up the handful of cartridges he carried in his pocket, and calling, "Cam along, Tom! The birds, Tom, the birds! Quickly!" at regular intervals.

Those who witnessed Tom holding out full gun, squashed cartridges and shattered cartridge bag as he staggered manfully, very slowly and full of apologies toward His Lordship, reckoned that John Wayne had won an award for a similar performance. Eventually gun and loader reached each other and could actually begin to shoot again; that was when Liam's call from up on the ridge was heard.

"All out? OK! Load up on the trailer. Lunch!"

The drive was over.

Liam moved along the ridge. "Derek. Gather up that sewellin' an' chuck it in the back of my Land Rover, then get yourself an' Bob round to fetch the transport for the pickers-up; it's in the gateway at Jacksons. Eric, I'll go and see the Guv'nor."

"Do you want me with y'?"

"No. You get off back. See to the beaters. Dave, can you go and give the pickers-up a hand." David grunted in the affirmative as they each moved their separate ways. "And bloody cheer up, you! Things can't be that bad!"

When Liam arrived at the peg line, His Lordship was nowhere to be seen. His eldest son was though.

"Mister Stephen. Sorry 'bout the flushes an' the way they went out, Sir, all of a rush like that. Pair of foxes; went straight through the lot..." The heir apparent raised a quizzical eyebrow. "Lifted all our wires in there about a week ago, His Lordship's request. Said he wanted a fox or two about for the hunt next week, otherwise they'd be hung on the gibbet by now. Went straight through the lot of 'em, like I said... Nothin' we could do." Liam cast a glance across the ride. "Is His Lordship about, do you know, Sir?"

"Foxes, was it?"

"Yes, Sir. Foxes... a brace."

"I heard the beaters' call." He paused, staring along the riding. Liam stood square on looking directly at Stephen. "Yes, well, if that's what father wants... It's been a difficult morning all round so far, Liam. I'd think it was the last thing you wanted to find in here today. Foxes. Hm?"

"Was, Sir. Last thing... Last straw."

"Yes. You'll be wanting a word then. About the foxes?"

"I think one's called for, don't you, Sir?"

"Yes. Father's gone back to the vehicles. Heard the call for lunch and set off. I'm sure the break will allow common sense to prevail." He paused. "I'll have a word too, if you like... if it will help. Ah, good girl Ringer." Stephen's black Labrador came back with a cock bird and delivered it to hand.

"I'll take that, Sir." Liam relieved him of the bird. "Thank you, Sir."

Stephen watched the dog move back into the wood's edge. "Eric, Liam? He's not too happy about all this, I suppose? Difficulties... his beat and such."

Liam paused for a moment before answering. "Understatement, Sir. No, he's not."

"No. I can understand. All the trouble he went to on my behalf for today. Doing it first time through, for us... youngsters."

"Yes, Sir."

"Well, can you make sure you tell Mister Cornby that I am appreciative of his efforts? Saw the re-pegging. Earlier birds were more spread than usual. Might be worth a repeat one day; foxes notwithstanding, of course."

"Of course, Sir, an' it might." Liam paused before continuing. "He wants to do right by you, Sir. Eric. Just that. Wants to do you proud; you an' your guests. His Lordship aint givin' him that chance."

"Quite right. Can be quite tricky some days, father... Do I need to tell you that?"

"No, Sir, you don't. If all the years 'ere have taught me nothing else they've taught me that."

"Then you've earned the right to speak up."

"Thank you, Sir. What it is, if you'll forgive me for sayin'... well, it might be his estate, Mister Stephen, but it's your day an' this certainly can't continue, we all know that."

"No. I'll have a word too. A two-pronged attack might help."

"Right... Back on the pegs at what time, Sir?"

"Quarter past two." Stephen paused and turned toward the vehicles before turning back. "Quite right Liam, thank you." He smiled. "Not harsh... Our day, us boys. Quite right." He began to leave. "Right. Quarter past two." He looked back over his shoulder. "On the pegs."

—✺—

"You should've 'phoned t' check. I could've told y'. Same one I saw not two week ago. Custom Zodiac… not many of them about. Clean bumpers, knackered springs?" David nodded. "Same one then."

Eric and David were sat once more in a hedge bottom, whiling away the time before they split for the final check. "Well, we'll all know it next time. Give it a wide berth, unless a beer shampoo's in order!" continued Eric. There was a long pause then he added quietly, "Nothin' worse is there? Hearin' somebody else shaggin'; unless you recognise one of the voices as y' missus that is." They sat silently then Eric looked across. "You alright, Dave? Is summat wrong?"

David rubbed his eyes, coughed and then looked into the middle distance. "No, nothin'. Just me eyes are tired, y' know… long days."

"You've not been 'ome yet, 'ave y'?"

"No. Well, by the time we'd hung up the bag, sorted the guns' birds an' tomorrow's rota with the beaters an' farm staff… didn't seem no point."

"You are you kiddin' me, aren't you? Jesus, Dave. You should've got back for a cup of tea at least. All this runnin' around won't do you nor that lovely lass of yours any good, you know that, don't y'?"

"Maybe."

"No maybe about it, an' anyway, we'd sorted the bag out by half seven; you buggered off straight after that. I thought you'd got off home so if you didn't then where'd you go?"

"Just thought I'd take a stroll round by The Clump."

"You what?"

"Well, you know 'ow the poachers time things after a shoot day. They reckon we'll all be too knackered or too busy early in the evenin'. They're right on the first count, not on the second."

"Bloody hell. Did you hear anythin'?"

"Nope."

"Well then."

"Still worth it. That fuckin' Stratton might've been about; I'd like to catch him..."

"Wouldn't we all, but you shouldn't be out on your own, Dave. You know the routine we follow here."

"Always?"

"Well, I know there's times when you need to act on the spur but even then a 'phone call or summat, when y' can, ar. Other than that you need to tell folk your route. You've always done it before. That way, if you go missin', we know where to look. You never know what situation you might get into an' there's some bad bastards in the poachin' game, lad."

"I know all about that."

"So, if you know all about it why slope off on your own? Eh?" David sat quietly. "Trust me, Dave, best to be in twos, eh? Don't do that again, alright? Let folk know."

"Bollocking accepted."

"Done with the best intentions."

"I know."

"An' remember, if you're with someone else you've got witness corroboration. That way you can beat the shit out of 'em an' say they tripped over a tree root." Eric smiled at him but none came back. "By, but you're miserable today, lad."

"I've said, I'm just tired. Days blend into one."

"Ar, no let up is there?" Eric took out his cigarettes and lit one. "Right, I'm off."

"Thought I could smell summat."

"Thank God!"

"What?"

"You! At last, a joke out of y'."

"Oh."

"First bloody time today."

"I've not been that bad."

"You bloody have! Was afeared you'd crack your face if y' smiled."

"It's just this headache been gettin' me down. I said."

There was a short silence as Eric resettled. "Look, I know it's not my business but me an' my Hattie..."

"Y' right, it's not."

"Oh. OK. If that's how it pans out."

"Eric. Look, I don't mean to sound... ungrateful for your concern, nor Hattie's... nor Liam's, I'm not. But, can we just leave it there for tonight? When I sort things out, then I'll talk it over, maybe, but 'til then can we leave it, eh?"

"Ar. Right. If you say so."

"I do."

"Right." He got up. "I'll feed me outside woods on the way back 'ome. I'm fucked." He yawned and offered a hand to help David up. "You'd better make a move too, lad. Big day for you tomorrow. After my fucked-up session of today you'll shine."

David took Eric's hand and was hauled up. "That wasn't a fucked-up anythin', Eric. Went very well after lunch, I thought. Three forty three brace is a nice day in anyone's book; no records broke but you gave us a bloody good day for all that."

"No thanks to Little Lord Selfish. Mister Stephen must have stood up to him... at last."

"After Liam's little chat? I'd guess he'd have no choice, was either that or face a walk-off midway through the afternoon."

"We may have a decent one takin' over then. Not before time neither."

"Careful what you ask for, Eric. Lordy's mad-keen on his shootin', the lads less so an' that could spell changes. Don't wish Lordy into a grave just yet!"

"After this morning's little opera? Pass me the fuckin' shovel."

Rubbing his hands over his cheeks, David sank his knuckles into his eye sockets again in an effort to stir his alertness. "Cheerful sod. Better the devil, Eric, better the devil... I think I'll feed Stonepit and do a last run round before I go 'ome."

"Well done, letting folk know where you are."

"Ha, yeah, right." David paused. "Yeah. Right. Big day tomorrow."

"Much on the feed?"

"A few... Enough."

"Better had be, or Lordy'll want y' scrotum for an 'andbag."

"Small clutch-purse anyway."

"Two jokes in the space of a minute; excellent!" Eric smiled and looked at his watch. "Time." He took out his cigarettes again and lit another from the stub-end of the last.

"Two fags in the space of a minute; stupid," said David, a slight smile on his face.

Eric smiled back at him. "Blimey, you'll be on telly before long – comedy host!" He looked up into the sky. "Gonna get colder. You'll be feedin' the pens in seven hours, you'll know then." There was a long pause. "Right!

I'm away." Eric moved off into the darkness. "See y'
tomorrow..." He looked at his watch again "...In a bit.
You've got any sense you'll get back home to that lovely
wife of yours an' bugger Stonepit."

"Yeah. See you in a bit. Big day..." David said this last to
himself as by now Eric had gone and he was quite alone.

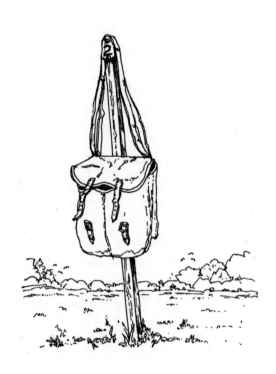

Chapter Eleven
Month 2 – October 1985

"Where...? Oh right, I know, near the rail track end... right. You fetchin' your ferrets? Right, I'll leave mine then, but I'll fetch along some nets. Ar, we may well... See you in about a half hour... yup... see y'."

David put the 'phone down and came back into the kitchen. Stephanie looked up from the baking tray of hot scones she had just taken out of the oven. She began to place them on a wire rack to cool. "So, that'll be a slight delay on the scones and tea, will it?"

"Ar. Sorry, love. Them rabbits on Parker's land, by the rail track..."

Her concentration moved back to the scones. "I see."

"They've cleared a patch of winter barley the size of a football pitch, so he says, an' he's chosen now to tell us. Liam's gonna finish feedin'..."

"I don't know why you can't let them clear their own rabbit troubles."

"Because you an' I both know it'd not stop at rabbit clearance. Before we knew it tenant farmers would be bowlin' over hares and deer and swearin' blind they thought they was just big rabbits."

"Bit of an exaggeration, that."

"Not much."

"Still boils down to the fact that, once again, they snap their fingers, you keepers jump and we've lost yet another precious and very rare morning to ourselves. That's 'we' as in 'you and me', by the way"

"I know, but..."

"You said earlier. Told me you'd be here this morning." She indicated the scones. *"Otherwise, what's the point?"*

"Sorry, pet."

"No you're not."

"I am."

"No you're not! If you were then, alright, maybe you can't tell Mister Parker to look out for his own, but you could have told Eric you were busy, that you'd got something important on."

"I haven't..." As soon as he said it, David realised his mistake and he tried to back-pedal. "Not, y' know, not... what I meant was..."

After a very brief glance up, Stephanie turned her attention back to the scones. "I know what you meant, David."

"No you don't, Steph."

"Yes, I do." She stopped her scone stacking. "You meant, as is usual in these things, that the job comes above all."

"Steph... I meant nothin' of the sort."

"Then why did you agree to go?"

"Because this is my job!"

"Hear that?"

"What?"

"That's what coming first sounds like."

"But..."

"And what's this?"

"What?"

335

Stephanie pointed to the scones then the kitchen in general. "This." David said nothing. "This is what coming second looks like."

"You don't come second to anythin'!"

"Then where were you on my last three shopping trips?"

"That's just shopping."

"No it's not, it's more than that! It's time together! 'Just shopping' it may be to you, but its still time together. The only time we ever get!"

"Some time together that is."

"Well, thank you very much."

"Well it's hardly happy-hour, is it?"

"It's the only time we get!"

"That's not true neither."

"No? Oh, alright, so the last opportunities we've had to spend any time together, 'just shopping' as you choose to call it, they've been missed because affairs of state have called, is that it?"

"No..."

"No, it's affairs of the es-state have ruined our time together!"

"Now you're blowin' it out of all proportion an' gettin' irrational."

She slammed the spatula down onto the table. "Don't you dare patronize me, David! The only irrationality going on here is your irrational fear that the estate will somehow collapse if you take so much as five minutes away from it!"

"Steph..."

"It's true! No time for me, for us, for just...!" Her exasperation showed in her frantic efforts to take off her apron, the ties of which she had now pulled into a knot. "Look at me! I can't even untie an apron!" She tugged and pulled as the tears of frustration began and David moved *forward and took hold of the apron strings. Stephanie stopped crying immediately and slapped his hands down. "Leave it! Just leave it, I'll do it...!"*

"Jesus, Steph, calm down, it's nowhere near as bad as..."

"Then what's this?"

"What's what?"

"This! This isn't shopping; this is 'us' time! A warm scone, a mug of tea, some chat. Us! But no, not to be! Some farmer rattles his cage bars and you're all over there fussing and fawning."

David flicked a glance at the wall clock and Stephanie registered it. There was a cold calmness in her voice now. "I know, I know, 'Look, Steph, I do have to go, I promised Eric...' What about our promises?"

"Promises?"

"Those ones we made, when we got together? That the reason we got together, got married, was to spend time with each other. That's what we said."

"We do spend time together."

"Yes, at mealtimes and then only if we happen to meet at the table."

"An' picnics."

"Which I arrange, cater for... make time for."

"Steph, you knew what the job was ..."

"Before we got together? Yes, I did. Sorry to be such a letdown."

"I didn't say that."

"That's the implication."

There was silence; eventually, David scratched his head. "Look, why don't we...?"

"Leave it, David! You need to get off otherwise Eric or Liam will be back on the 'phone. Leave it."

He looked at her then turned to go into the hallway to collect coat and boots. Back into the kitchen armed with his clothing he saw Stephanie staring deeply into the sink. After some thought, he scratched a non-existent itch on his hand and coughed. "Aha... look, Steph... I know this may come out the blue a bit but, why don't you get over an' see Alice, eh?" She turned and looked at him. "I know, I know. Just, you've seemed so down of late. She's always good for company so you keep tellin' me." She turned away again. "Steph? What? Have I said summat?" No reply came back. "Have you two fallen out?"

Stephanie looked out of the kitchen window and her reply came back small, lost.

"No."

"What is it, Steph?"

He rested his hand on her shoulder but she shrugged it off sharply. "It's nothing... nothing. Just not been seeing much of each other lately, that's all."

"You've not done this because of me, have you? I know I've not exactly, you know..."

"Ha! If only. No, it's me... You had nothing at all to do with this one, David. It was me."

"Well, for what it's worth, I'm sorry 'bout that. But... its more, aint it? I mean more than just that. What's to do with you, Steph?" He paused for a few seconds. "Got to be summat... you sound off at me for stuff you used take in your stride. You've stopped... you know, you don't seem to want me near you."

"I do, David, I do. It's... Oh, it's all... It's nothing. Just had a tummy ache for the last couple of days and it's getting me down a bit."

"I'm talkin' about the last couple of months, Steph, never mind the last couple of days."

"I know… Just before you came back from Scotland, I'd picked up this urine infection; I told you about it. It took so long to clear up. All to do with 'my condition', I suppose, if you get my meaning."

"Steph, we've not so much as…"

"And then I've had this tummy upset for the past few days."

"Summat you ate?"

"No, I don't think so. That urine thing has come back… maybe…" Stephanie's voice took on an angry, pleading quality. "Can we leave this, David, please? I don't want to talk about it, OK?"

"Crikey, love. Alright, alright…" He too looked out of the window then put his hand back on her shoulder. "Look, whatever it is, if I can help then let me, OK? I'm never too busy to help."

"You're always too busy, David."

"I'm not…" The telephone rang. "Fuck it!"

He stood by her and she shrugged his hand off again. "Go on, answer it. It'll be Eric no doubt."

David went into the hall and picked up the receiver. "Hello?" He looked back along the hallway to Steph standing by the kitchen table. "Hi, Eric… No, not at all… Yup, OK, I'll collect you on the way… No, fine. No… only scones an' tea. They'll be 'ere when I get back… Yup, see you in about ten m… Yup… Bye." He put the 'phone down and walked back into the kitchen. Stephanie was busy splitting and filling the first of the cooled scones with jam and cream and didn't look up. He stood there for a few seconds. "That was Eric." He stood a little longer. "You gonna have one then?"

"Yes. Why? Is that so surprising? I've gone to the trouble, no point in wasting them."

"It's not, I'm just glad to see you eating that's all. Save us a couple eh?" They stood in silence. "That was Eric..."

"There's a surprise."

"He wants me to pick him up on the way."

"What's wrong with his vehicle?"

"Nothin', he just wanted to chat..."

She looked up now. "So you thought you'd make time for him."

"Oh, Jesus. Steph, it's my job!"

"She put all her concentration back into filling the scones. "Don't worry, they'll still be here when you get back. A couple."

David recognised this as a shutdown and completed his dressing in silence. Returning from the sitting room complete with shotgun and cartridge bag he called out. "Sack, come on!" He looked at Steph. "Sorry, love. Keep forgettin'... bugger it!"

"You're not the only one. I do it too." David was about to speak but she talked over him, holding his gaze as she did so. "Off you go, Eric's waiting."

After a long look he moved towards the door. "I'll take Jill. See you later this afternoon."

The door closed and Stephanie threw the finished scone at the wall, lathering the cooker and wall cupboard with cream and jam.

—⁓—

Eric was waiting, complete with gun, net-bag and ferret box. He climbed into the Land Rover and, as David began to drive away, immediately lit up a cigarette.

"Do you 'ave to?" David slid open his window.

"If you don't want me to be in as bad a mood as you obviously are then, yes I do."

"Who said I was in a bad mood?"

"Didn't need to say it, the way you drove up said it all."

"What?"

"Like you were pullin' in for a pit stop at Monaco."

"I didn't, I just thought we'd best get on, that's all."

"Oh, right, so the skid marks left on the road and the bald spot on y' front tyres is nothin' to do with your mood then? Good, I'll be able to relax when you start swinging that pump-action shotgun about then."

"I'm a deal sight safer than most!"

"Not with that hair trigger on it, you aint! That bugger's lethal, set up like it is." There was a short silence. "What's up?"

David completed his turn into the lane that led to Parker's farm. "Nothin'... just things... home front."

"Oh ar?"

"Steph's just been acting a bit strange of late. Sort of... well, on the edge, I suppose."

"That usually means they're being shagged by someone else does that."

"Fuck me, Eric; you're such a fuckin' comfort you are!"

"A joke, Dave. Jesus... it was a fuckin' joke!"

"Well not fuckin' funny, alright?"

"Alright." He looked out of the side window as they approached the farm's inner yard then muttered, "That'll be the sex-police been stoppin' you of recent then will it?"

David pulled up alongside Liam's Land Rover. "Leave it, Eric, eh? Just... y' know, leave it."

"Ar, right. If I can do anything to help." David gave him a look. "No, I didn't mean that, just, you know, if you want to talk."

"Thanks, you're a pal."

"Although, you know, if you think Steph could do with, y'know...?"

David smiled and shook his head. "There's no limit to you, is there?"

Eric opened his door and got out. "None. I 'eard the angels stackin' my foldin' chair up against the walls of heaven years ago. Mornin' Liam!"

The three of them stood together in the yard as Mister Parker crossed to join them from the milking parlour.

The sobs came from deep within. It was all Stephanie could do to catch her breath between them. Sitting on the downstairs toilet, she pushed her flattened palms against the side walls in order to keep her balance such was the force of her crying.

Gradually the sobbing subsided to a long moaning cry as she began to rock back and forth, arms wrapped tightly round her waist.

"My baby, oh my baby..."

"Well, how close was he then?" David leaned into the conversation, eager for details, dreading their possibility. "Could they have mistook him for someone else?"

Norman Parker looked from keeper to keeper as he explained the events. "No, not my Glynis. She knows the family well; who doesn't. He was right at the start of it, I think."

"They're sure of it?"

"Yeah..." His voice tailed off. His information had rekindled some previous concerns and he was unsure what they were but was sure that Liam was less than pleased.

Liam raised an eyebrow and coughed. "Ah-ha... Well, I have to wish they'd said summat sooner."

Norman could sense the annoyance. "Well, they would I'm sure, but that were the day our 'Becca went down with the appendicitis so other things took precedence."

"Oh, ar. Right, yeah, sorry. I remember you mentioning it; she alright now?"

"Ar. Were a close call though. Just started out as a bit of tummy ache first thing in the mornin'. Came on strong when they were in town, doubled the poor lass over. Lucky they were there really, close to the hospital like they were. Ambulance straight to casualty. Next thing we know they're talkin' about possible peritonitis an' she's in the theatre losin' some bits."

"Ar. Must've been a bit of a scare for you both..."

"Ar, it were, an' her slow recovery too."

"Ar, 'course... So...?"

"Oh, ar, well, it was only when I mentioned this mornin', you comin' round to sort out our bit of a rabbit problem, that Glynis came out with it. Said she an' 'Becca saw him clear as day, just goin' up the track. He'd got nothing, you know, no gun nor nothing... not that she can recall anyway. Prob'ly nothin' to it, but not a social call neither was it? I mean, were too early for pheasant, August, an' your place is at the end of the track aint it, David? No poacher of Stratton's calibre's gonna take the chance of goin' past there, is he? An' in broad daylight?"

Liam closed the conversation down. "No, he'd not. He may have been scoutin' though. That lane runs right up to Brabham's Wood. Well, thanks for the information Norman, bit late but that can't be helped. We'll follow it up. Thank Glynis will y'... an' tell 'Becca I'm glad she's mended up now too."

"I will that. If they hadn't caught that Denham bus and been sat right at the back they would've seen nothin'." There was a short silence. "Well, I 'ope it helps."

"No doubt it will. Right, we'd best be off an' sort these rabbits out eh?" David and Eric nodded but kept quiet. Liam turned to go. "Right, Norman. We'll drop in a gang of coney on our way back, providin' we get any."

"No shortage along that hedgerow that I do know. So thick along the hedge they're juggin' in the open field. You'll see how much they've trimmed as well. I'm not exaggeratin', space as big as a football pitch they've cleared!"

"Right, see you later." The three keepers left the yard. At the field gate Liam stopped and left absolutely no doubt about his feelings. "Right, Dave, this need's t' be sorted."

"I know..."

"Can't continue."

"I know, I know."

Eric swapped his ferret box to his other shoulder. "We did say though, Dave."

"I remember. I know."

"Jesus, of all the days it has to be the one their 'Becca gets appendicitis; I can't believe that!"

"Careful, Liam," said Eric. "You might let a bit of compassion in through the back door."

"You know what I mean, Eric."

"I do, an' you know what I mean an' all."

"Ar. Y' right. It's what the job does to you sometimes. But what the hell was he doin' there?" Liam opened the kissing gate for men and dogs to weave through. "Parker's right. Too early for pheasant... partridge maybe, but past your place in broad daylight? Well, he's just not that daft is he?"

David's head was spinning. "No, he's not. I'll talk to Steph when I get back. Maybe she saw somethin'. My guess is he knew I was away on the grouse an' if Steph was meetin' his missus, which he'd also know, then he'd also know he'd have the track to himself. Fuck it! What a bloody mess is this!"

"Eric's right, we did say, but 'I told you so' aint gonna help here." Liam patted David's shoulder. "You may have to force the issue with Steph an' that other woman though, Dave, as unpleasant as that may be."

"Ar, I know."

"Keep it in mind, he's a poacher. Has been, is, always will be. The only thing to stop him is if he's caught, and it's not 'appened yet."

Eric cut in. "One day, Liam; one fuckin' day."

"Maybe, but it's not happened yet so until it does it aint gonna."

"We'll see." Eric's voice dripped contempt.

"That still don't shine a light on this dilemma though. Talk to Steph, Dave. See what can be done..." He paused, cleared his throat then stated calmly and specifically. "But if it does continue an' we get any more of these 'little difficulties', I'll be informin' His Lordship. I'll have no choice on that. Understood? Otherwise we're gonna look like the guilty party in all this; all of us."

David was silent for few moments. "Yup, understood," was all the reply that came back.

"Bloody hell, will you look at that!" The keepers had reached the far hedgerow and could see the winter barley Norman Parker had sown earlier that year. "Bugger me, he weren't kiddin' were he?"

Eric climbed the style. "By buggery but they've made a pig's ear of this. Why'd he leave it so long before he let us know?"

"'Cos he's a typical farmer. Always think they can dodge things an' not spend any money." Liam looked across at David. "Don't let it get at you, Dave. Come on. There's none *of us fallen out. We know you'll sort it. Come on, let's roll over a rabbit or two, eh?"*

"Yeah, right. I'll talk to her when I get back."

"I know you will."

"See what comes up."

"Right, good."

They set off along the hedgerow and it was not long before they were busy with ferret, net, dog and gun.

—ɯ—

"Did you get many?"

"Sixty eight."

"Goodness! Mister Parker wasn't exaggerating then."

"No, not this time. We dropped him off twenty for his freezer. Paunched 'em on the way to his place, so that'll pay back for some of the lost barley."

Stephanie poured boiling water into the pot and began to sort out cups and plates for tea. "It'll grow again though, won't it?"

"'Course. Blimey, they used to put sheep on sown crops not that long ago to take off first bite. They reckoned second growth was always stronger. It's only recent this terror of a bit of nibblin's bothered farmers, and that's only 'cos the crops they grow now are so bloody specific; can't take the pressure of natural growin' conditions. Soil's just a thing they use to hold 'em upright these days."

"I'll bet Mister Parker was pleased though."

"Ar, he was." David paused and watched Stephanie as she carried the plate of scones to the table. "You alright, love?"

"Yes, fine. Why?"

"Nothin', just you look, I don't know... blotchy."

"*Bad time of the month; you know.*"

"*Oh, ar, I see, right.*"

"*Probably what my tummy ache was earlier, what was making me so ratty. Sorted now, so...*" Her face momentarily held a look that did not match her speech but David missed it. "*Sorry I was snappy; sorry. Your two scones still here, see.*"

"*Ar. No need for apologies. I know your monthlies knock you about a bit.*" He paused, drew in breath and continued. "*Look, Steph... summat came up while we were at the Parkers.*"

"*Yes?*"

"*Ar, summat you need to hear. We were talkin', in the yard, before we went out to the rabbits, an' Parker mentioned that his Missus, Glynis...*"

"*Oh, yes, I know Glynis, we met...*"

"*Ar, well, Glynis, an' Rebecca?*"

"*Yes.*"

"*They was goin' to market, goin' in on the Denham bus. Left the car, knew parking was gonna be difficult, so they was goin' in on the bus.*"

"*Yes, you said. Going in on the bus.*"

"*Ar, well... an'... Glynis said they saw Alec Stratton.*" He indicated the direction with his head. "*At the top of the lane here, makin' his way up it a couple of month ago, August time.*" Stephanie stiffened at this and David saw the change in her colour. A realisation that this may be deeper than he thought filled him with dread. "*Was 'e here, Steph?*"

"*When was this?*"

"*When?*" He almost laughed. "*Ha... Jesus... don't be so daft, I've just said. August. When I were away on the grouse. When do you think?*"

"*How did she know it was him?*"

"What?"

"Well it was a long time ago, how can she be sure... what brings it to her mind after all this time?"

"Come on, Steph, you're stallin'. Glynis Parker's lived here all her life. She knows everybody and everythin', an' she remembers it because it were the day her Rebecca went down with the appendix, alright? So, was he?"

It took a long time for her to answer but eventually Stephanie stood still. "Yes... Yes, he was."

"Oh bloody hell, Steph! Why didn't you say?"

"I'm sorry, David. I was going to."

"When? Next week? Christmas?"

"I just..."

"It was a couple of months ago, Steph! Gave me the chance to look a bloody fool in front of Eric an' Liam; thanks for that. So, tell me now; what the fuck was he doin' round here?"

"There's no need for sarcasm and certainly no need for that tone and language!"

"There's every fucking need, Steph! Now, what was he doing here?"

She went back to setting the table. "If you're going to shout then this conversation is at an end."

"For Chrissake, Steph! Liam's about to go and tell Lordy I'm the poacher's friend!" She could hear the terror in his voice and this stopped her. David took a breath then continued in more measured tone. "OK, right. Stephanie, why was Alec Stratton round here? A courtesy call was it?"

"I'll ignore the further sarcasm. He came to tell me Alice was unwell, that she couldn't meet me at the market, that's all."

"That's all! That's...! Jesus, Steph, can't you see how this looks?"

"There was nothing going on."

David looked at her for a second, completely thrown by her remark. "Nothin' goin' on? What... what are we talkin' about here, Steph?"

"What do you mean?"

"What I just said."

"What are you implying?"

"I don't know... I'm... I don't... I'm implying it was less than sensible for him to come round 'ere. What do you think I'm implying?"

"Exactly that."

"R-i-ght... OK. Well, Alice should have known better than to have sent him. Did he come in?"

"No, 'course not!"

"And why not use the 'phone? She's got the number."

"He said he didn't know where it was, the number, where she'd written it down. And Alice, she was asleep when he was about to leave. She'd been so unwell and he didn't want to disturb her... so he came on here."

"Just like that."

"Yes."

He leant back onto the sink, winded. "Phhh.... Jesus."

"No one saw him."

"Except Parker's wife, Glynis ..."

"Well that's..."

"And his daughter, Rebecca ..."

"Yes, but..."

"Who told Mister Parker, who told Liam an' Eric."

"That's..." her voice fast-faded.

"That's what, Steph? That's alright then, no one knows? Is that it? Well thank God for that. I'm so relieved no one knows... that it's still a fuckin' secret."

"I've already said there may be a time and a place for sarcasm and bad language, David, but this is neither."

"I'm aware of that, Steph, but right now? Right now I'm bereft of anything else to say. I'm a simple bloke, y'know, so sarcasm and swearin' will have to do, OK?" David turned away from her and stared out of the window, shaking his head in disbelief.

After a silence Stephanie probed a little more. "And Liam said what?"

"Hm?"

"What did Liam say?"

"That if we can't get it sorted he'd have to tell Lordy."

"Get what sorted?"

"Why do you insist...?" He turned back towards her. "This! This, liaison you've had with the wife of the county's most proficient poacher and now, seemingly, a friendship with the man hisself! The man who's been the bane of this estate for the past twenty-plus fuckin' years Steph, that's what! Stop bein' so... so bloody protective of everyone else but me!"

Stephanie could see a wildness in David's eyes that was unfamiliar to her but even though she was frightened by it, she followed through in turn. "She's been a friend, David! A friend!"

"An' what's her husband to you Steph?" This direct question stalled her. "See? That's what people will think!"

"What will they think?" Her voice held a level of calmness she certainly did not feel but she was desperate to calm David a little. He really was scaring her.

"For fuck's sake, you can't be that dim, Steph!" He paused, collecting his thoughts, controlling his impulses. "Right, let me try and explain and spell it out... again.

They're simple country folk round here, like me, Steph, but they can add up. They'll think, one, you're not only on friendly terms with the wife of the county's most proficient poacher but that, two, with the poacher as well! You got that much?"

"David…"

"And then they'll think if that's the case then it's obvious information's bein' traded, not just by me but by all the keepers! But I'm the one most in the frame, an' Lordy will stand that for all of, oh, I don't know, ten seconds before he sacks me? You know what sacks me means don't you? Let me clear any mist you might have over this. It's as in, kicks me out of the job, out of the house an' off the estate! Out of the job I love, that I've worked so bloody hard at, sacrificed precious years of me an' you just to succeed in, to make summat of it, for me, for us!"

Stephanie held his gaze. "He wouldn't do that."

He slumped at the table. "Love, love… You don't know these folk at all do you?"

"I've asked you not to patronize me David, and I'm sure His Lordship won't do anything of the sort. Particularly when he knows I've severed all contact with them."

Now it was David's turn to be flummoxed. He was not sure whether she had decided this earlier or was just thinking on her feet, but his anger deflated rapidly and he looked hard at Stephanie before replying. "Is that what's gonna happen?"

"Has happened."

"What, you've stop meeting up? Tea and such?"

"Yes! Foolish I may have been, stupid I'm not."

"Thanks, Steph."

"Don't thank me, David! I'm doing it for purely pragmatic reasons. If it was for me, I'd tell them to go hang, but it's not. I may be guilty of lots of things but I'm not disloyal..." Her voice faltered and the catch in her throat took her by surprise as she echoed her last statement with force. "I have never been deliberately disloyal!"

He looked at her, puzzled again. "No one ever said you were Steph."

He stood up from the table and made a move towards her but she held out a palm and shook her head. "No hugs, David, not now."

David sat back down. "OK. Well... I'll let Liam know. I'm sure that'll soften the edges a bit."

"Yes."

"Make it good."

"Yes."

After a long silence David looked across the table. "Scones are still here." He sat down. "How about we try one, eh?"

She sat, slumped almost. "Can't. Don't want one. You can... I'll pour. Feel a bit sick..." The 'phone rang and they sat facing each other across the table listening to its indecent intrusion. Stephanie's face never flinched. "You'd best get that. It could be important."

"Yeah, right." David put his unbitten scone back onto the plate, got up from the table. Stephanie sat staring at the teapot, listening to the one-sided conversation.

"Hi, Liam. No, no, just about to. Erm... well we 'ave, yes. Just. Yeah, it's been sorted. No, no, all good. Oh, right... well, erm, can Eric do it? No, it's just I was about to have a bite of tea, with Steph... Ar, scones. She made 'em earlier but I couldn't then. No. 'Cos of the rabbits at Parker's. No, just think it'd be better if I stayed on, y' know? Sort of talk a bit more... ar. No, all good. Then I was gonna do a trap *round after feeding. Right, thanks Liam. Yeah... See you tomorrow... Ar, talk it through then. Right, 'bye."*

She heard the 'phone go down and the sound of David's footfall as he walked along the hall and up the stairs.

—᠁—

"Can you get us a new toothbrush tomorrow, Steph? This one looks like I've been blackleadin' the grate with it." David walked to the bathroom doorway. "Steph?"

A voice came from the bedroom. "Yes. Yes, right."

"Sorry, love. Wasn't meaning to shout... y' know. Just thought you might have gone downstairs or summat." David appeared round the bedroom door and smiled. "Same as this one."

"What?"

He held it up. "Toothbrush. Same one."

"Oh, yes, right."

David stood watching her as she lifted out a blob of face cream from the pot and began to rub it in. "Steph?" She continued to massage in the cream and looked at him in the mirror. "About earlier, shoutin'; swearin'. Sorry." Stephanie was about to reply but he talked on. "I mean really sorry. Was just worried, you know, about Stratton... bein' seen so close to here and you sayin' he'd come to leave a message. Not the best information I wanted to be given, 'specially by one of the tenant farmers. You understand that, don't you?"

"Yes. But, like I've said, there'll be no need for you all to worry now, will there? All over."

"Ar, right." David moved back into the bathroom. "Cold again tonight. October first and we've already had a couple of good frosts. Do you want a bottle?"

"No, fine thanks."

"Sure? Anythin' past July and you usually bleat about sub-zero bedclothes."

"Don't."

"Do. Look at what you've got on now."

"Just like to be snug, that's all."

"No hot water bottle then?"

"No."

"There's brave. I'll go and do you one if you want."

"No, really, I'm fine. Will you stop fussing."

David pulled the light switch, flushing the bathroom into darkness. He crossed the landing and once in the bedroom flicked back the bed covers and climbed in.

Closing the lid on the cream, Stephanie looked across at him. "How can you go to bed like that?"

"Like what?"

"In just a pair of pants."

"Rather than like you, y' mean, dressed for the Yukon?" David turned onto his side, facing away from Stephanie. She pulled the bedclothes back and her move into bed and the switching off of her bedside light was as one.

They lay there for some time, then Stephanie rolled over and fitted her form to his, draping her arm round his waist. "Can we start over again? Today, I mean. Can we?"

David rolled over to face her and she moved back slightly. "Been bad, I know."

"You have no idea. I'm sorry too."

"Was me, Steph, I know it. Just got a bit..."

"What?"

"Insecure. No, worried like, for you an' me; this... I couldn't face anythin' to come between us, don't know what I'd do."

"Turn over so I can cuddle you again." Stephanie lodged herself into his foetal form. David grunted at her presence.

"That's just right, our girl. We fit... You're the treacle my stone sinks into. If you weren't here I'd have to invent you; my other half. Just hearin' about Stratton, my head ran riot. Got really scared, lost. Knew I couldn't live without you. Wouldn't want to... You alright, Steph?"

She stiffened her arms preventing him from turning, her tears running onto the pillow. "I'm fine. Sleep, eh?"

"Ar. Sweet dreams."

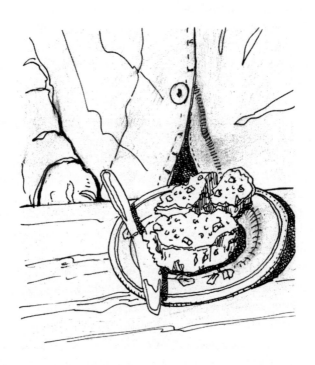

Day 02 – Thursday 29th November 1985

After feeding Stonepit, David knew sleep would at the very least be evasive and, to be honest, home was the last place he wanted to be right then. He completed another circuit of his beat before deciding to return and make tea.

He saw it as soon as he walked into the kitchen; the new teapot, standing on the table. It made him half smile but it fast-faded in the memory. After standing in the kitchen for some moments he felt the need to check on Stephanie, did not know why, and he climbed the stairs. She was fast asleep and he gently pulled the door to and looked across at the spare room. He swallowed, the saliva rattling down the sides of the shaft that led to the deep pit that was his stomach. 'What a fuckin' mess.' He sighed. 'Hmm; better a hot drink.' He looked at his watch. 'Twelve hours an' it'll all be over.' Back in the kitchen he put the kettle onto the Rayburn, sat at the table and opened yesterday's paper.

Snapped upright and semi-awake it took a couple of seconds before David worked out the alarm clock was the whistling kettle and he had nodded off. Shuddering off the remnants of his doze, he relieved the kettle of its torture and lifted the teapot off the drainer. 'Christen it right,' he thought. He moved to the sink and poured a little of the boiled water into the pot through the spout then poured it out of the top.

"Shall I do that?" David turned to see Stephanie in dressing gown and slippers, hair mussed, leaning against the door jamb. "Got the ceremony right, I see."

He looked at the pot then turned away from her, his tone flat and formal. "Ar. Old habits... Tried not to disturb you. Made a hash of it by the looks. You sleep?"

"Bits. Not a lot. You?"

He indicated the kettle, the creased newspaper. "What do you think?"

She glanced across. "No, guess not."

"How's the head?"

"Still on my shoulders."

"Ar. Sorry, Steph, really. Last thing I wanted..."

"I know. Bit, heat of the moment. All is forgiven."

"Ar."

"You didn't come back. I thought..."

"Stayed out. Was with Eric. Always a vulnerable time, after a shoot day; poachers to worry over."

"It's the first day over your beat today."

"As if I need remindin'."

"David. Can we please...?"

"Tryin', Steph. Tryin'."

"I know... sorry..." She started again. "You'll be fit for nothing. I just thought you'd want to talk, you said we needed to... and then maybe try to get a little sleep, you know?"

"Had time to think and reckon we about covered it all earlier. Could you pass us the tea caddy? You sure you don't want one?"

"No. Thank you." Stephanie handed the caddy to him and he spooned the leaves into the pot. "Have you given it any more thought?"

"Nothin' but; I said."

"And?"

"Don't know what to think anymore. All gets jumbled." He turned back to the sink. "All I know for sure is I loved you... still do; not sure what that means anymore."

"Everything. You saying that after all this... mess I've caused. Thank you."

"My thoughts exactly; mess, that is."

He moved across the kitchen to the fridge. As he passed Stephanie she caught his hand. "David, I've said it before and I'm saying it again. I've never stopped loving you and I never, ever wanted you hurt. If nothing else comes out of this, please understand that. What happened, what I did, was stupid, cruel, selfish... the lies... yes, all the things you said this morning."

"Would rather have been wrong." He wrested his hand from hers, opened the fridge and took out the milk. "Would give all an' a bonus to 'ave been wrong, Steph."

There was a long silence. Tea was made then Stephanie cleared her throat. "Ahem. How did yesterday go? I heard some of it... small world this estate. Incestuous."

"Then you'll know Lordy gave us an 'ard time with 'is temper."

"I did. Hattie called in."

"Ah, right. That explains it."

"What?"

"Nothin'. Stuff from earlier"

"Well, anyway, she told me. Your head must be full of the day, and you've all got such a lot on; all three of you."

"Ar. Clouds everythin' at times, shoot days. Takes you over. Was glad of it in a way."

"Yes."

"All went to the sick bucket when Lordy buggered up the pin draw. Was downhill from then on... well, you'll have heard."

"Yes. Hattie didn't stop long, but gave me the gist. She was on her way to the garden centre at Ripley."

"You didn't go?"

"No. Didn't feel like it. I just went as far as the village..." She pointed in its direction. "Teapot."

"What did she tell you then, about the day?"

"Said Sally Larsson had just got off the lunch shift at the big house; said Mister Stephen was less than pleased."

"Much like us then."

"I can imagine. Anyway, one or two harsh words spoken over the soup, Sally said; raised voices..." Stephanie paused and almost smiled. "Listen to me. Regular estate gossip, I am."

"Harsh words did some good then. Lordy was much better in the afternoon." He nodded as he spoke. "An' it's good to hear you chattin' on summat else, even if it is estate gossip."

She pushed off from the door frame with her shoulder. "Yes. Well, I've done a bit of thinking too. Sit down. We'll let this brew and I'll fry some bacon in a minute, just wanted to say something first."

"Yeah. OK." David sat. "What else do you want to say? No more surprises, I hope."

"David..."

"Ar. Right, sorry."

Stephanie sat opposite him. "Right." She took a deep breath. "No one knows more than me what a hash I've made of things, but I can't put the clock back or change it. I can only say again how sorry I am and that this whole mess is mine alone."

"Fairly obvious statement but..."

"Let me finish, then you can have your say... please."

"Yeah. OK."

"I think a lot of it has to do with me. How I've been feeling these last few months; but it's also about the job, your job, and how I see me fitting into it. And it's also about this, this baby thing we've been living under for what seems like forever."

"We've talked that through, Steph."

"Yes, I know..."

"For bloody years!"

"I know, and still it lingers on."

"Don't you try an' use that as an excuse for what you did!" His voice was becoming raised and the frustration showed in his eyes.

"I'm not, but it's a contributing factor."

"For what?"

"David, please..."

She tried to call a truce but he was too taken up with it to listen. "For what? Jesus; I thought you was tellin' the truth, about the urinary infection... all that bollocks you gave me about why we couldn't... couldn't make love."

"I felt so bad about it all, David. Felt... unclean. I just couldn't."

"Oh, that's rich! Then why do it at all? Eh? What ever in the name of all that's stupid made you think that you goin' out an' shaggin' another bloke would be the answer, the cure? Well done. That really solved all our problems... It were a bastard thing to do, Steph, that's what it were!"

Her hands were at her temples as she shouted out in tears and near hysteria. "David! Stop it, stop it! Stop it!"

It had the required effect and the silence that followed was razor-sharp. Eventually, Stephanie spoke, her tone creased and over-worn. "This was how the last discussion ended."

"An' why not? Was shit from start to finish."

"I know, I know. Please, I only want to rescue this mess, but I can't do it if you're going to fly off into a blazing temper every time we discuss it!"

"Fuckin' typical that. All of a sudden it's my fault."

"That's not what I said. That's your interpretation of what I said, and you only said it to make me feel even more guilty!"

"Well, don't you?"

It left her as a violent prayer. "Yes! Yes! Yes...! Yes! I feel guilty! Am guilty! Horribly so! I deserve no pity, no forgiveness; I. Am. Guilty! OK? You've won! All better now?" She saw the look in his eyes. "David, David... please. I can't... Nothing I say will change what happened. Nothing. All I can do, all I can ask you to do is try to help me repair it. Get back as near as we can to what we had before. I know that's going to be difficult..."

"You bet."

"Yes, I know, but I really want to try and I can't do it on my own. I need you there too. Please. I don't want us to be broken by this. Help me put us back together."

After a long pause, David spoke. "Don't know if I can paper over the cracks, Steph, an' that's the truth."

Stephanie was lost for a reply and stared at the Rayburn. "Then what do you want?"

"I want it back, Steph." He looked into her face. "I want it back as it was, that's what I want."

Her gaze never flinched. "Not possible, what's your plan B?"

He blinked first. Sighed. "Phhh… Like Liam yesterday, I haven't got a fuckin' clue; I'm makin' this up as I go along. What I have considered is my position here."

"I've already said I want us to stay together."

"No, I mean here. On the estate."

This brought Stephanie up short. The thought had crossed her mind during the past few hours but she had found it all too much to contemplate; certainly thought that David would find it the same. "Oh."

"Christ. When I think…" David cleared his throat. "Ahem, don't think now that I want to stay."

"You mustn't rush into any decisions. First we have to sort out us."

"This estate is part of us. An' right now? Right now I don't think I want it."

"OK. Maybe this will help. Let me tell you what I've been thinking. The big days are coming up so there's enough to do with that. But how about, after the season, I go back to mum and dads for a short while. Go back, just for a couple of weeks to recharge. How about that?"

"You go off to your folks?"

"Yes."

"An' how the bloody hell will that help?"

"I just think it'll give us both a chance to focus a bit. Let's stick it through here until the season's end and then, when I get back, when I've drawn breath a little we can decide how we move on."

"Ha! I know what it will give; it'll give your dad the proof that all along he was right."

"About what?"

"That you married a bloke as couldn't keep you happy. Not financially, socially nor… nor any other way."

"And he'd get his bloody answer! He has no idea what you mean to me!" She had never talked about her parents like this before, had always been on the defensive as far as they were concerned and David was surprised by her vehemence. "My parents can think what the bloody hell they like, which in their case is plenty, I know. You think I don't see it? It's what I grew up with! Mum never gets tired of telling what my womanly duties are and my dad just sits there, says nothing, but he's got that look... which isn't even close to the reality of who I am because they don't know me at all and that's because he's never had the good manners to ask! They don't count in this; I know how I want this to end!"

"Do you?"

"Yes!"

"How, Steph?"

"Oh, David... Isn't it obvious? I'm still here, still talking. I got things wrong. Got confused between what I'd got and what I was expected to make out of what I'd got; what was expected of me. I got lost... no string in the labyrinth." She could see he was looking puzzled and slowed down a little. "I look into the mirror and I don't recognise me. Do you understand that?"

"Think so."

"Now I need a little time to find my way back. I'm not happy. No, wrong... not as happy as I should be, as you deserve me to be and I want to find out why. A bit of time at home will maybe give me the space to look into my life here, not out of it... Do you see?"

"Not sure."

"I don't explain things well."

"No, no, you do, it's just me an' my brain." The familiarity of the phrasing hit them both and they smiled weakly at each other for what seemed like the first time in years. He looked around the kitchen, almost as if the units had the answer to it all. "Do you really care, Steph?"

"What do you think? Yes!"

"I mean really? Don't say it if it aint so." She gently took his hand and held onto it, looking into his face. "OK, if it's what you want, if it'll help you then you'd best fix it up."

"I already have."

"Oh."

"Not behind your back. I just wanted to make sure they would be around. Not gallivanting off somewhere before I said anything."

"When?"

"I was thinking the middle of February."

"No, I mean when did you 'phone them?"

"Oh. Yesterday evening. I 'phoned them last night."

"I bet they were elated."

She released his hand. "Heard mum call to dad, about 'our little girl coming home', etcetera, so… elated? Well…"

"What did you say?"

"That we were having the estate builders in to do some alterations and I didn't want to live in the mess…" Her voice tailed off a little at the reminder then she rallied. "Said you couldn't come with me because of the catching up to be done. Hope that was OK?"

"Ar. S'pose so. Not much sun around then; February."

"Sun's not what I'm going for."

"Dunno. Some sunshine inside of you would be good."

She smiled at him and tears almost started but she held them in check. "Sometimes you get me just right. Yes, it would. Some, sun… inside me."

"You used to be, when we first started out; sunny. Happy."

She stood up and looked him deep in the eyes. "I know, I did... but people change, we both have. I suppose part of growing up is how you deal with that change... but, through all that I've never stopped loving you, you know. Never. Not for one second."

"Funny way of showin' it." He lifted his hands in submission. "Not spoilin' for a fight again, just an observation."

"I know. I maybe haven't dealt well with the changes inside of me."

"Steph..." He paused, making sure of what he was going to say. "I only know a couple of things for certain from out of this... shit-heap we're standin' in the middle of right now. I've not played things right an' I've maybe not been fair to you. You say you've not dealt well with the changes and I can see now I've not recognised them, but what you did, that weren't the way to go about puttin' it right. You lied to me, hurt me, an' I mean like no one ever could, like I never thought I could be; took away all my oxygen... I told you a long while ago, said if I didn't have you I'd be lost, inside and out, an' that's still true; that's the core to it. You're the other half of my 'eart an' I want us to stick it out if we can, if I can, want to believe in us again. Bit of a rough road so you're goin' to have to allow me a bit of travellin' time though, eh?"

Stephanie began to cry and David watched her unable to react. Gradually her crying ceased and she dried her eyes on her dressing gown. "Then take this from me. I'll never be so foolish again. Never." They looked long at each other, no movement, no reaction, just a look, then Stephanie exhaled sharply and moved toward the Rayburn. "Now, tea. This is stewed. I'll make fresh... and bacon."

"Couldn't eat a thing."

"You've another hard day ahead; your day. You must have something."

"Just a cuppa then." He looked at the wall clock. "I need to get off an' feed, what's in the pot will do."

"No it won't. Go and put a clean shirt on, I'll make a fresh pot."

"You and y' tea."

"What?"

"Warm the pot. Only use leaf tea. Water just off the boil. Stand it for four and a half minutes, any longer an' it's stewed..."

"It's the only way to..."

"'Treat a beverage that built a nation'. I know." He smiled and looked beyond her and out of the kitchen window before looking her in the eye. "That's one of the reasons I want to stay. Took us years to gather this together, our little things, our secrets. Things no one else knows about us but us. Worth fightin' for, I think."

He turned and began to climb the stairs.

—⚍—

The sky was bearing the deeper scars of dawn as David reached the gateway that led into the central ride of Brabham's Wood. Once amongst the low firs the light weakened further, almost blue-black in the part daylight.

His head was still full of the recent conversation with Stephanie. Her going away for a short while, to her parents of all places, and of how he felt about that, them, her... 'an' that fuckin' Alec Stratton'. Even at that hour, when she had first told him, his first instinct had been to go round and face him out, to smash him to the ground and it had taken all of Stephanie's persuasive powers to try and prevent him. It was as she stood barring his path at the doorway, when he had pushed her and she stumbled, fell, and cracked her head on the coat-stand that he had been brought back to his senses. This was not what he wanted; not at all. He had not wanted to hurt her. She was what was most precious to him, even after all the admissions.

After the shock of the stripped-bare emotional moment had been soaked up by them both, he had listened, argued, listened some more and finally agreed to talk further. Even though the prospect of more detailed discussion filled him with dread and anger, anything was better than what they had had over the past couple of months. Their talk had uncovered much but there was common ground. Stephanie's real and genuine regret for what she had done and her reassurances that she wanted them be together, as well as David beginning to understand his part in the process, had meant the conversation had ended, if not on a positive note, then one that at least gave him hope for their future.

Out in the fresh air, David had sucked in the prospect of daybreak's beauty and chill as a drowning man grasps at passing timber. Now, and in spite of his hurt and confusion, the job's excitement and responsibilities coursed through his veins like a drug. It was what he lived for and he recognised his dependence on it; the thought of giving it up made him shudder. 'Not if I can help it; not if we can work things out.'

Entering the wood's womb, five steps along the ride and a sharp left turn brought him to the release pen gate and access to its inner sanctum. The fit of his hand on the latch was as if sculpted and the gate yielded to his unspoken sesame, lifting him out of the oppression of home and releasing him back into the world. The first birds had already dropped to the pen's floor as he was absorbed by the greenery.

Stretching a full two hundred yards ahead, the wide straw covered ride ran as straight as an arrow through low firs until it reached the older and taller mixed soft and hardwoods that formed the rest of Brabham's Wood. Roughly in the centre of the pen, round a slight bend, four smaller rides criss-crossed, creating a star shape and, not for the first time, David stopped and stared, savouring the uniqueness of his lot and the sanity it offered. The day started here; almost anything could happen. His good fortune was made tangible as the birds dropping from roost to ride grew in number. He stood still and the ghost of a smile showed. 'Just a bit longer before I bust the cobweb of another day', he thought. 'Just a bit longer.'

Looking along the ride, his concentration was arrested, not for the first time, by the incongruity of the feed hut ahead. Standing on its tall iron wheels, the green-painted retired navvies' hut was empty of pan-shovels and teapots. Now it reposed openly in the very place most of its past inhabitants had sought, illegally and under cover of darkness, to go.

For these itinerants, the labourers who dug the soil in turn of the century, welfare-less Great Britain, unemployment was the most feared working class disease. A dog eat dog mentality prospered back then, when 'working man' meant the same thing as 'forced labourer'. Contained in these small travelling communities, all centred on huts like these, were the ingredients for the formation of a separate state within a state. What this particular community lacked in order to prosper however was working class solidarity; philosophical discussion was easily ousted by the need to fill the belly.

The means to repel starvation could be taken from these workers at a whim by the despised gangers; kings in their own workforce. Through their brutality intellectual growth was stifled, power centralised and the workforce just did as they were told by the man who told them to do it. Any advances in equality would be stillborn, leadership challenges and the growth of dissenting groups could be dissolved with a cudgel; loyalty gained by the simple expedient of an extra crust of bread; support gained by the threat of loss of livelihood.

This was the hut's pedigree. The navvies used it as makeshift home and hearth, their lives consisting of work and of always, always being one meal away from full. The abundance of game and large tracts of growing crops were always in view, always a temptation, and so it was that many a hare, rabbit, partridge or pheasant kept the freshly scrumped swede, potatoes and cabbages company in the pots that bubbled in these iron wheeled huts. These were the days when, on any given field, grey partridges could be night-netted in double figures; when running dogs and gate nets were as much a part of the labourers' lives as were shovels and picks; when it was expected you brought along a dog which could be sent back to the hut with the sound of a single whistle if cornered; when men, finding themselves in that same tight corner, asked for no quarter and gave none. What they faced, if caught, were harsh punishments administered by the very landowners on whose estates they poached. They knew there was only ever going to be one verdict and you were hung for a sheep as a lamb, so being caught meant finding a way out, no matter who got hurt or how badly.

Over time and with the help of a revolutionary hand, this hut had seen a change of fortune. It was now a poacher-turned-gamekeeper and the wheat it held, that would have saved its past community from starvation, now went to fill the crops of the five-figure pheasant stock released each year onto the estate. Only the spirit and suffering of those workers remained, absorbed into the hut's planking. It was their sole surviving relative, bearing witness to the present state of England's sporting countryside, the efforts of its game keepers and the fitness of its game birds. On windy nights, David often heard the air trilling through the spokes of the hut's iron wheels and fancied it an echo of the poaching navvy's whistle sending lurcher to kennel.

Shaking himself from the reverie, David strode along the ride, pheasants moving out of his way just sufficiently to avoid being trodden on as they gathered for the morning feed. In the hut, he filled his shoulder bag with the mixture of wheat containing a sprinkling of pheasant pellet then, stepping back onto the ride, began to walk as he whistled the birds to feed, scattering the mix along the straw as he went. It was the falsetto click of alarmed pheasants and the dull crack of fluttering wings that stopped his progress.

'Summat up. Sounds like ground bother... Jesus, today of all days.' His pace quickened and even though he'd be loath to fire it in the pen, cursed the fact he had no gun. 'Bet it's a bloody fox... bet y'. Fuck, fuck it!'

A thick long stick lying on the ground just before the bend in the feed ride caught his eye. It may just be useful, was certainly better than nothing. Bending swiftly, he picked it up and, like a Christian bearing a crucifix, made his way round the bend and into the star arena.

Most birds were still scratching at the straw, albeit with some agitation. Those on the rides leading away from the centre, however, were alert, heads erect and concentrating as only those on death row can concentrate when they hear the jingle of the jailer's keys. David stood his ground and waited. Immobility and silence would give him all the details needed before deciding on a course of action. In this lull, his fieldcraft manual flicked across his mind.

'Not of the winged variety or all rides would have cleared at the raptor's first pass overhead. No flying pheasants so not a fox; they jump high, send shock waves out over a far larger radius. A cat? No. Such a lack of success in the midst of such plenty. No. So stoat or weasel or rat.' The sounds of agitation continued. 'This speed an' stamina? Not a rat. So, stoat or weasel.'

David moved into the centre of the star. Above his head, looking every bit as powerful as the sword that had separated Medusa's portable vivarium from her shoulders, the stick was raised ready for battle. He settled and, by listening intently, followed the chase's progress.

Gradually it became clear from the chorus of pheasants that the duet of hunter and hunted were headed towards the centre star. David gauged the probable entrance point, took three steps back, spread his legs well apart to maintain balance like a golfer at the tee, quickly slid his hands up the stick to correct its length and waited again. A little patience would mark his fieldcraft theory paper; the result came back fast.

Two hen pheasants immediately to his left scattered as a melanistic hen bird with a damaged right wing tip crashed onto the riding immediately followed by the brown sinews of a dog stoat, both of them partners in a real life cartoon chase. Absolutely intent on its goal of breakfast, the manic mustelid saw nothing but the endgame and, absolutely intent on escape, the hen saw nothing but possible annihilation looming. But this was no game ended by the timely intrusion of a plummeting grand piano; life and death were at stake.

The hen pheasant jinked sharply to her right, running directly between David's open legs. Not to be outdone the stoat, with a dash of white and a flick of a dandy's tail-tuft, followed suit. David swept the club down and it moved at hurricane speed and right on target. Only when inches from the head of the stoat, travelling at full power and correct trajectory, did the end of the stick come into contact with the ground proving the second theory of the morning; time spent in research is never time wasted. The bottom six inches of the stick snapped off and the shock wave that went up David's arm was sufficient to severely jar his shoulder. It did nothing, however, to lessen the inertia of the now severely shortened stick. His gripping fist, now freed from the full stop of the stick's initial impact, crashed into his testicles.

The gush of air from David's open mouth was just ahead of the sound his backside made as he crashed to the ground. He slowly rolled onto his side and into the foetal position; the feed bag's impact with the floor sent nine pounds of mixed wheat and pellet rocketing high into the air. The startled stoat skittered off in a ninety degree sweep, sending straw debris and stale pheasant droppings into David's face. The six inch tip of his now-shattered sword of freedom fell harmlessly alongside its head; all this was followed by a wheat and pellet hail storm. As silence and inactivity descended so the once terrified pheasants now gingerly made their way back onto the feed ride and began to peck at the scattered food.

David lifted himself slightly, on the edge of vomiting, trying desperately to breathe properly. Looking along the feed ride, his gasped words came through clenched teeth and a fit of coughing.

"Aaah...! Fuck... me knackersssssssaaah!"

With the words exhaled he flopped onto his side again, both hands still clutching his groin.

—⁓—

The midmorning sunshine ran its searching fingers over the autumn coat of the fallow doe standing motionless in the valley below Brabham's Wood. Her attitude was of one intensely alert, all energies channelled into her ears. Far off, like the popping of champagne corks, the sound of gunfire came across the valley and into her sensory computer. The distance was worked out in seconds, as was its relative seriousness. After a protracted period of listening the deer visibly relaxed, dropping her head to pull languorously at the frost-bruised grass that carpeted the valley floor. The line of gun pegs, sapwood sucker sentries to their giant, wood-bound brothers and sisters, stretched away from her.

She bent, plucked at the grass again then lifted her head at the sound of further gunshots. Brabham's Wood and the promise of better fodder and cover beckoned. With measured deliberation, the fallow doe began her trek up the slope and melded into the wood's flushing point, her autumn larder.

"Me nuts look like the arse end on a mandrill."

"Do what?" asked Liam as he and David, accompanied by assorted canine accomplices, walked out of Fir-Plant Slide after the first, very successful drive of the day.

"You know, one of them baboon-like things with the big blue arse an' humbug face... you know."

Liam smirked. "Bad as that are they? No sex please, we're bluish is it!" Liam laughed at his own play on words.

"Oh yes. Oh, very funny that. No bloody sympathy from you, an' Eric's compassion all but absent. Great. Fine bunch of mates you are... great."

"An' you sound brighter."

"Do I?"

"Better than yesterday, in spite of your stoat encounter."

"Yeah, well..."

"A good openin' drive does wonders for a body, eh?"

David smiled. "Ar, it does." Fir-Plant Slide had, indeed, been an excellent drive and its success gave cause for some beaters to begin talking about estate records under threat. "It's what defines my life, y' know?"

"I do."

"Sorry if I've been a bit of a shit recently; just things, y' know?"

"I do. Not the details, but I can work out from other stuff you've said, you know, that Steph's not exactly in love with the job, an' if the missus don't like it..."

"One way of puttin' it."

"Only way."

"Ar, Maybe." As they moved towards the tarpaulin covered trailer that would take beaters and keepers to the far side of The Old Railway and the next drive, David stopped and commanded Liam's full attention. "It may be

I'll be askin' a favour or two… some time off. Nothin' to put the season at risk, not in any way, just the odd break or two; February maybe."

"Ar?"

"Could do with the support, Liam… think I… my time, the job an' other bits might have caused some upset. Let's just say Steph's taken some strange action to bring it to my attention."

"Is it terminal?"

"Depends how it plays out. Maybe. Not sure, so I'd be grateful for some leeway an' not too many questions."

"Notwithstandin' what you've just said, is there anythin' you can pass on?"

"I can tell y' she's gonna go to her folks for a week or so, after the season's over."

"Right… like that is it? Right." Liam considered for a few moments. "Right, then you give me as much notice of events as you can an' I'll cut you as much slack as possible; how's that?"

"Thanks."

"Won't be able to sort things out every time."

"No, I know. Don't expect it, just whenever possible."

"Right. Can I mention this to Eric?"

"As much as you think he needs to know."

"Would you rather?"

"Well, we've already touched on things so he's not entirely in the dark."

"Right." Liam smiled as they covered the remaining few yards to the trailer. "All this lot then you smack yourself in the knackers. Some payback, eh?"

"Ar, with interest."

"You might say it was stoatally out of order." Liam laughed again as they reached the trailer and climbed into the covered back. The tractor set off to the yells of those inside who had not heard the full details of the stick-fight at Brabham's Wood, demanding David tell them exactly what had happened.

By lunchtime the subject of David's fight with the stoat had been exhausted and everyone involved in the day's sport was feeling particularly well pleased with the morning's events. Of the four drives completed, none had fallen short of expectations, indeed The Old Railway and The Clump had exceeded previous days.

Liam sent Eric and the trailer full of beaters on to the lunch break and he and David walked back to help the guns and pickers-up clear the ground of shot game. They could hear the level of praise and Liam spoke to the Duke of Arden in passing.

"That tested them, Your Grace. Sorted the men from the boys."

"Certainly did, Coyne." He moved over to them and addressed David. "Superb drive, keeper." David tipped his cap as the Duke turned toward his host and called over. "I think I must be a boy then, Reggie."

"Thought you did awfully well, Johnny. Not easy at number two peg, twistin' back like they do."

They moved on as Liam confided in David. "No signs of any tantrums yet. The day's goin' really well, last thing we want is him dancin' off his peg again, like that Fred Adair."

"Fred Astaire, you daft sod, an' I don't want him doin' it neither."

"Well, whose Fred Adair then?"

"Red Adair; Red! Do you not listen to the news? He fights oil fires!

"I'll bet Ginger don't like that."

David looked at him for a moment or two. "There are times when I can't tell whether you do this on purpose or not."

"Tell you what though, I think we might have a decent lad in Mister Stephen, y' know. I 'eard he said summat yesterday lunchtime. Good sign, that he had the gumption. Couldn't have been easy. Light at the end of Lordy's tunnel, eh? Only reason all's right today is 'cos Lordy's got what he wants. Right peg number for the first drive 'cos Christopher didn't forget his special pins today."

"Probably never will again neither."

"I'll lay money on it, not if he wants to remain entire; an' that's the measure of the man who's in charge, Dave. That's the difference between him bein' unbearable and halfway bearable – the simple fact he's had plenty of birds over him. An' y' know, the pity is, when he wants to, when he can control hisself he can bloody shoot an' all. Did you see that left an' right he had at the Railway, towards the end of the drive?"

"That pair of cocks? Yeah. He killed that second one a treat. It must've looked like a thrush when it went over him, took near on five seconds to hit the deck. Come down stone dead. Crackin' shot. Even Eric said so, an' that's after Boys' Day. He's in the pound seat at Brabham's Wood."

They climbed the stile out of the field as Liam nodded. "An' I'm glad of it, even if it is rigged. The way he's shootin' today, he'll keep the bag up, maybe get you a record; make up for that bloody Major Tranter! You'd think, him havin' been in the army, he should be able to shoot a bit; couldn't hit a tank with a sponge. An' that bloke next to him, what's his name?"

"Him with the blonde lass who can't stop talkin'? Got that spaniel as keeps whinin'?"

"Ar, him. Mister Thomson, aint it?"

"Delaney." answered David.

"Yeah, that's him; Delaney, ar," said Liam as David smiled at him. "How come he got an invite? For all the use he is, he may as well chuck that bloody spaniel at the birds... an' then he can chuck that girl he's with at me. Pretty little thing she is." Dave smiled again. "But, our Major Useless notwithstandin', you've given 'em an excellent mornin', in spite of gettin' mugged by that stoat."

"Done me best," David looked towards the horizon, "in spite of the home front. Still; time, events... folk can change, y' know?"

"Ar. I just hope you an' Steph can sort out whatever it is that's troublin' you both. Eh?"

"I hope so too."

"You gotta pull all the ingredients together then reduce 'em all down to what you really want, Dave, y' know? An' if it's really what you want then hang on to what you've got."

"That's very profound, comin' from you."

"Not me; Frankie Valli, 'Four Seasons'."

"How come, of all things, you can member that?"

"Teenage years, girls, fun...free time."

"Ar. Right." They reached the porchway of the beater's hut and, as they removed their boots, they could hear Eric holding forth on how the increase in the bag was due to the addition of his birds left over from Boys' Day. David smiled. "Listen; I can hear him claimin' the cup already."

They entered the hut and several voices broke into the theme song from '*Record Breakers*' followed by general laughter and conversation. The warm pork pies and two bottles of port sent up from the house lulled the chatter.

Gradually belly's filled, the conversation restarted and talk inevitably returned to the possibility of the beat's record being broken, even more so when the game-cart driver arrived with the morning's numbers.

With just two more drives to come after lunch and four hundred and sixty one and a half brace in the bag already it certainly looked precarious, even to David. A sweep was opened by the beaters as to the final count for the day, and some of the numbers suggested were mighty close to David's own thoughts as to what the day would yield.

The picking-up team arrived for their lunch just as keepers and beaters were leaving, and their fresh discussion was stifled in with the tobacco smoke as the door to the hut closed.

Outdoor clothing back on, Liam turned to David as he climbed up onto the trailer. "You gonna get that terrier of yours, we'll need her in that thick stuff? I'd ask Eric, but he hasn't got one."

Eric's voice floated out from the porchway. "Will have soon though."

"If you're lucky," David replied. "Ar. Pick us up at the gate will y', Peter?"

Peter Bennett, the tractor driver for the afternoon, nodded. "Ar. Will do."

David made his way to his home a short distance away as the rest of the beaters climbed aboard and sorted out their positions and dogs amongst the straw bale seating. Eventually the tractor arrived outside David's gate and he rounded the end of the house accompanied by Jill. Seeing he was alone, several of the beaters called out.

"Where's Steph?"

"Highlight of the day when we see her."

"Not hidin' her from us are y'?"

The shouts and laughter came thick and fast from within the trailer but Liam's voice cut short continuing comment. "Come on, settle down! The day'll be over before we get to Brabham's at this rate an' you all know how long it takes to do that drive. Let's get a move on!" The tractor set off as Jill joined the beating staff and the trembling canine crew huddled further inside the trailer, but David stood at its rear, his one hand holding the roof bar to steady himself as he looked back at the cottage and its empty front path.

As they drew close to the wood the chit-chat and friendly banter was halted by Liam who addressed his troops, involving old hands and newcomers alike in the plan, picking out trusted individuals and detailing them with specific tasks.

"OK you lot, listen up! After we're clear of the release pen, where the ground rises sharp and off to the left, the trees an' ground cover's thin 'cos we've had the timber blokes in to shift some of the stunted stuff. That was last February, so the cover's not had time to thicken out."

"Did they shift much?" asked Geoff Riley from deep inside the trailer.

"Ar, enough, an' they made a right mess in there an' all. Some deep ruts not been back-filled yet so everyone walk careful through there. An' keep your bloody dogs up. It'll be easy to get through so I don't want no dogs in the next county before we're five minutes into the drive. OK?"

The team dismounted from the trailer in relative silence and Liam led the way through the firs and into the pen. Jill was at David's heel panting hard with adrenalin-filled excitement as Liam called them round once more, dropping the level of his voice as he spoke.

"Simon and Geoff, when you get to the centre ride give us a call. The guns will be waitin' at the bottom gate; go down an' let the back guns in. Rest of you stand bloody still, just tap your sticks, an' no cluckin' nor whistlin', we aint callin' chickens in. An' no talkin'!" He indicated Simon and Geoff again. "Lordy'll see to the front line. Bring guns six, seven and eight up to join us in the line. They'll shoot their way to their pegs as usual then stand behind us."

"Are they still pegged on the feed ride?" asked Geoff.

"Yeah, but a bit further along this year, just to try an' miss them snowberry on the left. You'll see the pegs when you get to the ride. OK?"

"OK."

"There'll be two pickers-up behind 'em, but mark any early birds shot just in case. Dave, you'll be on the ride callin' the drive through. Arthur? Arthur! You'll be in the middle so make sure it don't get ahead of the right hand. Eric'll be waiting at the ride end but I want you to collect up the stops as you go. Don't leave it to no one else… understand? You do it." Arthur nodded. "Eric will let us know when Lordy's got the front guns in place. If this idle waster's done his job we'll have a few birds boxed in so I don't want 'em goin' out before time nor in one big flush neither. Let Dave an' Jill do their bit first, then we'll feed in the line a couple at a time. If you hear a rise of birds or get a call to hold still then bloody-well hold still! Don't move forward again until you're called on by either me, Dave or Eric. All good?" The assembled beaters nodded and whispered their agreement. "OK. Line out. Let's see what we can do about this record. Simon, keep a bit ahead for this first bit. On you go then beaters!"

The line moved off, the beaters close together at first but gradually spreading out as the pen and the wood widened, the beaters sticks coaxing Brabham's Wood to her eventual, hopeful orgasm of sporting birds. The weather was ideal. The sun shone brightly and the wind, a soft and unhurried breeze, bestowed the gift of a lingering caress to each leaf and tree trunk as it moved through the woodland in the perfect direction. All the omens were set fair. Notwithstanding the stoat, David had seen the feed rides stacked to bursting point that morning. This would be a drive to remember.

The vast majority of birds had moved deeper into the wood almost as soon as the tractor pulled up but any that were left were soon moved on by the line of human and canine bristles that swept the woodland clean. By the time the beating line emerged from the pen a familiar pattern was beginning to develop and the assembled guns, waiting silently by the bottom gate, had watched with growing excitement as large groups of birds continuously crossed the wide central ride. Early dogs drifted onto this centre ride like the first smoke from a forest fire and the beating team emerged close behind them then stood still as these assembled guns divided into their teams. The back guns, accompanied by their loaders and Simon and Geoff, moved into their starting positions as His Lordship took the remainder round the wood's edge and on to their pegs at the front of the drive.

After this brief halt the beaters moved on once more, right hand first, dogs now kept more firmly under control as the number of pheasants continued to build under the backward and sideward pressure of the advancing beating line. Odd birds flew back, the walking guns doing their best through the miasma of branches, and any birds that were hit were quickly gathered in by the pickers-up some thirty yards behind them, but the vast majority of pheasants kept moving forward on foot, into the flushing point ahead. Eventually these three back guns reached their pegs on the feed ride alongside the beaters and, after a short wait, Eric let it be known the front guns were in place. David, accompanied by an aloof and superior Jill, moved along the ride to inspect each gun-and-loader duo and brief them as to drive's idiosyncrasies. Once back to their position in the centre of the line, Liam's call went up.

"On slow now, tap them sticks, keep an eye on each end, just let it keep a bit ahead!" The beating line entered the start of the thick cover of the flushing point which acted as a sponge, soaking up the pheasants as they crept further into its density and darkness, feeling safe and secure in the confusion of cover.

After a short distance the beaters minds were re-focused by David. "Pay attention you lot, an' keep them sticks tapping! We'll have 'em slipping out if we don't keep our eyes open. Steady on the left! Jenny! Keep that kid on your left back a bit, it's not a bloody race tell him!" This was the culmination of the year's work for him; the reason for all the nights out, the long days, the missed meals and family company and, for David, of so much more. There was no way he was going to allow a lack of concentration in others spoil the drive. "Jill! Steady you little bugger!" Jill lifted a paw. "Sit up!" The terrier halted and waited, stump wagging bottom hovering.

The black Labrador belonging to Jenny Sawyer appeared near Jill, its mind so fixed on testing the light breeze for squatting pheasant that it never even noticed the terrier.

What was going through Jill's mind at that point would never be discovered.

What would eventually be discovered was that both terrier and hunting Labrador had completely failed to scent the fallow doe as she lay, marble-like just three feet from them. Caught inside the advancing line of beaters behind her and the guns positioned in front, she had reverted to the highly successful trick used by all species of deer for generations; she had become a leaf.

Fifteen minutes earlier, on hearing the arrival of the beating team, the deer had moved to the thick cover in the upper reaches of the flushing point and had secreted her bulky form deep into the undergrowth's colour and visual scribble. Selecting the thickest part of the briars that surrounded her, the doe moved backwards until she could feel the stems and their guardian of thorns gathering up behind her; this cat's cradle of blackberry formed an excellent barrier to her rear end. Next she needed to strengthen her invulnerable invisibility by pressing her tail to her tummy so that only the smallest amount of her white rump showed and the area giving out most scent was well wrapped up. Then, dropping down on her knees, the doe sealed the scent glands in between her front hooves by fixing them tight against her upper front legs as she gently lowered her rear end to the floor, pressing the scent glands in between the cleats of her rear hooves into the ground. Once in this position she moved just a fraction, a sort of snake-like wriggle as she exerted a slight, downward pressure into the leaf mould. Stretching her neck out straight to face the distant cacophony, she lowered her head onto the woodland floor. With ears erect, eyes unblinking and nostrils wide, she regulated then slowed her breathing so as to centralise all movement to an inward one. This completed parts one to six of the Fallow Deer's Green Cross Code, now all she could do was wait, motionless; see what developed.

What developed was the story the woodland creatures told as they passed her hiding place, confirming that her position was fast becoming more precarious. This was neatly underlined by the sound of Hades growing louder and closer and, like the hands of Armageddon's clock the deer pressed her ears flat onto the top of her head, their midnight positions a comment on her expected lifespan...

"Now you stay close. Don't go dashin' off." Jill's ears drooped fractionally as she wrestled to cross the chasm between canine understanding and human expectation. "On steady!"

Jill whipped round to move forward and, just for a nanosecond, terrier and fallow doe were nose to nose. Both sensed through whiskers and noses that here was unclear confrontation and so the actions and reactions of these two protagonists was neither considered nor rehearsed but came, rather, from the dim recesses of their subconscious, handed down by their ancestors.

The released nerves of survival in the stretched-taut fallow doe allowed her, even from her cramped position, to leave cover and clear terrier in one fluid movement as she made to exit by the front door, which was David.

Jill, unsure of just what this explosion was, did what any self-respecting and threatened terrier would do; she met the challenge head-on and with all guns blazing. Leaping back and up then biting down hard onto the fast disappearing deer's upper thigh she quickly became a Wall of Death sidecar passenger.

David, sensing not seeing the deer's direction of travel, had only enough time to sway to his left to avoid the fast-approaching fallow doe. The terrier's body was whipped away in an arc as the deer twisted to avoid David, which it did, but the thirteen pounds of battle-hardened terrier smacking David in the upper chest didn't.

The blow winded but did not remove the tenacious terrier.

It felled David with consummate ease. The air left his body in one great gush.

"Furrr-k!"

"Deer back!"

"Look out!"

These comments from the beaters in the immediate vicinity were all shouted at the fast disappearing canine-cervid duo, neither of whom was quite in control of their actions as they careered through the woodland in the direction of the line of waiting back guns.

On all sporting estates of any worth, the shooting of ground game was banned on driven days but, as far as the deer was concerned, death from every direction was imminent, especially from this terrier who was now growling savagely. It was as the line of guns came into view that the deer's first surge of sense-blinding adrenalin was overtaken by both her predicament and the power in Jill's jaws. For the first time since she had risen from the undergrowth the doe showed her fear, her pain, her distress and the seeming hopelessness of her case in the only way she could; she began to scream loudly.

This sound snapped the prostrate David back to the present.

"Jesus... H... Christ! What th' fuck...?"

He lay in the undergrowth struggling to weld together the physical pain and mental bewilderment caused by the last few seconds. In an unequal fight for both breath and voice, he called out.

"Jill! Leave... it! Leave...!"

The deer's screams of pain grew louder as the terrier's grip gradually affected its ability to move and then, in slow motion, she folded over onto the ground, her forward progress halted by numbing pain and sheer terror. Seizing the moment in all four paws, Jill released her grip and shot round to the throat end of the by now prostrate, wailing beast in order to administer the coup de grace', her body seemingly a good ten feet behind her jaws. Seeing the approach of teeth, the deer raised her head and folded her head and neck backwards, away from Jill's initial snap, then continued arching her body towards her own hind quarters to create living origami.

Missing her target, Jill's forward lunge carried her well past the spot where she should have made contact. In a desperate bid to salvage something from this fast-looming, ignominious defeat, the terrier put her rear legs into overdrive as she too reached for her own hindquarters in an effort to recover the overshot ground as the fallow doe unfolded like a whip-thong, her hooves skipping and slipping as she rocketed away; back in the direction she had just come. Leaves and debris fountained up and her rear hoof struck the terrier sending her yelping backwards, out of wind and out of the chase.

David staggered to his feet, gasping and disorientated, filling what was the deer's escape route and so received the full force of the returning doe's full weight full in the small of his back.

There was no expletive this time, David just collapsed.

"Ayup!"

"What the bloody hell!"

"Look out!"

All this from the beaters nearby was far too late to be of any help.

It was the limping, winded Jill as she wagged her stump and licked his face that stirred the flattened keeper sufficiently into consciousness to hear, with awesome clarity, the roar of fourteen hundred pairs of panic-stricken pheasant wings filling the air as they left the flushing point of Brabham's Wood as one bird, out and over the heads of the waiting guns.

The fallow doe ran on.

On through flushing cover and carefully gathered pheasant.

On and out into the valley.

On through the line of front guns in her blind effort to escape from this county.

Just as he fell back into a semi-faint, David heard His Lordship's shout from up front.

"Ho! Fallow deer out left! Leave her be!"

This was complemented nicely by Liam's unabridged version underscored with a continuous beating of pheasant wings.

"Fuckin' hell! Where's that bastard deer come from? All them fuckin' pheasants…! Hold the line… Oh, for fuck's sake!"

—⚉—

"Well, I'm still not convinced you'll be fit for tomorrow."

The guns had retired to their evening of dinner and deliberation, the beaters had gone home. At the back door of the big house the day's events were being discussed by the three keepers over a cup of tea, a slice of fruit cake and a shared part-bottle of single malt the housekeeper, Margaret, had brought out to them, compliments of His Lordship.

"I said, I'll be OK." David looked at Liam. "Honest. What time do you want me there?" Liam looked at Eric then back at David. "I'll be alright, I've said. What time, Eric?"

"Only if you're sure."

"Keep this bugger up an' I'll change me mind. Time."

"I was thinkin' about seven."

"Christ, early as that?"

"Well, to do any good, yeah. Them birds'll be on the move from daybreak, an' that maize still beckons. Threat of some rain tonight, no amount but tomorrow's forecast is for a bright start so that'll mean light that bit sooner... so yeah, on stop by seven really."

"Hm. Gonna be a bit difficult, unless I feed most of my beat tonight."

Liam stepped in on their conversation. "I want you to be able to function tomorrow, Dave. Some time at home is what's needed, y' know? Last thing you need to do now is bugger off without tea an' hump around a feed bag full of grain for six mile. Is there not another way we can do this, Eric?"

"Not that I can see. If I'm on stop at The Quarry how can I collect the early beaters to tap that maize into it an' feed my main coverts? Enough of a mad rush as it is. I've got Hattie feedin' the duck for me at half six so she's out the picture an' I'm feedin' my outside woods tonight; in the dark, if you please!"

"Well, yeah, if you're feedin' tonight it will be dark, that's 'cos the sun's gone in."

"Thank you for that observation. It just seemed to make sense for Dave to do it, if he feels able. You'll not be feedin your pen 'til later, will y'?"

"Well, no. Not shootin' my beat tomorrow so not 'til about half-eight, but my outsides will have to be done as usual an' before the day starts, that's where the time's soaked up... I reckon I'd not get there before half seven at the earliest, an' that's providin' things go to plan."

"Liam?"

"I'm out the equation. I've to do the guests' cartridge bags, see Douglas in the kitchen about the loaders' food for lunch, the game dealer's here first thing to collect today's lot then I've to feed what I don't get round to doin' tonight. Earliest I could be there is eight."

"Too late," said Eric. "Them birds'll be in another county by then. That bloody maize on Jackson's..."

"I suppose I could ask Steph to go, to be there by seven, I mean, then I can do my bits and get to her at half past. Where do you want the stop?"

"Dead centre, Dave. In the valley, base of the cliff. Would she do it?" Eric asked, grabbing at the possibility.

"Don't know... think so. If I ask nicely. An' it's only 'til I get there, so half hour at most, then Steph can get back an' sort breakfast; get her a bit involved, to feel part of things y' know. That be OK?"

"If you think she'll wear it, ar, that'd be grand, an' if she can tap in the hedgerows as well..."

"On the far side?"

"Ar. I'll come in the same way, bring beaters to the hedgerows as soon as I can and get them to take over, then we'll tap in that maize, move back what's been missed." Eric flicked a look across at Liam. "Things a little bit easier on the 'ome front now are they, Dave?"

David paused, unsure of how to answer. "Not completely right yet, no. Still work to do… both sides; still… a work in progress."

"An' you think she'll be alright about goin' on stop?"

"She's a good lass deep down; knows how important these days are for me, for all of us. She might get things wrong sometimes but she's not the sort to do bad things… deliberate like." David paused and considered what he'd just said as both Eric and Liam stood in silence. "An' anyway, we 'aven't got much choice 'ave we? So, me an' Steph then."

Eric picked up his scotch. "Thanks Dave, an' thank Steph for me as well. With it stopped-off early we might be able to rescue summat from The Quarry, 'specially after that daft bastard went roamin' about yester-Evenin', M'Lord!"

His Lordship, dressed for dinner, appeared in the doorway behind David and Liam. "Evening, Cornby, Coyne, Clarke. The three C's deep in conversation, I see?" His Lordship smiled, expecting a reaction to his oft repeated opening; there was none this time either.

"Yes, M'Lord," replied Liam. "Just talkin' through the drives for tomorrow, where the problems might lie."

"Indeed. Did you form any useful conclusions?"

"We did, Sir. Thought The Quarry would be a good one to start off with."

"Agreed. I must say, I'm looking forward to the day, as are the guests"

"Some more than others, M'Lord, I'll bet."

His Lordship smiled. "Yes, I would think so. The Quarry seems to quieten most guns down when it comes up for discussion." He turned slightly in Eric's direction. "We can just hope the foxes haven't returned."

"I can almost guarantee it, Sir."

"Can you, Cornby?"

"Yes, Sir. After what we saw the other day we've been careful to check things over this time. Probably moved on after the last scare any'ow, an' we've moved the pegs back to their usual positions, 'cos of doin' the drive properly this time, so we know where all the action will be takin' place."

"Good, yes, I see." Avoiding Eric's poorly concealed jibe, His Lordship played his opening gambit. "Bit unfortunate, those foxes."

Liam countered it. "Only there 'cos you'd asked for the wires to be lifted though, Sir."

"Yes, but…"

"For the hunt to find one you said, Sir."

His Lordship was in check. "Well, yes, you have a point, Coyne, although we saw neither of them come out." He raised a quizzical eyebrow.

Liam never flinched. "No, Sir. Sewellin' line turned 'em back; one went past me not twenty yard away. If I'd had a gun… but the damage was done by then, Sir."

Checkmate to Liam.

New game.

"And then the fallow deer of today?"

"You saw that one, Sir."

"I did."

"Heard you call on it; thank you, Sir." His Lordship was in check again.

"Heard you call on it too, Coyne. Caused a blush or two amongst the ladies present." Liam lost his queen.

"Yes, M'Lord; my apologies."

"Thank you. I'll convey them over dinner."

Checkmate.

One game all.

His Lordship turned to David. "So, just the one deer then?"

"Yes, M'Lord. Gave us all a surprise, one way or another."

"So I heard. How's the back, Clarke?"

"Been better, Sir."

"I can imagine."

David watered down the conflict. "Last time I try to make out with a fallow doe."

All of them smiled. "We're givin' him the night off tonight, M'Lord. Apart from a bit of night-feedin' which Dave assures us he's alright to do."

"Are you?"

David nodded. "Yes, M'Lord. Fine. Thank you for your concern."

"Then I've told him to get off 'ome an' rest before the obstacle course of tomorrow an' more night work kicks back in."

"Very wise, Coyne. Have we had much bother of late?"

"Odd bit of roadside poachin' Sir; some local losses, an' you know about the duck an' Eric's bit of success. The only big session we know of is those Coventry boys we caught; you know about that too."

"I do, and a well done comes from me to you all on that. Always a concern, when events happen; especially events on a shoot day... like random foxes."

"Always a worry, M'Lord."

"Yes, of course."

"Late nights are beginnin' to tell, but it's what keeps us free of blaggards."

"Yes, I can imagine." All fell silent, then His Lordship cleared his throat. "Ahem. Well, I'll get back. You have enough drink out here? Margaret brought out the whisky?"

"Yes, Sir, she did." Then all three keepers chimed by return. "Thank you."

"Good. Well, I'll wish you all a goodnight. You'll see to the cartridge bags for tomorrow, Coyne?"

"As usual, M'Lord, yes."

"Leave the list on the entrance hall table, so I can collect the money."

"Yes, M'Lord."

"Right, good. Well, goodnight." He turned and moved back into the house then stopped as the thought struck him. "Oh, by the way, we've had a gun drop out at the last minute, Lord Ashcliffe." Their faces showed alarm for such an announcement this late in the day as His Lordship continued. "But we'll still be up to strength; Miss Anne will be shooting instead. If you can sort out some sixteen bore cartridges for her, that would be much appreciated. Make a note of how many and add them on to the payment list."

"Yes, M'Lord."

"Right, goodnight all and see you in the morning."

After a few seconds, Liam turned to Eric. "Bloody hell, that were close!"

"It were. I just caught sight of the toe of his shoe reflected in that window in the door; could've been difficult if he'd been a second earlier." Eric shook his head. "Did you hear 'im, when you said about the hours out? 'Yes, I can imagine!' he said. No he bloody can't! He hasn't got a clue what it's like at this end of the stick; none of his lot 'ave!" There was a short pause then Eric spoke again, a glint in his eye. "Which way will y' be goin' then Dave – round y' beat I mean, for mornin' feed, before you meet up with Steph?"

"I'll come in from Rickett's Farm end, after I've fed The Railway and before I go into The Quarry, why... Oh, hang on."

"Well, if you're comin' that way you can lift them fox wires in Grey's Copse for us."

David looked across at Liam, smiled and shook his head. "I knew there were summat comin'. Can you believe this? Which fox wires?"

"You know two of 'em. There's one on Rickett's Farm end, by that gap in the thorns, and that other one on The Quarry side, by that broken post, but I've put another halfway up the bank, on that track. Charlie's been usin' it so I popped one down yesterday; shouldn't be surprised if it's full when you get there."

"Oh yeah, I'm sure. So, you want me to lift three wires then? In my delicate condition."

"Don't wanna catch any beater's dogs in there tomorrow when we blank it in, do we? Just think how bad you'd feel if that 'appened."

"How come all of a sudden it's my fault?"

"There's no blame bein' 'anded on; it'll just save me the walk back across after feedin' is all. That means I can collect the beaters sooner an' get over to you an' Steph a lot faster.

Liam cut short the chatter. "Yeah. Well, like I said to Lordy, give night duty a miss an' feed only what you have to tonight. Your back must be bruised as buggery the force that deer hit you."

David drained his glass and placed it back on the tray. Although the feeding he was about to do would take an hour or so and it was the spare bed that awaited him at home, he was pleased to accept the chance of a night off from poaching duty.

"See you tomorrow, Dave, an' no counterpane gymnastics tonight my lad."

Liam downed the rest of his Scotch and talked on hurriedly. "Right, Eric, let's get back to the game larder an' sort out the bag. I'll want thirty brace of pheasant, all the woodcock and forty brace of duck left for the kitchen, the rest can go. Game dealer's here at six."

David picked up his stick. "'Night, you two, see you on the ice in the fish market."

As he walked away, both Eric and Liam could see he was covering his feelings with a swagger.

"All's not well there, Liam. I know it."

"No. He said bits today, like he told you, but it was all misty, sort of unclear. I just hope whatever it is gets sorted. Bloody hell but that's turnin' cold! That's startin' to frost." Eric downed the whisky in his glass as Liam continued. "Right, game larder, I'm ready for me supper." He put his head inside the doorway. "Margaret? Margaret! We're off now! Thanks for the tea an' stuff! We'll leave it just inside the doorway here!"

An answer came from the depths. "Righto, Liam! See you."

"Ar! Let Douglas know I'll be in to see him about the loaders' lunches at quarter past five."

"Right!"

Eric and Liam walked out from the doorway's slash of light and into the dark yard.

On the other side of the estate, just as these first tentacles of evening frost were insinuating themselves into the crevices of Eric and Liam's clothing, so the last cock pheasant in Grey's Copse called its goodnights to Alec and fluttered to roost.

After three quarters of an hour sitting motionless in the hedge bottom that ran away from the copse and towards Rickett's Farm, Alec's body was ripe for a concerted assault by the elements; he shivered that inward, rippling shiver that causes the shoulders to roll. The forecast was for some rain but, as things stood, it seemed the night was going to be a still, sharp one; no night for the poacher. There was little point in him being there really, not in these conditions, gunless and listening to the birds go up to roost, pinpointing their position for later retrieval; a later retrieval now frozen out by the promised clear night and impending frost. No point that is except for the sheer pleasure of just being there. Shame really. Couple or three birds was all he wanted, and the copse would be the best place to get them.

Once part of a larger piece of scrub woodland, time and agricultural greed had honed Grey's Copse down to its present size and shape. The past efforts of limited stone mining had removed its heart, and the greeded-over ground now wore a plaster of nature's making – hawthorn and blackthorn scrub plus a mixture of youngish oaks and elder all in-filled with ground elder and bramble tentacles.

Although some distance from the centre of the estate, the copse's closeness to The Quarry meant it still had to be fed, but in silence, and as late in the day as possible. Alec knew all of this; the rough timings, the feeding routine. Only three fields short of the estate's eastern boundary and close to The Quarry, he also acknowledged that it made a tempting if high risk target.

'No point hangin' about now though,' he thought. 'Not on as still an evenin' as this.'

A clear sky and the start of biting temperatures were all the spur needed to deflate the balloon of his desire.

'Home an' a mug of tea...'

Rising, not without difficulty, Alec began to move homewards. Keeping close to the hedges that bounded the fields, he made his way to Rickett's Farm and the ink stain on the grey paper horizon that was The Clump, beyond which was home.

Chapter 12
Month 1 – November 1985

"Steph! Steph? You in the kitchen?"

Stephanie came out of the back door as David walked across the yard. "What is it?"

"Do you want to see a grass snake?"

"A what?"

"Grass snake, bottom of the garden under that old tin sheet."

"What were you doing looking under there?"

"Wanted to make sure there was no rats that close to the hen run. Took a peek an' there she were; snugged down an' ready to hibernate. You had one as a pet, didn't you, when you was a kid?"

"Erm... yes, I did."

"Just thought you'd like the memory."

"Well, wouldn't it be just as well to leave it be?"

"She's well set, not likely to shift as long as we're sensible... just thought you might want a look."

"How do you know it's a she?"

"Size of it. A good eighteen inches long, lovely markings. Matriarch, I'd guess." She stood by the door. "Well, you want a look-see?"

"No. Thank you... no. Not right now."

"Oh. OK." He looked crestfallen but managed a smile. "Well... just thought... I'll just make sure the tin's secure then. Back in a min.'"

In the kitchen, Stephanie bit her bottom lip as she poured off the last of the hedgerow jam she had been bottling. She had got it wrong, not going to see the snake. Too late now.

David came back into the kitchen and saw the arranged bottles. "Oh, right, I see. Didn't realise you were in the middle of summat. You should have said."

She grabbed at it. "Yes, yes I was. I thought you knew I was doing this today."

"How could I? You never mentioned it."

"Didn't I? Oh, sorry, must have been to someone else. Sorry."

"That's OK."

"Was she alright? The snake?"

"Oh ar, fine. Wish you'd had time to have a look, she were a lovely colour."

"Yes, sorry. Jam calling."

"Ar." He looked around the kitchen. "Thought I might make tea, do you want one?"

"Do you have time? I mean, it's not your usual time for tea. You're usually well occupied, traps and such."

"I've just got a breather 'til Liam comes to collect us for bale cart to the feed rides. He said he'd pick us up at the pigsties but I asked could he pick me up here and I'd grab a cup of tea... y'know, with you."

She stopped in her actions and looked at him. "Well, that'd be very nice. Then thank you, I'd love a cup."

He beamed. "Right, I'll get to it. Will there be a chance of tryin' that jam on some bread too?"

"The early batch should be set by now so, yes, I suppose so; made bread yesterday too, so you make the tea and I'll sort out plates and such."

They worked in companionable silence, just like any normal couple.

—◈—

The loaded straw cart bounced along the track. David and Eric, seated precariously on top of the bales, had to alter their centre of balance to avoid being sent over the edge.

"Don't mind his passengers." Eric indicated Liam sat in the tractor's cab and seemingly oblivious to their predicament.

"Why should he?" said David. "Perfectly comfortable where he is." He looked down onto the cab. "Oi! Fangio! Steady on there!" Liam turned in answer to the call, smiled, waved and carried on. "See? He could have lost us three fields ago an' not knowed it." Eric smiled.

Liam turned onto the riding of The Clump, dismounted and opened the gate as David slid down the rear bales ready to close it. After climbing back on, and with the tractor crawling gently along the ride, Eric and David threw off the replacement bales at each depleted stacking point. When they reached the far end of the wood, as Liam took the tractor and empty trailer out onto the field to turn it round, they both returned along the ride, stacking the bales neatly as they went.

With the tractor back at the entrance gateway, Liam turned off the ignition. "Did you leave me a couple of stacks open in the middle, for fox hides?"

"Ar, we did. Third an' sixth," called Eric. "Have we time for a smoke?"

"If you've got some we have, yeah."

David took off his jacket and removed a pack of sweets from the pocket. "That'll be fags instead of a sweet then will it?"

"I can do both."

David nodded in Liam's direction. "There's a level of greed goin' on 'ere that's unknown to the animal kingdom."

Liam watched Eric who opened his cigarette packet with one hand and shoved the other into the open sweet bag. "He fell into a pond of alligators once; ate three before they could haul him out." Liam took a cigarette from the pack and offered a light.

"Do you want a hand to spread some of this straw?" David waved the sweet bag at Liam who shook his head.

"No thanks, Dave, fag will do me for now. No, I'll do it this afternoon. Quite enjoy it really, up here on me own... nice."

"Ar, know what you mean."

Eric grabbed his feed bag from the back of the trailer. "Right, if that's the deal an' it's alright with you two, I'm gonna get off home."

"On a promise are we?"

"Ha! I've got two chances of that; a dog's chance an' no chance. No, I'm gonna lift the bottom of the pen wire in The Quarry. Need to give them birds full run now. Wire's just gonna be a net for Charlie to trap any slow risers against."

Liam looked across at David. "You lifted all yours yet?"

"Ar, all but the one in Barton's. I was gonna wait until after first shoot day through the main coverts before I did. What do you two think?"

"Reckon that's favourite. Liam?"

"Ar, me too. We're only in the first week of November, too early yet; it'll give the birds that fly in there from other drives a chance to get used to new quarters, an' a new feedin' time; will slow down their desires to bugger off over the border."

"What I thought." David pointed out a gang of pheasants that had sauntered onto the riding to scratch *idly at the ground. "Lunch queue formin', Liam. They always seem to know when fresh straw's goin' down, don't they."*

He looked up the ride. "They do that. Internal clock. No peace for the wicked, eh?"

"None," said Eric. "Right. I'm leavin'."

"On a jet plane?" asked David.

Eric shouldered his feedbag from the back of the trailer. "An' with that cheerful reply, I'll bid you both sod off."

Liam stubbed his cigarette underfoot. "Ar, right. Dave, can you take the tractor and trailer back to the yard. Drop the trailer by the gateway and hitch up the flatbed, then run it across to the wood yard. Garry and Neville want to load some cordwood for the big house."

"Right." David looked after the disappearing form of Eric and called out. "See you've finally spent some cash!"

"What?" Eric turned back.

"On a feedbag."

"Oh, that. Ar, well, it were no good waitin' for Lordy to do it." Eric looked at the bag. "It'll do 'til he buys the next one."

"Be out of fashion by then." David waved to him. "See you later for rabbitin'?"

Moving off, Eric waved regally. "Ar, I'll fetch along me ferrets."

"An' a dog; terrier would be useful," said Liam.

Eric stopped and turned again. "Not mine... wanted to chat about that."

"Oh, ar? What's that then?"

"Not now. Pen to get to. Later maybe." He turned, went through the gate and was gone.

"David looked at Liam. "What was that all about then?"

"I think he's lookin' to replace Patch. Said summat about it a while ago. Have you not heard him?"

"I've heard him mention it a few times, but after a while I stopped payin' attention. She not well then?"

"Just old."

"Oh, well..." David shook his head. "Don't know what he thinks I can do about it."

"Nor me."

David took another sweet from the pack. "He refused a pup from Jill's one an' only litter on account of the cost, tight-fisted bugger." He offered the pack to Liam.

"I remember, an' there'll be no replay neither... no thanks Dave... so he'll have to look elsewhere."

He pocketed them. "Y' right there. An' you didn't have one for the stud fee neither."

"No, well, too many dogs at the time. Nor you."

David shook his head. "No, same reason. Not over bright, were we? I reckon folk wantin' advice from us would be leanin' against an open gate." Liam smiled as David moved to the tractor and climbed aboard, talking as he went. "I'll get off then." He looked up the ride to where more pheasants were gathering. "You'll 'ave a mutiny on your 'ands if I keep you much longer."

Liam followed his gaze and made a move to the gateway. "Ar; best get to it. See you at the Brickyard, about three. Only want to do an hour, clear that thorn brake in there."

"Yup."

He stopped. "Oh, Dave. How's things with you, you know, with you an' Steph? Not that it's my business, just wondered... hoped all was well... or a bit better at least."

David smiled. "Some good days, some not so. Thanks, Liam. Bit better."

"Good. See you at three. I'll get the gate."

Driving through the gateway, David paused and leant out of the cab door. "Thanks, Liam."

"Ar. Right; three."

"Ar."

Liam watched him go, then the call and rapid wingbeat from a cock pheasant on the riding arrested his attention and he closed the gate.

"Yes, alright. Comin'. Keep y' feathers on."

Closing the freezer door, Alec left the back shed and went into the kitchen. Alice was half inside a tall cupboard in the hallway and he called to her as he closed the back door.

"Alice? What you doin' in there?"

"Nothin'. Just putting away some bits. You want some tea, I suppose?"

"Yeah; er, I'll make it... shall I?"

She pulled herself out from the cupboard and looked at him. Alec was leaning against the door jamb, arms folded. "You feelin' alright?"

"Ar. Why?"

"No reason. I'll have one as well then, if you're offerin'."

"'Course." He shoved himself upright. "I'll put the kettle on."

Alice watched him then busied herself for a few seconds more inside the cupboard before closing the door and going into the kitchen. Alec was just putting the kettle onto the range and she moved to the sink, picked up two mugs and went to the fridge.

Alec looked at her. "I'll do that. I said."

"Oh, right." She relinquished the mugs. "Just thought..."

"I can manage. Sit down... Where's the sugar?"

Alice smiled at him and pointed to the wall cupboard over the work surface. "In there. I'll get it."

Thanks." She picked up the sugar, placed it by the mugs and went back to the fridge. "What you doin'? I'll get the milk, sit y'self down."

"Just thought..."

"No, I'll get it." He opened the fridge door and took out the milk as Alice sat. "Is it this one?"

"The other's not opened yet?"

"No."

"So that's the one then."

"Right. Do you wanna biscuit with it?"

"Erm... yes, alright."

"Are they..."

"Still in the pantry? Yes. I'll get them..." She stood up "...And a couple of plates."

"Ar, right. Which pot are the tea bags in now?"

"Same one as always, the blue one, with the flowers on it. I'll get it, it's on my way to the pantry."

"Ar, right."

"Along with the biscuits."

"Right."

Putting the biscuits and teabag pot on the table, Alice opened the wall cupboard and took out the plates. "You alright for a minute?"

"Ar. Why shouldn't I be?"

"No reason." She put the plates down and left the room. "Back in a bit."

"Where you goin now? I'm makin' tea!"

"Won't be a second, gettin' summat." After a few moments she was back and handed Alec a large brown paper bag. "Here. Was goin' to leave it 'til Christmas but you may as well 'ave it now."

"What's this?"

"Tell you what, live dangerous, open it and 'ave a look."

"Sarky. I mean, what's this for? Not me birthday or nothin.'"

"Just a little summat for Christmas; I said. Well, open it."

"Ar, right." He began to open the bag tentatively.

"It's not tickin', you're safe."

"Ar. Thanks." He pulled out a woollen something or other from the bag and looked at it puzzled, unsure. "Er... thanks. It's lovely."

"You don't even know what it is yet."

"I do, it's a... a, summat you knitted, very soft, from that alpaca farm you went to, I'll bet. With that Stephanie."

"Go to the top of the class an' give out the pencils, you remembered! It's a scarf." She saw his expression. "Well, go on, try it on."

"A scarf!" He almost laughed. "Since when 'ave you ever known me to wear a scarf?"

"You're not gonna wear it?"

Now he saw her expression and smiled. "'Course, 'course I will..." He unrolled it. "It's very... big; did you do it to a pattern?"

"No. I just knitted 'til the wool ran out." She stepped forward and began to wrap the lengths around Alec's neck in order to shorten the ends. "It is a bit on the long side."

"A bit! There's enough here to rig out a small sailin' ship an' 'ave sufficient left over to wrap a whale up for winter." He smiled. "Joke. But it's very nice. Very... soft, ar, soft." He began to uncurl it. "What did your mate knit?"

"My mate?"

"Stephanie."

Alice shrugged as she took the scarf back and began to fold it. "Not sure. A cardigan, I think, or a jumper..."

"You don't know?"

"No."

"Unusual."

"What is?"

"That is. You two usually share all sorts. Just thought you'd know."

"Well I don't."

"You not seen her of late?"

"No. Well, not as much as we used to."

"Why's that?"

"Just… don't know, just not seen her."

"Fallen out?" He was fishing now, unsure, insecure, overly interested.

"What's it to you? You think it might be summat to do with you then?"

The answer came back fast. "No!" Almost too fast.

"Well then. She's just been busy. Season comin' up an' one thing an' another…" She looked at Alec. "Her husband out all hours."

"Alice…"

"Anyway, not the end of the world. We'll probably pick it up again if things go alright for her." She moved out of the kitchen and up the stairs waving the bag-wrapped scarf high. "I'll just put this away. I expect tea when I come back down."

He had to keep it calm, but the worry was near the surface of his question. "What things? Alice? What things?"

Alice answered on her travels. "What do you think?"

"I… don't. Just interested in your doin's, you know?"

Alice turned on the stairs still carrying the bag and stopped halfway down, talking to Alec over the banister rail. "Since when?"

"Since when, what?"

She sighed. "Since when have you developed an all-consuming interest in my friendship with Stephanie?"

"It aint all-consumin'! Just, interested. You were good friends, weren't y'?"

"Yes."

Month 1 – November 1985

"So, now you say you've not seen 'er for a bit but you know things aren't goin' quite right for her... was just, y'know, wonderin'. What things?"

"You really want to know?"

"Asked, didn't I?"

Alice sat on the step and looked at Alec through the bars. "OK, well, back in September, she... an' this is between just you an' me, right?"

"'Course."

"Well, she thinks she might be pregnant."

The only outward sign to this news was a twitch of Alec's right eye. "Well... that's good aint it?"

"Only if you're sure who the father is."

He rubbed his eye. "Not her husband's?" Alice stayed quiet. "Did she say who's?" Alice still stared silently through the bars. "Well, that's for 'er to sort out then, aint it? Nothin' to do with us."

"Soon forgot whose friend she is, haven't you?"

"No, you know what I mean. You can only do so much for folk." He turned back into the kitchen. "Right, I'll get on with tea."

She watched him go. "Bored with it now are you, once we start in on women's problems?"

He didn't turn round. "No. Just don't see what we can do so no need to trouble ourselves about it."

"Fine friend you'd be." She got up.

This stopped him and he turned round. "Friendship's one thing, Alice, but once you start gettin' involved in other folks' marriage problems that's when trouble starts. They expect y' to take sides; 'aint for me then you're against me' sort of stuff. Not what I'd want and not what you'd want either I'd guess, so I'd suggest you keep well out of it."

"That's very caring, comin' from you."

"An' that's harsh. I have me moments y' know. Now, can we 'ave some tea?"

"I thought you were makin' it?"

"I am, I just... yeah, I am makin' it."

She made her first move back up the stairs. "Ar. Right. Well, get on with it then." Alec watched her go then busied himself with tea.

Chapter Thirteen
Day 1 – Friday 30th November 1985 – Part One

David stirred in the bed. His first action was to reach out. Finally rousing himself sufficiently, it was confirmed to his sleep-bruised senses that he was, indeed, alone and that outside it was, indeed, tipping down with rain.

He began to roll over to look at the clock; that was when the pain hit home. His head fell back onto the pillow and he sucked in his breath, muttering "Jeeeesussss!" A tentative tilt of the head showed him the time. 'Half two.' A blast of wind-blown water hit the window, threatening to break in and mug the curtains. "Hark at that weather!" He was talking to himself; he was alone in a single bed and talking to himself. Then he recalled the conversation of earlier. 'No great amount, Eric? Right. Thanks.'

Reaching out he took hold of the edge of the mattress and began, with oaths and intakes of breath, to haul his body upright. He finally eased his legs out of the bed and to the floor in a move vibrant with pain and sat panting, willing away its shrillness. 'Bodes well for the day this does,' he thought. He attempted to get up and go to the door and eventually the bathroom. "Aghh...! Blooo-dee hell!"

Stephanie stirred and climbed the slope from doze to semi-consciousness. She switched on her bedside light, awake but unsure why until she heard sound in the spare bedroom.

'David,' she thought. 'Back must be painful.' She listened further and heard the door open. 'Now what? Leave him? Go and ask if he's alright? Pretend I didn't hear, that I was sleeping soundly? What's the matter with you? He's your husband, 'course you can ask… no, he's not, he's a stranger in a spare bed. Oh Lord…' She heard the bathroom door open, saw a sliver of light glide under her door then shrink to mourning as it closed. 'No, this is silly.' She got up, slipped on her dressing gown, opened her door and stood by it.

The wait was interminable. Then the bathroom door opened and light exploded onto the landing and the motionless Stephanie. David stood on the threshold, one hand on the pull-switch the other on the door handle, looking across at her.

Eventually Stephanie spoke. "'Morning."

"Half two? Yeah, s'pose…" David stared at her for many seconds then sighed and began to move. "You want the bathroom?"

"No, thank you."

"Then what?"

"Heard you…" She cleared her throat. "Ahem, heard you, and that rain. Just wondered if you were alright."

"Fine; thanks. I'll, erm…" He switched the light off, closed the door and stiffly began to cross the landing to the spare room.

The backlight from their bedside lamp framed Stephanie in silhouette. "That back still bad then?" Her question stopped him. "I heard you, just."

"Still givin' me a bit of gyp, not surprisin' really." They stood silently, the chasm of their understanding yawning open between them. "You not sleepin' well?"

"No. Not surprising really." She half smiled and even in this reduced light, David saw it and a clenched fist gripped the inside of his chest. "Not at all well."

"No, s'pose not." He motioned with his head. "Well… best try an' get a bit of shut-eye; big day."

"Yes. Right."

He stopped as he passed her. "An' thanks, for goin' on stop. Eric an' Liam much appreciate it."

"And you?"

"Aye." He thought for a moment. "It's just that, with everythin' else goin' on… I just didn't want to load more."

She could see the helplessness in his eyes and it hurt her deeply, inwardly, but Stephanie's reply was firm and controlled. "I really don't mind David, and we have to keep it under control, do the daily things. And it's important for you, for all of you; and my doing it won't make any difference to… to us."

"Won't it?"

"No."

He half turned to her and his question came back fast, bare. "So it won't make you love me again?" It stopped her breath.

She reached across and tried to take his hand. "I've never stopped loving you, David; never. I told you that. Know that above anything. Never."

He avoided the contact. "Fine." He twisted back to the door. "Ow, bugger!" He caught her look. "Bound to stiffen up. Once I get moving, in the mornin'… later… it'll ease up."

"Not on that spare bed it won't."

"It's alright."

"No it isn't, I know. It's like sleeping on an oar." She put her hand on his shoulder and gave it the gentlest of squeezes. "Come back to bed, David; our bed. Please? No agenda, just from me to you, to help your back."

"Hmm..."

"And..."

"And?"

"And, I miss you... Please?"

David looked into the depths of the spare room. If he entered there would be no way back, he knew it. His gaze fell onto the warmth of their double bed still ruffled. The bedside light glowed beckoningly yet still he resisted its call. "Don't know."

"Please?"

"I hurt, Steph."

"I know."

"Not me back." He clutched his fist to chest. "In 'ere, I mean... in 'ere. Goes clean through, out the other side... away."

The rain dashed itself against the landing window and Stephanie shuddered. "Come to bed."

He surveyed the two rooms again. "Ar. Right."

She led the way into the bedroom and as David flicked back the covers, so the scent of her hit him and he plunged into it.

Alongside him now, Stephanie flicked the bedside light switch to darkness. They lay back-to-back, their breathing controlled lest the other should feel the movement.

Moments later, David slid his hand across to Stephanie. She sensed this and dropped her hand behind her.

They intertwined fingers and she squeezed his hand in return.

—⁓—

"That you love?"

"Better 'ad be." Alec's voice reached Alice from the bedroom's pitch dark. "Go back to sleep, it's only half three."

Alice stirred further from sleep and switched on her bedside lamp. "Blimey, is that rain I can hear?"

"Yeah. It's been tippin' it down. The forecast for tomorrow's fine; no one said about this comin' in-between whiles. Still, weather forecasts... Wind was a bit frisky earlier on but it's dropped now an' the rain's slowed a bit. Still a nice breeze through them firs back of the house though; more than enough to kid the keepers. Too good to miss is this." Alec's voice took on a childlike anticipation, as if Father Christmas had come a month early. "An' if I didn't expect it then neither will them keepers. I know just where to go, you get off back to sleep."

"Do you have to go?"

"Miss a night like this? Ideal cover."

"No, I mean do you have to go?" He said nothing. Alice lay staring at him for a good few seconds before she stretched her arm down the length of the bed. "Have I lost you, Alec Stratton?"

"What lost me?"

"To that estate."

"What, Barn Tor? Don't be daft; just a visit for pheasant is all it is."

"Is it?"

"'Course. Why? What do you think it is?"

"More."

"Than what?"

"More than just pheasant."

Alec sat back on the bed. "Is there summat you're not tellin' me, Alice Stratton?" She said nothing, just looked at him, her eyes tracing the contours of his face. "Speak up if there is, I've got to go. Is there summat you're not tellin' me?"

"No. Is there summat you're not telling me?"

Alec caught the inflection in her voice and cocked his head on one side like a puppy desperately trying to understand a new command. Alice could see the discomfort in his face and, for whatever reason, protected him from it. "You will take care, won't you?"

Alec grasped the exit line. "'Course I will. What's up?" Then he softened a little. "You've never said before. Is there summat I should know about?"

She withdrew her hand. "No, just care about my man."

He stood suddenly. "Your man aint worth the care."

"I'll be the judge of that."

"If you think otherwise then you're a pretty poor one." He continued to dress.

Alice smiled at him. "You sure I can't tempt you back?" She moved slightly up the bed and her nightie was tugged off her shoulder. "Sure?"

"What's got into you? You don't want me to go, do you?"

She was hurt by the seeming embarrassment of her situation, of a late middle aged woman acting like a coquette, of the feeling of foolishness, of having to state the obvious to a man who was old enough to know it, and it showed in the tone of her reply. "Thought you'd never cotton on; no I don't! What do you think this is all about?"

"All what?" He sat on the bed again. "Alice, I'm not about to give it up, OK? It's what I do."

"Yes, you said." She tugged the nightie back up.

"Don't go off into a sulk now."

"Don't you tell me what I should an' shouldn't do, Alec Stratton!"

He got up. "Right. If you're gonna throw a fit there's nothin' further to say, is there?"

"This is not me throwing a fit! All I'm asking is for you to stop poachin' Barn Tor; you want to see me throw a fit, I'll oblige."

"Christ, Alice... Look, I just need a couple of birds; two or three!"

"And then?"

"And then what?"

"Then! When you need just another couple of birds? What then?" Alec stared at the curtained window. "They deserve better, Alec. David... an' Stephanie. Do you not think?" After a long pause, Alec continued to dress. "You're still goin' then?"

"I am."

"Still runnin' the risk of getting' caught."

"Not me."

"Do you not think you owe any of them anything?"

"No. Look, you chose to 'ave a keeper's wife as a friend not me. I never made any pact, never made no promises, not to anyone."

"To Stephanie? Did you not make any promises to her?"

Alec was unsure just how far into the minefield he had walked but decided to tread firmly in any case. "What the bloody hell has she got to do with all this? You may 'ave had her as a friend but I'm not beholden to her for what I do."

"So. No promises."

"Met her once, on Seer's Hill, you know about that."

"Once?"

"Yes. Once."

"Once...?"

She was opening the door as wide as she could but Alec refused to step over the threshold. "Ar, I've said. Told you about that, an' no I never made no promise."

Alice's hurt showed in her sigh. "Oh; OK... so no promises. I'm not askin' you to stop poaching, just askin' you not to poach there."

"Alice... I just need a couple."

"Alright then, I'll settle for second best. After tonight then. Please. Don't go back."

He looked at her for a long while seeing something deeper. "You've never been second best, Alice."

"No?"

"No."

"You're sure about that? Nothing else to add, M'Lord?"

It was said with a smile but there were things wrapped up in Alice's look that he had not contemplated, their edges just showing. He moved toward the door. "I'll see."

"Thank you."

"I only said I'd see."

"An' I only said thanks. It sounds rough out there an' you'll be gone a while. Put a coat on, an' wear that scarf, it's in the drawer..." Her voice trailed off, its utterance seeming foolish in the shadow of the night and of deeds to be done.

Alec stood for a second, his voice took on a puzzled quality and he almost laughed out loud. "A scarf! What? You mean that scarf-scarf?"

"Yes that scarf-scarf! That scarf I knitted for you, the alpaca wool one."

"Alice, love... As lovely as it is, it's about six foot long." Her look demanded serious words for serious times. "Yeah. OK." He opened the drawer and took the scarf out. A long look at Alice was followed by him draping it round his neck with a single loop. "There y'are. An' I'll wear me long waxed coat, with the fixed hood, y' know... an' I'll take the air rifle, eh? They'll never even know I've been there." He paused a moment longer than normal. "I'd never knowingly go out to hurt you, Alice."

"No?"

"No, I'd not. I've been on the stupid side of daft sometimes, but never to a plan; what they call it in court?"

"Premeditated?"

"Ar, premeditated... ar, that's it." He was almost on the verge of saying something of incisive clarity; Alice knew it and she lifted up slightly to concentrate. He broke the spell. "See ya!" The door closed softly.

Alice looked into the empty space that he had so recently filled. The rain hit the window again causing her to switch off the bedside lamp and shuffle back under the covers and into a darkness of possibilities. 'Should've said summat, given him a chance... too late now...'

"Is it that time already? We're not going out yet are we?"

David sighed like a boy caught in the pantry. "Bugger... No, it's only just gone quarter to four. I was hopin' to get out without disturbin' you."

Stephanie roused further from her deep doze. "Has it stopped raining?"

"All but; a bit of drizzle, stiff breeze still about. An early walk will be a good thing to do in this... see who's about."

"You never had any intention of going to sleep, did you?" David stayed silent. "You did it just to get me off to sleep, didn't you?"

After another long pause David nodded and looked at the clock. "Ar, I did. You're on stop in a bit over three hours. Get off back to sleep now an' I'll see you in The Quarry. Seven thirty. I've reset the alarm for six."

"It's very early, David, what are you going to be doing for three hours?"

"Feedin' me release pen"

"It doesn't take you three hours to feed the pen."

"No, I know. I said I'd lift them snares in Grey's Copse, for Eric, on my way across."

"Do anything for anybody."

David ignored the comment. "Go back to sleep."

"Don't know I'll be able to. Do you want tea?"

"No. Thanks. I'll just have a glass of fruit juice..." Stephanie began to fold the bedclothes back. "I said I don't want tea. Thanks."

She pulled the bedclothes back and paused. "Well... just... you know. Take care, that's all."

He moved to the door. "Hark at us two; you'd never guess. See you at The Quarry; seven thirty." He closed the bedroom door behind him.

The rain had slowed to a misty drizzle by the time a hooded Alec reached Raynes Lane. He was amazed at how much water had fallen during the night, most of it lying verge-side courtesy of badly constructed, badly maintained drains.

The hood of his waterproof coat and the thick alpaca scarf that he'd looped once around his neck in deference to Alice's concerns, were keeping his upper parts warm and dry, but the puddlesome Raynes Lane had succeeded in completely soaking through his plimsolls, his choice of footwear for night work. Travelling the narrow lane was preferable, however, to moving across the fields for the softness of the ground would readily accept a footmark; he would have to cross some of them eventually but there was no need to make the keepers' job any easier than he had to.

Once on the Rickett's Farm side of Grey's Copse he turned off the lane and retraced his steps of earlier along the hedge, back towards the copse. A clock chimed in the distance and he adjusted the position of the rope over his shoulders in readiness. 'Just gone four thirty. Top end of this hedge, sit for five minutes or so, check out, then get the job done.'

Having eaten their fill of the fallen maize cobs on Jackson's land, the female muntjac and her six week old fawn had been making their leisurely way across to Grey's Copse to gain liquid refreshment, cover and rest when they sensed Alec's presence sixty yards distant.

Under the trees' shadow the doting family of two slipped like rumours into the cover. They were following a much-used track, one they had travelled along many times but which was now laced with the pungent odour of fox. The doe pushed the forever preoccupied youngster ahead as they reached the halfway point of the upslope. The fawn took a couple of steps then made a sideways jump and the doe snorted in impatience at its skittishness.

Life was one great big adventure to this fawn; there was fun in every innocuous object from a disorientated mole or the shadow of a crow as it passed overhead in the late autumn sunshine to a drift of sheep's wool. But there was no space for playtime tonight; safety had to be reached, but playtime seemed to demand attention.

The fawn backed up, ran forward, twisted its head and leapt a little... this was no game. It had pushed its head into the newly-erected fox snare and, although the non-locking clip ran smoothly, loosening and tightening with each movement of the fawn's head, the whole contraption was held fast by the drag pole. The mother began to panic, her panic communicating to the fawn. It was on the verge of squealing out in fear when the close proximity of Alec permeated even this dire situation. Pushing her muzzle against its head the doe forced the fawn's body to the ground and the fawn took this unspoken instruction without question.

With a hasty, all devouring look back at her prostrate youngster, she slid into a bramble thicket nearby to await an opportunity for rescue once danger had passed.

After placing the pump-action shotgun into the gun rack, David was eternally grateful that the vehicle started first pull. Hand cranking a nineteen sixty seven Land Rover this early in the morning with a very sore back would not be popular.

He switched the headlights on and they penetrated the virgin darkness, carving an arc as he turned the vehicle out onto the estate road and headed towards The Clump and Rickett's Farm.

The first pheasant was exactly where Alec had heard it rise into the hawthorns some ten or so hours earlier.

Putting gun to shoulder was somewhat harder due to the extra thickness of his topcoat and the scarf, so he flicked the hood off to ease movement.

Phhhttt!

The air rifle whispered the sitting cock pheasant its last rites and the bird succumbed to gravity and Alec's waiting hand.

The scent of the intruder's approach had filled the fawn with concern. The sound of an increased threat made by the air rifle now made it fret for its life, but, in these circumstances there was little to be done except lay still. Absolutely still. Wait for the danger to pass then continue with efforts to escape.

Its mother, beside herself with fear could only sit it out; the meek waiting for the will to be read.

Phhhttt!

The second pheasant followed its companion and Alec moved around the outside of the copse and away from the sculpted muntjac fawn in search of a third.

Now he had two birds, he could use the length of rope. Slipping the heads of the pheasants through the loops, he pulled the nooses tight, one pheasant dangling just below his waist on his left side, one on his right. Under normal circumstances and with the excess running down his back, the lashing point of the rope rested against his bare neck, but not tonight. Tonight it rested against Alice's scarf and, although its length meant the excess had to be gathered in a bunch inside his coat, he was not averse to admitting it was more comfortable for the thick woollen pad saved his neck being chafed by each move of his head. 'Trust her to find a better way to travel.' Alec pulled the industrial-strength zipper part-way down and fed the two still warm birds inside the coat, shuffling the gathered scarf ends aside so the birds could rest against his sweatshirt, freeing his hands for continued shooting.

As the danger moved away round Grey's Copse so the muntjac fawn relaxed slightly. Still under cover of the bramble, the doe tested the air with her polished jet nose and the involuntary trembling of her left front leg ceased as she lifted it off the ground in a grotesque parody of a point. The fawn held its position, its senses illuminated by the shaft from a ray of hope.

Alec continued to move round to The Quarry side of the copse when, from the direction of Rickett's Farm, two beams of light from an approaching vehicle sliced a path up and along Raynes Lane. He whipped back into the copse's thorns only to see the wedges of light die as the vehicle coasted to a halt.

The movement of Alec in the thorns caused the fawn to flatten in a taut freeze once more, its heightened terror sending an airborne, fear-soaked ripple of scent to its mother some ten yards distant. The snare pressed into the fawn's neck but, despite this pain, it knew it had to remain motionless and silent; these were its only defences against the unseen enemy.

David coasted onto the grass verge. He could see Grey's Copse up ahead.

'Thank Christ it's stopped rainin'. Hate doin' this when there's no moon through the cloud, never mind when it's wet. Last two feed rides were as dark as a coffin.'

He looked at his watch. 'Quarter past five. I'll slip them wires first then walk across to feed The Railway.'

He removed the shotgun from the gun rack behind his head, slipped in two cartridges, pumped one into the chamber and stepped out of the vehicle.

Alec changed his position as he heard the faint click of a door being closed. He moved slowly around the copse to get a better view.

The muntjac fawn, on hearing fresh movement, flattened even further into the copse's leaf-mould carpet.

Danger was approaching of the keepering variety; Alec knew it; even a blind man would know it. Escape back the way he had come was out the question as was any idea of any idea of cutting across the fields to the village. Grey's Copse was set on top of a slight incline and anyone moving off in that direction, even in the light from this grey, pastry-cloud-wrapped moon would be easily spotted, particularly by a keeper.

His choice was either to hide in Grey's Copse on the supposition that this was not the keeper's destination or, by using the copse as a shield, cross the field on the blind side and go through The Quarry; Alec's success and reputation had not been built on suppositions.

David kept a little way off from the double hedge for, even this late in the year, woodpigeons roosted in the large ash tree that stood gauntly in the hedgerow. Disturbing these one-eyed sentinels from their bare-leaf dormitory would alarm everything for miles.

He knew, with absolute certainty that the shadowy figure was moving towards the copse; this meant The Quarry was the only possible escape route left open to Alec. To try concealment in a copse of this size, which contained a number of already alerted pheasants, was a suicide mission. Stuffing the air rifle into a rabbit hole and quickly backfilling the entrance with leaves, Alec slipped round the copse and away.

The fawn, on hearing Alec's departure, relaxed once more and breathed less stertorously. With her head pushed slightly out of the brambles, the mother scented the air prior to moving back to her offspring.

David reached the edge of Grey's Copse and the first of the fox wires to be lifted. He swapped the gun from one arm to the other for he could see the knocked wire. 'Could've been charlie... or a rabbit or pheasant; whatever it was, it bloody missed.'

He took out and opened his pen knife. Cutting a short, forked twig from the nearest hawthorn, he sliced across the two branches of its fork, placing the 'Y' across the snare wire. Lifting it up and back he pushed the two points into the soft earth to pin the now closed snare loop to the ground. This operation was so familiar to him it took only seconds but, as he completed the move, his back gave a sharp reminder of the previous day's events and he groaned out loud.

An audible groan re-alerted the muntjac fawn and its mother. Now both fully aware of the direction and proximity of this fresh threat both deer stiffened again, their reserves of panic-control just about exhausted.

An audible groan re-alerted Alec. He quickened his pace. He had decided, even though its degree of difficulty would mean slower progress, to move along one of the narrow tracks half way up The Quarry's bank. It would be the most unlikely route for a pursued felon to take, certainly in this light and weather, and so be the least inspected. But more than this, Alec was also unsure whether the keeper behind him was alone. He knew the Barn Tor keepers usually hunted in pairs so it could be he was being forced to go this way, that there was another waiting at the gateway out of The Quarry base. The mid-height track would allow him to spy over these escape routes in relative safety before committing himself, for those on guard duty seldom looked up. This middle way would also avoid the large pheasant roost on the higher ground near the release pen.

Heading purposefully across the field towards an opening in the hedge he had used on many occasions, Alec began to breathe a little quicker. He was beginning to feel very exposed and the ground was slippery in these plimsolls, even on the level. The very end of the night was beginning to show over Rickett's Farm and anyone coming round Grey's Copse would be sure to spot and challenge him. Denial would be difficult, especially when he was wearing the fruits of his ill-gotten labours about his neck. Like Dracula, he was in danger of becoming a victim of the sunrise; this was going to be a close one.

David moved across the copse towards the new wire Eric had set. Pin it down and he would be on the far side of the copse in a few moments.

The fawn tried to reduce its already shrunken form.

Day 1 – Friday 30th November 1985 – Part One

The mother drew herself back into the cover. The brambles would offer her sufficient cover until flight became necessary but, with the snare loop holding fast, immobility was still the fawn's only compatriot in adversity.

When he was fifteen or so feet from the snare, David was aware something was amiss.

He slowed his step and checked the safety catch was in place on the shotgun as instinct took over. Almost caveman-like he searched for something suitable which would help him deal silently with the snared creature. He spotted the very weapon, a thick hawthorn limb lying just to his left. As he switched the gun from left to right hand and bent sideways to collect this cudgel, so his back twinged again and he let out another audible groan. "Ahhh... Christ." Then a thought struck him. 'You've been 'ere before. Check the length of the stick, my lad, check the length.'

Stephanie sat bolt upright in bed.

"What? Huh! Quarry." Awareness of where she was seeped in and she relaxed a little, wiping the back of her hand across her upper lip which was damp with sweat. She kicked the bedclothes to one side and slipped her feet into standby slippers. 'Dropped off.' She looked at the clock. 'Quarter to six... early; never mind, dress and cuppa.'

She cancelled the alarm, slipped on her trousers then opened the dresser draw to remove a pair of thick socks, slightly uncovering the christening dress.

'Why did you have to spoil it all?' She looking up into the mirror and spoke out loud. "You never saw this one coming did you, Stephanie Clarke?"

Moments passed. She closed the drawer firmly and continued to dress.

Alec gained the cover of The Quarry and rushed gratefully into its camouflaged arms. He made his way to a narrow track and scrambled up it with some difficulty, for the heavy rain of earlier had made it very slippery. Reaching the escape track some thirty feet up, he set off along it.

The extra clothing, scarf and brace of still-warm pheasants, added on to the threat of imminent discovery, were making him feel hot and bothered. He must be getting old; it had never been this close before. The greater the distance he could put between himself and what was obviously a keeper on his tail, the better he would feel but, as if to infuriate, now his progress was slowed further by having to traverse the dimly-lit crochet-work of slippery tree roots overhanging the drop. He opened his coat a little more and loosened the loop of scarf around his neck to let out some heat.

As David groaned again, so the fawn's nerve broke.

With the first in a series of high pitched, ear-shattering squeals of terror, the fawn lunged away from the enemy and towards its still silent but highly distraught mother, but was brought up short by the fox snare still firmly fixed about its neck.

Alec twisted sharply in the direction of the fawn's first scream and this sudden movement took his feet by surprise. With the algae-covered roots acting as an accelerator he flipped over; his head slammed onto the unforgiving timber, knocking him unconscious.

The speed of his fall catapulted the brace of pheasants out of his part-opened coat, their claws pulling the ends of the scarf out with them until, at the extent of the birds' very short and macabre flight, the excess scarf was tugged from their grip. The ropes crossed as birds and scarf fell behind and on either side of Alec's head, forming the first section of a noose as he continued to travel feet first over the roots toward the drop. His journey to the edge was interrupted when his legs flopped through one of the larger gaps and he began to flow liquid-like through it. Tumbling and turning, the pheasants' weight twisted rope and scarf as they endeavoured to follow his lead, only to stall as the knots and rings slipped snugly into the crossing point of two thick tree roots. This sudden halt snatched the rope under Alec's head and the completion of the noose was neatly achieved as the transfer of pressure to the back of his neck snapped the rope's binding string, allowing the excess to feed out. Cracking the side of his head once more as he cleared the roots' gap and with the hood flapping in the sudden rush of air, Alec began to free-fall.

The female muntjac quivered in fear for her fawn. David yelped in pain as he leapt backwards in fright from the still squealing fawn, all the while juggling the loaded shotgun to to a safe landing.

Alec's body was snatched to a full stop.

David, still locked into a sitting position, gripped the small of his back. He looked at the fawn and addressed it directly. "You little fucker." A pain in his hand registered and he looked down. His index finger was jammed between the shotgun's trigger guard and a stone. He raised his eyebrows. 'That hurts.'

In The Quarry, Alec's body swung in gentle circles below the roots beneath the gathering daybreak of another shoot day.

Chapter Thirteen
Day 1 – Friday 30th November 1985 – Part Two

The sudden, piercing volume of the fawn's first screams had sent David through a complicated jump routine. This left him with a pounding heart from the initial shock, weak legs from his rapid action, an adrenalin-soaked bloodstream that showed itself as sweat running down his sides, and a lower bowel that demanded immediate contraction.

Unable to defend her shrieking youngster, yet filled with an overwhelming urge to do so, the female muntjac began to follow a set of animal survival rules enacted by countless other creatures when faced with the possibility of annihilation. Almost without exception, creatures know where the tipping-point is placed between fighting for the family's survival and suffering severe injury or death in doing so, or the abandonment of the present offspring in order to remain fit and healthy to breed again. As for the human survival rules, had the fawn been a sabre-toothed tiger, David's instinctive evasive action would probably have saved his life, proof that humans really have not strayed far from their animal ancestors. But right now the imperative was that he deal with the damage being done to his eardrums. Back pain or no, the fawn would have to be caught, wrestled and silenced.

David decided to wait until the snare was at its most taut, for only then could he lessen the number of dodging choices left open to the fawn. It was at this point in the proceedings that movement out of the corner of his eye registered; there stood the exception.

Bathed in a mist that was vibrating with a dawn chorus of infant horror and soaked with the scent of a predator, in a selfless display of maternal bravery the doe muntjac had moved slowly through the shrubbery towards her struggling, hysterical youngster. Eight feet from her objective, her shivering limbs refused to move further. It was the emergence of her head from the shrubbery that caught David's eye and he could only guess at the state of her mind. And yet, in spite of it all, she had travelled this close; was prepared to risk all for her youngster whose squeals of terror were too much for them both to bear. He glanced her way. 'You must really want this,' he thought. 'An' I mean really.'

He looked back. The fawn had reached full stretch of the wire and was now holding its body rigid, all the while screaming and twisting its neck and head in its escape efforts. 'That's what a broken heart sounds like. OK. Let's see what we can do about it, eh?'

He stooped to place the shotgun gently on the ground, checking the position of the safety catch. 'Last thing I want; blow me bloody legs off.' Then, like a tiger at the culmination of a stalk, he took in a deep draught of air and gathered himself for the catlike spring and the promising, painful landing.

Stephanie sat for a few moments, waiting, car window open. Even at this early hour, the first light was sufficient for her to see the tresses of mist draping the river valley.

In the distance she could hear the first calls of wake-up pheasant and the last calls of home-to-bed mallard. She sighed deeply as thoughts tumbled one on top of the other. 'Just look at what you've got. Folk would kill to keep this and you're on the edge of chucking it away. You've lost your senses, girl...'

The distant call of something in distress interrupted her train of thought. She could neither pinpoint nor identify the sound.

'Sounds like a fox... long way off though. Other side of The Quarry.'

She got out of the estate car, opened the boot and sat just inside to slip off her shoes and pull on thick socks and wellingtons.

The cock robin, perched on its usual winter-song bough in the oak tree, stared warily at the unfamiliar, shadowy object hanging underneath the tree roots that stuck out of the quarry bank.

Every morning had been much the same since the dispersal of his second brood of chicks. Since then this pugnacious little song bird had defended his territory with vigour and many a robin-rival had been seen off, the red of their breast feathers flicking his tantrum thermostat to full. After these encounters The Quarry's Red Baron was ready for anything; anything, that is, except this unusual fruit.

The distant squeals of terror had been of sufficient intensity to tempt the robin out from his near-daybreak singing practice to investigate. After a dicey flight between bushes, for he was somewhat out of his element in this not-quite-crepuscular light, the continuing sounds of distant distress appeared unconnected to any immediate threat and he had just decided to return to his shrub rehearsal room when he registered the new shape in his landscape. So large, so new, so sinister in this light... and so still; discretion was definitely the better part. The cock robin bobbed and weaved his head the better to catch any slight movement, but there was none, just an eerie stillness and silence.

Using the surrounding vegetation to move closer, the robin's alarm call became more incessant, bolstering his state of hypersensitive suspicion. This scolding note rang with sufficient authority to arouse the attentions of a gang of long-tailed tits who were next on the scene. Their numbers were quickly augmented by a clicking wren and an ever-alert pair of magpies. All were puzzled by the shadowy shape and slightly alarmed by its size, but this did not deter them from moving towards the object of their annoyance. Large or small, friend or foe, dead or alive it had to be sorted; they moved in mob-handed to deal with the uninvited guest.

The launch of David's attack at the still yelling fawn was borne out of grim determination; he needed to make it count. His one-deer audience and aching back had a strong interest in the proceedings.

Like a shark, he memorised the position of the fawn and, on impact, closed his eyes to avoid damage from the now wildly flailing limbs of his target; both his direction and timing were spot on, it was his landing that left a lot to be desired. He gathered in the fawn, taking a kick to the chest in the process as the volume and pitch of its hysterical squeals reached new heights. With his face pressed against the fawn's flank in an effort to contain its struggles, David was made aware of every filling in his mouth.

Stephanie stopped pulling on her wellingtons.

'What on earth?' She paused and listened, then stamped her foot into the boot's sole and slid the duck's-head stick out from under her jacket. Its familiarity and history acted as a conduit to a rainbow of emotions and, as she caressed the shape, so she snatched at breath as the suddenness and depth of feeling hit her.

It took a good few moments to regain control.

She eventually stood up but put a hand on the doorframe for support. 'Came from nowhere.' The distant yelling continued and she listened again. 'That's not a happy creature, whatever it is.' She grabbed her coat and closed the boot. 'Right; concentrate, Stephanie Clarke.'

David would have said something, but there was no expression in the English language he could call to mind to adequately describe the pain in his back.

'Exquisite' was the word he wanted.

With teeth gritted firmly together against the pain, he bent all his energy into securing the still struggling fawn to stillness and silence... above all silence; to do this he needed to plunge it into darkness. Pressing further weight onto the still protesting fawn, he flipped his right arm out and back in a deft movement that forced one side of the jacket off his shoulder. With a series of circling arm movements coupled with several shoulder shrugs, horizontal disco-dancing almost, he flipped the sleeve free, reached across the fawn and yanked the jacket across its head. Stillness and silence descended on the copse; it seemed even the trees were grateful.

He lay there, his half-on-half-off jacket wrapped round the fawn, his waistcoat scuffed and dirty, his shirtsleeves muddy and growing wet from the tree-locked dew dripping from the hawthorns above, an awareness of the stare of his audience gripping his neck and his back throbbing with pain.

He spoke out loud.

"Now lie there... an' don't you dare die of a fuckin' 'eart attack."

The muddy soil was building up again and Stephanie stopped for the second time in her progress along the hedgerow. Using the fence post for support she flicked great clats of soil off her boot and realised the distant yelling had ceased.

'Moved on...' She removed the mud from her other boot and set off again.

As the avian circle of raucous agitation closed in so their boldness grew.

The distant squealing had ceased and this collective could now give its full attention to the mystery in their own backyard. In any other baiting exercise there had always been some show of either annoyance or peevishness from the recipient of their woodland manifesto. This silence bordering on disregard caused their calls to become more hysterical as they tentatively tightened the circle. The robin gradually gained in bravado and curiosity, sufficient for him to venture to within two feet of the object of their frustration. Such carelessness could not be tolerated. There had to be a way of obtaining a response and, if vocal threat was unsuccessful, then direct approach and challenge was the only option left.

Flicking up and over the target, the robust redbreast swooped with a precision mastered by two seasons of landing on branches stirred into erratic movement by fickle winds. It landed momentarily on the rope then flicked onto the top of the hood looped over a thick spike of root projecting out from the cliff face; this bold and decisive move caused a silence to descend over the scene. If nothing followed the robin's challenge then the magpies could take over. They had already sensed blood on this strange creature, for these small-bird muggers made their living by plundering the eyes of the innocent, the unwary, the newly born... the nearly dead. What they needed was proof-positive that no surprises awaited... discovered by a third party of course; magpies were ever hungry, never stupid.

The robin, ticking less frequently and with less assertiveness than before, gradually moved down the rope. Further encouraged by total lack of movement, it hopped onto Alec's damp and green-stained head.

Nothing.

Recognition dawned.

The robin hopped from head to shoulder. There was no longer any threat and the other birds showed their agreement with his conclusion. A single wing flick carried the wren to the gathered folds of Alec's partially open waterproof coat, the zipper making a good perch; it bobbed its tail and chirruped. The long-tailed tits were more wary as they tinkled and tripped over and above Alec's head.

The magpies, satisfied as to the condition of the victim, closed in with a purpose of chuckles.

Reaching under his jacket, David felt for the head of the temporarily motionless, now thankfully silent, fawn. He needed to trace an accurate cervid map, find the snare loop and slip it open; not an easy task for the fawn struggled every time he altered his position or grip. As he realigned his body the better to achieve the aim of his fumbling fingers, a slightly suppressed but fully audible snort from behind him added urgency.

This was the first sound the mother had uttered and his admiration for her diligence and fortitude was increased tenfold; even his back eased a little. Any respite in pain would be short lived, however, for time was getting on and he needed to give the fawn its freedom, the mother the gift she so richly deserved and himself the chance to meet Stephanie on time.

Twisting to his right reintroduced him to the pain in his back and legs, as he lay lengthways along the body of the fawn. Lifting his full weight slightly, so as not to crush the youngster, he waited for the fresh struggles to subside. The fawn paused and he quickly thrust one hand back under the jacket. Pinning the fawn's neck to the ground he felt for the snare's slipknot; it was only the work of a moment to loosen the noose and flip it over the fawn's head.

David lay still. He now needed to alter his position just once more so that, on releasing the fawn, it would be given a free run to its mother. Decisions made, he lifted his body and rolled over the prostrate creature. In a move akin to the majestic sweep of a bull-fighter's cloak, he released the fawn from his jacket and into the fast growing light of day. He even managed a weak "Ole!", though the sharp stab of pain that followed this movement quickly elongated it to "Ole-fffuck!"

Catapulted so vigorously and rudely into the big wide world when it really thought all was at an end was a little too much for the fawn. It took a second snort from the doe to interrupt its disbelief and it turned its head towards the familiar sound. David could now see the mother still peering from out of the bramble thicket. The fawn spotted her too and, with rapid if somewhat shaky steps, moved towards her squeaking plaintively in welcome. David's broad smile stayed in place as the fawn, buoyed up on a sea of maternal love, melted into the cover.

The robin was on the verge of returning to the woodland coverts in a continued search for spiders and for any other cock robin within singing distance of his territory. It was then the oozing blood, gathered at the hairline of Alec's temple, gained sufficient weight to trickle rapidly down his ghostly white face.

Confronted with such an open challenge, the robin launched itself at this red gauntlet. With all its well fed two ounces, the robin whipped into the side of Alec's face on its first territorial sortie, accompanying this first blow with a loud click of hostility which blasted into Alec's ear. With a deep and resonant grunt that shook his whole body, Alec announced his condition to the mixed group of woodland civil defence members, border guards and potential muggers; this was no corpse.

Immediate silence from the other birds was followed by a Richter scale of reaction. Chattering, ticking, clicking, and a whistle from the wren on a frequency that went straight to the back of Alec's head, the startled team each took evasive action. The robin lifted away to the left as fast as a slingshot stone to land on a bare teasel some ten yards away and blast out its alarm call. The wren dropped a few, free-fall inches then flicked its wings sufficiently to carry it to a rootlet that stuck out from the cliff face and began a rhythmic scolding. The long-tailed tits burst upward like a fancy rocket in their mad scramble for safety and a convenient position from which to whistle their contempt, and the magpies, as ever putting personal safety first, leapt back on flicking wings to the top of a hawthorn tree fully twenty yards away before setting up their raucous call of aggrieved suspicion.

David sat up suddenly, disregarding the pain this time. 'What th' fuck's that noise about?'

The light was now such that Stephanie could see a fair distance along the narrow belt of mixed saplings and mature trees that ran out to meet the hedgerows, and was glad she had got there just a little earlier than planned.

Along this green artery were a dozen pheasants which had obviously roosted nearby and were feeding on the fallen mast under one of the beeches before snacking their way off the estate and into the maize. She lifted her stick and tapped gently on a hazel sapling. The reaction from the pheasants was instant. To a bird they stopped feeding and looked in the direction of the noise. Stephanie kept up a rhythmic tapping and, adding the odd tongue click, began to move gently towards them. Her increased level of threat was not lost on the birds and they began to move back the way they had come.

'Mission accomplished,' she thought. 'David will be pleased.' The thought, coming like that, reminded her of how things had been, could be, might never be again; then...

"Damn!"

To her left, along a hedgerow running at right angles to hers, were a further gang of twenty pheasants she had failed to spot. They had heard her approach and were all standing alert and poised for flight, the line of which would send them over the road and onto Jackson's ground.

She weighed up the possibilities. 'Back and along the road? Yes, then up to them from the far side. Should be able to chivvy them the right way.' Then other sounds intruded. 'Magpies sound annoyed. Fox about maybe? That'll please Eric.'

With a further glance in the direction of the chattering magpies Stephanie set off back along the hedgerow to the road.

David instinctively reached for the shotgun, the smile disappearing from his face as the woodland postal service delivered its message.

'Steph?' He looked at his watch. 'Can't be. Not yet. Fox... owl? Possibly – bit late. Human company? Not likely... not this near to the start of a shoot day. Only a fool would risk it.' He glanced at the shotgun. 'Daren't fire it off this close to the start of the day... Bugger!' The noise continued offstage. 'Well, whatever it is them birds are onto summat sneaky that's for sure.'

Alec coughed once more. The convulsion shook his body and caused a note of panic to enter the already hysterical calls of the birds that had now been joined by a blackbird and one of a pair of resident jays. Its partner had fallen victim to a Ladder trap not forty eight hours previously, but although that partnership had been broken there was still a need to protect his territory for a future mate, and this intensity of disturbance could be ignored no longer.

David rose in stoic, lip-biting silence. 'Got to sort this lot out. Christ, it's enough to wake the dead.'

He leant against the hawthorn trunk, took in four, long draughts of late-autumn vintage champagne and, with aching torso, crooked the gun under his arm and set off across the field.

Due to the lower temperature in The Quarry, the moisture just hung, sulking in the trees and grasses, just so much heavy water.

This damp had failed to douse the birds' ardour however. After a further cough had erupted, the assembled birds continued to call at Alec, but louder now since they had been obliged to move to a more discreet distance.

"What the hell?"

The sound continued to confuse. David could not understand why any creature, subjected to this level of avian abuse, should choose to stay around.

Reaching the hedge that formed the field's boundary, he eased up a little but, although his back fully agreed, locating the reason for the continuing commotion demanded otherwise.

Alec coughed again, this time with sufficient force and volume to cause his eyelids to flicker; he was gradually coming round.

David listened more intently. 'That's no bloody bird that much I do know.'

It was only a half-heard noise mixed in with the dripping from the trees and the already identified avian choral society, but whatever it was it was most certainly alive. David's mind raced through the various predator permutations once more. It was obvious the mystery creature had moved; had made clear to the gathered mass exactly what it was and how it was, and a gradual cessation in the intensity of the alarm calls told him the ornithological equivalent of 'fighting another day' was being invoked.

'Don't think there's any cattle near here... Jesus, in The Quarry on a shoot day? A dozen heifers on the feed ride will just about make Eric's day... an' Lordy won't believe this one.'

His interest now fully engaged, David began to move along the hedge and toward the quarry's gate.

Alec's eyes gradually opened as the cerebral world slipped into the tangible. He became aware of breathing, of wetness... and of a splitting headache. His thoughts were like a pack of playing cards dropped; why was he upright yet not touching the floor?

He shook his head in an effort to clear it and immediately regretted this action for the movement put an edge on the already deep pain in his temples. It also caused the rope to move a little.

'I'm hangin'?'

Alec bent his head very slowly downwards.

There, just below his chin was a knot of woollen material that disappeared up and over his shoulder in a straight line. 'Jesus, my arms hurt.' He blinked, hoping the movement of his eyelids, like a conjurer's sleeves, would reveal all.

It didn't.

He puzzled over this visual confusion until, lifting his head, he looked gingerly upward and found another clue. There, above him was the continuation of material, his stretched-taut hood... and a rope.

'The rope's comin' from them branches...?'

He lowered his head again and gave the situation more thought. It would seem politic to figure out where he was for a start. To begin to build a hypothesis... any hypothesis really so long as it gave him some idea of just what the hell was going on.

The constant dripping of moisture muzzied David's hearing and now the birds had left the scene there was no destination point picked out by their calls.

He stood still; listened again.

All he could do was plant belief in the mental map he had drawn when he had first heard the noises, then make for that spot with as much quiet circumspection as he could muster.

'This rate I'll be there well before Steph.'

The thought of her, fast like that, brought him up short. It was as if nothing had happened, as if all was right with the world. It was only in the following seconds that the rest of the ingredients poured into the mix and he sighed inwardly at its compression. After a few seconds, he breathed deeply and moved forward, his footwear heavy with the clinging lumps of soil picked up during his travels across the ploughed field from Copse to Quarry.

'What's those lumps...?'

He looked more carefully.

'Not lumps, pheasants… they're pheasants! Rope? Grey's Copse! This aint Grey's Copse.' The thoughts were running in a sluggish fashion. 'Pheasants… I was in Grey's Copse.' He paused; sighed. This was hard work. 'The Quarry! That's it! I'm in The Quarry.' Moisture splattered his hand and he stared at the blood that now streaked it as though it were a chemical formula that would provide the miracle cure for his complaint.

'Red…? Blood.' He looked upwards again. 'The pheasants? Mine. I fell, fell…'

His head began to spin so he shut down these fervent mental gymnastics, closing his eyes to take five or six deep breaths before allowing his thoughts to run on.

'There's got to be some sense to all this… there's got to be.'

The off-road hedgerow was reached without incident and Stephanie climbed the fence and began tapping her stick once more. Immediately the pheasants ahead of her reacted as one and their necks stiffened as they all made a first tentative step away from her. A couple of the birds ducked into the hedge bottom.

'Damn! Should have brought Jill… never get them out if they squat… damn!'

Rattling the hedge shoots harder she increased her speed in order to keep the rest of them on the move. The birds sensed this human was on a mission and also set off rapidly on foot and, thankfully, back to The Quarry.

"Brrrrrrr!" Stephanie added a vocal hurry up.

Reaching the spot where the two birds had sneaked into the hedgerow, Stephanie pushed her stick into the hedge bottom, much like a bad guy pokes the hay stack that hides the hero. There was an immediate kerfuffle right at her feet and a cock and two hen pheasants exploded from the hedge and streaked away in the right direction, all shriek and wing-flap.

David's thoughts were further confused by the faraway sound of alarmed pheasant.

'Now what? There's got to be some sense to all this. Maybe whatever's in The Quarry has laid still an' that's why the birds have stopped callin' on it, and maybe that noise on the far side, were pheasants droppin' from roost, or cocks fightin' so not connected... Oh, for fuck's sake! I've left me jacket back in Grey's Copse!' He looked up. 'Got the gun, forgot the jacket: bollocks! I don't believe this! Jesus, I thought I were cold." Then the thoughts followed on. 'I ought to be at home, that's where I ought to be; home... what home? Oh, bloody hell, what a fuck up... Because I'm doin' this? Because I'm doin' this when it should be Eric sortin' his own beat out?' The pain in his back increased in agreement and his head throbbed with the jumble of emotions and contradictions. 'I can't do anythin' anyway, even with the gun; let that off and I'd frighten everythin' away as far as Kent. So what then? Shout 'boo' and 'ope it's got a weak 'eart? This is bloody silly. I ought to be at home... in a hot bath, sortin' out my own problems... with Steph. A fucked-up marriage an' where am I tryin' to sort it out? In a bloody quarry! This is stupid.'

Alec opened his eyes.

'This is stupid. Now. Take it steady, Alec Stratton.' His eyes followed the rope line upwards. 'That's a scarf! It's the scarf, Alice gave it me... that I put...?'

Placing his right hand on the rope and trapping the scarf under his chin, he very carefully traced its line upward with his fingers. 'Not tight. Not…? Why do my arms hurt so much?' Clearing his head with a slow deliberate blink he looked down, beyond scarf and rope… beyond his chest… beyond his feet to the mist-blur below. He looked up bringing the overhead into focus. 'Roots! That's what they are! They're not branches, they're roots! Roots… the quarry bank… I fell…'

Gradually, slowly, his eyes widening all the time, Alec lowered his head once more to look below. Now it was all becoming numbingly, stomach-churningly, ice chillingly clear as he spoke under his breath.

"Fuuuckin' hell… I can't be. Oh, fuck!"

'Know where I want to be; know where I will be.'

Even in possession of all the facts, all the information, all the emotional turmoil for his future the estate still had hold of him and his life; he recognised it, accepted it. So he would meet with Stephanie, they would talk, talk and get a resolution, an agreement, a commitment and above all forgive… but only after he had solved this conundrum. The Quarry. That was where he would be.

He reached across, picked up the shotgun and climbed awkwardly over the gate.

'Sit an' wait. That's the thing. If it's still about, I'll soon know.'

He dropped into the nearest cover, slipped onto his haunches and, placing the shotgun across his knees, prepared to sit it out.

The puzzle now facing Alec needed some thought, but above all a quick solution.

Here he was, not only in The Quarry and in semi-possession of two pheasants, but also suspended above ground by a rope that somehow had failed to become his executioner. Him. A known poacher. 'My suspended sentence...'

He almost chuckled but this turned into a coughing fit that pushed against the iron band constricting his head and caused his body to shake; not recommended in the present fix. After a couple of unhealthy barks he managed to bring it under control.

Stephanie was pleased with her work. All the birds had headed back and now she could finish gently tapping up the last hundred and fifty yards, then head into the heart of The Quarry to await David's arrival.

David registered the cough as soon as it erupted. The air was whipped-cream still so even the stifled bluster had been sufficient to give the game away.

'Knew it! The bugger's still there, up ahead. An' that's no cow, that's human.' Then the thought struck. 'If it's that bloody Eric prattin' about there'll be a fuckin' row, I'm just in the mood.'

With a firm plot on the target, David moved forward with confidence. He knew where it was and what it was; now he needed to find out who it was.

The obvious answer was to reach over his head, haul himself up his own hangman's noose, grab onto the root-gibbet and either pull the rope out and climb through or do the drop.

'Then what? What if I slip? What happens if I can't tug the rope free? Then what? Alec, concentrate! Right, climb up the rope first... Climb up an' through? Looks tight but I came in that way so... but then there's no goin' back an' if I can't get through or the loops give out, or I can't shift 'em...' Alec sighed as he thought on. 'Well, you've got to do somethin', Stratton. You can't spend all day here, they're shootin' in here today...!' It just popped into his head but it struck him like an electric shock! 'They're shootin' in here today! Then try an' talk your way out of it.'

David moved through the slowly dispersing mist, eyes facing front, letting his other senses do the work. Each step since he had heard the last cough had been done at a snail's pace; each shred of cover scanned in search of telltale signs for he felt he must be almost on top of his quarry.

Alec decided to climb.

'Hope the roots aren't too slippery; hope my arms support me; hope the rope aint jammed too tight; hope I can get it free and it comes out clean and in one go. Jesus, Alec, that's some gang of hopes'

He looked downwards. Below him amongst the mist-draped saplings and scrub cover he stared hard at a landing place between two oak saplings. If it all went wrong and he ended up scrabbling for release, at least he had something to aim for.

He reached up with one hand in readiness to take hold of the rope but snatched it down immediately as he felt his body shift and swing slightly as he registered a slight tightening of the scarf around his neck.

The thickness of the soil on her boots demanded that Stephanie stop once again. 'Now I know how a diver feels,' she thought as she grabbed the only section of the post-and-rail fence not dressed in old-man's beard.

The soil's weight dragging on her boots had gradually drawn one of her socks down and under her foot but she had chosen to ignore it up 'til now. Holding the top rail, she scraped her left boot on the lowest one, the soil falling in clats into the long grass, then began to repeat the process with her other foot but lost balance and shoved her leg through the gap between the rails. Lurching forward, she steadied but as she drew her foot back the boot caught on the rail and it was dragged further off her foot.

"Oh, for goodness sake!"

Now her sock was nearly off. She pushed it back into the boot hoping it would be alright to stand on; it wasn't. Leaning against the fence and using the toe of one boot, she lodged it into the heel of the other. Boot and sock came off in one and as she bent to pick it up so she lost her balance, plumping her foot down into the damp grass.

"Lord...! All I want to do is pull my sock up!"

She snatched her foot up, bent over to upright the fallen boot then leant back on the fence.

"Now... come here!"

She grabbed the sock and pulled it back over her muddy foot and trouser leg, folding the top over just below her knee.

"And you. Come here."

She drew the boot closer and slipped her re-socked, damp foot back into it.

The suddenness of overhead movement in his peripheral vision caused David to flinch and duck as if to avoid a blow. Almost immediately, instinctively, he lifted the barrel of the shotgun and slipped the safety catch off.

451

The object was stationary and he slowly tilted his head off the stock.

As if transfixed by an invisible beam their eyes met.

Silence punctuated the scene.

Alec eventually cleared his throat.

"Ah-hem. G'mornin'."

Stephanie climbed the gate and moved quietly along the riding that led to the cliff face of the quarry. A water-dressed spider's web spanned the track and before moving through it she looked at its beauty, its perfect symmetry and the crouching inhabitant near its centre.

'There's a life,' she thought. 'No yesterday, no tomorrow, just now.'

David stared then spoke, the words leaving him of their own accord seemingly oblivious to Alec's previous utterance.

"How the fuck...? Alec Stratton?"

"You couldn't put that gun away an' 'elp us down could y'?"

There was a further lengthy silence as David looked beyond Alec to the roots above him. "What's that round your neck? Is it a rope?"

"Not sure... could you 'elp us down before it is?"

Another shorter silence followed then David was snatched from his amazed state.

"Help you down?" He re-seated the shotgun. "I'll fuckin' shoot you where you are, you bastard."

Stephanie slowed her pace a little. She could hear voices, mumblings up ahead. Then she began to move more quickly as the thought of David being there ahead of her struck home. 'Don't think I've been that long. Can't be Eric, I'd have seen his vehicle.'

"Jesus, it's only a couple of pheasants!"

"A couple of pheasants! Is that what you think this all about?"

"Look, alright, I've been a pain in the arse for Barn Tor, I know. You've got me where you want me after all these years... just, it'd be much appreciated if you could put your anger to one side for a few more seconds and 'elp us out, y' know? You can still kick the shit out of me, but after you 'elp me down."

David stood his ground. "You don't know, do you?"

"Please? The gun?"

"The gun stays..."

"David! David, what are you doing?" Stephanie's voice led her onto the clearing and captured both men's attention. She looked up. "Oh my God! Alec? David, what...? What are you doing to him?"

"What am I doing to him? For fuck's sake, Steph! I'm doin' nothin'; I just got here! Ask him! Ask your lover, the world-famous fuckin' poacher; ask him what's goin' on."

"He's not my lover, David, I told you what happened!"

Alec's mouth dropped open. "Oh, Christ...! You mean he knows?"

"'Course I fuckin' know!" David shouted back. "What do you think?"

"It was a stupid mistake, David, I told you; my stupid mistake!" Stephanie controlled the panic she was feeling as she tried to wrest the situation away from the abyss. "I got it wrong, was stupid, slipped up just once. I know that and told you. I know how you feel about that, you told me. Shooting Alec won't put it right."

"She's right…"

"Shut it, Stratton! You've no say in this!"

"No, alright, I'll shut up, but can you please put the gun down? Please!"

"David, he's right. Put it down. If you shoot him they'll know it wasn't an accident; they'll know it was you."

"How? How will they know? I could've fired in fright, an instinctive reaction. There's no one 'ere to see;"

"I'm here, David."

He looked across. "You what…? You'd sell me out over this bastard?"

"Yes."

"But, Steph… you wouldn't." His voice choked and his aim slipped a little.

"Yes, I would. Could you live with someone who'd committed cold-blooded murder? Could you? I only want to stop the man I love putting himself in prison for the next twenty years." She held his gaze. "They always find out, David, the guilt shines through and I want them to have nothing to find; I want you here, with me, because we love each other; I love you. The gun… please."

He lowered it and an audible sigh came from above them. "Is there a chance you could help us down now?"

Without taking his eyes off Stephanie, David snapped back. "I told you to shut it, Stratton!" He looked up. "You're the cause of all this!"

"Just me then. No one else involved."

"Alec Stratton! Be quiet!" The strength in Stephanie's voice surprised even her.

David lifted the gun slightly. "You're in no position to argue the toss, Stratton! You may have got off from bein' shot but it don't help you out on the poachin'."

"No, alright. Look, I know now there's other stuff goin' on, but me bein' up 'ere don't 'elp that, does it? I've been poachin', you've caught me, so how about helpin' me down. I'll not be goin' anywhere. I owe you that much."

"He's got a point, David."

"He's got nothin' but my contempt, Steph, and he does owe me." He looked back up at Alec. "You bloody well do."

There was a short silence then Alec spoke. "I know. So, 'elp us down an' I'll say sorry properly."

"David, what about your back."

"It'll cope." David exchanged looks with Stephanie then leant the shotgun against a thin oak sapling. "One time; for you."

She smiled at him. "Thank you."

"Ar." He began to size up the situation. "I'll 'ave to get above you." He began to retrace his steps in order to reach the pathway Alec had taken earlier. "Couple of minutes. Hang on. An' I wasn't tryin' to be funny."

"That's OK," ventured Alec. "I think a sense of humour's needed."

David ignored it. "Steph? Keep an eye; make sure no pheasants try an' creep out."

"I'm strung up here an' you…? Don't you never stop?"

Alec's comment snapped David to a halt as the bile rose in his throat. He turned and took a couple of paces back to look up at Alec.

"No, I don't! See? I can't! You know why? Because slippy sods like you are out all hours tryin' to get us the sack, that's why! So no, it never fuckin' stops… never! An' everythin' else suffers 'cos of it! Should make you so proud, eh? That even now, even though I'm knackered beyond belief, even though you've hurt me beyond imaginin' Stratton, an' left me with this... this shit state of a marriage... even now with you hangin' there, I still 'ave to worry about these bloody pheasants. You've no justification for what you've done to this estate, to my Steph. My Steph! To me! So just shut your trap an' think yourself lucky! The only reason I'm doin' this, the only reason is 'cos Steph's asked me to; it aint for you. Right now you dead counts as nothin' to me; fuck all!"

"I get the point. Thanks."

Stephanie glanced up at Alec but spoke to David. "Yes, I'll keep a look out. Will you be alright; your back?"

"'Course, I will. I'm alright... I've got you."

"I know you are, and yes, you have."

He smiled weakly, turned and scrambled stiffly up the slope, noticing the scuff marks left by Alec's earlier ascent. Moving along the ridge, and after a couple of slips, he reached the mesh of tree roots. "Jesus, it's like a skatin' rink up 'ere. Not surprised you ended up where you are."

"Surprised I aint dead, you mean?"

"Disappointed is the word for that." Lying on his stomach, David slid his way across the roots. "My first instinct is for you to stay right where you are, Stratton. Let the world see you for what you are. The one thing you aint gonna get is away with this."

Stephanie moved slightly to get a better view. "David, please be careful!"

"Don't concern y'self, Steph; I'll not risk bugger-all over him." He surveyed the situation; the trapped pheasants, the slack rope, the scarf. 'How the hell...?' He gently moved the scarf to one side, looked through the roots then shook his head and spoke under his breath. "Jesus..."

"What?"

"You. You are one lucky bugger is all I can say. It's not the rope what's holdin' you up nor the scarf; it's the hood. It's hooked over a limb… the rope's still slack." He focused on Alec. "You know the rope I'm talking about? The one with the two estate pheasants tied up in it?"

"Oh, them pheasants! Ar, I know the one's you mean. I wondered where they'd got to."

"For a bloke in your position you've a lot to say. You'd not be talkin' so smart if that limb hadn't have been there or that hood was only press-studded to the back of the coat, I can tell you that. Now, shut up an' let me think." David weighed up the options. "I'll 'ave to unhook you, that'll just leave rope an' scarf…" He looked again at the open root work then at the floor below. "You'll not get back through this way. How do you feel about the drop?"

"A lot 'appier knowing the rope'll be cut before an' not after the event." Alec looked up. "It will be, won't it?" David just looked back and Alec swallowed with difficulty.

Working the rope from side to side, David forced the knots and rings more firmly into the wood. "They're well jammed now, even more when you put your full weight on it. You catch hold of the rope and lift up, I'll free the hood then cut the rope as quick as I can, but you're gonna 'ave to hang there for a good few seconds; up to it?"

"Have to be."

"Right, when you reach up you're as like to slip straight through that coat even though it's a good fit so you'll need to grab hold of the rope real fast; move yourself sort of one arm at a time, but fast. You'll swing about a bit… just don't do it too much, in case."

"That's reassurin'." Alec paused. "I'm trustin' you with the rope so when I hit the floor I aint goin' nowhere. I'll owe you that much; maybe more."

"Ar, you damn well do, an' don't think this lot is gonna make us friends. It don't." David adjusted his position slightly. "OK, take hold."

"Can't believe I'm doin' this." Alec breathed in deeply then snatched at the rope over his head, feeling the immediate change in status as the rope stretched taught to his grip. Gradually his body steadied.

David leant through one of the gaps in the roots. "Now, lift... more, more, that's it." The hood buckled in the centre and he lifted it off the limb. "Hood's free, don't let go now or you're fucked." He pulled himself back through onto the root platform. "Keep a good grip; gonna free the other end."

"Hands are slippin'." There was a note of panic in Alec's voice.

"Not yet, Stratton. I've to make sure there's no surprises up here first... just, hold on!" A further few seconds passed before the scarf flopped down to hang limply from Alec's neck. David quickly checked the position of the rings. They were biting deep into the crossing roots now and he took the knife from out of his trouser pocket. "I can put an edge on this." David showed the knife and called down. "Move back a bit, Steph! He's gonna fall mighty fast when he lets go."

Stephanie stepped back a few paces, watching intently as David reached through the roots, the dead eyes of the pheasants watching his every move. "You gotta lift a bit more."

"Can't; me hands are slippin'...!"

David reached rapidly through the roots and gripped onto Alec's wrist. "Right, I've got y'; now, get a better grip, one hand at a time."

David felt the pressure on his chest as he briefly took Alec's weight. Having adjusted his grip Alec looked up. "Thanks."

"Huh. Now you need to lift again, for me to cut." David placed the blade on the rope between Alec's gripping hands and his bloodstained head. "Right, you ready?"

Alec looked at the ground, at David, and then nodded.

"Lift."

Alec saw the blade move.

"You're free."

Alec let go.

The length of time he had been suspended meant the normal shock-absorbing abilities of his body were totally unprepared to cope with the force and suddenness with which he hit the ground. As his feet made their first contact the shock travelled from the soles of his feet, clacked his jaws together and yet missed out the rest of his body completely, making breathing difficult and speech impossible. He rolled in what seemed like slow motion, eventually coming to rest and trying hard to concentrate the several pains away.

Stephanie hovered for a second but was unable to keep away and she rapidly moved to Alec's side.

"Alec, are you alright?"

David watched from his high perch. The closeness of these two bored deeply, cruelly into his head and heart and he wanted to scream, to yell and roar at the injustice, at their disregard for him, then he steadied. She had told him she loved him, had chosen him; suddenly all seemed in balance; all was safe.

He looked at the two pheasants. "I don't suppose mouth-to-mouth will do much good up 'ere so I'll toss these birds down too, shall I?"

There was no reply from the pain-wrapped Alec but Stephanie looked up at him. "Thank you, David. He's alright, just winded."

"Makes my day, does that."

She smiled up at him. "I don't deserve you... you certainly don't deserve me."

"Maybe so."

Alec managed to speak between gasps. "There's neither... of you deserve me. Sorry..." He tried to loosen the remains of the rope and the clothing round his neck.

"The scarf..." Stephanie said quietly as she took it and pulled it gently from round his neck. "Is that better?"

"Ar. Thanks, Steph..."

She gathered its folds and placed them into her lap.

Above them, David tried to pull pheasants and rope out from under the crossing roots but he slid across them in the process. The green, slippery surface would offer no grip and, as he had surmised, the ring of metal and knots had been well and truly bedded home by Alec's weight. He sliced through the rope, removed the pheasants and pocketed the rings. Balancing on one knee he tossed the pheasants towards the drop.

"Below!"

Like the result of a successful left-and-right, the two pheasants began their descent, the one bird falling fast and true straight to the floor. The second bird bounced off the edge of the roots, the tail catching the top-most branches of a thin oak sapling causing it to flick end-over-end, its feathered beauty flashing in the sun shafts that had just begun to show over the cliff's top edge.

The bird rattled though the leafless twigs before hitting the shotgun leant against the sapling's trunk.

As gun and bird smacked onto the ground so the hair-trigger flicked and the shot discharged. The blast hit Stephanie full in the chest, throwing her up and back like a rag doll. Peripheral pellets ripped into Alec's legs and he yelped, jumping up and back as if stung by a hornet cloud; the gun did a single somersault before coming to rest alongside the discarded scarf.

A silence followed and then David's voice cascaded down from the roots. "Steph! Stephanie! Oh, God, Steph...!"

He scrambled backwards across the roots and along the ridge. Reaching the slope, he practically tumbled down it, landing full tilt at the cliff's base. Running to her, the sobs and wails came thick and fast, but they ceased abruptly when he saw Alec cradling Stephanie in his arms.

"You! You... fuckin'...! Put her down, put her...!" He kicked out catching Alec on his damaged leg as he snatched up Stephanie's arm and dragged her back over shotgun and scarf, away from Alec's grasp. "Oh, Jesus... Steph! Steph... please...!" He looked across at Alec who was holding his leg, his face creased with pain. "You bastard, Stratton, this is your fault! You an' your poachin, your fuckin' poachin'!" He dropped to one knee and gathered her close. "Oh, Steph, Steph, pleeeeease...!" He shook her. "Wake up, c'mon, c'mon! Wake up!" His sobs began as the reality sank in. "Don't leave me, Steph, please don't leave me!"

Alec pointed across at the shotgun lying between them. "She's dead, David. The gun... Steph's dead."

David's reaction was immediate and savage. "Don't you call her that! Don't you fuckin'...!" His mouth was twisted with rage, his eyes wide and bulging, the blood from Stephanie staining his face and chest. "You're not fit to say 'er name!" The two birds were where they had landed and David leant forward, grabbed one and threw it with full force at Alec as he bellowed out to the woods. "Pheasants! Fuckin' pheasants!" Alec's reactions were sufficient to catch the bird as David's rage continued. "You! You couldn't leave 'em be could you, Stratton? Had to come back, an' for what? All for a fuckin' pheasant!" He loosed his grip on Stephanie slightly and her head flopped back, her open eyes staring sightlessly into the blue. "For this!" He softened slightly as he stared at her face. "For this? Oh, Steph, noooo...!"

As the trees soaked up his cry so another sound caused him to look up and he saw Alec adjusting his position. Their gaze fell in unison onto the shotgun and their eyes narrowed in recognition as the rage returned to David. "For that? Eh, Stratton! For that! For your fuckin' heartbeat? Eh? You bastard...!"

The long-wheel-base Land Rover pulled up at the end of the hedgerow, a hedgerow full of meandering pheasants.

Eric spoke as he dismounted from the driver's side. "Right lads let's get these escape routes blocked in an' Dave an' Steph off home... Bloody hell, there's a lot of birds on the move! Surely she must've stopped it off by now?" The beaters, climbing out the back, murmured their agreement.

A single shot rang out from within The Quarry, its sudden noise causing one of the assembled cock birds to chortle and thrash its wings in display as the rest of the birds stood to attention gauging threat and distance.

"What the...?"

"That'll be Dave will it then, Eric?" asked Geoff Millar with a smile.

"It better 'ad be an' he'd better have a damn good reason even if he is shootin' vermin. He'll ruin the bloody drive lettin' a gun off this close to start time; ought to know better."

Eric hurriedly collected his stick from inside the vehicle.

"Geoff, take Paul and Phil along the road and tap those pheasants back along that hedgerow. Get 'em back into the wood. Mike, stay with the vehicle. Graham, you get the other side of this hedge and we'll run it back fast an' sort out The Quarry." ...

Peter Webb

About the author: Born in Wolverhampton and so a genuine Black-Country Boy, Peter has had a chequered career; rock drummer, zoo and game keeper, gundog trainer, conservation officer, writer, actor, director, designer and stage manager. He now lives in Cornwall with his wife and two running dogs. '*The Quarry*' is Peter's second novel; his first, '*Ladies of the Shire*', was published in 2009.

www.peter-webb.com